STEALING A KISS

"I bought locks for all your windows and dead bolts for your doors. The security in this place stinks. So as a precaution, I'd like to install them tomorrow."

"Brady, that was very thoughtful of you," Sloane said, "but I'm perfectly adept at taking care of myself."

"I have no doubt about that. But sometimes a man likes to feel useful. Humor me, would you?"

"Since I wouldn't want to put a crimp in your manhood"—she tossed him a wicked smile—"then go ahead and get your tools out and do what you need to do."

"Yeah?" Brady leaned over to kiss her. Just something quick and sweet in case he'd misunderstood.

But when she opened her mouth for him and slipped her arms around his neck, he went all in.

It was a supremely bad idea, but he couldn't help himself. . .

Books by Stacy Finz

GOING HOME

FINDING HOPE

SECOND CHANCES

STARTING OVER

GETTING LUCKY

BORROWING TROUBLE

Published by Kensington Publishing Corporation

BORROWING
TROUBLE A NUGGET ROMANCE

STACY FINZ

LYRICAL SHINE
Kensington Publishing Corp.
www.kensingtonbooks.com

LYRICAL PRESS BOOKS are published by

Kensington Publishing Corp.
119 West 40th Street
New York, NY 10018

All Kensington titles, imprints, and distributed lines are available at special quantity discounts for bulk purchases for sales promotion, premiums, fund-raising, educational, or institutional use.

Special book excerpts or customized printings can also be created to fit specific needs. For details, write or phone the office of the Kensington Sales Manager: Kensington Publishing Corp., 119 West 40th Street, New York, NY 10018. Attn. Sales Department. Phone: 1-800-221-2647.

Lyrical Press and Lyrical Press logo Reg. U.S. Pat. & TM Off.

First Electronic Edition: February 2016
eISBN-13: 978-1-61650-923-1
eISBN-10: 1-61650-923-6

First Print Edition: February 2016
ISBN-13: 978-1-61650-924-8
ISBN-10: 1-61650-924-4

Printed in the United States of America

To my brother and sister-in-law, Noah and Kendra Finz.

ACKNOWLEDGMENTS

A special thanks to fire captain John Darmanin for his fire knowledge. Any mistakes, technical or otherwise, are mine.

Thanks to Kairee Krause for coming up with "Gold Country" for Tater's band name.

Thanks to my beta readers: Jaxon Van Derbeken, Wendy Miller, and, as always, my family.

And to everyone who made this book happen: My agent, Melissa Jeglinski of the Knight Agency, editor John Scognamiglio, production editor Rebecca Cremonese, and all the other folks at Kensington Publishing who worked tirelessly on the entire series. Thank you.

Chapter 1

Sloane McBride didn't know what to make of Chief Shepard. He was young for the top cop of a police department—somewhere in his thirties if she had to guess. Good-looking and cocky. Not a good mixture for a boss, in her experience.

The good-looking ones tended to have roaming hands and the cocky ones tended to be spineless.

Of course she'd been jaded by her experience at LAPD. Not by the work. She'd loved being a homicide investigator in the gritty city. Her father and brothers liked to tease her that Los Angeles—filled with palm trees, swimming pools, and movie stars—was amateur night compared to the South Side of Chicago. But she'd seen the devil in the City of Angels.

This place, Nugget, was nothing like it. Serene as the surrounding Sierra Nevada mountains. The place even had one of those old-time burger drive-throughs, and the citizens actually knew their neighbors. It was the epitome of Small Town USA. Although a few months ago there'd been a murder and a drug bust that rivaled some of the gangland slayings down South. So maybe she could do good work here.

"We're a team." The chief continued spewing platitudes about the department, trying to sell her on the job. She knew her former LAPD colleague, Jake Stryker, had told Rhys Shepard about her difficulties in Los Angeles. The chief had offered her the job anyway. "We've got each other's backs here."

Yeah, yeah. That's the way it was supposed to be at LAPD. What a joke.

The dispatcher—Sloane thought her name was Connie—lightly tapped on the glass door, then barged in. "Maddy is on the phone. She said you're not answering your cell."

The chief immediately picked up his line. "Everything okay? . . . Sure, sugar, that'll work. But I'm in the middle of an interview right now. Can I call you back?" He smiled over something she said and hung up. "Sorry about that. My wife."

Connie still loitered in the chief's office, checking Sloane over. "You taking the job? It would be good to get some estrogen in this place."

The chief shot the dispatcher a look.

"What? I'm just saying." The dispatcher turned to Sloane. "When you're done in here come find me. I'll give you the real skinny."

After Connie left, shutting the door behind her, Chief Shepard apologized. "We're a little loose around here. But we're a good department. Before I came back from Houston, the town contracted with the Plumas County sheriff out of Quincy. That's more than a half hour away. Folks here are real appreciative to have us."

He didn't have to push so hard. So far, this was Sloane's best option since the larger departments around the state wouldn't touch her with a ten-foot pole. The good-old-boys' network at LAPD had made sure of that. But here she had Jake advocating for her, and if she had to guess, Nugget PD was hard up for officer candidates. The rural railroad town, four hours northeast of San Francisco, was way off the beaten path. Too small a department to attract ambitious, experienced officers. It wouldn't have appealed to Sloane if she didn't need the job so badly.

At least it was a pretty place—lots of trees, rivers, and lakes—and since she'd originally come from Chicago, the cold and snow didn't scare her. She'd make the best of it until her situation changed.

"How is the rental market around here?" she asked.

Chief Shepard lifted his shoulders. "Not the best, I'm afraid. A lot of rental cabins that aren't really fit for year-round living. There are lots of homes for sale in Sierra Heights, our only gated community. But they'll run you close to a mil. Griffin Parks, the seller, might be willing to rent you one, but we're talking big bucks. I own a duplex on Donner Road. One of the apartments is vacant. I don't know how you'd feel about me being your boss and your landlord. But it's cheap and clean. I'll give you the key and directions. You could drive up and have a look at it. If you're not interested, you could swing by Sierra Heights. See if you can make a deal."

A half hour later she chugged up a craggy road in her Rav4. Good thing it was four-wheel drive. Although people she'd talked to said the winter so far had been mild, the place typically got sixty inches of snow a year. And it was only January, after all.

She hadn't wanted to offend Chief Shepard, so she'd agreed to look at his duplex. But after what she'd gone through in LA, Sloane didn't want her private life overlapping with her professional one. She'd just make an excuse why the apartment wouldn't work and try to find something else.

At the top of the hill she nosed down the driveway, parked on a well-maintained pad next to an old van, and got out to take a look around. The duplex was nothing fancy from the outside, just a single-level rectangular box made of wood shingles with two apartment doors and a nice front porch. On one side sat a pine-log rocking chair and a matching swing. Cozy. The view included downtown Nugget, which up close wasn't much, but from this height looked like a Christmas card with the snowy Sierra mountain range looming in the background. She had to admit that it was way more picturesque than the glimpse of the bougainvillea-covered cinder-block wall she got from her Echo Park apartment window. Lots of pine trees and a river on the other side of the railroad tracks.

In her jacket pocket she found the key and climbed the porch stairs. One of the doors creaked open and a man came outside.

"You Sloane McBride?"

She took a step back. He had startled her for a second.

"Rhys said you were coming over to look at the place." He stifled a yawn, and from his smooshed hair she got the impression that he'd been taking a nap.

"I'm Sloane. You must be Brady." The chief had mentioned the tenant, something about him being a chef at the chief's wife's hotel, where Sloane was staying. Given that he wore a pair of baggy black-and-white striped pants and a chef's jacket, Sloane thought this had to be him.

"You don't smoke, do you?" he asked. "The duplex shares the same ventilation system."

She blinked up at him. "No." And she wasn't taking the place, so it didn't matter.

"Good. I've got to get back to work." He headed to the van and opened the door.

"Hang on a sec," she called and jogged over to him. "Have you lived in Nugget long?"

"Since summer. Why?"

He had about six inches on her, so she had to look up. "I'm just trying to get a feel for the place."

He gazed at his watch. "I've got about fifteen minutes. What do you want to know?"

She shrugged. "Anything you can tell me."

He smiled and she noticed he was nice-looking. Really nice-looking. Brown hair, hazel eyes, and a day's worth of stubble on his chin. She hadn't missed his Southern accent either. She was a sucker for a Southern accent. Between him and the chief, she had to wonder what the rest of the guys in Nugget looked like.

"Good people," he said. "But gossipy as all get out. Great skiing a half hour from here in Glory Junction. If you like to hike, there's a ton of trails. Great fishing and hunting too. Lucky Rodriguez will hook you up with a horse over at his cowboy camp if you like to ride. It's a great way to see the countryside." He nudged his square jaw at her. "What are you into?"

"I like to run." And until she'd gotten promoted to the robbery-homicide division, she'd liked to dance. Salsa. "Go to the gym."

"No gym here. But there's a yoga studio on the square. And you can run anywhere. It's safe as long as you don't mess with the wildlife. A couple of the women in town organize bowling parties over at the Ponderosa. It's probably slower paced than what you're used to, but it's a welcoming little town. So, you taking the job?"

"Yeah, I'm pretty sure I am."

"LAPD, huh?"

"Uh-huh. How'd you know?"

He chuckled. "Everyone here knows everything about everybody. What they don't know, they make up."

She waited for him to ask her why she'd left the department, but he didn't. Maybe the whole town knew already.

"I've got a wine and cheese service in thirty minutes. You renting the place?" He cocked his head at the apartment next to his.

"I haven't looked inside yet." She wasn't about to tell him the truth. "I was hoping for something a little closer to town."

"You can walk from here," he said, and started getting into his van. "I'm over at the Lumber Baron Inn if you have any more questions."

She waved goodbye, then let herself inside the apartment to have a look around. It wasn't much, but it was roomier than her LA place. It had a decent-sized living room and her queen-size bed would easily fit in the bedroom. The bathroom was right off the kitchen. She assumed the layout was what people called a railroad apartment, because it resembled a passenger car on a train. It made sense, given that this was a railroad town. The chief hadn't been lying when he'd said the place was clean. More like spotless.

After Donner Road she headed to the subdivision called Sierra Heights. For a gated community, the security sucked. She got right past the empty guard kiosk and zipped around, looking at the mammoth houses, their elaborate decks and giant yards. The chief had been correct in assuming that this place was too rich for her blood. Gorgeous, though. If she had the money, she'd live here.

On Main Street she found a real estate office and popped inside. A woman named Carol said she had a couple of rentals Sloane could look at, but her hopes deflated after the house tour. The first stunk like a dog kennel and gave Sloane the creeps. Lots of chain-link fence and gaudy statuary in the yard, including one of those boy-peeing fountains. The second was a cabin that hadn't been winterized. The third would've been perfect. It was right in town with a sweet little rose-garden backyard, but it was also for sale. The owner would only rent it on the condition that it be made available for showings. No go. Not only didn't Sloane want the inconvenience, but she didn't want to have to move again in a few months.

Disappointed, she drove back to the Lumber Baron. If only she'd found an apartment or a house half as comfortable as her room at the inn. The bed and breakfast was pretty spectacular with its period architecture and elegant furnishings. Sloane hadn't realized that the chief's wife owned the place until he'd mentioned it during their interview. Last night, when she'd gotten in, there was only the young guy, Andy, manning the desk. And this morning she'd rushed out to meet Jake for breakfast at the Ponderosa, the kooky Western restaurant/bar/bowling alley across from the inn on the town square.

When she walked in the lobby she nearly collided with Brady, who looked to be on his way out. He had changed into jeans and a long-sleeved waffle-knit shirt—and he was seriously ripped. Not like a gym rat, but like a guy who spent a lot of time outdoors. Mile-wide chest, big pecs, flat stomach, and muscular arms.

"You staying here?" he asked by way of a greeting.

"Yeah. I checked in last night. Is that hamburger place any good? I was thinking of grabbing something before it closes and bringing it up to my room."

"It's good," he said. "Or if you want to be around people, you can go to the Ponderosa for happy hour. The food's good there too."

She wondered where he was off to since other than bowling there didn't seem to be anything to do. Unless he was headed to the Ponderosa's happy hour or to meet a girlfriend.

"Okay. Thanks."

"Chicken-fried steak and eggs for breakfast," he said, grabbing a down jacket from a closet behind the check-in counter and slinging it over his shoulder. "Catch you later."

"You must be Sloane." A dead ringer for the beautiful woman in the wedding picture on the chief's desk came into the lobby. "I'm Maddy, Rhys's wife."

"Nice to meet you."

"You taking the job?"

Whoa, people around here get right to the point. "I'm gonna sleep on it, but probably . . . yeah."

Before she knew what was happening Maddy enveloped her in a hug. "You don't know how happy that makes me." Sloane didn't usually get this kind of reception from the wives of other cops. "It'll just be nice to have a fourth person on deck, you know what I mean?"

Yeah, they need someone to work graveyard and holidays. "Sure," she said, and tried to pry herself loose from Maddy's embrace. She was stronger than she looked.

"Rhys said you might be taking the apartment on Donner Road. That used to be my apartment. It's where Rhys and I fell in love."

"Really?" A little TMI, but sweet just the same. For whatever reason, it made her feel better about Shepard. She didn't know why he'd left such a bad taste in her mouth in the first place. The chief seemed completely professional—even decent.

Then again, they all did until you broke the code of silence. That's when the people who you thought had your back left you to fend for yourself while the world blew up.

"It's a great apartment," Sloane said. "Conveniently located, clean, spacious. But to be completely honest, I feel a little weird about having my boss as a landlord."

Maddy nodded. "Rhys feels weird about it too. We decided that if you take the apartment we'd have my brother, Nate, act as the go-between. Nate and I co-own the Lumber Baron."

"How would that work?" Sloane asked, thinking that this might be a more comfortable solution.

"You would just have all your dealings concerning the apartment—rent, deposit, repairs—with Nate or my sister-in-law, Samantha. Rhys and I would stay out of the picture."

That seemed better—less company town. "I'll let Chief Shepard know what I decide tomorrow, then."

"Great. And, Sloane, I do think you'll really like it here. I know you're from Los Angeles and a small town like this can be a culture shock, but it's a wonderful place. People look out for one another. I came from San Francisco and never thought I'd get used to the slow pace of small-town living. What I found was that the big city had been pretty darn alienating. And of course I'm biased, but I think my husband is a wonderful boss."

Sloane laughed. Jake had said the same thing, and she respected his opinion. The man had been a cop while Sloane was still a toddler. And unlike her, he'd survived the snake pit.

"It'll take some getting used to, but I'm up for the challenge." She wanted to stay positive.

"And Brady will be a great neighbor. If you're lucky, he'll cook for you."

"He seems nice." And hopefully quiet, since they'd be living right on top of each other and her hours were bound to be odd, given that she'd be the newbie.

"Very," Maddy said. "We're crazy about him."

Sloane bet most of the female population was, anyway. After a little more small talk with Maddy, she made her way across the square to the hamburger place. It was called the Bun Boy, which cracked her up. There were walk-up and drive-through windows, but no indoor seating. Just a smattering of picnic tables on a swath of lawn, under a few big trees. Nice in summer, but way too cold this time of year. She got her food to go and took it up to her room. She probably should've gone to the Ponderosa for happy hour to get more acquainted with the town, but between her interview with the chief and all the new people she'd met today, she was talked out. Nugget was a chatty place.

She ate at the writer's desk while flipping through the channels on the flat-screen. Nugget at least had cable. The food was better than expected, she thought while wolfing down a large order of seasoned curly fries. In LA, she and her girlfriends liked dining at all the trendy bistros and cafés. Sloane didn't consider herself a foodie by any stretch. Not like her friends who read the *Times* restaurant reviews religiously and traded names of hot new chefs like little boys did baseball cards. Sloane couldn't name one famous cook unless it was Paula Deen or Gordon Ramsay. But she enjoyed eating and experiencing new cuisines and flavors. Everyone in her family cooked, except her. Her mother was an avid baker and her father and three brothers worked in a firehouse, where kitchen duty was as much a part of the job as putting out blazes.

She could've gone home to Chicago—her father had actually insisted on it when he found out what had happened on the job. "No one messes with a McBride," he'd said. But Sloane preferred to stand on her own two feet. So Jake's suggestion that she come here seemed like the winning option. Still, she had to wonder whether she was making a huge mistake. Having never lived in a small town, it would take a lot of adjustment. *Like what kind of place doesn't have a gym?*

The room phone rang, making Sloane jump. In LA, she'd had to change all her personal numbers. Not that that had helped. The problem with cops was they could always find you.

With trepidation she picked up. "Hello."

"How'd it go?" Jake's reassuring voice came across the other end.

She took a deep breath. "Good. I'm planning to take it."

"Wise decision," he said. "It'll help get your confidence back. It's good work, Sloane. People here are appreciative of what we do. You'll be welcomed with open arms."

She thought about Maddy and bit back a laugh. "The chief has a vacant apartment. What do you think about me taking it?"

"The place up on Donner Road? It's perfect."

She told him how the chief's brother-in-law would act as landlord to prevent any awkwardness.

"That'll work," Jake said. "But, Sloane, Rhys is a fair guy. You don't have to worry about him."

"He certainly seems to be in a rush to get me here. Is there something you guys aren't telling me?"

"Nah. He liked you from the phone interview—likes your résumé too. Most of the candidates we get up here are retirees. Rhys wants young blood."

"Looks like a lot of cowboys up here, going by all the hats and boots in the Ponderosa this morning. Will I have trouble with the town accepting a female cop?"

Jake laughed. "These are ranching people, not Neanderthals. You'll do just fine."

"I'm meeting Connie for lunch tomorrow. What's her story?"

"She grew up here, started up the department with Rhys, and is a coffee snob—her sister lives in Seattle. She's an excellent dispatcher, has a smart mouth, and we love her to death. I'm glad you're having lunch with her. She knows where all the bodies are buried. What are your plans for dinner tomorrow?"

"I haven't thought that far ahead," Sloane said.

"Cecilia and I would like to have you over. She's a marvelous cook and desperately wants to meet you."

Sloane accepted the invitation and Jake gave her directions to his house before signing off. Instead of going straight to bed, Sloane decided to take a soak in her slipper tub. Since she'd never bathed in one, the charming claw-foot had called to her the first time she'd seen it. Everything about the inn did. It was just so warm and inviting.

On her way to the bathroom she swiped her cell off the bed and checked emails. The first one was from her parents, who wanted to know how the trip had gone. All three of her brothers had left texts, demanding the scoop on Nugget.

But it was the last message, marked urgent, that filled her with a deep foreboding, convincing her that the sooner she got out of LA, the better.

Sloane McBride, you can't hide. We're coming to get you.

Chapter 2

Brady had a full house. Unusual for a weekday in January. But tourists were taking advantage of the particularly dry winter. So far, no chains required to get over the pass.

Maddy rushed into the kitchen. "What do you need me to do?"

"Take those out." He nudged his head at plates of chicken-fried steak and biscuits, with country gravy ladled over the top. "The vegetarian plate is for room 207."

Maddy balanced several plates on her arm and made her way to the dining room. She couldn't cook, but she knew how to serve. Brady assumed it was from growing up in the hospitality business.

He had a sweet deal working for the Breyers. Nate was wound tighter than his sister and wife; still, Brady had taken to the guy, who owned nine other hotels in the Bay Area and a resort near Glory Junction that he was in the midst of refurbishing. Even though Brady was overqualified for the Lumber Baron, the three Breyers made up for it by letting him do whatever he wanted. Devise his own menus, buy his own ingredients, even cure his own meats. And they gave him a hefty budget with which to do it.

Little by little Nate was using Brady to head up catering for big events at his other hotels, including weddings and parties as part of a joint venture with a neighboring dude ranch.

Last summer, when Brady had run from a bad situation and stumbled upon this little town, he'd never dreamed that it would take care of him the way it had. Of course, he still had to keep his guard up. Trouble could come at any time.

Interesting that now he'd be living next door to a cop. Although Sloane McBride didn't look like any cop he'd ever known. She was certainly fit enough, but her golden hair, cornflower-blue eyes, and that dazzling face of hers reminded him more of one of the fairy princesses in his niece's Disney books than a peace officer. According to the word around town, she was a friend of Jake's; he'd recommended her for the job.

Brady measured out enough beans to brew a fresh pot, and poured the stale coffee down the sink.

"We have two more couples and Sloane McBride." Maddy set down a tub of dirty dishes on the counter and began loading them into the dishwasher. "Make Sloane's extra good. She's the key to my marriage."

He stepped back and looked at her, wondering what she was talking about.

"Do you know how much overtime Rhys works?" Maddy said. "Emma and I barely see him anymore."

Given that the department was a three-man—four if you counted Connie, the dispatcher—operation, Brady suspected it was a lot.

"You take these out to those other couples." He pulled four plates from the warming oven. "I'll take this to Ms. McBride."

"Good idea." Maddy loaded up and started out the door. "Fabulous food and a hot guy—the perfect incentive for her to stay."

Brady rolled his eyes. The women around here were a little nuts. Sloane sat at a corner table, reading one of the pamphlets from the front desk that told the history of the area.

"If you want the real flavor of the town you should check out the *Nugget Tribune* website," he said, and placed her plate on the table. "*Bon appétit.*"

She lifted her head and the power of her smile floored him. Pretty lady. But if she planned to move into the apartment next door, she was off-limits lady.

"The *Nugget Tribune*, huh?" She reached for her phone, which sat on the table, and started searching for the site.

"All the news that's fit to print—and then some."

She laughed. "Thanks for the suggestion . . . and for breakfast." Her eyes grew large as she took in her plate. "This is enough food for an army."

"No bitty portions up here in the mountains. Dig in before it gets cold."

He walked away so she could eat in peace. When he got back to the kitchen, Maddy was adding more plates to the dishwasher.

"Is that coffee fresh?" She motioned to the pot he'd just put on.

He nodded, and she poured herself a cup. "Well, did she say anything?"

"Like what?"

"Like whether she could start right away?" Maddy opened the fridge, pulled out a carton of half-and-half, and poured a dollop into her coffee.

"No. Why don't you go ask her?"

"I did last night. She said she was pretty sure she was taking it. But I was hoping she'd start soon. Like tomorrow."

Brady laughed. Then again, he'd practically started the day he was hired. The Lumber Baron's former cook had left without giving notice. Emily Mathews, the town's famous cookbook-ghostwriter to the stars, had filled in as a favor. But she'd been in the midst of planning her wedding to Clay McCreedy, taking care of his two boys, and trying to make a book deadline. To say that the Breyers had been desperate for help was an understatement. The timing couldn't have worked out better for Brady since he'd needed a job. Fate.

"You don't know what it's like with a toddler." Maddy shut the dishwasher door and started the wash. "Even when Rhys can break away from work, we hardly have any time together."

"My guess is she'll need time to pack and move. What's her deal anyway? Why is she leaving such a big department?"

"All I know is that she needed a change," Maddy said, and looked directly at Brady. "She's pretty, isn't she?"

Brady held up his hands, palms out. He knew what she was up to. The entire town was filled with matchmaking mamas. Sam, Nate's wife, had already tried to set him up with Tawny Wade, Nugget's resident cowboy-boot designer. Tawny, who as far as Brady was concerned was the only sane woman on the face of the earth, happened to be in love with Lucky Rodriguez, the town's bull-riding champion. The two planned to get married in the spring and Brady, who considered Tawny his best friend, was catering the reception.

"Very pretty," Brady said. "But not for me."

"Why not?"

Because the change Sloane allegedly needed was probably code for *I have to get away from a bad boyfriend*. And Brady didn't want any part of that. His last romantic escapade had left him more than gun-shy—scared to death would be a truer statement. And Sloane McBride was packing more heat than he cared to handle.

"Never a good idea to start up with your neighbor."

"In most cases I'd say that's true. But that duplex is where Rhys and I fell in love. Maybe it has the *kavorka*, the lure of the animal."

Brady rolled his eyes. "You've been watching too many *Seinfeld* reruns. Not interested, Maddy."

"We'll see."

No, we won't. "What do you got going today?"

"Probably take a ride up to Gold Mountain to check on the renovations. Right now, we're mostly consumed with whether Lina will get into the University of Nevada, Reno."

"I thought your sister-in-law was going to USF." Brady had only met Lina Shepard once or twice since she lived full-time in San Francisco and only occasionally came for visits.

"Yep. But she really wants to transfer into Nevada's engineering department and learn how to build bridges."

"Bridges as in the Golden Gate Bridge?"

"Mm-hmm. She interned over the summer with a structural engineering firm and became obsessed. USF doesn't have a program. But it just so happens that Nevada's is one of the best. And she'd be close to home."

"That's great," Brady said.

"Yeah. Except it's really competitive. There's no telling whether she'll get in."

"I'll be thinking good thoughts."

"Thanks, Brady. How 'bout you?"

"I'm making savory palmiers for the wine and cheese service and have a meeting later with Jake and Cecilia to go over their wedding menu."

"Full day," Maddy said.

"Yep."

He left Maddy to finish what few dishes were left while he checked the dining room for stragglers. Except for Sloane, who he noted had cleaned her plate, the room was empty.

"You want seconds?" he asked, and she pulled her face from her phone.

"I'm stuffed. That was fantastic."

He grinned and cocked his head at her phone. "The *Trib*?"

"Mm-hmm. The police blotter. May as well know what I'm getting myself into."

"A lot of henhouse thefts in these parts." He tried to keep a straight face.

She smiled, and again he had a hard time thinking of her as a cop. It was probably all kinds of wrong to stereotype that way, but when you looked like a prom queen . . .

"You going back to LA today?" he asked.

"Tomorrow. I still have to meet with the chief to finalize a few things."

Maddy had made it sound like she was taking the apartment next to him. He thought it would be pushy to ask. By the end of the day whatever decisions she'd made would be all over town anyway.

"Good luck," he said, and started walking away when he heard a ruckus in the lobby.

By the time he got there, he found Andy, the inn's reservationist, pinned to the wall by Andy's clone. Both were dressed in the uniform of cookie-cutter nonconformists everywhere: dyed black hair, studded belt, combat boots, and piercings. Nate made Andy tone it down when he worked the front desk.

"What's going on here?" Brady asked.

"He owes me money," said Andy's doppelganger, wannabe Sid Vicious.

"I do not," Andy croaked. He couldn't really talk because Sid had him in a choke hold.

Brady plucked the kid off Andy and held him away. That's when Andy used all his force, which was surprisingly considerable, to ram Brady and Sid Vicious into the wall. Andy started pounding on Sid, and Brady knew that if he let go of the kid, they'd have a full-fledged brawl on their hands. Not exactly the best impression for guests.

Before Brady could do anything, Sloane, who'd evidently followed him, restrained Andy in some sort of hold. Probably a police maneuver.

She told Maddy, who must've heard the commotion and had come running like the rest of them, to call 9-1-1. Brady didn't think it was necessary. Both idiots, who continued to spit obscenities at each other, just needed a kick in the ass. Obviously, though, Sloane was a by-the-book kind of cop.

A few minutes later Rhys showed up. Sloane still had Andy controlled. Looks were deceiving; the woman wasn't cotton candy, that's for sure. Brady had loosened his hold on Sid, who seemed to have run out of adrenaline. Rhys gave them a stern talking-to and sent Sid on his way. Andy slithered back behind the check-out desk. If Brady knew Maddy, she'd give Andy a pass—she was soft like that. But if Nate had been there, he would've fired the kid.

"Everyone okay?" Rhys asked, and got nods all the way around. He looked over at Sloane, who leaned against the wall, unruffled. "Thanks for stepping in. I'll see you over at the station in a few. Hopefully, you've got good news for me." And with that he sauntered off.

Maddy grabbed Andy by the arm. "You, come with me."

Brady watched them disappear behind Maddy's office door, shook his head, and turned to Sloane. "You've got some moves."

She shrugged like it was nothing. "That happen a lot in the inn?"

"Never before. Andy's a slacker, but he's harmless. He's in a band—they're god-awful. I suspect that was one of his bandmates."

Again, she smiled, giving Brady a kick in the gut. "Weird town."

Wait until she got a load of the other characters. "A little bit. You staying?"

"I am." She nodded.

"Well then, welcome to Nugget, California. As the entrance sign proclaims, we're the Pride of the West."

Two weeks later, Sloane moved into the duplex on Donner Road. She hadn't been sure whether her furniture would go with the whole rustic setup here. Sloane had liked cruising the trendy shops in Santa Monica and West Hollywood and had amassed a collection of shabby-chic pieces—lots of overstuffed, ruffled, slipcovered sofas and chairs. Oddly enough, they actually looked better here than in her LA apartment.

Nate, her new landlord, said it would be fine if she wanted to paint. She thought a palette of cream, yellow, and robin's-egg blue would make the bland apartment cheerier. In Reno, there were a couple of good paint stores, according to Yelp.

As she stood staring at the walls, visualizing how she could give the place pizzazz, someone knocked on her door. Reaching for her service weapon, which she always kept within arm's reach these days, Sloane peered out the peephole.

No one.

Slowly she opened the door, her finger on the trigger. There'd been two more menacing messages since the night in the Lumber Baron, and she wasn't taking any chances. Even if the threats were only intended to scare her, she planned to stay vigilant.

On her doormat sat a pie. She gingerly lifted it one-handed and sniffed. It smelled like apple. She shut the door and brought the pie into the kitchen for a closer inspection. Then she found the note and sighed in relief.

Welcome to the hood.
Brady

She could hear him moving around next door. Clearly, he wanted to give her space to get unpacked. The pie was the perfect gesture. Considerate and welcoming, without being overly friendly. She liked his style. And then there was the fact that she was starving, having had no time to stock the refrigerator.

Sloane managed to find the box with her silverware, grabbed a fork, and ate pie right out of the dish. It was still warm . . . and sweet Mother of God, was it good. Like possibly the best thing she'd ever eaten, although his chicken-fried steak and country gravy ran a close second.

Well, damn, now she had to go next door and thank him. Leaving a mere thank-you note seemed chintzy for a pie of this caliber. Plus, if Sloane didn't get out of the house soon, she'd inhale the whole thing.

She checked her hair in the mirror, walked across the porch and knocked. A few seconds later, he pulled the door open, wearing a pair of running pants and a long-sleeved compression shirt. And if she'd thought the pie was good . . . *Hello, Superman.*

"How's the move going?"

"Better, now that I have pie . . . outstanding pie. I just wanted to thank you."

"No problem."

"You going running?" *No, Sloane, he always dresses like that.*

Brady stuck his head out and looked up at the sky. "Yeah, but I think it might rain. I have to be back at the inn in time for the afternoon service."

"Well, I won't keep you. Thanks again for the pie, and I'll return your pan as soon as I'm finished."

"No rush. I've got lots of them."

She started to head back to her side of the duplex and stopped. "Where do you run?"

"There's a fire trail at the top of the hill. If you want to go sometime, I'll show you."

"I'm not sure what my schedule is yet, but yeah. Thanks."

"Sure," he said, and went back inside.

The guy had to have a girlfriend, she told herself as she retreated behind her own door. No way was someone like him single. Her cell rang and it took her a few minutes to find it in all the clutter. These days she always checked caller ID before answering. If she didn't know the number, she let it go to voice mail. That way she had a record.

"Hi, Chief."

"How's the unpacking going?" He sounded harried.

"Uh, good, thanks."

"Look, I hate to do this to you, but Wyatt's sick as a dog. Jake is taking his graveyard shift. Any chance you could ride along with Jake, get to know the place? I have a feeling we're gonna be short an officer for a few days."

She gazed around the disaster that was currently her home. "No problem. In fact, I'd love to."

After hanging up, Sloane got her new uniform out of the closet. In the robbery and homicide division, RHD, she'd worn plain clothes. The last time she'd donned her blues at LAPD was for the funeral of a fellow detective shortly before she'd left. A man whose death had been laid at her feet. The harassment had started even before Sweeney died—nasty looks, even nastier gossip about her, and no one wanted to partner with her in the field. But after they'd found Sweeney dead in his house, she'd been blamed and the persecution got so bad that Sloane couldn't stay in the department any longer. If she had, the next funeral would've been hers.

Chapter 3

"What do you think of the new lady cop?" Donna asked Emily. For an hour Brady listened while the members of the Baker's Dozen, the local cooking club that commandeered his kitchen the second Saturday of every month, gossiped.

"You ladies ever consider doing some actual cooking?"

Donna, the proprietor of the Bun Boy, swirled a glass of wine and sipped. "What bee flew up your butt? We're talking about the new girl, the one who happens to be your neighbor."

All eyes turned to Brady, who threw his hands up. "I've got an inn full of people and a wine and cheese service in three hours. If you want to learn the French technique for making *pâte à choux*, it's now or never, ladies." Why he'd agreed to join this klatch of crazies, he'd never know. He was the only male in the group and the only one of the bunch who didn't spend their meetings nattering.

"Let's do it," said Emily, the only sane one of the bunch, who already knew how to make a killer *pâte à choux*. "Show us your technique, Brady."

Brady preheated the oven to four hundred degrees and quickly added the first few ingredients to a large saucepan. He planned to use the puff pastry for cheese *gougères* to serve to the guests—and the Baker's Dozen.

"Some measurements would be nice," Donna said, taking notes.

"Measurements?" Brady smiled. "We don't need no stinking measurements." He couldn't remember the last time he used a scale or a cup or a spoon. Maybe culinary school.

From memory he said, "About a cup-and-a-half of water, a stick plus a tablespoon of unsalted butter, a teaspoon of sugar, half that much salt, two hundred grams of flour, and eight eggs."

"So it's a recipe for high cholesterol," Ethel, owner of the Nugget Market, quipped.

Brady chuckled. "Nah, this is health food."

"Easy for you to say," Donna interjected. "You don't have an ass the size of a barn."

"I don't know, Donna, your ass is looking pretty good to me." She was old enough to be his mother.

"Not better than Officer McBride's. I heard she signed up for Pam's yoga class."

That was news to Brady. Then again, he wasn't keeping tabs on his new neighbor. Rather, he was trying very hard not to. He had, however, noticed that Donna was right: She looked damned good in that Nugget PD uniform of hers.

A few mornings this week she was getting home as he was leaving. The poor woman had evidently pulled the graveyard shift. He supposed newbies had to pay their dues. Somewhere he'd heard that she'd been a homicide detective. Whatever she'd left in LA had to be pretty bad for her to start from the bottom again. He certainly knew what that was like.

The water, butter, sugar, and salt came to a boil and Brady added the flour, instructing the women to stir vigorously with a wooden spoon until the mixture formed into dough. A few took pictures with their phones. Brady removed the pan from the heat and proceeded to beat the eggs, adding them a little at a time to the dough until it was glossy.

"This is what it should look like." Brady demonstrated how the dough should slide off a wooden spoon like a thick ribbon, then transferred the batter to a pastry bag fitted with a half-inch tip. "Got it?"

The women nodded their heads and Brady proceeded to show them how to pipe small mounds of the dough onto cookie sheets.

"This is the part I have trouble with," Grace, owner of the Farm Supply store, said. "You do it so fast and so perfect."

"I've had a lot of practice." He'd worked his way through culinary school catering. Before that he'd helped out in his aunt's restaurant in South Carolina.

"Today, I'm making *gougères*." He sprinkled each mound of dough with shredded Gruyère. "But you can fill these with pastry cream for cream puffs or éclairs."

Emily helped him pop the cooking sheets into the Lumber Baron's large industrial oven, where they'd bake for thirty minutes or so. In the meantime, Brady tossed together a Caesar salad with chicken he'd grilled earlier. They'd have it for lunch along with the *gougères*.

"Well, Brady, dish. What's Sloane McBride like?" Donna wanted to know.

"You mean beyond being a nice lady and the newest member of our fine police department? Because if that's what you want to know, I've got nothing."

"She came into Farm Supply to introduce herself and seemed lovely," Grace said. "I for one like having a woman in the department. It adds a different sensibility. Did you all get an invitation to Jake and Cecilia's wedding?"

Everyone said yes in unison.

"I never did understand why Cecilia never joined the Baker's Dozen," Ethel said. "The woman is a marvelous cook."

"Maybe because you women gossip too much," Brady put in. "You ever think of that?"

Ethel stared at Brady over her spectacles. "Cecilia can hold her own in the gossip department."

"We should probably approach her again," Donna said. "But after the wedding. She's got her hands full."

"Brady, aren't you catering the wedding?" Emily asked.

"Yep. If you know of anyone looking to make a few extra bucks, I could use servers."

"Lina might want to," Emily said. "She's saving for a new car."

"Did she get into Nevada?" Ethel asked. "Last I heard they were waiting to hear."

"She's in." Emily beamed. "Rhys and Maddy are ecstatic. She's getting a place in Reno, but will be home all the time now." The forty-five minute drive was a cake walk compared to the four hours it took to get to San Francisco.

"I know she's taking some weekend shifts at the inn and is looking for any other odd jobs she could work in with her class schedule," Emily continued.

"We're always looking for checkers at the market," Ethel replied. "I'll let Maddy know."

By the time the Baker's Dozen had finished eating and left, Brady got started on laying out a spread for the guests. The weekends were particularly busy at the inn, when people from the Bay Area and

Sacramento flocked to the Sierra to commune with nature. He usually took weekdays off, preparing dishes in advance that could easily be reheated. In LA, his restaurant closed on Mondays and he'd had a staff of fifteen, including a chef de cuisine who did the heavy lifting when Brady wanted a day off.

Here, he had no staff. But the Lumber Baron was slower paced, giving Brady more time to be creative. And hopefully Nate would continue using him for his big hotel events. Eventually, when Brady determined it was 100 percent safe, he'd resurface and take up where he'd left off. For now, though, this was a nice life.

After the guests had devoured the last cheese puff, Brady cleaned up the kitchen, packed up, and went home. He'd just gotten out of his van when Sloane drove up.

She slammed her door shut. "We have to stop meeting like this."

"You just getting home from work?" She had on her uniform.

"Yep. And you?"

Brady nodded. "How's the new job going?"

"So far, so good. I'm still trying to familiarize myself with the area."

"I guess it's different than what you're used to."

"You can say that again. I was thinking of taking a run. You wouldn't by any chance want to show me that fire trail you were talking about?"

"Sure," he said. "Give me five minutes to change."

"I'll meet you on the porch."

He got there first and waited in his rocker. Sloane came out a few minutes later and the first thing Brady noticed was she had a semiautomatic holstered in an elastic-band carrier around her hips. The second thing he noticed was she had very nice hips. And ass. Nice everything, come to mention it.

"You always run with that?" He pointed at the gun.

"I feel naked without it." She cocked her head at his chair. "Where'd you get that?"

"Colin Burke. He's local—makes mind-blowing furniture. His house and studio are just over the hill."

She reached out to touch the pinewood. "It's nice. I may have to get me one. You ready?"

"Yep." Brady got to his feet and looked at the sky. "It's gonna be dark soon. You need to warm up or anything?"

"No, I'm good."

He started out slowly since part of the trek was uphill and he didn't know what kind of pace she liked to keep. So far, she kept up just fine.

"It's really pretty here," she said as they reached the top of the hill where the terrain flattened out.

"It is. Cold too." He noticed she'd worn short sleeves.

"I'm originally from Chicago, so this doesn't faze me." Her voice hitched slightly from exertion. Brady was surprised she could carry on a conversation at all. "How about you? I detect a Southern accent."

"South Carolina."

"You came to Nugget by way of South Carolina?"

He laughed. "I went to Los Angeles first."

"Really? How long were you there for?"

"Three years." He didn't want to get into the details. It was a small world and the fewer people who knew where he was and what he'd come from, the better.

Brady hadn't bothered to change his name, figuring it was common enough. But he stayed off Facebook and Twitter. When Harlee Roberts had wanted to write a feature story about him for the *Nugget Tribune*, he'd politely declined. No need to borrow trouble. But if trouble found him, he'd be ready.

"Chicago, huh? What brought you out here?"

"Job. LAPD was looking for officers."

"You didn't want to stay in Chicago?" Brady cut over to the fire trail and they took that for a while.

"California appealed to me, but mostly I didn't want to work in the same city with my father and three brothers."

Brady lifted his brows. "All cops?"

"Nope. Firefighters. My dad's a battalion chief. My oldest brother is an arson inspector."

"They wanted you to join the family business?"

"Not exactly." She stopped, bent over, and put her hands on her knees. "You mind if we rest for a second?"

"Sure."

She looked over at him. "You're not even winded."

"The high altitude is probably getting to you. I'm just used to it."

"No. It's that I do all my running on a treadmill at the gym."

"We've done five miles. You want to walk back?"

"Would you think I'm a wuss?"

"Anything but." He deliberately stared at her pistol and let his eyes wander a bit, trying not to be too obvious about it. "So, are you one of those competitive women?"

"A little bit," she said, and grinned. "Kind of have to be in my line of work."

They turned around and started heading to the duplex. "Word on the street is that you signed up for yoga."

"On the street?" She laughed. "Who told you?"

"The Baker's Dozen—a group of meddlesome old ladies. We're all in a cooking club together."

"Seriously?"

"Yeah. You want to join?"

"I don't cook. But I'll come to eat. Is that allowed?"

He shrugged. "From what I can tell they don't have a lot of rules. They just like to gossip—and drink. These women can seriously hold their liquor."

Sloane laughed. "Are you the only guy?"

"Yep. Nuts, huh?"

"I think it's awesome. How long have you been a chef?"

"Ten years. Went to culinary school right out of college. Got my first job in Charleston. How long have you been a cop?"

"Nine."

That probably put her right around his age of thirty-three. Maybe a little younger. "You didn't like LAPD?"

"Uh, let's just say I needed a change of scenery after some difficult circumstances." She made it sound ominous.

The sun had set and the sky was streaked in red and blue. Pretty soon they'd be out of light. They were more than halfway home when the distant rumble of a train sounded.

"How often do they come by?" The duplex was a stone's throw from the tracks.

"A few times a day," Brady said. "Not so much at night."

"That's good." She smiled, and the sheer power of it caught Brady off guard.

He was almost tempted to ask her what she was doing for dinner. But the run had been enough. He wouldn't want to seem interested. After all, she'd clearly come here with a past and Brady was in no position to deal with her complications. He had enough of his own.

* * *

It was Sloane's first day on the job solo, and years since she'd worked patrol. At least she'd pulled a day shift. The chief was fair about spreading around the crappy hours. He even worked them himself, which at first surprised Sloane. According to Connie, no one was exempt from pulling holiday and night duty.

She turned left on Main Street, thinking about lunch. Possibly a burger at the Bun Boy, or maybe she'd dash home and pop a frozen burrito in the microwave. Just about to head back to the square, Connie's voice came over the radio.

"We have a 10-91V at the Nugget Gas and Go. Animal control is ten minutes out."

Sloane hung a U-turn and put on her flashing lights. At the gas station she hopped out of her police SUV and went inside the store. A guy in coveralls greeted her and she couldn't help but notice that he was rather nice-looking. Not as knock-your-socks-off as Brady, but right up there. What was it with this town? She'd yet to meet an unattractive man here, making her wonder what they put in the water.

"Around back," he said.

He led her outside, past the garage bays—where a mechanic had his head under the hood of a pickup—and behind the shop. On a flat concrete pad that butted up to a grassy embankment sat a large Dumpster and . . . oh shit, a bear! He'd pulled out heaps of garbage and was sitting down to a picnic lunch.

Sloane had absolutely no experience with this sort of thing. "Isn't he supposed to be hibernating?"

"Not all of them do. I read somewhere that fifteen percent of the black bears up here don't sleep in the winter. I'm Griffin Parks, by the way. You must be Officer McBride. Nice to meet you. Welcome to Nugget."

"Nice to meet you too." She glanced over at the bear, wary, her hand on her holster. The creature didn't pay them any mind, just continued to chow on trash. "When I got the call I thought it would be a dog . . . like a pit bull."

"It's my fault for keeping the Dumpster unlocked. It's a hassle otherwise. He'll likely take off when he's done, but I can't risk it, especially with tourists. You'd be surprised how many of them think it's a good idea to pose their kids with a bear for a close-up. Or try to feed them."

"Animal control is on its way." Hopefully she sounded like she knew what she was doing because she didn't have the foggiest notion what the protocol for dealing with wildlife was.

Griffin nodded. "How you liking the town so far?"

It's different, that's for sure. "I'm liking it. You grow up here?"

"Nope. Visited when I was a kid and the place stuck with me. So I bought the gas station two summers ago. Best move I ever made. I hear you're living in Rhys's duplex on Donner Road next to Brady."

"Uh-huh." She didn't know how she felt about people knowing where she lived, but apparently there was no getting around it in this town.

"If you're looking to buy a house, drop by Sierra Heights."

"That big gated community? On my salary?" She laughed.

"I'll cut you a good deal."

Was this guy joking? "How's that?"

"I own it."

Surprise must've been written all over her face because he smiled. "I thought it would be a good investment, but the truth is, I'm having trouble selling them. Mostly people just want to rent them on a weekly basis for vacation houses."

A million questions flitted through her head, like how in the world could he afford an entire upscale development? Perhaps it was the grease-splattered coveralls, but she just wasn't buying it. They both perked up at the sound of an engine.

"I'll check to see if that's our friends from California Department of Fish and Wildlife," Griffin said, and left her standing there with the bear. Fish and wildlife, huh? And here she thought it would be a dog catcher.

With one hand on her weapon, she got as close as she safely could, pulled out her phone, and snapped a couple of pictures. Her brothers were gonna die. She quickly shoved the phone in her pocket as Griffin returned. The fish and wildlife guy trailed behind him.

"This is Ty," Griffin told Sloane. "He's our go-to guy for bears."

"You the new girl?" Ty winked. Since he was a white-haired, grandfatherly looking fellow, she didn't take offense.

"I'm the new girl and a little out of my depth here," she said. "What do we do with him?" Sloane nudged her head at the bear.

"Unless we think the animal is a danger, I monitor the site and make sure he eventually returns to the wilderness. Spread pretty thin these days, we'll often bring in local law enforcement to keep an eye on the situation until we get there."

"You won't kill him, right?"

"Nah. But Griffin here needs to keep that Dumpster locked."

"I know, Ty. I got lazy."

"So do I stay with you?" Sloane asked.

His lips curved up into a playful smile. "You can if you want. But it's not necessary."

Well, in that case she needed to get going and patrol a few of the neighborhoods left on her beat list. Sloane said goodbye to Griffin and Ty, and radioed Connie to let her know she was leaving the Gas and Go.

"Rhys wants you to come back to the station," Connie told her.

She had no idea what that was about, but she pointed her vehicle onto Main Street and headed for the square. A few minutes later, she ducked inside the office, hoping that Jake would be there to give her a heads-up. No such luck.

Rhys came into the main area, an open room with cubicles and a few desks, and beckoned Sloane into his office. "I heard you tangled with a bear. Bet you didn't get too many of those in LA."

"No, sir."

"Just call me Rhys."

"Okay, sir . . . Rhys."

The chief shut the door behind them. "Take a seat."

Sloane wasn't getting a good vibe and wondered if someone had complained about her. Although she couldn't imagine who. All her contacts so far had been nonconfrontational, downright pleasant in most instances.

"I got a call from LAPD today," Rhys said.

Here it starts all over again. "Yeah, I bet you did." She wouldn't even pretend to be surprised. "It didn't take 'em long, did it? Who was it? Jacobs?"

He didn't say anything. Just watched her. It was an investigative trick to get the other person to talk. Did he think she didn't know that?

"What did Jacobs say?"

"It's not important since I'll judge your work for myself."

"He told you I was crazy—a hysterical female with a persecution complex—didn't he?"

"Are you?"

That certainly didn't take long. "No," she said, but what was the point. He'd just believe whatever the lieutenant told him. The brotherhood.

"Look, the only reason I'm telling you this is because I don't want you thinking I'm taking calls behind your back. I have the utmost faith in you, Sloane, or else you wouldn't be working here. I also want you to watch out for yourself. I didn't like this guy's tone."

"Did he threaten me?" She should probably tell Rhys about the voice mails, but running to her new boss would make her seem hysterical. The calls couldn't even be traced. They just sounded like idle threats. Pranks, really.

"No. He wouldn't be stupid enough to do that publicly. Although I did get the impression he thought I was a Barney Fife type and that I'd be real beholden to him for passing on the information."

Sloane knew that before becoming chief in his home town, Rhys had been a narcotics detective in Houston. He'd left a big promotion—homicide lieutenant—to come here. That folksy Texas drawl might fool some people, but Rhys Shepard knew the workings of a big metropolitan police force.

"Just keep on your toes," he continued. "And if you've got a problem, come to me. Or if you're more comfortable, go to Jake."

"All right. I'm sorry Jacobs bothered you, Chief."

"Don't apologize for other people. Go grab some lunch."

She couldn't get out of the office fast enough. Halfway home she started to cry. Sloane wasn't typically a weeper, but the barrage of harassment seemed to be starting all over again. For months she hadn't felt safe in LA and thought Nugget would at least offer security—it was eight hours away from LA. But even here trouble shadowed her.

She took the turn on Donner Road and bumped along the rutted road until she came to the duplex's driveway. After parking in her usual spot, Sloane blew her nose and started for her apartment only to run into Brady on the porch.

He tilted his head. "Hey, you okay?"

"Allergies," she said, and quickly turned the key in her lock. "I only have a half hour for lunch so I've got to . . ." She pointed at her door.

He stood there anyway. "Something happen at work?"

"I saw a bear," she said, and in a move that was so out of character for her, burst into yet another round of tears.

"Must've been some bear." He somehow maneuvered her onto his porch swing and scooted next to her. "Tell me what's wrong."

She wanted to hide, she was so embarrassed. What kind of cop cries on the job? This is why women got reputations for being too emotional in the workplace. "It's nothing . . . just stuff I left behind. I really don't want to talk about it, Brady."

"Okay. But just sit here for a second and take a couple of deep breaths."

She wished she had more tissues. Brady reached into his back pocket and pulled out a handkerchief.

"Use this. It's clean."

She wiped her nose. "Are you on a break from work too?" He had on the baggy chef pants.

"Yeah. Usually I just hang out at the inn and work on menus, but I was out late last night and thought I'd catch an hour's sleep."

She wondered where he'd been. Not a lot going on in this town past nine, unless he'd gone to Reno.

"So you saw a bear, huh?"

"It was eating garbage at the Gas and Go. Ty from fish and wildlife came."

"I still haven't seen one. Everyone says they're all over the place."

She pulled out her phone and showed him the pictures. "I took them to send to my brothers."

"He's a big fellow." He bent over to get a better look and his leg skimmed hers. It felt nice. Warm and solid.

"Do you know Griffin, the guy who owns the Gas and Go? Does he really own Sierra Heights too?"

Brady nodded. "The guy's loaded. He's half Wigluk and gets proceeds from the casino."

"Wow." She never would've guessed he was rich from looking at him. Just a working stiff like the rest of them.

"You feel better now?" he asked.

She had started to shiver and he put his arm around her shoulders.

Whether it was the comfort he offered or the crying jag, she did indeed feel better.

"I do. Thank you, Brady."

"No problem. Next time you want lunch, come over to the inn and I'll feed you."

He probably felt sorry for her and wanted to save her. A lot of men she'd known were like that. Sloane was perfectly capable of saving herself. But she could always use a good meal.

Chapter 4

Brady came into the Lumber Baron Tuesday morning to find Lina behind the desk.

"Hey, good to see you again. You remember me?" he asked.

"Of course I do. Brady Benson, best chef in Nugget."

Not that that was saying much, but Brady appreciated the compliment just the same. "Don't you have school?"

"The spring semester doesn't start until the twentieth."

"You settled in?"

"I got an apartment off campus. Rhys and Maddy are helping me move in this weekend. Just trying to earn a few bucks in the meantime."

"I have a catering gig . . . Jake Stryker and Cecilia Rodriguez's wedding next month . . . if you're interested. Although it'll crimp whatever Valentine's Day plans you might have. The wedding is on the fourteenth."

The girl was a knockout and Brady imagined she had no shortage of guys chasing after her. He'd heard that she and Griffin Parks used to be an item. Although Brady thought Griff seemed a little old for her. Lina was just a kid.

"I'll take it." She said it with such enthusiasm that Brady laughed.

"Okay. I'll give you the details later."

Right now he had breakfast to make. This morning they had only three couples and a businessman staying at the inn, so preparations would be easy. When he got to the kitchen he found Jake sitting on a stool, sipping a cup of coffee.

"Nice kitchen," Jake said. "I don't think I've ever been in here before."

"Welcome," Brady said, and immediately started on a frittata. "You come to drop off Cecilia's list?"

"Yep. She keeps changing her mind."

"Brides tend to do that. But we've got a little time and I'm pretty flexible. I've got to say that I like the idea of doing a tapas bar. A little something for everyone."

"She's sticking with that," Jake said. "She just keeps changing the types of appetizers. One day she's gung ho about shrimp, the next she wants tuna."

"Why don't we just do both?"

"Something about it clashing with the wine. I don't know. I'm leaving it to the two of you."

"I'll sit down with her and we'll hash it out." Cecilia liked to cook. In Brady's experience good cooks were the most finicky about the food at their receptions. He couldn't blame them. The food made the event.

"How's it working out with Sloane living next door?" Jake asked, and Brady got the impression that the detective looked out for her. He'd been the one to bring her to Nugget, according to Maddy.

"Good. We don't see a lot of each other . . . different schedules." No way was he telling Jake about her minor breakdown the other day. She'd want that private.

Brady suspected that the tears had been over a boyfriend thing. Sloane was probably in the midst of a bad breakup, hence her relocation to the ends of the earth and a need for a "change of scenery." Perhaps the guy had been another cop and LAPD wasn't big enough for the both of them. That's why it was best to steer clear of romances too close to home.

Unfortunately, Brady had learned that the hard way.

After breakfast, he threw together a couple of hors d'oeuvres for the afternoon service. They expected a few more guests, but like most winter weeknights, bookings remained light. Lina popped in and made lunch out of leftover frittata and fruit salad. He heated some of yesterday's biscuits for her while he prepared menus for the rest of the week.

"So you want to build bridges, huh?"

"Yep. Specifically suspension bridges like the Golden Gate and the Bay Bridge."

"Sounds complicated," Brady said as he cleaned the range. When it came to the kitchen, he was a neat freak.

"It is sort of, but I find it fascinating." Her dimple showed when she smiled and once again Brady noted how pretty Rhys's baby sister was. Dark hair, dark eyes, and olive skin. She reminded him a little of Eva Longoria.

With both her parents gone, the police chief probably had his hands full keeping the boys away. Lina took her dishes to the sink, washed them, and headed back to the reservation desk. It was nice having someone competent for a change. Truthfully, he didn't know why Maddy, Nate, and Sam kept Andy around. Brady had never hesitated to fire one of his slacker line cooks.

He pulled out his laptop and was about to check his email when Lina escorted Sloane into the kitchen.

"You still willing to feed me?" she asked and looked a little sheepish.

"Absolutely. Grab a seat at the island."

He pulled out what was left of the frittata and fruit salad from the refrigerator, made up a plate of the appetizers, and started heating everything.

"I don't think I can stand another Bun Boy burger, and I've been living off dinners at the Ponderosa," she said.

"We've got limited options." It was on the tip of his tongue to invite her to this great Indian restaurant he'd discovered in Glory Junction, but stopped himself. "If you're willing to drive a half hour there are a couple of good places in Glory Junction."

"That's what Jake was saying. For a small town the Ponderosa is phenomenal and the fries at the Bun Boy can't be beat, but I like a little variety. In fact I'd kill for sushi or a *bánh mì*."

He liked a woman who was passionate about food. Hell, if he didn't watch it, he could really like her. Beautiful, nice to talk to, and not afraid to eat. Half the women in LA were anorexic, and the other half lived on protein drinks because they considered sitting down to a meal a time suck. He pulled her plate out of the oven, added a scoop of the fruit, wiped the edges, and placed it in front of her with a mock flourish.

"So what were your favorite restaurants in HelLA?" he asked, and cocked his hip against the counter to watch her eat. Today she had her hair tied back in a ponytail, which kind of did it for him. Sporty and a whole lot sexy.

"There were so many. Pizzeria Mozza of course; Mexicali Taco and Co.; Picca."

He nodded his head in agreement, although he thought Kiriko was better than Picca.

"Let's see," she continued. "Gjelina, Lucques, Langer's . . . ah, the pastrami . . . Hunan Mao and my favorite, Pig and Tangelo."

Before he could stop himself, Brady blurted, "That was my place."

"Pig and Tangelo? The best, right?"

Apparently she thought he meant his place to eat. He kept quiet. A quick search on the Internet and she'd know in an instant, but why advertise? The greatest thing about Nugget was that he could hide in plain view—as long as word didn't get back to LA, where six degrees of separation really did exist.

"This is good," she said with her mouth full. "Really good."

"Glad you like it." He searched the refrigerator to see if any of the chocolate *pots de crème* were left and found one hiding in the back behind the milk. In a mixer, he whipped cream, spooned a dollop onto the chocolate, and slid the ramekin and a spoon to her. "Try this."

She dipped the spoon in, held it up to her mouth and licked. It about drove him crazy.

"My God, this is good. If you leave it here, I'll eat the whole thing and then I'll need a nap."

He shrugged. "So, take a nap."

"I have to go back to work." Sloane pushed the dish toward him right before Connie came over the radio, saying something about an 11-84 near the high school.

"What's that?" Brady asked.

"They need me to direct traffic." She hopped off the stool. "Must've been a fender bender. I hate to dine and dash without doing my dishes . . ."

"Don't worry about it." He waved her off, happy that it wasn't anything more serious.

By the time he got home the sun had started to set. Brady sat in the van for a few seconds watching color paint the sky. They'd had an unprecedented number of clear nights. But it was cold when he got out. Sloane's police SUV was parked in its usual spot. She'd beaten him home. Now didn't that sound funny?

He was halfway to the porch when she came jogging down the driveway. "You ran the fire trail?"

She nodded, then bent over with exhaustion. He waited a few seconds for her to catch her breath and noticed that she had her sidearm again. He didn't know much about police protocol, but it seemed odd that she would run with a gun, especially in a place like this. Unless she was afraid of mountain lions.

"I managed to run it the whole way this time," she said, huffing. "I would've waited for you, but it was getting dark."

He didn't want their running together to become a habit, yet he felt an acute sense of disappointment that he'd gotten home too late. Her top was tied around her waist above the elastic holster, and the cold did nice things to her sports bra.

"I better get inside," she said, sounding self-conscious. Maybe she'd caught him looking.

"Good night." He waited for her to get inside, then unlocked his door.

But not before checking that the piece of paper he'd stuck between the top rail and the casing was still there.

A couple of days passed without incident and Sloane started to think that the troublemakers in RHD had moved on. Out of sight, out of mind. Isn't that what they said? They were probably so inundated with robberies and homicides that they'd finally forgotten about her. They'd gotten what they wanted, anyway. They'd pushed her out.

She looked outside to see if Brady's van was gone. She knew he typically took off Wednesdays, when the inn was the least crowded. Today was her day off as well, and she wondered if he wanted to hit one of the slopes near Glory Junction if there was even enough powder. Just two people sharing a mutual interest in skiing. She'd seen his gear in the shed and noticed that he had a rack on his van.

Other than Jake, she didn't have any friends here. Connie had reached out, but Sloane was leery of getting too close to anyone in the department. That left Brady. She still couldn't figure out whether he was seeing anyone. There'd been no signs of female life on his side of the duplex, though a couple of nights he'd gone out until late. Not that she was keeping track.

She dragged herself into the kitchen, turned on the coffeemaker, and went to take a quick shower. After dressing, she assessed the stack of boxes that still lined her living room wall and decided to stay home and finish unpacking. Later, she'd go to Reno and buy paint. And groceries. At least sandwich meats for lunches, and dinner meals she could pop in the microwave.

She'd just poured herself a cup of coffee when someone knocked. She grabbed her weapon off the kitchen counter and made her way to the front door. Through the peephole stood a dark-haired woman about Sloane's age and a dog. Some kind of an Australian shepherd mix.

Sloane tucked the gun in the back waistband of her jeans, covered it with her baggy sweatshirt, and opened the door. "Hi. Can I help you?"

"I'm Harlee Roberts. I live just over the hill in the big log cabin house."

Sloane had probably driven past the house during patrol. "Would you like to come in?"

Harlee told the dog—Max—to stay on the porch and followed Sloane into the living room.

"Sorry about the mess. I haven't had time to completely unpack or organize." Sloane cleared off the couch so Harlee could sit. "You want something to drink?" In LA, neighbors never came over to introduce themselves. Sloane had begun to think it was only a Midwestern thing.

"Some coffee if you have it made." Harlee probably could smell the fresh-brewed pot. It was a small place, scent traveled.

"Sure. You want cream and sugar?"

"Just a little cream."

Sloane went to the kitchen to fill a mug for Harlee and grab her own.

"You have really nice stuff," Harlee said on Sloane's return, and took the cup from her. "My mom owns a store in the Bay Area that sells a lot of things like yours. You'd like it. She also carries some of my husband's pieces."

"Your husband wouldn't by any chance be the guy who made Brady's rocking chair and swing?" She couldn't remember his name off the top of her head. Something Irish.

"Yep. He also made the rockers at the Lumber Baron, the planters in the square, and the tables and benches at Lucky's cowboy camp."

"Brady said his studio was nearby. I'd love to come over sometime and get one." She wondered if they were very expensive.

"Anytime," Harlee said. "His studio is right behind our house. He built that too."

"Have you guys lived here long?"

"Colin, about four years. I met him here when I moved into my family's vacation cabin last fall. But I've been coming up since I was a kid. So you're from LA, huh?"

"Chicago, originally."

"Welcome. It's a really nice town. Do you like to bowl? The reason I ask is that Darla . . . she runs the barbershop with her dad, Owen . . . and I are always looking for young, single people to come to our bowling parties. When we started, both Darla and I were single. Now she's engaged to Wyatt Lambert."

"Wyatt from Nugget PD?" Uh, duh. How many Wyatt Lamberts could there be in this town? Sloane had liked him instantly.

"Uh-huh. And Connie too. We've been trying to get Brady to come, but he says he hates bowling."

Sloane wondered if that meant Brady was single. "I'll come," she said, thinking that it would be a good way to meet people.

"Great." Harlee smiled. "Griffin, of the Gas and Go, and his mechanic, Rico, come. And Tawny Wade and Lucky Rodriguez recently joined the group."

"Sounds like fun. Although I have to warn you, I'm not much of a bowler."

Harlee laughed. "Neither are we. We mostly use it as an excuse to drink beer and socialize."

That worked for Sloane. "When's the next one?"

"I'll talk to Darla. We'll try to do it on a night both you and Wyatt aren't on duty."

"Sounds great," Sloane said. "So do you work with your husband in his furniture business?"

"Occasionally I'll pitch in with some of the office work. But I have my hands full with the *Nugget Tribune*. I own it, run it, and pretty much write all the stories."

"Seriously?" After Brady told her about it, Sloane had gotten a subscription and scanned the online newspaper every day. The website had everything from national wire stories to local news. Even birth, wedding, and death announcements, recipes, a ranching column, and a fish report. "It's a great newspaper."

Harlee looked surprised. "Thanks. I don't get that too often. The Nugget Mafia likes to say that if it was a 'real newspaper' "—she made finger quotes in the air—"they could at least use it to wrap their steelhead in."

Sloane knew the Nugget Mafia included the mayor, barber, and a bunch of other old guys who hung out either at the barbershop or the gas station, playing cards. They liked to call her "Blondie" and tell her how to do her job. The chief had told her to ignore them.

"The *Nugget Tribune* is the other reason I came," Harlee continued. "I wanted to do a profile on you since you're the newest addition to our police department."

Caught off guard, Sloane sputtered. "Uh . . . I'd have to check with the chief." The last thing she needed was to draw attention to herself.

"Rhys won't care," Harlee assured her.

Sloane shrugged and tried to sound apologetic. "In LA we always had to go through the public information office to talk to the media. I'd feel better if I checked with him first."

She didn't want to seem difficult, she really didn't. In this town, she got the sense that more than half the job was public outreach. But she didn't want a reporter dredging up what had happened in Los Angeles and slapping it on the front page with a banner headline. She'd been lucky to have escaped the press in LA, especially after they found Sweeney dead.

The scandal had been mostly confined to the department. There was a slight chance that if the story had been leaked to the media, she would've had protection from the ceaseless threats, the awful phone calls in the middle of the night, and the dead rodents in her locker. Maybe she would've been transferred to a unit that had her back, instead of being stuck with the same detectives who nearly got her killed. But Sloane was more inclined to think that media attention would've made things worse. Much worse. And it had only been a matter of time before the *LA Times* or the *Daily News* had started sniffing around.

"Okay." Harlee took another sip of her coffee and smiled like she was onto Sloane. "Brady didn't want to do it either. Some people are shy about being in the paper. I get it. It took me a while to get Emily Mathews to do a cooking column, given how the press treated her when her daughter went missing."

Sloane hadn't met Emily Mathews, just knew she was a famous cookbook author and was married to the chief's best friend, a cattle rancher. "What happened with her daughter?"

"She was kidnapped several years ago from Emily's backyard in the Bay Area. The police and FBI never found her or the culprit."

"Ah, Jesus," Sloane said. "I remember reading about that case. The father was some big Silicon Valley lawyer, right?" Harlee nodded. "I had no idea she lived here now. Gosh, that's just terrible."

"Yeah. But you must see a lot of terrible things in your line of work."

Why did Sloane get the feeling that Harlee was interviewing her? "I'm sure you do too."

"When I worked for the *San Francisco Call*, yeah, all kinds of horrible crime and tragedies. Not here, though. I thought I'd miss the big stories, but not so much."

Maybe Harlee didn't, but Sloane knew she'd miss it after a while. She'd gotten into law enforcement to make a difference. How much of a difference could she make in a town where the bulk of the job required directing traffic and minding a wayward bear?

"She's remarried, huh?" Sloane couldn't stop thinking about Emily Mathews.

"To Clay McCreedy. He's a former naval fighter pilot and the town hottie."

Since Harlee had brought it up, Sloane asked, "About that: Does there seem to be a freakishly large number of good-looking men in this town? I mean, I lived in LA, land of beautiful people, but I'd say per capita Nugget has it beat. Am I crazy?"

Harlee busted out laughing. "You're not crazy. It's something about this mountain air. Although we have our fair share of nut jobs. Have you met the Addisons yet?"

"No. Who are they?"

"They own the Beary Quaint, that motor lodge outside of town with all the chainsaw bears and the swimming pool." She made the cuckoo sign. "They wear creepy matching bear hoodies and are constantly accusing people of breaking the law. Don't worry, you'll get to know them."

From Harlee's description, Sloane couldn't wait. She desperately wanted to ask about Brady's status, but couldn't find a casual way to slip it into the conversation. Harlee stayed another twenty minutes, regaling Sloane with stories about the town and its characters. By the time she left, Sloane felt like she'd made a new friend. She'd been invited to join Harlee, Darla, and a woman named Sam—one of Brady's

bosses—to the Ponderosa for happy hour. As long as Sloane didn't
have to work, she planned to take Harlee up on the offer.

*This may not be my dream job, but I may as well enjoy myself
while I'm here.* She took her and Harlee's mugs into the kitchen, did
the dishes, and spent much of the afternoon unpacking and decorating the apartment with her pictures, knickknacks, pillows and rugs. It
was too late to go to Reno for paint, but she'd make it next on her
agenda. She was just leaving to go to the Nugget Market when Brady
pulled up.

He got out of his van, looking ruggedly windblown. From the
backpack he lugged with him, it looked like he'd been hiking.

"Hey." He nudged his head at her, sat on the porch rocker, and removed his hiking boots. "You have the day off?"

"Yep. Spent it unpacking."

"Where you headed?"

"To the grocery store," she said. "You need anything?"

"I'm good." He had that right. "See you later."

Sloane would've invited him over later for a bite, in reciprocation
for the pie and frittata he'd fixed for lunch the other day. But she felt
intimidated cooking for him. Her best dish was spaghetti carbonara,
which was neither original nor particularly good. But it was fast, and
fed an end-of-the-day carb craving. Maybe she'd call her mother and get
a few good recipes from the McBride family repertoire. She needed to
check in anyway.

The market was nearly empty. Ethel, the nice lady who owned it
with her husband, Stu, gave her a warm welcome. While on patrol
she stopped by a few times a day and usually bought a bottle of water
or a pack of gum. According to Jake, a couple of years ago the place
had been held up by some strung-out guy. Weeks later, the robber
took the chief's wife hostage at the inn and Rhys shot him. Because
they didn't get much crime like that in Nugget, people were still talking about it. That, and the recent shooting and drug bust at a local
ranch on the outskirts of town. It was the one everyone called a cowboy camp, which as far as Sloane could tell was a dude ranch. The
owner was that Lucky Rodriguez guy who Harlee had mentioned was
a member of the single bowlers group. According to Jake, he was
also a world famous bull rider.

"You off today?" Ethel asked her.

"I am. It's quiet, huh?"

"It got busy around two."

Sloane grabbed a cart. "I'm stocking up."

"You let me know if there is anything you can't find, dear."

"Thanks, Ethel."

Healthy eaters always said you were supposed to shop the perimeter of the grocery store. Produce, dairy, meats—the fresh foods. Sloane always headed straight to the middle, where they kept the boxed and canned goods, then over to the frozen section. Today, she cruised each aisle, checking out the selection. It was a nice little store. No Trader Joe's, but it carried all the necessities.

She filled her cart with her usual provisions, grabbed a couple of packaged meats from the deli section, and headed to the condiment shelves. On her way to the cash register, she perused the magazines. "Twenty Ways to Get Your Man." She tossed the *Cosmo* into her cart.

After checking out, she went home. Brady's van was gone again. Maybe he'd gone out to dinner. She unloaded, put her groceries away, and called her parents before it got too late with the two-hour time difference. Afterward, she warmed a can of tomato soup on the stovetop and made herself a grilled cheese. Good comfort food on a cold night. She listened for Brady's van, thinking that if she timed it right she could bump into him while taking out the garbage.

But when ten o'clock rolled around, she gave up, changed into her pajamas, and crawled under her down comforter with her *Cosmo*. Sometime around midnight she heard movement next door, turned over, and went back to sleep.

Chapter 5

Nice of Lina to tell him that she'd moved back to Nugget, or at least was spending the bulk of her time here, now that she'd been accepted to the University of Nevada. Instead, he'd had to hear it from Owen, who'd found out about it from Darla, who'd gotten the story from Maddy while cutting her hair at the barbershop.

It pissed Griffin off.

Just another example of why she was too immature for him. That's the reason they'd broken up in the first place. He'd wanted to give her space to be a college student and she'd misinterpreted that as him not being into her enough. Ridiculous.

Next month was her twentieth birthday—still too young for a twenty-eight-year-old man. He polished the chrome on the new bike he'd finished building. The owner, a corporate attorney from Reno, was scheduled to pick it up today and drop off a check for the remaining fifty thousand dollars he owed Griff. His custom motorcycle business, repair shop, tow service, and gas station had flourished since he'd bought the Gas and Go. Griffin wished he could say the same for Sierra Heights.

Morris, his financial adviser, had warned him that selling off the million-dollar homes in the gated community would take time. But Griff just wanted to enjoy living there without the hassle and upkeep of the whole development. When he sold most of the houses, the association fees would cover the maintenance and an elected board would enforce the covenants, conditions, and restrictions of the community. Although he could certainly afford to do it on his own, he didn't want the headache. He'd prefer to have more time to focus on the Gas and Go.

Watching as three vehicles lined up for the automated car wash, Griff thought that had been his best innovation yet. It didn't make money, but it got people to fill up their tanks for the free wash voucher. He started to head into the garage when he spotted an old International Harvester Scout pull up to one of his gas tanks. Lina's truck.

He could ignore her or take the bull by the horns. Since it was just a matter of time before they ran into each other, he decided to get it out of the way now, rather than later.

He walked over to the pumps, took the gas nozzle out of her hand, and proceeded to fill the Scout's tank "Hey. Heard you were back."

She looked as beautiful as ever bundled up in a ski jacket and knit cap.

"Sort of. I live in Reno now."

"Yeah, that's what I heard."

She shifted from one leg to the other. "I heard you're seeing someone . . . I'm glad for you."

He wasn't seeing anyone, at least not anymore. Dana was a terrific woman. Smart, beautiful, good at her job. But he just hadn't felt that zing. They still occasionally got together for a movie or drinks, but just as friends. Griff didn't say anything, though. Last he'd heard Lina was involved with a student at USF. Someone more age appropriate. Maybe the guy would follow her up to Reno.

"I'm looking for a good used car," she said, and motioned at the Scout. "This thing isn't very reliable." Sixteen months ago, when she'd left for college in San Francisco, he'd put a new transmission in for her. "So if you hear of anything, could you let Rhys or Maddy know?"

Not her. God forbid they talk to each other.

"Yeah, sure." The nozzle clicked. He pulled it out of the tank, hung it back on the pump, and put her gas cap on. "Drive carefully."

Griff walked away, climbed the stairs above the convenience store to his office, which formerly served as the old owner's apartment, and buried himself in paperwork. At about four his client showed up with his wife, to pick up the bike. She'd driven him so he could ride the motorcycle home. Good evening for it, Griffin thought. Although the temperature hovered around thirty degrees, nothing but clear skies.

The guy seemed pretty psyched about his new toy.

"Tell your friends," Griff said.

He decided to hit the Bun Boy on his way home, drove to the square, and parked in front of the fast-food joint. Colin Burke was in line ahead of him.

"How's Lucky's house coming along?" Griff asked him. The two had ordered and stood at the take-away window, waiting for their burgers and fries to come out.

"Pretty good so far." Besides making kick-ass furniture, Colin worked with a local contractor, building homes. He shoved his hands in the pockets of his down jacket. "Just hope the weather holds. I heard Lina Shepard's back?"

Griff nodded. "Yep."

"How you doin' with that?" The winter he and Lina had broken up, Colin had been his sounding board.

"Good," Griff said, and lifted his shoulders. "Water under the bridge."

"Yeah, right. Is she old enough to vote yet?"

Griffin pierced his friend with a look. "I'm staying away from her."

"Look over there." Colin cocked his head across the square, where Rhys Shepard got into his police-mobile. "If you feel your willpower slipping, just remember that her brother's a hell of a shot."

Griff had heard all the jokes before. Robbing the cradle. Jail bait. You name it. But in his mind, the age difference wasn't all that terrible. If Lina were thirty and he thirty-eight, no one would give a damn.

Their food came out and Colin carried his over to the *Nugget Tribune*. Griffin figured Colin's wife, Harlee, was pulling a late one. Unlike Colin, Griff ate in his truck and hurried home to nothing.

That evening, Sloane had been on shift less than an hour when she got a call from Connie that kids had found skeletal remains on the shore of the Feather River, not far from the high school. The light was fading fast, but she assumed the call wouldn't take long. The bones more than likely belonged to an animal that had washed up.

She parked in the school lot, crossed the highway, and following Connie's directions, scrambled down the embankment to a rocky beach below. Apparently, the spot was a popular hangout for kids after school. There wasn't a lot for a teenager to do in this town. A small group had assembled at the base of the trestle bridge and waved her over. They were yelling something, but she couldn't hear them over the sound of the rushing river.

By the time she'd hiked to where they were standing, one of the kids had climbed up the embankment to a small turnoff where cars were parked, and turned on his headlights. Smart thinking.

"It's right there." A tall boy with dark hair pointed to a pile of rocks. "No one touched it so we wouldn't contaminate the scene."

Sloane smiled to herself. Everyone nowadays watched *CSI*. "Good job."

She stumbled over the rocky terrain to get to the spot where the boy had directed her, and sure enough, there was a skeleton. And damned if it didn't look human. A torso, if Sloane was to guess. But she'd need the medical examiner to make an official determination. Given the lack of light it was difficult to see much, and she needed to be careful not to disrupt the area in case it was a crime scene.

A couple of the kids came toward her. "Stay where you are. I want to keep this area clear."

"It's a person, isn't it?" the dark-haired boy asked.

"Looks like," she said, and got on her radio to ask Connie for reinforcements. They'd have to take pictures and do a grid search for the rest of the remains before carting off what they had.

When she got off her radio she asked the boy, "Are you the one who found it?"

"Yes, ma'am."

She'd need to take his statement. A crunching noise made her look up to see a man coming down the bank.

"Sir, I need you to turn around."

"That's my dad," the boy said.

"You must be Officer Sloane." The man totally ignored her and kept coming. "Clay McCreedy." He stuck out his hand.

She refrained from rolling her eyes and shook it. "Okay, everyone, let's take it over here." Sloane herded the group as far away from the remains as she could.

"Was the person murdered?" a girl with curly hair wanted to know.

"More than likely not. But we'll investigate." She wondered if anyone—a hiker, hunter, fisherman—had gone missing from the town recently. Surely, she would've been briefed on something that important.

"As soon as the chief gets here, I'll need to individually interview you. Does anyone need to call home?"

A couple of the kids got on their cell phones.

She turned to the McCreedy boy. "Were you the one who called 9-1-1?"

"I did." This from the boy's father. "Justin called me."

She couldn't help herself and ruffled the boy's hair. To this day she still called her dad when things went wrong. As far as she was concerned, there was nothing Marty McBride couldn't fix.

"I'll need to interview you as well," she told him.

"No problem."

A few minutes later, Rhys and Jake parked in the turnout. From the top of the embankment, with a rope, Rhys began lowering large klieg lights. Clay helped Sloane untie them and sent the rope back up. Jake hiked down and Sloane showed him the skeleton. Together they strategically placed the lights to illuminate the area.

"Looks like an adult from what I can tell," Jake said. "Probably was unearthed after the last snow thawed, and floated down the river."

That's what she'd thought too. "I scouted out the area the best I could, but I don't think we'll find the rest of the remains tonight." Or ever. Animals had probably scattered much of them.

"We've called for the coroner from the Plumas County sheriff. Someone from the office should be here soon."

"No one has gone missing in recent months?"

"No one in the county who hasn't been accounted for. It was the first thing Rhys checked."

Rhys came up on them, got as close to the bones as he could without disturbing anything. "It's hard to say, but they look like they've been around a while. That, or animals and weather conditions picked 'em clean."

Sloane looked up to see Harlee coming down the side of the ridge on her butt. "We've got company."

Clay helped her down and she started taking pictures with her phone camera. Sloane suspected she wanted to get as many photos as she could before they kicked her off the scene.

"Want me to shoo her away?" Sloane asked.

"Nah." Rhys let out a breath. "Before long the whole town will be here. Just keep her to the side."

"Okay." She walked off to get witness statements and say hi to Harlee.

"Is it human?" Harlee asked.

"Yep. We think an adult, but can't be sure."

"Any theories? You think it might've been foul play?"

"Way too soon to know," Sloane said. "I've got to interview the kids. Rhys wants you to stand back here."

"I'd love to get a close-up of the skeleton."

"I don't think so, Harlee." Sometimes reporters and cops forgot about the survivors. Not because they were naturally callous, but because the job could desensitize you. "So that's Clay McCreedy, huh?" She nodded her head in his direction.

"Yeah." Harlee raised her brows. "What do you think?"

Sloane's lips quirked and in a low voice she said, "If word ever got out about this place, single women would flock in from all over the world."

She finished up with the witnesses. Got Clay's statement too and sent everyone packing. It had gotten quite dark and Clay volunteered to take the kids without wheels home. Given that the man was Rhys's best friend, she felt okay about him providing transportation. Sloane headed back to Rhys and Jake when her phone beeped with a text. She checked to make sure it wasn't an emergency.

Sloane McBride, you can't hide. We're coming to get you.

They were back at it. Just when she'd thought they were finished making her life miserable. She let out a breath. It wasn't worth changing the number again. They'd only find the new one. It was nothing more than a prank, Sloane told herself. Rhys flagged her over and she put the phone away.

"This is your case," he told her, and she felt a rush of excitement. Sloane could use the distraction—something a little more challenging than directing traffic.

It would probably turn out to be nothing. Some of these old historic ranches were bound to have family cemeteries on the property. One of the graves had probably been unearthed in a recent storm. But Sloane liked a good mystery.

After the coroner's investigators came and combed as much of the area as possible using the spotlights, they carted away the skeletal remains. Tomorrow they'd send the torso to the sheriff's lab and hope to get DNA. A forensic anthropologist would also determine the sex and age of the John/Jane Doe.

With nothing left to do, Sloane went home, planning to return during daylight to search the area for more remains. Fingers, teeth, a skull, anything that would help them identify the body. But it could be tough. Even if they got DNA or dental records, if the person wasn't in the system, they wouldn't have anything to match them to.

At the duplex on Donner Road, she found Brady sitting on the porch with the light on.

"Heard they found a body over by the high school," he said.

"By the river. Skeletal remains." By now, Harlee must've posted the story.

"I gather you were there?"

She nodded. "It's my case."

"What kind of case is it?"

"Too soon to tell." She sat on the swing.

"You eat dinner?"

Her stomach rumbled in answer.

"Come in, I'll make you something." He led her inside his apartment, an exact replica of hers, except without much furniture. At least it was warm.

"You live light?" No pictures on the wall. No knickknacks. No nothing.

Brady gazed around the living room at the thrift-store sofa, crate-turned-coffee-table, and flat-screen, and shrugged. "I'm hardly ever here."

She followed him into the kitchen. He'd hung all manner of pots and pans—good ones if Sloane had to guess—from hooks on one wall and lined shelves with cookbooks on the other. This clearly formed the bulk of his possessions.

"Grab a seat and I'll heat you up some potato-leek soup."

She watched him move efficiently through the kitchen, opening a bottle of wine, putting bread in the oven, and stirring the soup on the stovetop. Within seconds he put down place settings and the wine in the center of the table.

"Let it breathe." He must've known how badly she wanted a glass.

"Can I help?"

"I've got it covered." On a board he diced vegetables. His big hands working the knife like it was a third arm. His biceps flexing through the sleeves of his thermal shirt. "A lot of people out there at the scene?"

"Rhys and Jake. A bunch of kids, Clay McCreedy, and Harlee from the newspaper."

Brady smiled. "She gets around. What was Clay doing there?"

"His son Justin was the one who found it. He called his dad. Clay called us."

"Did it freak the kids out?"

"Probably a little."

"How 'bout you?" He smiled at her and she could've sworn that her heart skipped a beat.

"I've seen worse. Hopefully we'll find more. All we've got is a torso. We think the person was an adult." She moved the wine to make room for the salad bowl he put on the table. "What did you do today?"

"Met with Cecilia Rodriguez to finalize the menu for the reception. You going?"

Everyone knew that Sloane had worked with Jake at LAPD and that he'd brought her here for the job. "Yep. I'm looking forward to getting dressed up and dancing."

He shot her another one of his amazing smiles. "It'll be a good wedding. They're nice people."

"I've only met Cecilia a couple of times, but I like her a lot. I met Jake's ex number three once or twice. Her, not so much." Then again, Jake had been a dog back in those days.

Sloane was still on patrol when Jake was with the department. They met at the scene of a triple homicide. As the responding officer she was eager to help, doing any scut work the investigators needed. Jake, the lead detective, must've sensed her ambition because he let her stay involved in the case long after most patrol officers returned to the field. A few of the guys said he was probably trying to get in her pants. But Jake had always treated her with the utmost respect. Sloane suspected that she reminded him of his daughters. Besides, she got the feeling that he only catted around with women outside the department: police groupies who hung out at the bar where the RHD guys drank, hoping to get lucky. Some called them holster sniffers.

Jake had been the one to encourage her to take the detective test.

And he'd been the one to back her when she'd called him in a panic and told him how the department had turned on her.

"Will you have to work the entire party?" she asked Brady, hoping that she might get a chance to dance with him. Feel those strong arms around her.

"Pretty much," he said, and ladled the soup into two bowls and pulled the bread out of the oven, serving Sloane first and then himself. "You want butter for that?" He didn't wait for her to answer, just pulled a crock from the refrigerator.

She waited for him to sit, gave them each a big portion of salad, and dug in. The soup was extraordinary—maybe the best she'd ever eaten. "Is that bacon in there?"

"Yep." He poured the wine, cut a slab of bread and put it on her plate. "Try that."

She spread butter on the slice, took a bite, and closed her eyes. "Holy cow, that's good."

"I baked it this morning before I went to work."

She must've slept through it. Ordinarily she could hear him moving around and smell his coffee brewing. Thin walls. "You'd make a great husband." The words were out of her mouth before she could stop them.

"I don't think so," he said like it was a matter of fact.

Since she started it . . . "Why not?"

"Just not a settling-down kind of guy. I get itchy when I'm in a place or with a woman too long. How 'bout you?"

"If I found the right guy. Not a cop, that's for sure. You'd be surprised, though, how many civilian men have a problem with what I do."

"No I wouldn't be surprised."

"Don't tell me you'd have a problem with it."

"I don't know, since it's not an issue for me. But I can see why a man would worry about his woman. It's a dangerous job."

"But a woman shouldn't worry about her man being a cop?"

"I didn't say that. What I said is it's a dangerous job. For either sex. You ever have any close calls?"

"Once." But it shouldn't have been a close call. It wouldn't have been if her own guys hadn't been gunning for her.

"What happened?"

"It was a domestic call. Robbery-homicide doesn't typically handle those, but the husband was wanted for questioning in a liquor-store holdup. I wound up embroiled in a hostage situation without backup."

"Why didn't you have backup?" he asked.

Because no one came when she'd radioed for help. "It was a screwup. But it ended fine." She really didn't want to go into it. "Where in LA did you say you cooked?"

"I didn't."

She threw up her arms. "What's the big secret?"

"No secret. I'll tell you my story if you tell me yours."

He really was an exceptionally good-looking man, but she wasn't telling him anything. "Some other time." She finished her soup.

"You want more? Dessert?"

"I'm stuffed. And I really should turn in. I've got a big day tomorrow." She got up and started clearing the dishes.

"I'll get that, Sloane."

"Nope. Rule in my house was the chef didn't have to do KP duty."

"Suit yourself." But he came up behind her while she stood at the sink and looked over her shoulder.

Sloane was no little wisp of a thing, but with his front pressed to her back she felt small, almost fragile.

"My place didn't come with a dishwasher, did yours?" he asked, and she shook her head, afraid if she talked she'd stammer. "I'll wash the pot."

"I've got it." It came out like a croak and she pretended to cough.

He backed away and busied himself putting away the leftovers. Together they got the kitchen cleaned up in record time. She grabbed her jacket and scarf and headed for the door.

"I'll walk you," he said.

"I live three feet away." Not to mention that she had a Glock strapped to her hip.

"Indulge me. I know you can take care of yourself, but I'm a Southern guy. It's a manners thing."

"Okay." She actually thought it was nice. And maybe, just maybe, he'd kiss her good night.

The more she got to know him the more she liked him. After all she'd been through, it was nice to have someone she felt safe with. And the best part was he seemed so comfortable in his own skin. He didn't have to one-up her or act macho to prove his manhood just because she wore a gun and carried handcuffs. With Brady Benson there was no question that he was all man. From his hard body to the confidence he exuded in everything he did. It was so appealing that she wanted a taste . . . his lips on hers.

But when they got to her door and she turned the key in the lock, he went back inside.

Chapter 6

"Did you hear that they found a body yesterday at the Meet Up?" It was the first thing Lina said to Brady when he walked into the Lumber Baron the next morning.

"What's the Meet Up?"

"It's a stretch of rocky beach, across from Nugget High, where the kids go after school or after games, to hang out. And yesterday, Justin McCreedy almost tripped over a skeleton."

"I heard," Brady said.

"Then why did you ask?"

"I didn't know it was called the Meet Up. So what's your brother saying about it?"

"You know him. Rhys doesn't tell us anything. But he put that new officer, the pretty blond lady, in charge of the investigation. Do you think it was a murder?"

"I have no idea. What does the *Nugget Tribune* say?"

"Not much. Hey, can I ask you something?" Lina followed him into the kitchen. "Do you know a real estate agent named Dana Calloway?"

"I met her once." She'd had clients who'd stayed at the inn. Came to pick them up to show them properties and wound up staying for breakfast. That was the extent of his knowledge of her. "Why?"

"I just wondered what you thought of her."

"Is this about Griffin?" He knew Parks had dated the real estate agent.

"Sort of. I'm just curious about her."

"Can I give you some friendly advice?"

"Sure."

Brady pulled a package of Canadian bacon and a dozen eggs from the refrigerator and started on a hollandaise sauce. "Don't go snooping into Griffin's life. Guys don't like it. If you're interested in him, be straight with him about it. If he's interested back, great. If he's not, let him go."

"He was interested in me and I blew it."

"How?" Not that he really wanted a front-row seat to the girl's love life.

"He wanted to keep it casual because of our age difference and because I'd gone off to college, and I pushed for more until I drove him away."

He looked at her. "So don't make the same mistake twice. Men don't like needy."

"But I care about him," she said.

He let out a strained sigh, not wanting to get involved in a young woman's drama. He had enough of his own. "I'm not the best guy to talk to about this kind of stuff. Maddy seems like she'd be better."

"She'll just tell my brother. You, on the other hand, can give me a guy's perspective. Plus, you're hot."

What does being hot have to do with anything? Brady decided to ignore that comment. "You want my perspective? Finish school. Then worry about men." Jeez, now he sounded like the kid's father.

She blew out a breath. "What about you? You seeing someone?"

"Nope," he said, and checked the list he'd taped to the oven hood with the number of guests he'd be serving this morning.

"Maddy says the new police officer moved in next door to you at the duplex. You know that's how Maddy and my brother met, don't you?"

"Yep, so I've heard." He melted butter on the top of the stove.

"She's pretty . . . that new cop."

He stopped what he was doing and turned to Lina. "Don't you have work to do?"

"You're no fun." She fluttered her eyelashes at him and headed back to the front desk, only to pop her head back in five seconds later. "Hey, don't forget to give me the info on Jake and Cecilia's wedding. I need the cash."

"I'll get it to you before you leave today."

"Thanks, Brady."

The girl was a little flirt—and a handful.

"Good morning." Sam wandered into the kitchen as Brady dropped eggs into a pot of simmering water. "I'm pulling breakfast duty for Maddy. She and Nate went over to Gold Mountain. What do you need me to do?"

"You can set the sideboard with the usual spread." In addition to a hot entrée, they put out cereal, yogurt, fruit, coffee cake, and a couple of juices. "I got the coffee going."

For the next hour, Brady served up more than a dozen plates of eggs Benedict. Most of the guests had come down to the dining room early, wanting to get a start on their day. With few stragglers, they had the kitchen cleaned up in no time.

"So did you hear about this body they found at the Meet Up?" Sam asked Brady as she loaded the dishwasher. "Nate and I got in late last night from San Francisco. But I saw Harlee's story this morning."

"Yeah, Sloane told me about it. It was just bones . . . a torso, maybe. She went back today to see what else she can find."

"You think it's someone who's been dead a long time and just washed up from the river?"

"Could be. I suppose they'll run tests. They can probably determine stuff like that."

"What else did she say? Did she think it was foul play?"

"She said it was too early to tell. But it's her case."

"Good. You can pump her for information. How's that going, by the way?"

"How's what going?"

"Living next door to her. I figure you must be happy for the company. It's a little isolated up there on Donner Road."

"Harlee and Colin live just over the hill."

"Still." She added soap to the dishwasher, turned it on, and straightened her back. "Are you at least neighborly?"

"Of course." He left it at that. The whole town liked to play matchmaker. "Our schedules are different. We don't see all that much of each other."

"She seems nice . . . and adorable. Harlee invited her to the next bowling party. She said Sloane seemed excited about it."

"Yeah? When's that?"

"They have to figure out schedules so Wyatt and Connie can be included." They were half the department. "You planning to go?"

"Maybe." He shrugged.

"Wouldn't want to commit to anything?" Sam teased.

"I commit to the Lumber Baron every day."

"Yes, you do. And we're incredibly thankful." Sam kissed him on the cheek. "I'm taking a ride out to Lucky's cowboy camp to help Cecilia with sketching out a table arrangement for the barn. Wanna come?"

Brady rubbed the bristle on his chin. He'd forgone shaving this morning. "Nah. I've got some errands to run. But it's nice of you to help Cecilia. I know they're trying to do as much of it as they can on their own to save money."

"I love helping Cecilia. Compared to the bridezillas I deal with at the Breyer hotels, I ought to pay her for the privilege. It'll be such a great wedding. I watched them fall for each other, you know? It was at Clay and Emily's wedding . . . at our table. You were too busy running the kitchen to sit with us."

"It'll be Lucky and Tawny next." The whole damn town was getting married. Brady hoped it wasn't contagious.

"That'll be quite a party." Sam sighed. "I'm so happy for them."

Brady was catering that one too, and of course he'd done Sam and Nate's wedding back in September. After Sam left, Brady pulled out some of the leftover bacon and made a BLT, wrapped it in plastic wrap, grabbed a bag of chips from the cupboard, gathered a couple of cookies from the jar, found a banana on the sideboard, and filled a thermos with coffee. He packed it up and jumped in his van. Five minutes later, he spied the spot everyone called the Meet Up. It wasn't difficult given that the place crawled with police and sheriffs' vehicles.

He parked over at the high school and crossed the road, scanning the rocky beach below for Sloane. It was cold but clear, and the river ran full, despite California's devastating drought. Brady supposed that the snow pack from the mountains continually fed the tributary. Yellow tape had been haphazardly strung across a roadside turnout used for parking—mostly by kids who hiked down the steep grade to the beach—to keep rubberneckers away and to free up more space for law enforcement.

He finally spotted Sloane near the river's edge, talking to a small group of men. She had on plain clothes and a Nugget PD baseball cap. Her blond ponytail swung through the back of the hat every time she moved her head. He tried to catch her attention without crossing the tape. His height gave him an advantage and eventually she lifted her head and saw him standing there. She flashed a beatific smile and he held up the lunch he'd packed. Signaling to give her five, she went back to talking to the men, then started her climb up the embankment. He couldn't help himself and crouched under the tape, went to the edge of the ridge, and lifted her the rest of the way up.

Her nose was red from the cold and her breath came out in white puffs. And for a minute he almost lost himself and kissed her. It surprised him. Kisses inevitably led to more, and his ordeal in Los Angeles had been enough to turn him celibate for the last nine months. But Sloane, who seemed so normal and beautiful, made him feel virile—and interested—again. She also scared the crap out of him.

"I thought you'd need fuel," he said. "I parked my van across the road. You could sit in there and eat."

"I only have about fifteen minutes, but that sounds like heaven right now."

He put his hand at the small of her back and led the way. As soon as they got inside, he turned on the ignition and cranked up the heat. Sloane used her teeth to pull off her gloves.

"It's a lot colder here than LA."

"But not as cold as Chicago?" He handed her the lunch he'd made and poured her a cup of coffee from the thermos.

"Well, not as windy." She pulled the sandwich out of the plastic wrap, took a bite, and sighed in appreciation. "I can't believe you did this for me."

"Just trying to be a good citizen. How's the investigation going so far?"

"I found the skull."

"Shit."

"No, it's good. With dental records we may have a better chance of identifying the person."

"You any closer to that?"

"No. But after I'm done here, I'll go through law enforcement databases for missing people. Hopefully by then we'll know the sex and a possible age—whatever the forensic anthropologist can tell us. We might even get DNA."

She ripped open the chips. "You want some?"

"I'm good."

"I rushed off without breakfast." She took a sip of the coffee and warmed her hands on the cup. "So good."

He grinned because she was so damned pretty. "Are all those guys down there sheriff's deputies?"

"It's their crime-scene team. I kind of thought they'd be ... you know ... but they're really good." She looked around the van. "You've got a lot of stuff in here."

It's pretty much where he stored his sports and camping equipment: spare skis, snowboard, snowshoes, a sleeping bag, tent, and kerosene stove. Why clutter the apartment?

"Hey," she said. "As soon as things slow down, I'm gonna make you dinner. I'm not much of a cook, so you can't judge."

No one ever invited chefs to dinner except other chefs. Call it an occupational hazard. "No judgment."

"You better keep to that." She inhaled the cookies and took a few more gulps of the coffee. If she wasn't careful she'd burn her mouth. "I've got to get back. Thank you, Brady. This was the sweetest thing anyone has ever done for me."

He doubted that because it wasn't much. Just lunch.

Brady watched in his rearview mirror as she crossed the road. She looked good in jeans and the blue ski jacket that hugged her curves. On the days she wore the uniform, she looked good in that too. He supposed a woman like her looked good in everything. And out of everything.

As she disappeared down the embankment, Brady drove out of the parking lot with the scent of Sloane's powdery perfume still fresh in the air. She was a nice woman and he enjoyed cooking for her. That's all.

Everywhere Griffin went he ran into Lina. At the Ponderosa, the Nugget Market, the Bun Boy, on the sidewalk in the square. Granted, there weren't a lot of places to go in Nugget. But did she always have to be wherever he was?

It was more than a man could take. Especially considering how beautiful she'd become. She'd always been gorgeous. Even the first day he'd met her in the Sierra Heights parking lot, puffy eyed from crying over her father's death. But in San Francisco she'd blossomed into a full-fledged woman. She even carried herself differently—

more self-assured, more poised, more feminine . . . ah hell, he didn't know how to describe it. But she was different.

Also different was the fact that she barely gave him the time of day. There was a time when she couldn't get enough of him. And that had been the problem. She'd wanted more than he'd been willing to give due to their age difference. Now he wondered if that had been a mistake. Because if Griff wanted to be honest with himself, he was miserable.

He tried dating other women. He went to Harlee and Darla's bowling parties. He even let a few friends set him up. But he was just going through the motions. His mind was always on Lina.

The strange thing was, he and Lina hadn't even been together very long when she'd gone off to school. Yet, the first time he'd laid eyes on her he'd been spellbound. It was as if destiny had brought them together that day in the parking lot. He knew it sounded like a bunch of woo-woo crap. Until Lina, Griffin had never bought in to love at first sight or any of that other romantic nonsense. Before his inheritance, life had been too brutally realistic to believe in fairy tales. His mother had been a starry-eyed dreamer, and look where it had gotten her. Penniless and buried in a potter's field.

"I'm taking off." Rico poked his head inside Griffin's office. "Got a date."

Rico always had a date. Recently he'd been seeing a dealer over at the Atlantis in Reno. "Stay out of trouble."

"You too, man."

Griffin gathered up his stuff and followed Rico downstairs. Maybe he'd head over to the Ponderosa. Have a drink. If he was lucky, Lina wouldn't be there. He took his truck instead of his bike. Despite another clear night, the weather had turned chilly. At the Ponderosa he grabbed a seat at the bar, noting that it was crowded for a weeknight. Hank Williams's "I'm So Lonesome I Could Cry" blared. *Great.* Just what Griffin needed.

He ordered a beer, used it to mark his spot, and got up to feed the jukebox. Something a little more upbeat. Willie Nelson's "Roll Me Up and Smoke Me When I Die," Ray Wylie Hubbard's "Screw You, We're from Texas," and the Beat Farmers' "Gun Sale at the Church." The Ponderosa cook, Tater, was in charge of the music and he liked to mix it up. Very few people knew the cook used to be in an alternative country band. But all the touring had gotten to him, so he'd retired. His parents used to own a diner in nearby Glory Junction before rents went through the roof. They'd sold the business, but Tater had learned how to cook there and got hired by Sophie and Mariah when the couple had bought the Ponderosa.

As he walked back to his bar stool he bumped into Lucky Rodriguez, who was coming out of the john.

"You hear about the body Clay's kid found at the Meet Up?" Lucky asked.

It was all anyone talked about. "Yeah. They figure out who it is yet?"

"Not according to the *Nugget Tribune*. I just hope it doesn't have anything to do with the stuff that went down at my place." A couple of months ago there'd been a shooting on Lucky's property over cattle rustling. It turned out that his workers were stealing livestock and dealing meth. The police bust had been big news.

"I doubt it," Griffin said. The poor guy had had enough problems—a daughter recovering from leukemia. "How's Katie?"

Lucky's face brightened. "Come over to our table and see for yourself."

Lucky's fiancée, Tawny, and their daughter, Katie, had snagged a corner booth. Griffin squeezed next to Katie and gave her a kiss on the cheek. The stem-cell transplant had worked wonders. He'd never seen the girl look so healthy; her cheeks were flushed with color and her eyes shone bright and lively.

"You're looking good, kiddo."

"I got a horse today. She's a chestnut."

"Yeah? That's awesome. I heard you're an amazing rider." He turned to Lucky and Tawny. "How's the cowboy camp coming along?" It was a dude ranch, but Lucky didn't like anyone calling it that. The champion bull rider thought it sounded lame.

"Great," they said in unison, and smiled at each other.

"The house too," Lucky continued. "It's all finally coming together."

"Hey," Tawny said, and leaned across the table. "I heard Lina's back . . . that she's going to school in Reno now. So?"

He shrugged. "So nothing."

"You don't even want to try?"

Lucky kissed her. "You want romance, I'll give you romance. Leave him be."

"How's your ma's wedding plans coming along?" Griffin asked. Cecilia and Jake's upcoming nuptials were the talk of the town.

"Good." Lucky grinned. "You're coming, right?"

"I wouldn't miss it. I better get back to my seat before someone steals it and my beer. What's up with this place tonight?"

"It's the only sit-down game in town, and the food's decent."

Lucky was right. Yet Griffin owned the only gated community in town and you didn't see anyone busting down his doors. "I'll catch you guys later. Hey, Katie, I want to see you ride that horse." The girl gave him a big smile and he made his way back to the bar.

Griffin saw Owen walk in the door, waved him over, and gave up his stool for the old guy. "What are you drinking? It's on me."

"Well, in that case I'll have something fancy like one of those Sex on the Beach drinks."

Griff wondered if anyone even drank those anymore. "Knock yourself out."

Owen flagged over the bartender and ordered a Coors—in a can. "You hear any more about that skeleton they found by the Meet Up? Blondie's working the case."

Griffin narrowed his eyes. "You mean Officer McBride?"

"Yep. I wouldn't be surprised if it was one of those drug dealers from the ring Rhys and Jake brought down. Probably a kingpin slaying." Owen made a gun with his fingers. "Execution style, right between the eyes. I tried to tell Blondie my theory, but she didn't seem too interested."

Big shocker there. "Owen, I don't know where you come up with this stuff. More than likely it's a hiker who got lost in a snowstorm."

"Could be." He scratched his whiskers. "But it seems to me that we would've heard about a missing person by now, don't you think?"

He had a point. "What's Darla doing tonight?"

"Wyatt's off work. They were going to some Indian restaurant in Glory Junction. What's going on with that real estate girl?"

"We're just friends," Griffin said, and drained the rest of his beer. "I've gotta roll." Yeah, if he was lucky he might be able to catch the tail end of *Judge Judy* on cable.

"Suit yourself."

Griffin put down enough money for both drinks and a tip, and headed to the front of the restaurant. Almost out the door, and who should come along but the entire Shepard clan, including Lina. Griffin lifted his face skyward.

"Hi, Griff," Maddy called. "You leaving?"

"Yeah. It's a madhouse in here." He peeked at Emma, Rhys and Maddy's daughter, who was bundled up in her stroller. Cute kid. "You guys have a good dinner." He managed to make his getaway without having to meet Lina's eyes.

Still, he'd been very aware of her. Too aware.

Chapter 7

Sloane wasn't home when Brady got back from work. He figured she was burning the midnight oil on her case and it was just as well. Although he'd wondered if she'd want to go for a run now that the days were getting a little longer. February already, and less than two weeks until Jake and Cecilia's wedding.

He made himself a sandwich, grabbed a beer from the fridge, took it into the living room, and sprawled out on the sofa. His laptop sat on the coffee table and he flipped it open and went on Facebook. He had four notifications. Never a good sign.

He took a few more fortifying slugs of his brew and clicked on the first notification. He'd been tagged in a photo. A two-year-old picture of him on the beach in Venice with his arms around psycho Sandra. She'd written, "Brady and I. In love." She'd posted it two days ago along with three other pictures of them in various poses, though they'd never been photographed together. He hadn't even known her when the picture was taken.

A week ago there had been nothing, and he thought maybe she'd finally tired of him, or better yet, had been committed to a mental institution where she could get the help she needed.

One by one he checked all the usual social media sites she loved. Twitter, Pinterest, Tumblr. On Pinterest she'd recently pinned similar romantic photos of them in various locales. At the Trevi Fountain in Rome, a café in Paris, a wine bar in Manhattan, the top of Mt. Everest, surfing in San Blas. He'd been to all those places, just not with her. The most disturbing of her postings, though, was Tumblr. She'd somehow managed to put up a looped video of them having sex. It was amazing what you could do with Photoshop these days.

He switched to his old email account. There were dozens of emails from her—all written in the last two days. Something had obviously set her off, but who could read the mind of a madwoman? He quickly scanned through them, hoping to find something threatening so the police could finally haul her in. But they weren't threatening, just scary as hell because she was not only demented, she was delusional.

I was thinking that if you didn't have to work too late at the restaurant tonight we could have crab for dinner. Or should I just come to Pig and Tangelo and we can have a drink at the bar?

He hadn't worked at the restaurant nor lived in LA in nine months. The last time he'd seen her, he'd told her in no uncertain terms to never darken his door again. What the hell was she talking about?

I bought you the sweetest tie today. You can wear it when my folks take us to brunch.

The emails just got more and more bizarre, as if Sandra lived on her own planet in a perpetual dreamworld.

Despite knowing it was of no use, he copied the emails and sent them to the Santa Monica police detective on the case. He knew it was a waste of time. The police had already told him that there was no law against sending crazy emails unless they contained threats of physical harm. And while it was illegal to post sex videos of a person without their consent, she hadn't identified him in the video and the police said the images were too obscured to completely make him out. Uh, could be because he never actually made a sex video with her. But she had somehow managed to Photoshop his arms into her pornographic show. Because those were definitely Brady's one-of-a-kind tattoos. Nope, not good enough, the detective had told him, saying his best bet was to change email accounts . . . phone numbers . . . jobs . . . and eventually addresses—to the other end of the state. *Welcome to the United States of America, land of the free nut-jobs.*

He switched to his other email account to make sure it hadn't been breached. Just some spam and a note from his sister in South Carolina. She, her husband, and their little girl were his only family after his parents had died in a car crash ten years ago. They tried to talk to each other either by phone or email at least once a week.

Kendall worried if he didn't check in. Apparently Daphne had lost a tooth and Jack was taking Kendall to Myrtle Beach for Valentine's Day. Nice.

Brady tapped out a quick response to his sister, told her to kiss Daphne for him, signed off, and put the laptop away. Next stop was his old cell phone. He had switched services entirely. But the police had told him to keep his old number just in case psycho Sandra left a threatening phone call. Then *booyah*. No such luck. Just more of the same drivel about how much she loved him and all the things they were going to do together. Three messages in total. In the beginning, she'd leave so many messages that his voice mail would be full an hour after he'd cleared it. Nowadays she was like hepatitis. She could lie dormant for days, weeks, even months, and then just like that, erupt into a liver-eating disease.

He sent the messages to a service that time-stamped and archived them so he could keep a permanent record. The police had told him to document everything, which he did. To no avail.

He brought his plate to the sink and washed it while peering out the window. Still no sign of Sloane's police SUV. He'd put new bulbs in the motion lights so she wouldn't come home to a dark house. Tough case she had there. But truth be told, it seemed to put a little pep in her step. Not that she was happy that someone was dead, just the contrary. But he got the impression that she needed to feel useful. He didn't think bear duty cut it.

He still wondered what had happened with her in LA—whether it was a bad breakup or something traumatic that happened on the job. Maybe that close call she'd had during the hostage situation she'd told him about. Brady figured Sloane would confide in him in good time. From the refrigerator, he grabbed another beer and channel-surfed from the sofa. Nothing good on. Outside, he heard a car door slam and got up to see who was there. Sloane got out of her SUV and walked the short distance to the porch. From her sagging posture, she looked beat.

He opened the door. "Hey, how you doin'?"

"Tired . . . and frustrated. We didn't find anything else."

"Like more bones?" Brady wasn't exactly sure what she'd hoped for.

"A wallet with a driver's license would've been nice." The corner of her mouth quirked up, like she knew it had been a long shot.

It was cold outside, so he opened his door and asked her if she wanted to come in. "I could heat you up something."

"Uh, I'm hungry, but I really need a shower and to change. After slogging through the dirt all day, these pants are ready to stand on their own."

"Go clean up and I'll make you something to eat."

"Oh, Brady, I don't want to take advantage. You already brought me lunch."

"No big deal. This is what I do. Go, get cleaned up. Food will be waiting for you when you're ready." He didn't give her a chance to argue, just shut the door and went into the kitchen to see what he could dig up.

He had enough ingredients to throw together a baked ziti—good comfort food that wouldn't take too long. While he boiled the water, he broke out a jar of the marinara sauce he'd canned during tomato season and grabbed a package of ground beef—McCreedy beef—from the refrigerator. Brady could hear the water going in the apartment next door and let himself imagine Sloane taking a shower. Yeah, he wouldn't mind seeing that, which lifted his spirits somewhat. Since the Sandra ordeal, Brady hadn't had an appetite for sex. Sure, he still thought about it like any other normal guy, but the thought of taking another woman to bed filled him with apprehension these days. You know what they say, *Once bitten by a lunatic, twice shy.* Maybe it was a good thing. Before Sandra, he'd gotten around. Unlike a lot of folks in the restaurant business, he'd never become involved in the drug scene. Cocaine had ruined a lot of good chefs. But he'd partaken in the after-hour parties and sex . . . and had gotten ruined by that instead.

He heard the water shut off and hurried the ziti along. By the time Sloane knocked on the door, the dish was in the oven, baking. He yelled for her to come in and uncorked a bottle of wine. She came back into the kitchen and had on black yoga pants and a skintight athletic turtleneck. He was so busy noticing how the outfit skimmed that body of hers that he nearly missed the fact that she was wearing her gun in the holster around her hips again.

He pointed. "You wear that everywhere?"

"Yep."

Brady might not know much about police protocol, but he'd known cops. He'd played ball with a few back in South Carolina and jogged with two vice cops in LA. He couldn't recall any of them packing while off duty. It struck him as strange.

"You mind if I ask why?"

"A lot of guys on the force do. Men just have more places to hide them."

"You don't feel unsafe with me, do you?"

She jerked in surprise. "Of course not. Should I?"

"Never," he said, wondering if she'd had a bad experience with a date, someone who'd tried to force himself on her. Maybe that's why she'd moved away. "The ziti should be out of the oven in another thirty minutes. Want a glass of wine?"

"Absolutely." She saw the bottle on the counter and poured them each one. "Thank you, Brady. You've probably already eaten and are doing this just for me."

"Nope. I just got home a little while ago."

"Working late, huh?"

"Just sending a couple of emails and catching up with people. My sister's in South Carolina. It's hard with the time difference to talk on the phone."

"Do you have any other siblings?"

"Nope. Just Kendall. My parents died ten years ago in a car accident. Kendall's married and has a five-year-old daughter, Daphne. We're tight, though I don't get to see them much—just Skype."

"I'm sorry about your parents. That must've been awful."

"I guess it was the reason I came out West. Without them, and with Kendall having her own family, there wasn't anything to hold me there. How about you and your family? From what you've said, I gather you're not close."

She shook her head and swallowed her wine. "We're very close. That's the problem—four alpha males always trying to dictate what I do. My oldest brother, Aidan, wouldn't even let me go to my prom without playing chauffeur so he could keep an eye on my date."

Brady laughed. "What about your mom?"

"She's great—my only ally. But I needed to get out of there before they smothered me to death."

He nodded and together they set the table. When Brady could, he snuck peeks at her moving around his kitchen. Sloane McBride was seriously nice to look at. He quickly tossed a salad and pulled the ziti from the oven.

"That smells like heaven," Sloane said, and sat while Brady served them both.

"It's nothing special, just fast. Were you out by the river the whole day?"

"Pretty much. Normally, I wouldn't eat this late, but I probably burned four thousand calories today. Wyatt Lambert helped me for a while, but it was mostly me and the sheriff's guys."

"You're looking for anything that would help identify the body?"

"Or anything that would point to a crime."

"Is that what you think this is?"

"We didn't find anything to indicate foul play, but that doesn't mean that the person wasn't killed somewhere else and moved."

"Will the forensic people be able to determine the cause of death?" Brady asked.

"Maybe. It depends on how degraded the skeleton is."

Pretty interesting stuff, Brady thought.

Sloane took a few bites of the ziti and moaned in pleasure. "This is so good. It's like with the BLT this afternoon. It's just regular stuff, but somehow you manage to make it taste gourmet and amazing. Don't take this the wrong way, Brady, but you should have your own restaurant. The Lumber Baron is wonderful, but . . ."

"Nate Breyer owns nine luxury and boutique hotels in San Francisco and a cabin resort in Glory Junction. The Lumber Baron isn't the only place I cook. Besides, there's more to the quality of life than a job." *Like not having a crazy woman sneak into your home and slit your throat while you sleep.* "What about you? How's having Rhys as a boss?"

"I'll be honest; I was worried in the beginning. But so far I've got no complaints."

"Why were you worried?"

She seemed hesitant but finally said, "He's only a few years older than me, very nice-looking, and I thought he would be full of himself."

"Like he'd try to put the moves on you?"

"Not necessarily, but like he'd be difficult to work for, especially if you're a woman. But that does not appear to be the case."

"I can tell you this, although you never really know a person for sure: He's dedicated to his family and openly dotes on them. He doesn't strike me as the type who would make a pass at another woman. I think his relationship with Connie should tell you a lot. He comes on gruff with her, but there's no question she has the upper hand. She's always calling him on crap and you can tell he's amused."

"Yeah, I kind of noticed that. I also like how he defers to Jake a lot. Someone with Jake's experience could be very threatening to a young chief. But Rhys is always consulting with him. Did you know they all play basketball at lunch—even Connie?"

"Nate and I sometimes join in if the inn's not too busy. Anyone can play. You too."

"It's been too hectic," she said. "But I might when things slow down."

He smiled at her because she was so solemn—and pretty. For a crazy second he wondered how bad it would be if they made out for a while on the couch. Then just as quickly nixed the idea. Not because he thought she'd go scary Sandra on him, but they had a nice friendship and he didn't want to ruin it. First, by making Sloane a sitting duck if Sandra ever found out about them. And second, by leaving.

When things got too hot, Brady always left.

Brady walked Sloane the three feet to her apartment again, stuck his hands in his pockets, and rocked on his feet. She got the distinct impression that he wanted to do more, but she wasn't about to throw herself at him, even though she wanted to. He was driving her crazy with all his surreptitious sultry glances . . . and the Southern accent. Whew, that Southern accent. Just the tenor of his voice made her hot. And the way he fed her constantly . . . didn't he know that was a freaking aphrodisiac?

"Thanks for dinner, Brady."

"You're welcome, Sloane." He grinned, and Sloane considered going up on tiptoes and placing a small peck on his lips. Nothing overt. Just, *hey*. Perhaps she'd rub up against him a little, you know, by accident.

Instead, she went inside and shut the door. She was just about to change into her pajamas when her phone vibrated with a text from Rhys. The Ponderosa had a 415. Shrugging into her warmest jacket and grabbing her badge, she ran to her vehicle, turned on the siren and flashing lights, and rocketed down Donner Road. By the time she got to the Ponderosa it was total mayhem. Bottles broken, chairs knocked down, and a frightened bartender cowering behind the bar. The cook—she thought his name was Tater—guarded the door to the kitchen with a broom. Two women and three men were going at it. Arms swinging and legs kicking. One of the men spun wildly, wielding a chair as a weapon.

Rhys was doing his best to defuse the situation, but there were too many moving parts for him to handle it on his own. Not without shooting someone.

He motioned for her to take the two women, who were both on the floor, clawing and tearing at each other's hair—probably why he'd called her instead of Jake or Wyatt. One's blouse had been ripped, exposing a good amount of flesh. The other was about to smash a plate over Ripped Blouse's head.

"Hold it right there," Sloane said, drawing her weapon. The woman raised the plate a little higher. "Don't even think about it. Slowly, put the plate down."

"Or what, you'll shoot me?"

"You really want to risk it?" It was difficult to sound authoritative in yoga pants. Sloane nudged the woman's arm with the toe of her tennis shoe. "Put the plate down, please."

"Only because you said please." The woman placed the plate on the floor next to her head and Sloane kicked it out of the way.

"Roll onto your stomach, place your hands on the back of your head, and spread your legs. *Please.*"

Both women complied. The other one looked the worse for wear. Besides the torn blouse, her lip was bleeding. Sloane pulled a handful of plasticuffs from her jacket pocket and restrained both women.

"You need some of these?" she called to Rhys, who had all three men down on the floor.

"Yeah, that would be good." He darted a look her way to make sure she'd cuffed both her suspects. "I only brought the one pair."

She helped him restrain the three men and said, "One of these women needs first aid. Should I call an ambulance?"

"I'll take care of it when I call for a sheriff's van," he said. "Separate the two women, read 'em their rights, and try to find out what the hell was going on here."

"Okay. I just want to get a blanket from my vehicle first." When Rhys looked at her funny she said, "One of them has a torn blouse."

"All right."

Sloane had expected him to tell her to forget it. In her experience male officers didn't care too much about modesty, especially if it meant getting a peep show.

"How you doing back there, Floyd?" Rhys called to the bartender.

"Okay," Floyd replied, and started cleaning up the broken glass. The cook also left his kitchen post and began righting tables and chairs.

As Sloane headed to her vehicle, one of the owners—she couldn't remember which one—met her at the door, looking panic-stricken.

"I can go in, right?" she asked.

"Yes," Sloane said. "Just be careful of the glass."

"Great." The owner blew out an exasperated breath.

"It's not as bad as it looks, but take pictures," Sloane called over her shoulder, and got the police-issued blanket from the back of her SUV.

Upon her return, she tucked the blanket around the woman with the ripped top, and like Rhys had requested, separated the two for questioning. Rhys had done the same with his three. A short time later, two paramedics came through the door and treated the woman with the bloody lip and checked the other four for injuries. By the time Sloane had gotten both women's statements, a sheriff's van had come to transport the five brawlers to the Plumas County jail in Quincy. Between the bartender, the cook, and the owner—Mariah, Rhys had called her—the place was almost back to normal.

"How much you think in damages?" Sloane asked her.

"It's mostly liquor and glassware," Mariah said. "I'm just glad no one got badly hurt and the place wasn't completely trashed. Insurance will cover the rest."

Sloane took in the dining room and bar. The Victorian millwork and vintage light fixtures looked original—and expensive. Thank goodness none of it had been destroyed.

"You mind getting Tater's statement while I get Floyd's?" Rhys asked.

"No problem." She headed toward the cook, who looked like a cross between a Hells Angel and a farmer. Railroad overalls, steel-toed boots, a red bandana holding his long hair back, and a few tattoos.

"I don't think we've formally met. I'm Officer Sloane McBride. I have to take your statement," she told him, and he nodded. "Did you witness what started the fight?"

"Yep."

Sloane waited for him to say more, but he just stood there.

"You want to sit at one of the tables?" She thought it would be less formal that way and would hopefully make him feel more comfortable.

He led her to one of the booths and waited for her to scoot in before taking a seat.

"What happened?" she asked.

"The lady in the short skirt accused the dude she was with of paying too much attention to the one in the jeans. He told her to shut her pie hole and continued to stare at the other one's table. The one in the skirt got up, went to the other table where the lady with the jeans sat, and told the two men with her that they were being disrespected by the guy at the other table."

Sloane stopped him. "You heard and saw all this from the kitchen."

"No. The kitchen had closed for the night. I'd come out to sit with Floyd for a bit, help him clean up, since he's new."

"Show me where you were when you heard all this." So far, Tater's account seemed the most plausible. The other two women's stories were so convoluted that Sloane hadn't been able to follow them.

"Right there." Tater pointed to the corner of the bar. "Short Skirt and Jackoff were sitting there." Just a few feet away.

"Okay. So what happened when Short Skirt went over to the other table?"

"The two guys flipped Jackoff the bird and one of them put his hand on Short Skirt's rear end. She laughed and sat on his lap. Jackoff didn't like that, so he got up and pulled the chair out from under them. That's when the shit went down."

"You mean they started fighting?"

"At first, it was just Jackoff, Short Skirt and the guy whose lap she'd been sitting on. The other two just stood there kind of shocked. But then Short Skirt pushed the lady in the jeans and ripped her shirt and the other guy got involved. Before Floyd and I could step in, all five of them started going at it. I went in the kitchen to call 9-1-1. That's when Jackoff vaulted himself over the bar, started grabbing bottles and throwing them at the others."

"Were there other customers in the restaurant?"

"Nope. Those two tables were the last ones."

"Tater, can you describe which guy stood there before Short Skirt pushed the jeans lady?"

"He was the one with the beanie hat on. As far as I can tell he and the jeans lady were just protecting themselves. The other three"—he shook his head—"troublemakers."

"You see them in here before?"

"Never. I don't think they're from around here. Were probably up for the car show in Clio."

"Thanks," she said. "You've been very helpful. And good work calling 9-1-1."

He got up and started to walk toward Mariah, but stopped and said, "You handled yourself real well."

She doubted he would've said that to Rhys, Jake, or Wyatt. The corners of her mouth turned up. "I appreciate it."

"You ready to go next door and do some paperwork?" Rhys came up alongside her while a deputy started loading the brawlers into a van.

"According to Tater's description of what happened, we may want to cut two of them loose."

"The one with the beanie and the lady you wrapped in a blanket?"

"Yeah," she said.

"I already let them go." He looked at his watch. "I've gotta call my wife. I'll meet you over at the station."

Sloane went to say goodbye to Mariah. They didn't know each other, but getting called away in the middle of the night because a bunch of rowdies decided to toss your restaurant had to stink. Tater and Floyd were helping her sort through the liquor shelves.

"Looks like we're done here," Sloane said. "Sorry you guys had to deal with that."

"I'm just glad you and Rhys came as fast as you did," Mariah said, eyeing Sloane's athletic wear. Not the most professional, but she'd been off duty. "Tater says you both got here in record time."

"The chief must've still been at the station. I was home and got here as fast as I could. Luckily you didn't have any other diners."

"Thank goodness it was late for our regulars. Usually that time of night it's mostly truckers coming through town to gas up. They're never a problem." Mariah came from around the bar. "Thanks for breaking it up. We're just really lucky to have you guys."

Sloane couldn't remember the last time someone thanked her for doing her job. "That's what we're here for. The chief is waiting for me, so I better get going."

She walked to the police station. Rhys was inside making a pot of coffee, his phone cradled to his ear. At her desk, she turned on the computer and started on her report while hearing snippets of Rhys's conversation. Something about going away for a couple of days and leaving the baby with someone's mother. Sloane couldn't tell. She knew Rhys and Maddy had a little girl named Emma, but that was about it.

Rhys said goodbye to whoever he was talking to and asked Sloane if she wanted a cup of coffee.

"I'll get it," she said.

"I'm right here." He filled her mug and walked it over. "Thanks for getting here so fast. I know you weren't on call. But Wyatt lives a ways out of town and I know Jake was doing wedding stuff tonight."

"No problem." She just wanted to file her report and get out as quickly as possible. It was weird being alone here with her boss.

"Were you at yoga or something? I know Pam holds late classes."

The truth was she'd signed up and had yet to go. Something always seemed to come up. "No. I was home."

"How's that working out . . . the duplex, I mean." He was quite the Chatty Cathy tonight.

"Uh, great."

"Brady's a good neighbor, right? I tell you, the man can cook. Nearly every night he sends my wife home with dinner." So apparently she wasn't the only person Brady cooked for.

"He's a nice guy," she agreed, and wanted to say *Don't you have a report to file?* Of course she didn't.

"You're doing a good job, Sloane. You're an asset to the department and we're really happy to have you."

Uh-oh.

Next thing he'd want to know is if they could have dinner together one night to talk more about her *future* with the department. She knew how this went. "Thanks."

"Maddy and I are thinking about going away for a few days—our first time since we had Emma. Maddy's mom's in town and can babysit. Ordinarily Jake takes over when I'm on vacation or out sick . . . but his head is on that wedding in two weeks. How would you feel about being in charge?"

She straightened in her chair. He was pulling out all the stops. "Wouldn't that upset Wyatt, since he has more seniority at Nugget PD than I do?"

Rhys shrugged. "He knows you have a lot more experience than he does. Wyatt has come a long way, but this is the only police department he's ever worked for. You don't have to make a decision right now. Think about it. And just know that the future of my marriage—and happiness—rides on your decision. But no pressure."

He went inside his office while she sat there feeling a great deal of pressure.

Chapter 8

Brady had heard Sloane haul ass out of the driveway shortly after he'd walked her home the previous night. She'd returned sometime in the wee hours of the morning. He wondered if it had something to do with her John or Jane Doe, but by the time he got to the Lumber Baron everyone was talking about a big bar fight at the Ponderosa.

According to Donna, Tater had had to guard the kitchen from the marauding crowd with a broken beer bottle, and when Mariah had seen the damage, she'd broken down in the middle of the restaurant and cried. Brady wasn't buying any of it. So after breakfast, he went over to the Ponderosa himself.

The place looked the way it always did and Mariah stood behind the bar, putting away glassware.

"Something happen here last night?" he asked.

"You didn't hear about it?"

He glanced around to make sure he hadn't missed anything during his first inspection. "That World War Three broke out and Tater had to smash heads."

She cracked a smile. "Not exactly. Two tables of people got into it with each other. Rhys and that new officer broke it up."

"Anyone we know?"

"I wasn't here. But neither Tater nor Floyd recognized them and they know everyone. Tater thinks they may have been up in the Sierra for that car show."

"No one was hurt?"

"Thank goodness, no," Mariah said. "They did manage to bust up a lot of dishes and premium bottles of booze."

"Ah, that sucks. I'm sorry, Mariah."

"Hey, it could've been much worse. According to Tater, the new cop was amazing. She took his statement afterward. I think he has a crush on her now."

Well, that explained where Sloane had rushed off to. Today, she was probably back to investigating the mystery skeleton. He'd left before she did this morning.

Rhys came in. "How y'all doin' today?"

"We're good," Mariah said. "Pretty much back to normal."

"Good. Just wanted to let you know that the three we arrested bailed out today and have agreed to pay restitution."

"Seriously? That's great." Mariah made room on the shelf for pilsner glasses.

"You need to come up with a figure in the next couple of days so we can submit it to the court. Pictures would be good too."

"I'm glad Officer McBride told us to take them. I never would've thought of it in all the excitement." She bobbed her head at both men. "You guys want something to eat before the lunch crowd gets here?"

"I'm fine," Rhys said, and turned to Brady. "How's it going?"

"Good. I hear your mother-in-law's in town and that you and Maddy are planning to go away for a few days."

"Yeah, if we can swing it. We're thinking Nate's hotel, the Theodore, in San Francisco." Brady supposed they didn't get too much alone time with a seventeen-month-old.

"Sam, Andy, and I have the inn covered."

Rhys nodded. "I'm a little worried that it's bad timing with Jake's wedding around the corner. But Maddy's mom is leaving in a week."

"What about Lina?" Brady asked.

"The spring semester just started at Nevada. We'll see." Rhys called to Mariah, "Don't forget to get me those numbers. I'll see y'all later."

Brady also left. On his way to the inn, he scanned the square. Sloane's police rig was parked in front of the station.

At lunch she wandered into the Lumber Baron kitchen in her uniform. Brady suspected she must be done searching the area around the Meet Up.

"Did you hear about last night?" she asked in a soft voice.

"About the fight at the Ponderosa? Yeah, the whole town is talking about it. Word is you and Rhys broke it up."

"I got called out as soon as I got home from your place. You probably heard my siren." She grimaced. "Sorry about that."

"No problem." He started heating her a plate of the leftover baked omelet soufflé with a side of grits, and threw together a small fruit salad. "You want coffee, iced tea, or juice?"

"Juice would be good." She smiled at him and grabbed a stool at the island. "Shouldn't I be paying for my food and drinks here?"

"Nope. If I took your money I'd get the Lumber Baron into big trouble."

"How's that?" she asked, her expression dubious.

"We're only licensed as a B and B. If we serve food to non-guests and accept money, we're acting as a restaurant. The Addisons hear about it and they'll raise holy hell."

"Harlee told me about them. The Beary Quaint owners, right?"

"Yep." Brady put silverware and a cloth napkin down for Sloane. "They're Nugget's official gadflies. Every small town has to have a few."

She laughed. "This place is bizarre. What's up with that Tater guy over at the Ponderosa?"

"I don't know much about him. Why, you interested? I hear he has a thing for you."

"He saw the fight last night and I took his statement. I thought he'd be difficult . . . inarticulate . . . but he turned out to be a great witness."

"That'll teach you to judge a book by its cover."

"You're right. As a cop you make snap judgments all the time—sometimes it's a necessity to stay alive. But I certainly don't like it when people think I'm less effective as a police officer because I'm a woman—or overly sensitive, or hysterical, and all the other labels that go with being female."

"See," he said, and leaned over so that their noses were nearly touching. "And I bet it doesn't help when you also happen to be extraordinarily attractive."

A flush crept up her face. "I don't know about that."

He pulled her plate out of the warmer and poured her a glass of juice. "Eat."

"Let me ask you something." Sloane picked up her fork. "Rhys asked me to oversee the office while he and his wife go away for a few days. Ordinarily he has Jake do it. But being in charge of a small department is a twenty-four-seven job, and Jake needs to focus on his wedding right now. What do you think I ought to do?"

To Brady it was a no-brainer. "Why wouldn't you want to do it?"

"You think the others will resent me, being the new kid on the block?" She started on the soufflé, making good work of it.

"I don't know a lot about the dynamics in a police department," he said. "But I do know some of the players there, and they don't seem like the types to be resentful. A: You're helping out Jake. B: You came from a big department. I think Wyatt was in the military before joining Nugget PD. Not really the same thing. And it would buy a lot of love with Rhys. He is jonesing to have some time alone with his wife. And Maddy's mother is here to watch the kid."

She smiled up at him, those big blue eyes of hers twinkling. "You're a very rational person, aren't you?"

"I try to be." Although his thoughts at this very moment weren't too rational. He was thinking about kissing her in the middle of his kitchen. She did that to him. Made him feel like he had all the answers. Like he was a he-man. And the physical chemistry . . . he'd never felt anything like it.

And of course that's when Tawny chose to walk in. "Uh . . . you look busy . . . I'll come back."

Sloane turned around to see who it was.

"I'm not busy." Brady waved her in. "Come meet my new neighbor, Officer Sloane McBride. Sloane, this is Tawny Wade, boot maker to the stars."

"Hi," Tawny said. "I've been dying to meet you. Jake has such nice things to say about you."

Sloane looked flustered, then gazed down at Tawny's Day of the Dead boots. Hard to miss, as they were hand stitched in about ten different colors. "Do you really make boots for the stars?"

"Brady exaggerates."

"No I don't," Brady said. "Country-western singers, major-league baseball players, rodeo stars, you name it, Tawny has made them boots. Remind me to show you the ones she made me."

"Did you make those?" Sloane pointed at Tawny's feet.

"I did."

"Wow. They're amazing." Sloane smiled but Brady thought she seemed uncomfortable, which struck him as odd, since she was usually very at-home with people. "I've got to get back. It was nice meeting you, Tawny. Thanks for lunch, Brady."

She took her plate to the sink, rinsed it, and stuck it in the dishwasher. As she walked out of the kitchen, Tawny turned to Brady and mouthed *Oh my God*. When Sloane was out of earshot, Tawny said, "She looks like Reese Witherspoon. Brady, you've been holding out on me."

"I haven't been holding out on you. She's a nice woman—that's all."

"What do you mean, that's all? Jake said as far as he knew, she was single."

"I told you, I'm not in the market."

"That's ridiculous. You can't swear off women because of one bad experience," Tawny said, and Brady shot her a look. *Bad experience* was the understatement of the year. "Okay, granted, Sandra should be in a mental institution, but—"

Brady cut her off. "Let's drop it. What's going on with Cecilia and Jake's wedding?"

She shook her head at him. "Everything is going as planned. Back to Sloane. It looked like you guys were getting cozy when I walked in."

"I remember not too long ago someone saying that about us." Brady laughed, remembering how Lucky's ex-girlfriend had spread it all over town that he and Tawny were an item.

"Come on," she said. "This is me you're talking to. You like her, don't you?"

He shrugged. "It's not a good time to get involved."

Tawny's expression grew concerned. "Did Sandra post more stuff . . . send more emails?"

"Not since the other day. But who knows with her? She strikes when you least expect it." Brady poured her a cup of coffee and got the one-percent milk out of the refrigerator.

Tawny fixed it the way she liked it and sipped from the mug. "What did the police say about the latest batch you sent them?"

"Same old. Nothing they can do."

"Brady, maybe you should talk to Rhys."

"It's not his jurisdiction. She'll go away eventually." He didn't want to talk about this anymore. "You and Lucky starting on your wedding plans yet?"

"There's not that much to do. We're having it at the lodge at the cowboy camp. Since it'll be summer we may do a few tents outside. I've already got my caterer." She winked. "So other than finding a dress, what more is there to do? Katie has already picked out twenty for herself."

She glared at him over her cup. "What are you grinning about?"

"I'm just happy for you."

"Well, I want something to happen for you."

"Yeah? What did you have in mind?"

"I don't know. Maybe something blond in a police uniform."

He rolled his eyes. "Don't you have boots to make?"

Tawny let out a sigh. "Always." She leaned over the center island and gave him a peck on the cheek. "I'll see you later. And, Brady, can't you just get to know her?"

Oh, if she only knew all the different ways he wanted to get to know Sloane McBride. "We'll see."

"I have a nine-year-old. I know what that means."

He just shot her a smile.

That must've been who kept Brady out on the nights he didn't come home until late, Sloane thought as she walked back to the police station. She was certainly beautiful. At least Sloane now knew why Brady hadn't made a move, not that she thought she was irresistible or anything. It's just that after he'd brought her lunch—and made her dinner twice—she'd gotten the impression that he might be interested. Her mistake. No big deal.

In the office, Jake sat at his desk, Connie and Wyatt staring over his shoulder at the computer screen. Sloane couldn't help herself and went over to see what they were looking at.

"He's trying to decide which boutonniere to pick," Connie volunteered. "Tell him the one on the right is ugly, will ya? He won't take our word for it."

Sloane wrinkled her nose. "Uh, Jake, the one on the right . . . not good. It kind of looks like a flower shop threw up."

"Right?" Connie reached over his shoulder, moved the cursor to the other boutonniere, and hit the Buy button. "There, you're done."

Jake glared at her, but before he could say anything Rhys came out of his office.

"It's one," he said to Jake. "Aren't you supposed to be meeting with the reverend?"

"Crap." Jake jumped out of his chair. "I'll be back in an hour."

Once he'd left, Connie said, "Good. We can talk about the shower now."

"What shower?" Rhys asked.

"The one we're throwing him tomorrow. So we can do it before you and Maddy go on your trip."

"I didn't say we were definitely going." Rhys glanced at Sloane.

"I thought we could do a potluck, decorate the place, and chip in for a gift—maybe a certificate for a restaurant or the spa in Glory Junction," Connie continued.

"I could bring my famous chicken wings," Wyatt volunteered.

"All right," Rhys said. "I'll bring the drinks."

"I'll do the decorations and something to go with the wings. Probably veggies or a salad," Connie said.

They all looked at Sloane. "I'll bring a cake." There was probably a bakery around somewhere where she could buy one. Have them write something on it.

"Perfect," Connie said. "Everyone give me fifty bucks and I'll buy the gift certificate online."

"Fifty bucks?" Wyatt protested. "Then I still have to get him a wedding gift."

"I'll put in a hundred," Rhys said. "Everyone else just do what you can. It doesn't have to be fifty."

"God, Wyatt, you're so cheap."

"Connie, knock it off." Rhys pulled out his wallet and shoved a bunch of bills in her hand.

Sloane didn't have any cash on her. Privately, she told Connie to put her down for a hundred and she'd get money from the teller machine at the Gas and Go. She also wanted to swing by the Nugget Market and see the cake selection there.

After Rhys settled in his office, Sloane wandered back there and knocked on his glass door. He motioned for her to come in and take a seat.

"What's up?" He leaned back in his chair and threaded his hands behind his head.

"I'll take over for you while you're gone—if you still want me to."

"That's great. You're sure?"

"I just don't want anyone to feel slighted or like I'm too ambitious."

He sat quiet for a few seconds. "It's not like that here, Sloane. But there is nothing wrong with being ambitious. That's why I hired you. I don't want this to be a department where people think they can skate because it's a country town that doesn't have a lot of crime."

"I don't mean it that way . . . I mean as far as moving up the ranks." Now she felt ruffled.

"What's going on with our John or Jane Doe?"

"Everything has been sent to the state Department of Justice's Bureau of Forensic Services. We're hoping to get DNA. In the meantime, I've been searching NamUs—National Missing and Unidentified Persons System—and any other databases I can find."

"Okay. Just keep me up to speed on it. So, do Thursday, Friday, Saturday, and Sunday work for you? In exchange, I'll give you four days off next week."

"Who'll work during Jake's wedding?"

Rhys sighed. "Wyatt and I will split it."

"That's not fair. If we cut the shift up three ways we'll each get to attend the reception, at least for a little while."

"You sure?"

"Of course. Now I have to go find a freaking cake."

He laughed. "You're not planning to bake it?" She looked at him like he was out of his mind. "Why do you think I volunteered to bring the drinks?"

"Good trick. Don't think I won't remember it for the next time," Sloane said.

When she left Rhys's office she was smiling. On her way out, she grabbed her purse and headed to the ATM. Griffin was working under the hood of an old station wagon but came into the convenience store when he saw her.

"Hey, how goes it? You find out anything more on the skeleton Justin found at the Meet Up?"

"Not yet. It'll probably be a while. Unfortunately, the lab guys don't have a lot to go on. But I'd like to spread the word. You know, in case someone remembers a ranch hand who never showed up to work or an out-of-towner looking for hiking trails, that sort of thing."

"I don't think you have to worry in this town," Griffin said. "Word is getting spread as we speak."

She laughed. He had a point. The town was rather gossipy. She couldn't get a hamburger at the Bun Boy without hearing Donna Thurston talking about this one or that one. Nothing mean, but rumor-mongering did seem to be a favorite pastime.

"Hey, Griff, do you know Tawny? She makes boots."

"Of course. Everyone knows Tawny. Why do you ask?"

"She had on a pair I liked. Are they terribly expensive?"

"On average about three thousand bucks."

"Whoa. Then they're definitely out of my league." Sloane had never been one to spend a lot on clothes or shoes. But she'd been curious about Tawny ever since she walked into Brady's kitchen.

"She also sells samples and seconds. You can probably get a better deal that way if she has your size. She and Lucky are building a house and a new studio. But for now she sells them out of her garage. I can give you directions if you want."

"Lucky, the guy who owns the cowboy camp that everyone talks about? How is he related to Tawny?"

"They're engaged. They have a nine-year-old together."

"Really? Uh . . . I'll get her address from you later. I'm supposed to be on duty." She started for the door. "If you hear anything about my case let me know, okay? And ask Owen and the other guys too." She couldn't bring herself to call them the Nugget Mafia.

It was ridiculous, but when she got in her truck she did a mental happy dance. Tawny and Brady must just be friends, then. Although she didn't know what she was so excited about. If Brady had been remotely interested in her, he would've made a move by now.

On her way back to the station she stopped at the Nugget Market.

"Hi, Ethel, you have any cakes?"

"Just what we have in the freezer cases. I think there are a few Sara Lee pound cakes in there."

"You don't have any bakery cakes?"

"Not at the beginning of the week, I'm afraid. Not enough of a demand. We have mixes in the baking aisle. Just make one."

She went over to the baking stuff and perused the shelves. It's not like she even had cake pans. Maybe she could borrow some from Brady.

"Chocolate or vanilla?" Sloane called to Ethel.

Ethel came down the aisle. "What's that, dear?"

"The cake is for Jake. We're throwing a shower for him at the police station."

"Now isn't that sweet."

"What flavor do you think I should go with?"

"You can't go wrong with white cake and vanilla frosting."

Okay, she thought, and grabbed a cake mix and a frosting can off the shelf. "Maybe I'll get one of these icing things to write on the cake with, too."

"I'm sure you'll make it lovely," Ethel said. "I'll meet you at the cash register."

Sloane grabbed a jar of candy confetti just for good measure, paid for everything, and put it in her SUV. She hadn't driven her Rav4 since she'd gotten here. Rhys let her take the department vehicle home with her every night.

Back at the station, she briefed Wyatt on what areas she'd patrolled, headed home and unloaded her groceries. She changed into jeans and a sweatshirt and nuked herself a frozen burrito in the microwave. At the table she watched the window for Brady's van. If he didn't come home soon, she'd be screwed for cake pans. But a half hour later he drove down the driveway and parked. She didn't want to ambush him so she waited until he went inside his apartment and had time to unwind.

In the meantime, she set up her ingredients and thought about clever things she could write on the cake.

Wishing you a long and happy marriage, since the other three didn't work out.

A little cop humor that she'd keep to herself. Sloane decided that enough time had passed since Brady got home, crossed the porch to his apartment, and knocked on the door.

It took him a while to answer, but when he did he was shirtless and rubbing a towel through his wet hair. He was insanely ripped, beautifully toned, and his arms . . . seriously inked with intricate designs. Whoa, she'd never seen him without long sleeves.

"It's cold," he said. "So come in and shut the door."

She was trying very hard not to stare at his chest . . . his six-pack . . . or his tattoos. Without thinking, she reached out and touched his bicep where an image of a fork and knife crossed like an X.

"Did it hurt?"

"Nah," he said. "You hungry?"

Jeez, did he think she was a food mooch? "No. I had a frozen burrito. You want one?"

He seemed to be thinking about it. "Sure. If you have an extra."

"I have a whole bag of them. Come over when you're dressed and I'll microwave it for you." She kept sneaking peeks at him. Tattoos weren't usually her thing, but on him they were hot. Truth be told, she'd never wanted a pair of arms around her so badly.

"Okay," he said, breaking the spell. "Give me five minutes."

"Just come over whenever you're ready." She started to leave. "Oh, and Brady, do you have a cake pan I can borrow?"

He continued to dry his hair and she watched his arms flex with every move.

"What do you need a cake pan for?"

"We're throwing Jake a shower at the station tomorrow. I got cake duty."

"You want round, square, or rectangle?"

"Uh, I don't know. I better look at the box."

"You got a mix?" He pulled a face.

"Yes. Not everyone is a trained chef, Brady."

"I'll bring a couple different ones over."

She hurried home to make sure she hadn't left any bras or panties hanging in her bathroom. About ten minutes later, he came into her kitchen—unfortunately wearing a shirt—carrying an assortment of baking pans. He lifted the cake mix off the counter and shook his head.

"What?"

"It's lame. You bake a cake, you do it from scratch."

"No, *you* do it from scratch. I do it from a mix. Actually, I would've bought a cake if I could freaking find one in this town." She grabbed the burritos from the freezer. "How many do you want?"

He eyed the bag. "I'll take two."

She wrapped them in a damp paper towel, put them on a plate, and stuck them in the microwave. "I make an excellent frozen burrito," she told him.

He cocked his eyebrows. "I can see that."

"I have four days off next week and I plan on making you that real meal I told you about, the one you promised not to judge."

"I don't judge. Just to prove it, I'll help you make the mix, even though it goes against everything I stand for."

The microwave dinged and she set a place for him at the table. He didn't make gagging noises when he bit into the burrito, so she figured he didn't mind it.

"Your place looks nice." He grinned. "Girly. I wouldn't have figured you for the flowery, ruffly, throw-pillow type."

"No? What would you have figured me for?"

"I don't know. But I like that you're unpredictable."

"What about you with all those tattoos?"

"You don't like them?"

She felt her face heat and got up to start on the cake. "I like them."

He cleared his dishes, rolled up his sleeves, and washed whatever was in the sink. She pretended to read the cake box while slyly sneaking peeks at his arms. *Mmm.*

"Let me see that." He took the box from her hand and read the instructions. "We should do two rounds." He preheated the oven and dumped the box into the batter bowl she'd set out.

Next thing she knew, he'd taken over her project, which was fine. At the rate they were going, her cake would be done in no time. She watched him butter and shake the pans until they were evenly coated with flour.

"You're good at this." She laughed.

"Not really. Baking isn't my thing."

"Don't you have to learn it in culinary school?"

"The basics, but pastry is typically a different program."

"I liked Tawny," she said. Clunky segue, but she was curious about their friendship.

"When I met her she was having a real rough time. Her little girl had leukemia and it was touch-and-go there for a while. But a couple of months ago Katie had a stem cell transplant and seems to have made a miraculous recovery. Lucky, Katie's biological father, was the donor. Now he and Tawny are getting married."

"How did you guys become friends?"

"Through Sam. Then I started bringing food over to help out."

"That was kind of you."

"Everyone in town rallied. That's just what it's like here—we take care of each other."

Sloane thought it was a nice sentiment if indeed it was true. In her experience no one took care of you if you went against the status quo. Even if it was the right thing to do.

Brady added the wet ingredients into the cake mix, stirred, poured the batter into the two pans he'd prepared, and slipped them into the oven. On the counter, he picked up the canned frosting. "We really gonna use this?"

"Yep." She pulled out her tube of icing and jar of confetti and held them up. "For decorating."

He sort of wrinkled his nose but didn't challenge it.

"What do we do now?" she asked.

"Hang out." He let his eyes move over her and she wondered what he was thinking. "After it's done baking we'll have to let it cool for a while before frosting it."

"Let's go in the living room then." She led the way, thankful that it wasn't a mess.

Brady stood in the middle of the room for a few seconds, taking it in. "What?" she said.

"Nothing. Where did you get all this stuff?"

"Santa Monica, Melrose Avenue, Venice." She shrugged "Wherever. Don't make fun of it."

He sat in her overstuffed chair. All that testosterone looked funny there. "It suits you."

"My choice of furniture? How's that?"

"You're pretty and so is your furniture. Are you getting over someone in LA?"

"No." She tilted her head, surprised by the question. "What made you think that?"

"I figured that's why you left . . . a bad breakup."

Before Sloane could answer, her phone vibrated with a text. "Damn. I'm probably getting called out again." She leaped up, grabbed her cell off the hall tree, and read the text. The color must've drained from her face because Brady came up beside her and wrapped his arm around her.

"What's wrong?"

She just stood there, shaking.

"Sloane, what does it say?"

Trying to get a grip, she handed him the phone so he could read it for himself. "This is why I left."

Chapter 9

"What the hell? Is this some sort of a sick joke?" Brady stared at the picture in disbelief.

"It's sick, but it's not a joke."

"This guy isn't . . . it's staged, right?" The man was swinging from a rope. His feet weren't touching the ground.

"His name is Lance Sweeney. He hanged himself two days after a grand jury indicted him on police corruption charges . . . stealing evidence and valuables from homicide victims."

"Jesus Christ." He read the text again.

Sloane McBride, you can't hide. You're next.

"Who sent this and why is he threatening you?" He heard the oven timer go off. "Sit down. I'll take the cake out and get you a drink of water."

By the time he returned, her face had gotten back some of its color. "Here. Drink this." He handed her the glass and sat beside her. "Tell me what's going on."

"I was the whistle-blower." She said it so softly he could barely hear her.

"On the corrupt guy?"

She nodded. "Him and a ring of detectives in RHD." When his face went blank, she said, "The Robbery-Homicide Division. It started with them stealing drugs from victims, which should've been evidence—a bag of weed, a half gram of crack, that sort of thing—and giving it to their snitches. We all had informants. In return for information we'd give them money, buy them a drink, and occasionally bail them out of trouble. We solved a lot of big crimes that way. A good many of these informants were junkies. So this ring of RHD detectives would pay them in stolen drugs. I was new to the division and had no idea what they were doing."

She stopped to take a drink. "Quite a few of our homicides involved large quantities of drugs, and these detectives grabbed everything they could before an evidence team got to it. Soon they were sending their snitches out to sell it. Some of these cops were making thousands of dollars on the side."

"Is that when you figured out what they were doing?" Brady asked.

"No. It was happening right under my nose and I didn't even know it. I looked up to these guys. They were everything I wanted to be—at least I thought they were. It wasn't until they got more brazen."

Brady noticed she was shivering and put his arm around her. "You want a blanket or for me to turn up the heat?"

"I'm fine," she said, and snuggled closer to him.

"Finish telling me."

"They started upping their game, stealing money and pretty much anything of value they could get their hands on. Some of it they had their snitches fence, the rest of it they kept or gave as gifts to their wives and girlfriends. I started getting a bad feeling when we'd show up at a house where someone had been killed and I'd see a twenty-dollar bill on a coffee table, and at some point it would disappear. But the scenes were so hectic with investigators coming and going that I didn't think too much about it.

"Then one night we got called to a home in the Hollywood Hills. There'd been reports of a man peeping in windows. Someone had caught him the night before trying to break into a home, but he got away before the police arrived. Well, this woman wasn't so lucky. He'd broken in, sexually assaulted her, and strangled her with a pair of pantyhose. Her husband had died the year before from a stroke. I remember that because she had pictures of them, their children, and their grandchildren everywhere. You could tell that this was where they'd raised their family—a place they'd loved."

She stopped and he pulled her closer. "You okay?"

"Those sons-of-bitches went through her jewelry box. They filled their pockets with her pearls, her locket, her husband's wedding ring. They would've taken hers if it hadn't been on her finger."

"They did it right in front of you?"

"No. Later I saw them divvying up their loot in the locker room back at the station. They didn't know I'd seen them. At first I didn't want to believe it. They were supposed to be the good guys."

"What did you do?"

"I went home, tossed and turned all night. I kept seeing the pictures of her family, thinking how some piece-of-shit pervert had violated this poor woman and then we came in and did it all over again. It made me sick." She blew out a breath. "The next morning I called my dad. He told me to go to internal affairs."

"Did you go?"

She nodded. "They opened an investigation immediately and started pulling detectives in for questioning. I never hid the fact that I was the one who went to IA. The entire division, plus the Police Protective League—my own union—did everything under the sun to discredit me. I was seeing a counselor to work through a shaken-baby case I'd investigated. Those are difficult for even the most jaded investigators and I just needed someone to talk to. It was supposed to be confidential. But somehow they got hold of the information and started spreading that I was in the midst of a mental breakdown. Then they pulled a new one out of the hat. Months earlier, I'd dated one of the targets of the investigation. He was going through a divorce, and in the end he wound up going back to his wife. No hurt feelings whatsoever. Yet, all of a sudden he and the rest of the division are making allegations that I'm a woman spurned. That after he dumped me, I went nuts and threatened to make him pay—hence the trumped-up charges. Like what kind of woman would do that?"

If she only knew, Brady thought. "Wait a second. Wasn't it an open-and-shut case . . . I mean once the family reported that the jewelry was missing, what defense could these guys possibly have? You saw them with the stuff."

"The family did report it missing. But it could've just as easily been stolen by her killer, who we still hadn't caught."

"Ah, Jesus." Brady scrubbed his hand through his hair. "Sorry, keep going."

"These were really respected guys, Brady, and soon cops from other divisions were avoiding me in the hallways. Someone put a dead rat in my locker, someone scrawled 'liar' in red paint on the door of my apartment, and no one would ride with me. The lieutenant, who was supposed to step in and have my back, just looked the other way."

Sloane leaned her head against the couch. "A few of the detectives' snitches had begun to talk to the IA investigators, who got enough to get warrants to search a number of the RHD guys' houses. They found some of the jewelry at Lance Sweeney's. Soon after, the case was brought before a grand jury and heads began to roll. Instead of vindicating me, it made people in the division even angrier. And when Lance committed suicide they were out for blood. He'd been everyone's best buddy in RHD—the guy you confided in, the one who took care of your dog when you went out of town, and who had your six in a crisis."

"But he was a thief and a liar." It bothered Brady that these cops made the really good ones look bad.

"I know," Sloane said. "I don't blame myself for his death. But everyone else did."

"What did they do?" Brady had a bad feeling he already knew.

"I got called out on a domestic violence case. Usually RHD doesn't handle those, but like I told you before, the suspect was a person of interest in a liquor store shooting. When we got there, I went to the front door and my partner took the back. The guy had barricaded himself in and afterward we learned that he was holding his ex and two kids hostage. As soon as I knocked, he put a bullet through the door, missing me by inches. I took cover and called for backup, not knowing if my partner had been shot at too. I waited and waited while the crazy guy in the house took a few more shots at me. It took them twenty freaking minutes to respond. In a situation like that it's an eternity."

"Where was your partner?"

"To this day I don't know what the hell he was doing all that time. He claimed that he'd been under fire too and couldn't get to me." She rolled her eyes. "I don't even think the shooter knew he was back there."

The thought of Sloane in danger, waiting for help while no one came, made him want to hit someone. "After that?"

"I quit," she said. "How could I do my job effectively under those circumstances? When I left, my dad and brothers came out to stay with me, worried that I wasn't safe in my own apartment. They begged me to come back to Chicago. But in the incestuous community of law enforcement, my name was already mud. I couldn't get a job to save my life. Then a miracle happened. Jake, who is still pretty plugged in at LAPD and has friends in IA, had heard what was going on, and knew how vicious it could get when you broke the so-called code of silence. He hooked me up here."

"The whole thing pisses me off," Brady said. "These guys were goddamn thugs—no better than the dirtbags they arrest."

"Please don't think badly of police," she told Brady, who'd balled his hands into fists. "Most of them are good people, but just like with everything else, there's always a chance of a few rotten ones. There were a lot of cops at LAPD who were appalled by these detectives and what they had done. They just weren't in a position to help me."

"So what's with the text? You think it's one of them?"

"I know it is. Ultimately, four guys, including Sweeney, were indicted. Sweeney's partner blames me for his suicide, and many in the division blame me for ruining the other three's careers."

"But you quit and left town. So why now?"

"They never stopped, Brady. My lieutenant even called Rhys and told him I was crazy—that he'd better watch his back. Even though it's a tiny department, they're furious that I have a job in law enforcement. They're hoping to discredit me."

"That text you just got is more than someone trying to end your career. It's a death threat. Have all the texts been like that?"

She shook her head. "This is the first time they sent me a picture. Until now it's always been vague, like, 'we're coming to get you.'"

"There's nothing vague about that. It's a blatant threat to do you harm. Is Rhys tracing them?"

She suddenly grew quiet.

"Sloane?" He gently grasped her shoulders.

"I didn't tell him about the texts and phone messages."

He jerked his head. "What do you mean, you didn't tell him? This is serious, Sloane."

"I won't let them intimidate me." She stuck her chin out.

"I'm not telling you to be intimidated. I'm telling you to have these bastards arrested. Why the hell wouldn't you tell Rhys?"

"Because I came here with enough baggage," she said. "I was lucky to get the job at all. The last thing a small department—any department, for that matter—wants is a headache. This"—she held up her phone—"makes me a headache."

"No." He pointed to the phone. "That makes you a victim. Jeez, you're a cop, for God's sake."

"That's right. And for that reason I'm handling it my way."

It was plain to Brady that these detectives were out for blood, and no matter how good a cop Sloane was, she was no match for them. He got up and paced the room. "Sloane, honey, you have to tell Rhys. Because if you don't tell him, I will."

Sloane sat through Jake's shower with a smile plastered on her face. The party was an unqualified success, but all she could think about was the text. And Brady's threat.

If you don't tell him, I will.

At first, his high-handedness had angered her. Then she'd come to realize that he was genuinely worried about her. Brady had always struck her as the kind of guy who didn't let anything bother him. The type to let trouble roll off of him like a raindrop. But last night she'd seen another side of him—a protective, authoritative side, which was supposed to be her role. She was the cop, after all. Everything he'd said, though, had been right. She couldn't disregard the last text as a nebulous scare tactic. She didn't believe for one minute that the sender planned to kill her, but it had been a death threat just the same. And that was illegal.

So sometime between the sun coming up and her first sip of coffee, she'd made up her mind to tell Rhys. Just not now. She'd wait until after his getaway with Maddy.

"You made this?" Connie said, then shoveled a forkful of Jake's cake into her mouth.

Actually Brady had made it—with a little help from Duncan Hines—and she'd frosted and decorated it. "It's a mix."

"It's good," Connie said. "Want to go to happy hour with me at the Ponderosa?"

"Sure." She wasn't on call and Brady was doing wedding stuff, which meant she'd have to fend for herself for dinner. Although Wyatt's chicken wings were still sitting in her stomach.

"Three-dollar margaritas." Connie punched her in the shoulder.

"Hey." Jake joined them, holding up the card and gift certificate they'd all gone in on. "Thanks for this and the whole party. And, Sloane, thanks for filling in for Rhys."

The chief had told everyone that starting Thursday she'd be running the show until he got back.

"No problem." Sloane took Jake aside when Connie went to grab her purse. "Wyatt isn't angry, is he?"

"He's not like that. No one is, here."

She nodded, not really believing it, although Jake had always been a straight shooter. For a while she'd contemplated telling him about the threats, but with his wedding coming up . . . well, he had enough to deal with. "Okay. I just don't want to step on any toes."

"How's your case going?"

"I'm still waiting to hear back on the person's sex and age range. At least it'll help me narrow down the field of missing persons."

He pulled Sloane in closer. "Hey, I know this is a little slow paced for you. Hell, at your age I would've died of boredom in a department like this, but it's a good group. And there is plenty you can learn here—things that will make you a better cop no matter where you go in the future."

"I know. It's all good, Jake. I don't think I'll ever be able to thank you enough for hooking me up here."

Connie approached. "You ready to go?"

"Three-dollar margaritas, here we come."

They threw on coats—Sloane had already changed into something more festive for Jake's party—and went a few doors down to the Ponderosa. Mariah waved to them from behind the bar, motioning that they should take any table they wanted. The restaurant's happy hours were popular, but the after-work crowd hadn't yet shown up, so they had the pick of the place. They settled on a table for two tucked under the staircase. She'd heard the second floor was Tater's apartment.

"Want nachos?" Connie asked.

"That sounds good."

"What about potato skins, fully loaded?"

"Aren't you still full from the shower?"

"No," Connie said. "That's why you're a skinny bitch."

Not if she kept eating Brady's food. "Okay. Let's get both."

"And a pitcher of margaritas."

A server came, took their orders, and returned with two margarita glasses.

"So you're the big boss while Rhys is away, huh?"

"It's just because Jake is busy with wedding stuff."

"It'll be good to get Rhys out of the office for a few days. He's been driving me up the wall. Don't get me wrong, I love him like a brother, but he needs to get laid."

Sloane nearly choked on her water. "I don't think we should talk about the chief's sex life."

"I do. It's not like I have one to talk about. How 'bout you?"

"Nope. But I just moved here. What's your excuse?" Sloane figured Connie, who was cute in a tomboy way, was in her early thirties and should have no problem meeting men.

"Slim pickings."

"What are you talking about? I've never seen so many good-looking guys. It's like they grow on trees here." Sloane bent over the table. "What about Griffin? You can't get hotter than him."

The server put down their appetizers, poured them two margaritas, and put the pitcher down in the center of the table.

When she left, Connie said, "Everyone knows he's in love with the chief's sister."

"Everyone but me. Who's the chief's sister?"

"Lina Shepard. She just moved back from San Francisco. She's going to the University of Nevada now and is splitting her time between here and Reno. They used to be lovers."

"But they're not anymore? If not, you should go for him."

"Not my type."

"All right, what's your—" Before Sloane could get the rest of the sentence out, the server returned with a plate of fried calamari. "Uh, we didn't order this."

"Compliments of the chef." The waitress rolled her eyes and in a low voice said, "They're from Tater. He made me say that."

Connie laughed, and at the top of her lungs yelled, "Thanks, Tater."

When the waitress walked away, Sloane asked, "What about Tater? Is he single?"

"He's single but I'm not into him. What about you? Got your eye on anyone?"

"Not really," Sloane said and played with the potato skin on her plate. "I'm still getting a lay of the land."

"What about your neighbor, Brady Benson?" She made a purring noise that made Sloane snort with laughter. Sloane tried to imitate it but couldn't pull it off.

"How do you do that?" she asked Connie, whose attention had turned to the door.

"Here come the Addisons."

The couple grabbed a table on the other side of the dining room. "So that's them, huh?"

"Yep. Be prepared for them to come over to say hello. They think they're friends with my parents. Secretly, my folks hate them. They'll also want to suck up to you, since you're the po-po and all."

Just as Connie had predicted, the minute they spied her they came trotting over. And they had on the matching bear hoodies Harlee had mentioned.

"Hi, Connie," the woman said, and then just stood at the edge of their table, gawking at them.

"Hey, Sandy and Cal. This is my friend Sloane McBride. She's our new officer—well, not so new anymore."

"Pleased to meet you." Sloane stuck out her hand. Neither of them shook it and Sandy eyed her margarita. "Connie and I just got off duty."

"What's going on with that body you found?" Sandy asked.

"We're awaiting lab results. Do you have any idea who it might be?" Sloane had been putting out feelers everywhere she went.

"It's probably one of those drug dealers left over from Lucky Rodriguez's cowboy camp. Ever since he came back to town we've had nothing but trouble."

Not from what Sloane had seen. "Well, if you hear of anything just let us know."

They didn't even say goodbye or nice to meet you, just turned on their heels and left.

"Asperger's," Connie said.

"What's up with the Garanimals?"

Connie laughed. "Yeah, they're a freak show. No one really likes them, but they have clout because they own the Beary Quaint. Before the Lumber Baron, it was the only game in town and brought in a fair amount of tourism. People are afraid to cross them."

Sloane remembered what Brady had said about them giving the Lumber Baron a hard time over their food permits. "Just as long as they're law-abiding."

"I doubt they're running a brothel out of that hellhole they call a lodge, but maybe while Rhys is gone we could raid 'em."

"What are you two laughing about?" Tater pulled a chair up to their table.

"Hey, that's the most I've ever heard you say at one time." Connie got up, went to the bar, brought back another glass, poured a margarita, and slid it over to Tater. "We were laughing at the Addisons."

He turned his head to where they were sitting, and grunted something unintelligible.

"You on a break?" Sloane knew that in an hour the place would be packed with diners.

"Mm-hmm. What's going on with the body?"

You'd think it was the O. J. Simpson case the way everyone talked about it here. In LA they found bodies all the time. Unless it was a movie star, the discovery rarely made the news. "Nothing yet. But if you can think of anything that might help us . . ."

"Will do," he said. "You like the calamari?"

They'd barely touched it. "It was delicious, Tater. Thank you for sending it out, but it probably isn't a good idea in the future."

"Why not?" He looked slightly offended.

"Because the police can't take free stuff."

"Oh," was all he said, and gave a half shrug. "I wasn't giving it to you because you're a police officer."

"I know. You were just being nice. But others might see it as currying favor. It's just the rules."

"But you can give me free stuff," Connie said. "I'm just a lowly dispatcher."

Tater smiled and Sloane noticed he wasn't that bad looking. Not up there with the rest of the Nugget hunks, but less scary when he smiled.

"Brady said you used to be in a famous band. Is that true?"

"Gold Country." Tater nodded. "But we weren't that famous."

"What did you play?"

"Bass." Connie was right, Tater wasn't much of a conversationalist. "I've gotta get back to work."

After he disappeared inside the kitchen, Connie said, "They were a pretty big deal. They opened for Ryan Adams."

Sloane didn't know who that was. Her tastes ran more toward pop music. "Why do you think he quit?"

"He didn't like all the touring. Plus, his parents are getting up there in age. I think he wanted to be around to help them out. He'll occasionally sit in with a couple of the local bands. We could go see him one night."

"I'd be up for that." Why not? It would be fun.

Sloane's cell phone vibrated with a text. She considered ignoring it, not wanting to end a fun evening with another gruesome picture of Sweeney swinging from a noose. Then again it could be work. As it turned out, the text was from neither. It was Brady.

Chapter 10

L ina came into the Gas and Go looking ready to spit nails.
        "Uh-oh," Griffin muttered to himself, and shut the hood of the
car he'd been working on.

"My truck won't start," she said.

"Careful where you walk there." She had on a skirt and high heels.
The garage was covered in grease. "Where is it?"

"In front of the Lumber Baron, parked in the square."

"You walked all the way over here?" He eyed her shoes again, letting his eyes drift up her legs.

"It's only five blocks. In San Francisco I walked everywhere."

People in Nugget drove two blocks to go to the grocery store. It
was a ranching town, folks liked to be close to their trucks.

"All right, I'll take a look at it." He grabbed some tools and jumper
cables and told her to hop in his truck.

They drove back to the square in awkward silence. Fine with him.
He pulled his truck up to the Scout and told Lina to pop the hood.
Frankly, he was surprised the old truck had made it this long. After
she got inside the cab and pulled the latch, Griff took a look at the engine. Lina came up behind him and watched over his shoulder.

"See that?" He poked at her battery terminals with a wrench.
"Corroded."

"Can it be fixed?" She was so close he could smell her perfume. It
was different than what she used to wear, less sweet and more spicy.

"I can clean it, but more than likely you need a new battery." He
turned to face her. "Weren't you looking for a new car?"

"I'm looking, but anything decent is out of my price range."

"How much you looking to spend?" He hadn't come across anything for her anyway, but when he did, it would be good to know her budget.

"A few thousand." She seemed embarrassed, even though there was nothing to be embarrassed about. It was a lot of money for a full-time college student.

"I'll continue to keep my eyes out." He nudged his head at the Scout. "What do you want to do about this?"

She chewed on her bottom lip. "What do you think I should do?"

"I'll take a stab at cleaning the terminals. See if we can get it started that way. If not, and you need a new battery, you'll have to decide whether you want to spend the money. It might not be worth it if you can find something else."

"All right. How much will cleaning the terminals cost?"

He gave her a hard look. "Give me a break, Lina."

"Well, I don't expect you to work for free."

"Then find another mechanic." He started to walk away, but she came after him.

"This is your business, Griffin. Do you go giving away free labor to everyone?"

"First of all, you're not everyone. Second of all, it's a lousy fifteen-minute job." He didn't wait for her to respond. "Go to the inn and bring me back a cup of water with a tablespoon of baking soda. If you could find me a toothbrush, that would be good too. Try to hurry—we're losing the light." Griff looked at his watch, then across the square at the folks rolling into the Ponderosa. Happy hour.

She hurried into the Lumber Baron. Every time he saw her she seemed to get more cosmopolitan. He guessed now that she was working part-time at the inn, she had to dress up. Lina looked good in skirts and high heels. Who was he kidding? She looked good in everything.

It didn't take her long to return with the things he'd requested.

"Thanks," he said, and loosened both cable nuts and unfastened the cables from their posts. "I don't see any cracking or acid, so maybe you don't need a new battery."

He dipped the toothbrush into the baking soda solution and scrubbed the corrosion off the top of the battery, the clamps, and posts until they were clean. In the back of his truck, he grabbed a water bottle and rinsed everything off, then dried it with a rag. He squirted some protection spray on the exposed metal, reattached the cables to their proper terminals, and twisted until they were tight.

"Try to start it," he told Lina.

She climbed behind the wheel and turned the ignition. After a few coughs and sputters the engine finally turned over.

"You fixed it." She beamed so bright it was like sunshine and he wanted to bask in the glow forever.

"Let's let it run for a few minutes to make sure it won't stall while you're driving." He stood with his arm resting on her window, listening to the engine. "Were you in a hurry to get somewhere?"

"No. I was on my way to Rhys and Maddy's. They're going to San Francisco for a few days while Maddy's mom watches Emma. I'm planning to stay the weekend to help her."

"What about Sam?" That was Rhys and Lina's little brother. "He's staying with Cody McCreedy. That way Clay can take the boys to their basketball practices. They're inseparable anyway."

"You liking Reno?"

"I am. My classes are great and it's a lot cheaper than San Francisco, plus I get to be near my family."

He wondered if she'd be going to Jake and Cecilia's wedding. If she'd be taking a date. He didn't ask, though. It might send the wrong message.

"You're probably good to go now. But, Lina, try to get something soon." He knocked on the roof of the Scout. "This old thing doesn't have too much left in her."

"I will. And, Griff, thanks so much."

"*De nada*," he said, and watched her drive away.

Sandra was back with a vengeance. Brady had found eight more emails in his old account, a few voice mails, and a Facebook post boasting about their wonderful time together in Cabo last month. Except he hadn't been to Cabo in January. Not with her, or anyone else. And it was pretty safe to say that between freezing his ass off in Nugget and soaking in the Mexican sun with Sandra, Nugget would win every time.

As usual, he sent everything off to Santa Monica PD, knowing full well there was nothing they could do. At least he was being proactive, unlike Sloane, who actually had a crime to report. As much as he didn't want to get involved with her, most days he found himself gazing at the clock, waiting for lunchtime, hoping she'd come to the Lumber Baron for a meal. At home, he listened constantly for her truck coming down their driveway. When he heard her rustling around next door after work . . . well, he thought about things he shouldn't, like watching her strip off her clothes.

A few minutes later he heard the crunch of gravel and positioned himself at the window. Sloane parked in her usual spot, slid out of the driver's seat holding a six-pack, climbed their porch steps, and knocked.

He opened the door. "I thought you already ate."

"I did." She handed him the beer. "This is a peace offering."

"For what? Going to happy hour without me?" He grinned.

"For getting pissy with you about going to Rhys."

"I was just looking out for you." He raised his arms, palms out. "Not that you're not capable of looking out for yourself, but I don't like the tone of those texts, Sloane. I don't like 'em at all."

She nodded. "I'll tell him when he gets back from his mini vacation."

Frankly, he didn't think it should be put on hold, even for a few days. The person, or people, harassing her needed to be dealt with immediately. But last time he'd stuck his nose in, she'd gotten defensive. *I'm a cop; I can take care of myself.*

He opened the door wider and swung his arm for her to come inside. "Have a beer with me."

"Let me change first."

"Okay. You sure you don't want anything to eat?"

"Positive. When you texted, Connie and I had worked our way through nachos, potato skins, and fried calamari. I may never eat again."

While waiting for her, Brady stashed his laptop in the bedroom and stuck two pilsner glasses in the freezer and the beer in the fridge. Sloane came back in her typical after-work attire. Yoga pants and some kind of stretchy top that crisscrossed under her breasts. And not for the first time he noted she had a hell of a body. Her hair was down and she'd also put on perfume. He was trying not to read anything into that.

Like always, she had a pistol tucked into her elastic holster. He pointed to the gun. "Are the threats the reason you always wear that?"

"I never know when I'll get called out," she replied, but Brady got the sense she was evading the truth. She wasn't wearing her badge or carrying her car keys.

Although the glasses hadn't had time to get frosty, he pulled them out of the freezer, grabbed two beers, and poured them each one. Sloane followed him into the living room and sat next to him on the couch.

"How was Jake's party?"

"Good," Sloane said, and her lips tugged up. "The cake was a big success. What did you do today?"

"I went to Reno to stock up on cooking supplies for the inn and for Jake and Cecilia's wedding. Other than that, it was pretty uneventful. You get any more texts?"

"Nope. Hopefully it was their last hurrah." She hitched her shoulders, trying to act blasé about the whole thing. Brady knew better. "I have to work for part of Jake and Cecilia's reception. We all agreed to take short shifts so everyone could at least attend some of the party."

"Seems like a good compromise. How's your case going?"

"I'm still waiting for lab results. Once they identify the sex and approximate age, I'll have a better idea of where I should focus as far as searching missing persons databases. So far, no one is missing from around here."

Brady put his feet up on the coffee table and took a slug of his beer. "Sounds like it could take a while."

"Yep. But I won't give up."

He didn't think she would. Not in her DNA. In the short time he'd known her; she'd struck him as the type to take the job to heart. She'd gotten herself ostracized for doing the right thing. Yet, there was no doubt in his mind that Sloane would do it again. That's just how she rolled. And it made him even more attracted to her. The fact that she could take care of herself was damned hot. Although Brady was a Southern man with a protective streak as long as Alaska, a strong, smart, capable woman was sexy as sin. And Sloane had all that in spades, not to mention looks that slayed him. She was the whole package, all right.

"You'll figure out who he or she is," he said, and moved a little closer to her on the couch. "There's no doubt in my mind. Let me ask you something, and I want you to be honest. You rattled over that text yesterday?"

She sucked in a breath and took some time to answer. "A little."

"Good." When she looked at him like he was an insensitive jackass, he continued. "Being rattled will keep you on your toes." It had certainly worked for him. "Given how you reacted when I told you to go to Rhys, this'll probably piss you off too: I bought locks for all your windows and dead bolts for your doors. The security in this place stinks. So as a precaution, I'd like to install them tomorrow."

"Brady, that was very thoughtful of you, but I'm perfectly adept at taking care of myself." Her eyes moved to the gun around her waist.

"I have no doubt about that. But sometimes a man likes to feel useful. Humor me, would you?"

"Since I wouldn't want to put a crimp in your manhood"—she tossed him a wicked smile—"then go ahead and get your tools out and do what you need to do."

"Yeah?" Brady leaned over to kiss her. Just something quick and sweet in case he'd misunderstood.

But when she opened her mouth for him and slipped her arms around his neck, he went all in. It was a supremely bad idea, but he couldn't help himself. Not when they'd been playing footsie for weeks now.

She hummed her pleasure, so he took the kiss deeper, exploring her mouth with his tongue. God, she tasted good. Like minty tooth-paste, beer, and desire. He slid his hands to her back and slowly took her down on the couch so that he was on top of her. The handle of her gun pressed into his belly.

"You think you could take that thing off?"

"Sorry." She lifted up, undid the holster, laid it on the coffee table, and plopped back down on the sofa.

He moved over her again and she pushed into his erection. "Yeah, that's better," he said, covering her breasts with his hands.

Again, she purred her appreciation. Her top had been pulled down just enough so that the lace edging of her bra peeked out. He wanted to see more, so he pushed the shirt up to her chin. God, she was gor-geous. All smooth, toned skin and a pink push-up bra.

"I like this." He traced the cups with his fingers. "It reminds me of your apartment. Girly." Definitely a contrast to the nine-mil she kept as her constant companion.

The bra had one of those front clasp deals that Brady was fond of. He unsnapped it, freeing a pair of killer breasts. Round, pert, and ample, with pink, erect nipples.

"Mmm." He held them in his hands, taking each one in his mouth.

She squirmed under him, tugging his shirt up. With one hand he pulled it over his head, then removed hers. The bra went too, and they were skin to skin. She watched him fondle her, taking in his tattoos.

"This okay?" he asked.

"Beyond okay." She kissed his arms, then his chest, and his chin, licking her way to his mouth.

At some point she'd wrapped her legs around him and he was so hard it hurt. "I don't want to take this too far."

"Why not?" she asked in a breathy voice that made him grow to bursting.

"Not a good idea." But he was already working his hands down her hip-hugging yoga pants. Her panties were wet and he couldn't resist testing her with his fingers.

"Oh God." Sloane tilted her head back and closed her eyes. "Take them off."

"Yes, ma'am." In one fluid motion he tugged off her pants and underwear.

He took her in from her head to her Brazilian bikini wax, then let his eyes wander down her long, lean legs. Jesus Christ, the woman was centerfold material.

He continued touching her, liking the way it made her come off the couch. But he wanted a taste too, so he dipped his tongue in her and she went off like a rocket.

"Brady, Brady, don't stop." They were a little past that now, he thought, and brought her to climax with his mouth.

She shuddered one more time and he kissed his way up her outstanding body while she tried to unbuckle his belt.

"What do you want there, sweetness?"

"You . . . more."

Somewhere at the back of his brain he knew this was a colossally bad idea, but right now another organ was doing the talking. So he lifted her up and carried her in all her naked glory to his bedroom, where he quickly got rid of his pants, found a condom in the nightstand, and checked the expiration date. They were still good, but not for much longer.

She pulled him on top of her and he laughed. "Just let me suit up, sweetness, then I'll give you what you want."

"Hurry."

Yep. His kind of woman—as long as she didn't turn out to be psycho. Brady ignored that last part as he slid into her warm tightness. Sloane had put him under her spell. He'd worry about the consequences later.

They spent most of the night and much of the early morning having sex. Sloane liked trying new things and Brady was all too happy to oblige. She blew him away. She was sweet and beautiful and sexy and . . . damn, was he in over his head. This was the worst possible time to get involved with someone. Not with psycho Sandra lurking in the background, waiting to pounce. And not when he'd always been a love-'em-and-leave-'em kind of guy. Having only a thin wall to separate them would make that hella awkward.

At least when he woke up the next morning she was gone. No kiss goodbye. No note. No strings attached. Just the way he liked it. But it didn't stop him from grabbing his shorts off the floor, pulling them on, and peeking out the window to see if Sloane's truck was gone and feeling disappointed when it was. She must've left for work.

He had the day off. Besides writing up instructions for the catering crew on Jake and Cecilia's wedding, he was free to do whatever he wanted. Since they hadn't gotten much snow in the last month, skiing was out of the question. Depending on the weather, maybe he'd take his kayak out on the lake. Or maybe he'd head into Reno and catch a movie.

But by the middle of the day he broke down and called Sloane. He'd forgotten that she was filling in for Rhys, and Connie patched him right through to her phone.

"Hey." She let out a nervous giggle. In a low voice she said, "I hope I didn't wake you this morning."

"Nope. Is it okay if I swing by and get your keys to install those locks?"

"Uh, yeah, sure."

"See you in a few, then." He clicked off, grabbed a jacket, and headed to his van.

Sloane was sitting in Rhys's glass office when he got there, and after Connie gave him the third degree about the menu for Jake and Cecilia's wedding, she directed him to go on back.

"How you doing, Chief?"

She giggled again and cocked her head at Rhys's big oak desk. "Pretty cool, huh?"

"Yep. Anything going on?"

"As Rhys likes to say, 'All quiet on the Western front.' But I'm using the opportunity to go through more missing persons databases."

"You have lunch yet?" He was hungry, is all. "If not, we can grab something at the Ponderosa."

"I haven't. But I don't know if I'm allowed to leave. Let me ask Connie."

She rounded the desk and headed for Connie's station. He laughed to himself, wondering who was really running the show. A few minutes later she returned.

"I just have to take the radio," she said, and shrugged into her jacket.

They walked over to the restaurant together and for a crazy second he almost took her hand. Sophie was on hostess duty today and told them to sit wherever they wanted. Sloane picked a booth in the back corner, where they sat across from each other.

The server brought them water and asked if they knew what they wanted. Sloane got a chicken Caesar salad and he got a steak sandwich with fries. They made small talk until the food came, and dug in.

"We've never been to a restaurant together," she said, and he caught something in her eyes that looked a lot like *we're a couple now*.

Not good!

Brady leaned across the table. "Sloane, last night . . . it was the best night of my life. But things got heated pretty quickly and, well, I should've been straight with you. I'm not looking for anything permanent."

Suddenly becoming fixated on the table, she said, "Okay," but her voice cracked and he felt like a first-class heel.

"Sloane, honey, look at me." She lifted her head and locked eyes with him. Man, they were blue. "I left some trouble behind in LA. It hasn't followed me yet . . . but now's not a good time for me to get involved." It wasn't safe for either of them. And then there was the fact that he didn't do involvement. Ever.

"What kind of trouble?" she asked, her chin held high.

"Bad trouble." He wanted to leave it at that, but she was looking at him skeptically. Like she thought he was either wanted by the mob or feeding her a lie after he'd gotten her in the sack. "I have a stalker. She's delusional and dangerous and I don't want to put you on the other side of that. You understand?"

He watched her morph back into cop mode. "What happened?"

"It's a long story. I like you, Sloane. You're beautiful, smart, and tough. And you've got enough on your plate. You don't need my pot of problems to add to it."

"Have you gone to the police?"

"Santa Monica PD is working the case. But my stalker is as canny as she is crazy. So far they have nothing to arrest her for. Their best advice to me was to get out of LA while the getting was good. That's why I'm here."

"You ran from her?"

He didn't like the way she'd phrased that, but yeah, that's exactly what he'd done. "She broke into my apartment, she trashed my restaurant, she violated the restraining order I took out on her . . . and that's not the half of it. But she didn't leave a trace of evidence. Just my word against hers. Sloane, hurting a woman goes against everything I know and believe in, but if I didn't get the hell out of there I was gonna hurt her."

"Was she your girlfriend?"

He gave a bitter laugh. "Nope. But she thought so. Still does. I met her in the bar of my restaurant, went home with her that night, and the next thing I know she's threatening to kill herself if I won't see her again. It's too surreal to explain. Even I have trouble understanding it, and believe me, I've read all the literature there is about this kind of warped obsession, trying to comprehend how this happened. But if she ever finds me, I don't want her finding you."

"Did you tell Nugget PD about this?"

He held her gaze. "I just did."

"So this is official?"

"Sloane, I'm not talking to you as a cop. I'm telling you because this woman is unhinged . . . seriously scary. Last night shouldn't have happened. But this chemistry between us . . . Ah, hell . . . it was selfish of me." He scrubbed his hand through his hair. "If anything happened to you, I couldn't live with that." It appeared that thinking with his dick instead of using common sense had become a pattern.

"Did you forget what I do for a living? If you're just looking for a way to disentangle yourself from me, be a man about it, Brady." She reached inside her handbag and got out her wallet. "Look, I've got to get back to work."

"I've got this." He quickly handed his credit card to a nearby server.

"Let me guess: This is the story you feed women because you're hiding from your wife." Sloane got to her feet.

"Hang on a sec." He went after her, wondering if that married detective she'd dated had done a number on her. "That was a cheap shot, Sloane. But check it out for yourself if you don't believe me. Just don't leave any bread crumbs. I've worked hard at staying under the radar. Now give me your house key for the locks."

"Don't worry about it."

"Ah, come on, Sloane, don't be that way." Not willing to take no for an answer, he held out his hand, waiting.

"Fine." She took the key off her chain and passed it to him. Then she walked out of the Ponderosa with her head held high and Brady's eyes pinned to her ass in those olive-green police pants.

No way would he drag her into psycho Sandra's sights.

Chapter 11

Sloane went back to the office feeling dejected. It's not like she wanted to marry him, but Brady was the first guy in a long time who'd held her interest. He was generous, kind, smart, amazing to look at, and he was right, the chemistry between them was combustible. She'd never been one to sleep with a man she wasn't already in a relationship with, but Brady had made her feel safe and comfortable. And the sex . . . well, it had been above and beyond anything she'd ever experienced.

His stalker story seemed like a handy excuse not to become involved. She was a cop, for God's sake, and could hold her own. Still, she got the sense Brady hadn't told her everything. That's why she shut the door to Rhys's office and picked up the phone. She told herself that it was official business. In order to protect its residents, the Nugget police should be privy to the case, especially if this woman was as dangerous as Brady had indicated. Clearly, he thought she was capable of coming here and making trouble. Furthermore, Brady had been the one who'd demanded that Rhys be thoroughly briefed on the details of her LAPD problems.

Well, Mr. Benson, what's good for the goose is good for the gander.

She found the number for Santa Monica PD, dialed, and within minutes was on the phone with the case detective. After making the proper introductions—McBride was common enough that he didn't seem to register her name—Detective Rinek spent a half hour getting her up to speed on Brady's stalker, making the hairs on the back of Sloane's neck stand at attention.

"She's slick," he told her. "Knows how to cover her tracks or stay within the narrow confines of the law. You ever see *Fatal Attraction*? This woman makes Glenn Close look like a pussycat. But there's not been a damned thing we could do about it. Off the record, I told the guy to get a gun. I don't know what you've got up there in that jurisdiction of yours, but I've seen how these things end . . . It's either him or her."

After they hung up, Sloane closed the blinds on the glass door and fired up Rhys's computer. It didn't take long to see that Sandra Lockhart was a busy beaver on social media. According to her posts, she and Brady had taken quite a few trips together in the last several months. The pictures were so obviously Photoshopped that a twelve-year-old could've done better.

On Tumblr, Sandra put on one hell of a show. Sloane had spent a fair share of her job in LA visiting porn sites, but this was pretty raunchy stuff. A lot of close-ups of genitalia and loud moaning and groaning. Brady's tattoos made a command performance, but while the man in the film doing the bumping and grinding had the same color hair and the same build as Brady, he wasn't Brady. After last night, Sloane could definitely attest to that. She compared Sandra's Facebook pictures to the woman in the video and thought they could be one and the same. Regardless, she had achieved the illusion that she and Brady were going at it like bunnies for the camera. Not the best image for a chef on his way to becoming the next Jamie Oliver.

He was certainly a cautionary tale against having a one-night stand with a stranger. But she wasn't blaming him. Sandra had turned his life upside down.

Someone knocked at the door and she quickly closed out of Tumblr. "Come in."

"What are you doing in here?" Connie glanced around the room.

"I was sifting through missing persons databases and the glare from the light was hurting my eyes."

"We've got a fight at the high school. Two girls. One had pepper spray. I thought it best if we sent you."

Sloane grabbed her jacket off the hook behind Rhys's desk. "Pepper spray? Seriously?"

Connie shrugged. "That's what the principal said."

"Okay. I'm on my way."

It took her less than ten minutes to get to the school. No traffic in Nugget. A nice perk, given that in LA, even with her lights flashing and her siren sounding, it could take thirty minutes to get to a crime scene in rush hour. Cars so thick, the roads were like parking lots.

Here you could zip around the city proper in no time at all. You just had to watch out for deer crossing the road.

She parked in the red zone in front of Nugget High, a stucco building with a red tile roof and double-sash windows. From the outside it looked a little like a fortress, but inside the walls were decorated with brightly colored posters and the floors—the same hardwood found in a gymnasium—held a polished shine. The lockers had been painted glossy royal blue and gold—the school's colors. The hallway carried that same familiar scent of schools everywhere: a mixture of ammonia and sweaty sneakers. It should've been terrible but was oddly comforting.

Sloane found the principal's office. Two girls sat at opposite sides of the room glaring at each other while a couple of secretaries clacked away on computers. The principal, a round woman with wiry silver hair that reached her shoulders, came out to greet Sloane and call her back into her private domain. Mrs. Saddler, that was her name, explained the situation, and by the time they went back out, one of the girls' parents had arrived. Mrs. Saddler escorted the family into her office, leaving Sloane to deal with the other girl.

"Is there a private place we can go?" Sloane asked one of the secretaries.

"There's a small conference room in the back." The woman pointed across the room.

"Let's talk in there, Rose."

The girl's head sprung up, like she was surprised Sloane knew her name. They went back to the room and Sloane shut the door. Rose sat in a chair at the table and folded her arms over her chest.

"When will your parents be here?"

"My mother works nights for Union Pacific." Rose gave a half shrug. "I doubt she's coming."

"Where did you get the pepper spray?"

Rose answered Sloane's question with a stony glare. Dumb question. You could get the stuff anywhere, including the Internet.

"Was it because Taylor and her friends were bullying you?"

More silence, but Sloane detected a slight twitch in Rose's right cheek.

"You can talk to me about it. I understand what it's like."

Rose snorted. "I doubt it, if you looked like that in high school."

Sloane couldn't really argue with that, since her bullying hadn't started until adulthood. "Don't pretend to know anything about my life and I won't pretend to know about yours."

That got Rose's attention. "Taylor is a bitch."

"Rose, I'm gonna be real straight with you. There are a lot of bitches out there. You can't take them all on with a can of pepper spray."

"Just Taylor would be enough."

"Mrs. Saddler said you dropped the canister and started to cry when she got in your face."

Again with the half shrug. "I didn't want to go all Columbine over some bimbo with bad highlights."

"What do you know about Columbine?" Rose hadn't even been born when that happened. "Because it was god-awful, Rose. The worst thing you can imagine."

Her bottom lip trembled. "I just want Taylor and her hos to leave me alone."

"What do they do to you?"

"I'll let you guess." Rose waved her hand over herself. She carried about twenty extra pounds, had a bad case of acne, and her hair could use a good washing.

"They do anything physical to you?"

"Four of them tried to shove my head into the toilet. Good thing I'm fat and could get them off me."

"Don't mistake strong with fat," Sloane said, trying to hide how much she'd like to haul those girls in and lock them in a jail cell. "What else did they do?"

"They hide my underwear and bra, so after gym I can't find them. They tape pictures of elephants to my desk, and generally make my life a living hell." Rose tried to act indifferent, but Sloane could see her pain clear as day. "You gonna arrest me?"

"Bringing a weapon to school and threatening another student with it is a felony, Rose. You've got to know you're getting suspended. The thing is, Mrs. Saddler says you're a good student. And I don't think you're a bad person. I just think you've been pushed to the edge. But that's not an excuse for bringing pepper spray to school. So there has to be some consequences. What do you think I should do?"

"How would I know? I'm only fifteen."

Sloane let out a long breath. "I'll need to sleep on it. Tomorrow, I'll expect you at the police station at nine in the morning. Make sure you show up or you'll be in even more trouble. Come on."

"Where are we going?"

"I'm taking you home."

"I can walk." Rose thrust her chin out.

"Not today."

Rose followed Sloane to her police SUV, raised her brows, and started to get in the backseat. Bullet-proof glass and steel mesh separated it from the front. "Nice ride."

"Sit up here in the passenger seat and buckle up," Sloane said, and got her address before starting the engine.

Rose lived in a cruddy part of town. A lot of tiny, run-down houses set on postage-stamp-sized lawns right next to the railroad tracks. A primer-gray Camaro sat up on blocks in Rose's front yard and half the steps to her porch were rotted.

As soon as they parked, Rose bolted out of the car. Sloane followed.

"What are you doing?"

"You said your mother works at night. I want to make sure you're okay alone."

But when they got inside there was a young man sitting at the kitchen table. There were dishes piled in the sink and a cat licking leftover food off of the counter. The man continued to sit there in his wifebeater, letting his eyes roam over Sloane in a way that gave her the creeps. Then he turned away, grabbed his Coors can, and took a swig.

"You get in trouble, Rosie?"

"That's my brother, Skeeter," Rose told Sloane.

"Hi, Skeeter. Is your mother home?"

"Nope." He popped the P. "She's working at the railroad. What can I do for you, Ociffer?" Skeeter let out a loud belch.

"Rose had a run-in with a girl at school today. She brought a can of pepper spray to use as a weapon, which is illegal."

"They picking on you again, Rosie?"

Rose started to cry; just fell apart in the kitchen.

"Fuck that school." Skeeter got up, put his arm around his sister, and looked straight at Sloane. "And fuck you too. These girls have been ganging up on her, and you people just look the other way. Who cares about a poor, chubby girl from the slums?"

"I'm not looking the other way, Skeeter. Those girls will get theirs. But Rose can't be bringing pepper spray to school."

He came toward her, invading her personal space. Sloane grasped the handle of her gun.

"You arresting her?"

She wiped the spittle from her face with the sleeve of her uniform. "I've told Rose she needs to be at the police station at nine in the morning. See that she gets there, you hear?" She turned to leave.

"I'm talking to you." He blocked the door. "You arresting my sister?"

"If you don't move out of my way, I'll be arresting you. Just make sure she's at the station by nine."

He slowly stepped away and Sloane got in her truck and drove back to the station. For the rest of the day she fielded phone calls, assisted Wyatt in taking statements after a minor accident on Main Street, and begged for Jake's advice on the Rose situation. By the time Sloane got home she was dragging ass. All she wanted was a hot bath and a glass of wine.

She went to unlock her door, realized that Brady had her key, and prayed he'd left it under the mat. The last thing she wanted was for him to see her looking like ten hours of bad day. Although she had plenty to say to him. She searched all the usual spots. The boot scraper, the pot of dead geraniums, and the mailbox. *Nada.*

No, Brady wasn't likely to leave her key lying around when he'd become fanatical about security, she supposed. So unless she broke into her own apartment, she'd have to knock on his door.

Crap! He beat her to the punch, coming out onto the porch, his hair mussed, like he'd been snoozing. And yet he still managed to be drool-worthy.

"You looking for this?" He dangled a shiny new house key off one finger.

"Thanks." She gingerly removed it and tried to make a quick getaway.

"I want to show you what I did." Brady followed her to her door.

"Now? Because I really need a shower."

"It'll only take a minute or two."

It was the least she could do after he'd done all the work. She really should've changed the locks herself when she'd first moved in. "All right."

The snick of the new dead bolt sounded when she turned the key. Inside, Brady took her through her apartment, giving her a 101 on the window locks, which were newfangled and seemed impenetrable unless someone smashed the glass. He took her through her kitchen and demonstrated how the dead bolt on the back door could only be unlocked with a key. No busting through the transom window and turning a knob.

"If you leave the key in it, it'll defeat the purpose," he told her. She didn't have the heart to tell him that the dead bolt wouldn't keep anyone who wanted in, out. Instead she turned her attention to a covered dish on the counter.

"I made extra," he said.

"Shouldn't I refrigerate it?"

"Not if you want it for dinner. It needs to be room temperature when it goes in the oven."

"Wow, Brady. I don't know what to say, except thank you. Did you do the same for yours?"

"Yep."

"Good." She looked at him directly. "I called Santa Monica PD."

"I figured you would."

"I think you're right: She's not gonna go away. And she's about as bonkers as they come—and I agree, dangerous. Did you get a gun like Detective Rinek told you to do? Do you know how to use one?"

He glared at her. "I grew up in the backwoods of South Carolina. What do you think? Don't worry about me; you've got enough problems of your own."

"Yet when you found out about mine, you got plenty involved." She stuck her key in the new kitchen dead bolt and jiggled it to make a point.

"That's different. You're going against a trained cop, maybe more than one. I'm going against a woman half my size. And if she thinks you and I are romantically involved, she'll come after you too."

"We're not romantically involved, so all's right with the world." She couldn't help the sarcasm.

"I'm gonna let you take that shower now, Sloane." He started to walk away, but she grabbed his arm.

"Thank you for securing my apartment—and dinner. I really do appreciate it. And, Brady, be on the alert. I'm worried about this woman."

"Right back at you."

The new locks didn't help her sleep any better, not when she wanted him the way she did. One night of Brady Benson hadn't been nearly enough.

The next morning she got to the station at seven and found Rose sitting on a bench out front.

"I said nine." Sloane unlocked the door. She and Rose were the first ones here.

"Skeeter dropped me. He has the morning shift at the railroad."

"What do you have there?" Sloane cocked her head at Rose's ratty backpack.

"Books. Skeeter said I won't be able to keep them if you lock me up."

"Skeeter have a lot of inside knowledge about these sorts of things?"

Sloane had meant to run a background check but had gotten caught up with the fender bender and all the other crap the police chief had to deal with. She did not envy Rhys his job. Nugget's crime rate might be next to nil, but a lot of whiny people lived here. One day in LA, or any other big city, would shut these people up for good.

"He's never been in lockup, if that's what you're asking." Rose dropped her head.

"Come in. As soon as Connie gets here she'll make coffee. I'm no good at it on that fancy machine."

Connie had a thing about her coffee, including grinding the beans fresh for every pot.

Sloane took Rose back to Rhys's office. "Take a seat. I'll be right back." She heard the bell over the door ring and wanted to see who came in. Connie.

"Morning." She waved to Sloane. "I'll get the coffee going."

"We've got company."

Connie walked over and peeked inside Rhys's office. "The juvie. She's early."

"Her brother had to work a morning shift and dropped her. You know him, Skeeter Jones?"

Connie shook her head. "I don't think so. Not by name anyway."

Sloane went back in the office.

"You the boss?" Rose asked.

"No, I'm filling in for Chief Shepard. He went away for a few days with his wife. My real desk is in there." She pointed to the cube farm.

"You don't seem like a cop."

"Oh yeah? What does a cop seem like?"

"Not pretty enough to go on TV."

There were plenty of beautiful female officers at LAPD. Sloane had never thought of herself in that category. "It's all I ever wanted to be. How about you?"

Rose seemed taken aback by the question. "I don't know. But I don't want to work for the railroad."

"Mrs. Saddler says you're smart, so I suspect you can be anything you want. But not if you keep getting into trouble. I've given your punishment a lot of thought. For the two weeks you're suspended, you'll perform community service by working as my assistant. No arrest. But I'll expect you every weekday and I'm going to run your butt off."

Rose blinked in surprise. "What'll I do?"

"You hear about the skeletal remains found at the Meet Up?" Rose nodded. "I'm trying to identify the person . . . determine whether the cause of death was criminal. You'll help me with that."

"How?" Rose asked, and Sloane couldn't tell whether the girl was intrigued or freaked out. It might be scary for a fifteen-year-old.

"By searching data banks for missing persons and flagging anyone who might fit our Jane or John Doe. I'm still waiting for information that will aid our search, but having a second pair of eyes will really help, Rose. You up for this?"

"Yeah. It beats going to jail, right?" But Sloane saw a flicker of excitement in the girl's eyes.

"Will your parents be okay with it?"

"It's just my mom and Skeeter," Rose said. "They won't care."

"Will you be able to get a ride here and home?"

"Skeeter has a bike he's fixing up for me."

"All right, we'll work around the transportation. You'll also have to keep up on your homework. Mrs. Saddler is getting all your class assignments together and will drop them here. Until we get the information I was talking about, you'll help Connie and the chief with anything they need."

Sloane spent the next thirty minutes showing Rose around the office and explaining how everything worked, then sat her at one of the empty desks to memorize police and penal codes—not that she would need them. But Sloane didn't have anything else for her to do. Jake came in with his cell phone pressed to his ear, looking stressed.

When he got off the phone, he said, "The minister has the flu." He sat at his desk, moved a stack of paperwork out of his way, and started booting up the computer.

"You've got a week until the rehearsal dinner. He'll be fine by then."

"How do you know?"

"Come on, Jake. You're just psyching yourself out."

He grinned. "Yeah, I am. But damn, I'm getting married."

"Yes you are. Hey, Jake, meet Rose. Rose, Jake's getting married."

Jake walked over to the girl and shook her hand, which seem to startle her. "Welcome."

The day went by fast. At two, Sloane lifted her head from the accident report she'd failed to file the previous day and realized she'd missed lunch. Figuring Rose must be starved, Sloane took them both to the Bun Boy for a couple of burgers.

Skeeter came to pick up his sister at four, just parked in front of the police station and honked his horn. Who knew that piece-of-crap Camaro ran?

"Have a nice weekend, Rose, and I'll see you Monday morning at nine, right?"

"Yep." The girl ran out the door and Sloane watched her get in the passenger seat.

Sloane went back in Rhys's office and called the coroner's office to see if they'd heard back from the CDOJ, which had its own forensic anthropologist and was better equipped than Plumas County for this sort of case. They were also getting tired of her prodding phone calls. Nothing yet, the person on duty told her. She spent the next half hour talking to her folks. Her father wanted to know when she was coming home.

She hedged just to keep him off her back, but no time soon. The truth was she didn't really mind the small department as much as she thought she would. Sloane might not be making a difference in the lives of Nugget residents, but this was a good place to reconnoiter for the time being. Eventually, she'd get back to saving the world.

By six she decided it was quitting time and called Harlee to see if it was okay to come by and pick out a rocking chair from Colin's studio. In another month it would be spring. She'd like to be able to sit out on the porch and listen to the birds sing and watch the occasional train chug down the tracks.

On the way up Harlee and Colin's mountainous road, Sloane

pondered which days she'd take off when Rhys got back. She still planned to tell him about the text, but since the Sweeney picture, there hadn't been any others.

Max greeted her in Harlee's driveway, racing around her car, clearly beside himself to have company. Harlee waved from her front porch and called the dog away so Sloane could get out of the car.

"Your house is fantastic." Sloane followed the lines of the ski-chalet roof. "Huge."

"Colin built it." Harlee skipped down the porch stairs. Sloane always marveled at how fashionable she was. Today she had on skinny black pants tucked into furry boots and a ski jacket that looked straight out of a magazine. "Come in. I'll show you around."

Sloane followed her back up the stairs and into one of the grandest living rooms she'd ever seen. The views of the surrounding mountains went on forever. And she could stand up in the stone fireplace.

"Wow. This is spectacular."

"Thanks." Harlee took her through the rest of the house. All of the furniture had been built by Colin and the work was breathtaking. "How's it going at the police department? You have any hot scoops for me?"

"Afraid not. I'm still waiting to find out the sex and approximate age on those remains. As soon as I do, it would be great to get a story on the website, spread the word."

"Absolutely. Just don't give it to anyone first."

Sloane smiled, liking Harlee's go-get-'em attitude. "You'll be first."

"Would you like a glass of wine or some tea?"

"Sure. A glass of wine sounds perfect, if it's not too much trouble." She really needed to be more sociable with her neighbors.

"Not at all. I've got a Russian River pinot noir in the cabinet." She took out the bottle and poured them both a glass. "We can take our drinks out to Colin's studio. He usually has a fire going back there."

Sloane had only met him in passing once or twice. A quiet guy compared to his bubbly wife. The studio was a mini replica of the house. Same tall ceilings and big windows. When they walked in, Colin had music blaring and the smell of pine hit her nose immediately. Sure enough, there was a potbelly stove in the corner, sending off plenty of heat.

Colin turned down the tunes and kissed Harlee sweetly on the forehead.

"Sloane is looking for a rocking chair," she told her husband.

"Maddy said you were filling in for Rhys while they went to San Francisco. How's that going?" Colin asked.

"So far no catastrophes." Sloane gazed around the studio. "You have a lot of great things here. Where do you sell it all?"

"Online, and Harlee's mom has a store. Between her and her other shopkeeper friends, word's taken off."

"Wow." There were four-poster beds, benches, farm tables, coffee tables, chairs, and porch swings. Sloane didn't know where to look first.

"In the summer I lug some of this stuff to the farmers' market."

"His pieces were in Della James's cookbook," Harlee said.

"The country-western singer?" Sloane didn't listen to her music but knew she was famous.

Harlee grabbed a book off a shelf, thumbed through the pages, and shoved it at Sloane. "See. That's Colin's farm table. The whole picture was shot at Clay and Emily McCreedy's ranch. Cool, huh?"

Colin's mouth quirked. "She shows that to everyone."

God, could they be any cuter? "So if I buy a rocking chair can I tell people Della James has a matching one?"

Colin laughed. "Not matching, but she occasionally has her people call to buy a few and send them out as gifts. Whether she's kept one for herself I don't know. We're not tight like that."

Sloane did another visual sweep of the room. "There are so many to choose from. Which one do you suggest?"

Colin walked around the studio, grabbing various rockers and lining them up together. "What are you looking for? One seater or two? Comfort or appearance?"

"One and both. My style leans toward shabby chic—kind of girlie."

Colin appeared to flash on something. "Hang on a sec. I'll be right back." He made his way around the furniture, out the door, and disappeared through the trees in the backyard.

Sloane looked at Harlee, who shrugged. A few minutes later Colin returned to the studio carrying a pine rocker that had been whitewashed.

"I forgot all about that one," Harlee blurted.

The wood grain still showed through the stain, reminding Sloane of old weathered barns and beach cottages. And the chair was less chunky than Colin's other work, more curvaceous and graceful. "Omigod, I love it."

Colin put the chair down in front of her. "Try it out."

She sat, wiggled her butt into just the right position, and rocked. Leaning her head back and closing her eyes, she said, "I may not even put this on the porch. I may keep it inside—at least until summer."

"You could do that," Colin said.

"It would totally go with your stuff," Harlee agreed. "You could even put a frilly cushion on it."

"I could. But it's beautiful just like this." Sloane reached into her purse for her wallet and whipped out some plastic. Whatever it cost, she planned to buy it. She'd just paid her bill down so there was plenty of room left on the credit card. "Sold."

Colin ran it on his smartphone and got her number so he could text her the receipt. She'd look at it later. Right now she just wanted to enjoy her new purchase. Sloane finished her wine while they talked about Jake and Cecilia's wedding, Harlee and Darla's next bowling party, and how Rhys's baby sister, Lina, was back in town. Apparently everyone was laying bets on whether Lina and Griffin would get back together.

Sloane was really starting to enjoy herself when she got a call. Wyatt needed backup on a DV situation up in the hills on the other side of town. No one was supposed to do those alone. Too volatile. And after her last domestic violence call, they made her especially twitchy. She ran to her vehicle with the promise that Colin would deliver her chair, turned on her flashing lights and siren, and jammed down the mountain.

Chapter 12

At about eight o'clock, Brady heard a truck motor down the driveway. He could tell from the sound of the tires that it wasn't Sloane. Hers were studded for better traction on ice. Rhys put them on all the police rigs in winter.

He got off the couch and looked outside the window to see Colin hefting a rocking chair out of the bed, and opened the door.

"You need some help?"

"I've got it. How you doing, Brady?"

"Can't complain. Sloane buy a rocker?"

"Yep. She got called out, so I'm bringing it home for her." Colin tilted his head at the sky.

"I think it'll be safe on the porch until she gets home."

"Isn't it for the porch?"

"She said she might like to put it inside."

"Why don't I keep it in here for her until she gets home." For a man who was trying to maintain a little distance, he seemed to be looking for every opportunity to get closer. When she hadn't shown up for lunch today at the inn, he'd been sorely tempted to march over to the police station to make sure she'd eaten.

"Sounds like a plan." Colin carried it in and set it down next to Brady's sofa. "Smells good in here."

"I just baked a couple of breads. You want one?"

"Sure."

Brady went into the kitchen and wrapped one of the loaves in foil. Colin followed him in.

"Your place could use some furniture." His lips curved up into a smile. "I know where you can get some."

"I'll get around to it eventually." Brady had always liked traveling light—nothing to hold him down. "You want a beer?"

"Nah, I've gotta get home to Harlee. One of the few nights she's home early from the *Trib*."

Brady thought Colin and Harlee had a good thing going. He'd catered their wedding and the two of them had struck him as a couple that would stick. He knew Colin had some phobias he was working through, particularly a fear of crowds. But it seemed that the furniture maker showed up more and more at the Ponderosa, so maybe he'd licked it.

"You know what Sloane got called out on?"

"Nope, just that Wyatt needed backup. But you can be sure my wife has her ear to the ground. That's why I've got to get home. Otherwise she'll go out sniffing after the story."

That made Brady chuckle. Yeah, they were a nice couple. "See you later, Colin."

"Thanks for the bread." Colin saluted him with the loaf.

After he left, Brady got a little anxious. Nugget was a safe town, but bad things happened everywhere. Hell, just a couple of months ago the town had a big drug bust and murder on Lucky's ranch. Crazy thing.

He stayed up past eleven waiting. Then decided to drive to the police station to see what was doing. That's when he saw headlights through his living room window and heard those studded tires coming down the road. His stomach settled with relief and he met her on the porch.

"Everything okay?"

She appeared surprised to see him. "Ruben Cottsfield got drunk and knocked his wife around. She wouldn't press charges, so we waited until he sobered up and left."

"I'm sorry." He tucked a loose strand of hair behind her ear.

"Me too, because he'll eventually put her in the hospital, and as long as she refuses help, there isn't a damn thing we can do about it."

"It sucks."

"It sucks. Brady, how come you didn't tell me you were the executive chef at Pig and Tangelo when I told you it was one of my favorite restaurants?"

He let out a breath. "It's cold out here. Come inside."

"I'm dead on my feet and need a hot shower."

"I'll tell you what, you go do what you need to do and I'll bring over your new rocking chair. Colin left it in my place. If you're not too tired after your bath, we'll talk. In the meantime I'll make you some herbal tea."

"All right. Just as long as we're not having a relationship." She enunciated "relationship" and rolled her eyes, then took that cute butt of hers inside.

Brady got the chair, lugged it over to her place, and put it in the living room. She could decide where she wanted it and he'd move it for her. He went back to his place and grabbed an assortment of teas and one of his loaves of bread before commandeering her kitchen. At least she had a kettle. He put some water up to boil and checked out her fridge for a beer. She didn't have any, so he went back to his place and grabbed a couple bottles.

By the time he got back, the water had stopped running. When she finally came out of the bathroom she had a towel wrapped around her head and wore a pair of drawstring pants and a clingy little long-sleeve tee.

"I just have to dry my hair," she said, and went back inside the bathroom.

Brady sat in the living room amid her frilly pillows, drinking his beer. Colin's rocker kind of fit in, he noted. But he thought the whole point was having something on the porch. She could sit on his, he supposed. Or the swing.

Sloane came into the living room, her blond hair down around her shoulders, and plopped next to him on the couch. Brady got to his feet, went in the kitchen, fixed her tea, and put a few slices of bread on a plate.

"Here you go." He put it down on the coffee table in front of her.

She wrapped her hands around the mug and took a sip. "This is perfect. Thank you. So, Pig and Tangelo, huh?"

"Yep. I don't tell too many people about it for fear that it'll get back to psycho Sandra."

Sloane laughed. "Is that what you call her?"

"That and a whole bunch of other things."

"So you only met her that one night and she went *Fatal Attraction* on you?"

"She came into the bar about an hour before the restaurant stopped serving. After a big night I'd hang out a while, have a drink, and schmooze with the bartenders. She was sitting a couple of stools down from me. A few guys tried to hit on her, but she wasn't interested. Somehow it came up that I was the executive chef. She scooted next to me, we talked food for about an hour, then the conversation got more flirtatious. We wound up going back to her place. I left her a nice note at around four in the morning and went home. By nine she was banging on my door."

"How'd she get your address?"

"When we'd left the bar she was tipsy, so I drove. My checkbook was in the van. She must've looked at it. We both only lived a few blocks away from the restaurant."

"What did she want?"

"I'd mentioned at the bar that I had the next day off. She said that we'd made plans to spend it together, which I never had. And she just went off. I told her she was coming on too strong. She cried, but finally went home, and I thought that was that. No such luck. By about eleven that night she comes banging on my door again, shouting that I'm an a-hole and that she's in love with me." He scrubbed his hands through his hair. "Sloane, we spent four hours together, max. Hell, I didn't even know her last name and I never gave her mine. It was just supposed to be a casual hookup. Never once that night did we veer into the land of a love connection. The whole thing's insane."

"From everything Rinek told me, this woman sounds nuts . . . It's her mental state that has me worried. Why didn't you change your name?"

He got up and went for that second beer. "You want something?"

"I'm good. The bread is out of this world, by the way."

Brady came back and took his place back on the couch. "I didn't change it because I shouldn't have to. She ruined my life . . . made me leave a great job, my friends, the beach. I'd be damned if I changed my identity too. If she wants to come here and mess with me . . . well then, bring it on. But I won't risk having her mess with you. What's going on with your issues?"

"Nothing." Sloane shook her head. "That picture of Sweeney was the last thing I got. Maybe they're over it."

"You'll still tell Rhys, right?"

"I'll tell him. I'll also be telling him about Sandra. Because, Brady, from the stuff I saw on Facebook, she's still obsessed with you. If she ever finds out where you are, she'll show up here. Rinek thinks she's capable of violence."

"She sure did a number on my apartment and restaurant. She clearly has a criminal mind, 'cause she never left so much as a fingerprint." He turned to Sloane and held her face in his hands. "So you understand why I'm worried about you . . . about us being together?"

"I think you should let me worry about myself."

"Not in my DNA." But he wanted her. He wanted her so much it hurt. She was different from any woman he'd ever known. Confident, tough, compassionate, and even a little vulnerable. A combination he couldn't resist.

"I'm realizing that about you." Sloane yawned. "I've gotta go to bed, Brady. Tomorrow I'm playing chief again and need to be at the station at the crack of dawn."

He gathered up his empties, walked into her kitchen, tossed them in the recycling bin, and headed out. "Lock up after me."

Halfway to the door he turned around, came back to where she was standing, and kissed her long and hard. She twined her arms around his neck, pressed against him, and he nearly lost his mind. *Time to go,* he told himself, but his body had trouble taking direction. Finally, he peeled himself away.

"Sleep tight, Sloane."

Saturday morning, Griffin went to the square for breakfast. He couldn't decide on sit-down at the Ponderosa or an egg sandwich to go from the Bun Boy. Seeing as he didn't have anywhere to be, he started to lean toward Tater's chicken-fried steak and potatoes. Griff had always liked lingering over the first meal of the day.

But as he walked to the Ponderosa he ran into Samantha Breyer, who coaxed him into having breakfast at the Lumber Baron.

"Brady made cinnamon-roll French toast that's off the hook," she said, shifting a grocery bag in her arms. "There's plenty extra."

"Here, I'll take that." He grabbed the bag from her and followed her into the inn.

Of course none other than Lina manned the front desk. She had on a purple sweater that made his eyes pop out of his head. "Hey, Lina."

"Hey, Griff." The phone rang and she immediately grabbed it.

He continued to trail Sam into the kitchen and put the sack down on the stainless-steel counter. For an industrial kitchen, the place felt warm, like a place for a big family to gather. Copper pots hung from a rack over the center island and gleaming white cabinets with glass fronts showed off the ironstone dishes inside.

Sam unloaded a couple of cartons of half-and-half, a jug of milk, and one of those squeeze-bear honeys.

Brady held the bear up to Sam. "You're kidding me, right?"

"I thought it was cute."

"Don't let Nate see it. He's liable to think you're in cahoots with those Beary Quaint idiots, the Addisons."

She laughed. "Oh God, I didn't even think of that."

"Hey, Griff, you want some breakfast?"

Brady didn't wait for an answer, just loaded up a plate and slid it down the center island for Griffin to take a seat. Maple syrup and butter magically appeared.

"You want coffee?" Griffin nodded, and Brady poured him a cup. First-class service.

"Here's some cream." Sam opened one of the new cartons and put the rest in the big industrial refrigerator.

"What about the guests?"

"They were up and at 'em an hour ago," Brady told Griff. "We're free until noon, when the Baker's Dozen gets here."

"I thought you met the second Saturday of every month," Sam said.

"We changed the date on account of next Saturday being Jake and Cecilia's wedding."

"Holy hell, this is good." Griff shoveled another forkful of the battered cinnamon roll into his mouth.

"I like to call it diabetes on a plate. Let me know when you want seconds. Sam, tell Lina to come get herself some breakfast."

Sam returned with Lina a few minutes later. Lina barely looked at Griff.

"Not so much, Brady." Brady pushed half her serving onto a second plate.

"Anyone hear from Rhys and Maddy?" Griffin asked.

All heads turned to Lina.

"They're having a good time. They went to Alcatraz yesterday."

"Cool," Griffin said. "I've never been. Have you, Lina?"

"No. I never got around to it while I lived there. I guess I thought it was too touristy." She dabbed at the corners of her mouth with a napkin, all dainty like.

Griff remembered when she used to wolf down Bun Boy burgers like a truck driver. It used to crack him up. Her being such a petite thing.

"I've been by a couple of times to see Emma and my mother-in-law," Sam said. "Looks like they're doing fine."

"I think between Maddy and Rhys they've called seven thousand times." Lina got up to pour herself a cup of coffee.

Nate joined them and Brady loaded him up with French toast. He found a seat next to Sam and doused his plate in syrup.

"It's already pretty sweet there, buddy." Brady took the syrup away from him, and Sam laughed.

"What are you laughing at?" Nate kissed her with syrup all over his lips. "Damn, this is good. Why aren't you cooking for all my hotels?"

"Because I only have two hands." Nate started on another batch.

"Who are those for?" Nate asked.

"Sloane's coming over. Why, you want more?"

Nate held up his hand. "I'm good. We've got a big dinner tonight."

"Where you going?" Brady asked.

"We're taking my mom to Reno for dinner. Lina is staying with the baby." Nate put Lina in a headlock. Nate had always treated her like an uncle even though technically they were only related by marriage.

Griff could've offered to help her, but she might've gotten the wrong impression. Ah, who was he fooling? Since Lina had come back to town she hadn't seemed to care whether he was dead or alive. At least before, when she'd come home from school for long weekends or holidays, she looked for every excuse to run into him. Griffin wondered whether she had someone.

"You find a car yet?" he asked her.

"Not yet. I'll have more money after next weekend. I'm working for Brady at Jake and Cecilia's wedding."

"I'm keeping my eye out for you."

"Thanks. That thing you did to the battery has the Scout running much better now."

He doubted that. The International Harvester was on its last legs. "Good. How's school?"

"It's great. I love my apartment and I love being able to spend long weekends home with my brothers, Emma, and Maddy."

"What about me?" Nate said.

Lina smiled at Nate and rolled her eyes. "And Nate and Sam."

"You sell any more places?" Nate asked Griff. "Not that Sam and I are desperate for neighbors."

"Dana's gonna hold another open house in March. The market's looking better and she thinks spring will bring more buyers to the Sierra."

Lina took her plate and cup to the sink and loaded them into the dishwasher. "I need to get out front."

As she walked out, Sloane came in and did a double take at the crowd in the kitchen.

"Hey, Chief," everyone said in unison.

She turned to Brady. "I didn't realize you were having a party."

"My cinnamon-roll French toast is a party."

"Here, Sloane, take Lina's seat. She went back to work," Sam said.

Brady fixed her a plate and poured her a cup of coffee. "Any crime today?"

She deadpanned and in a Rhys-esque Texas drawl said, "All quiet on the Western front."

Everyone laughed and Nate asked, "You find who those bones belong to yet?"

"Not yet, but I'm working on it. What did I miss?"

"Griff's real estate agent is holding a big open house at Sierra Heights in March," Brady said. "The market's coming back."

"I can't afford one," Sloane said. "But I'll come to make the place look busy."

Griffin chuckled. "We did that before. Had Harlee and Darla model some of the models. And boy, did we get action. This guy bought one." He slapped Nate on the back. "Sam's dad bought the one Sam used to rent before she married Nate. Why don't you buy one, Brady?"

Brady held up his arms, palms out. "Too fancy for me. Not to mention that it would feel too much like roots."

"You better not be planning to leave us," Nate said. "I need you, man."

"Not any time soon," Brady replied.

The discussion came around to Jake and Cecilia's wedding. Griffin took his plate to the sink and like Lina had done, loaded it into the dishwasher.

"I've got a bike waiting for me," he told the crowd. "Thanks for breakfast."

"How's that going? . . . The custom motorcycle business, I mean," Nate asked.

"Good. I've got a list of orders."

"And the Gas and Go?" Nate was a consummate businessman who could talk for hours about profits and losses.

"The best thing I ever bought. Between selling gas, food, and sundries; the tow business and the smog checks, I'm more than flush."

"What about the car wash?"

"It's a loss leader, but it works."

"I thought it was pretty genius myself," Nate said. "Especially in this drought, when people can't be running their hoses."

"Exactly. I paid up the ass for the car wash, but it recycles every drop of water used. I'll see you guys around."

On his way out he saw Lina sitting at the reception desk, thumbing through a textbook.

"Doing homework?"

"Just some background reading. You taking off?"

"I'm in no rush," he said.

"Are you upset that you haven't sold more houses in Sierra Heights?"

"Nah. You and I both know that I don't need the money. But I'd like to be rid of the headache of keeping up the place."

She nodded in understanding. "I'm sure it'll happen. It just takes time. Dana must be really good at her job for you to give her all those listings."

"Yep, she's good." He thought about telling her the truth about him and Dana, but what would be the point? Lina was clearly no longer interested in him and she was still too young.

"Are you both going to Jake and Cecilia's wedding?"

"I'm going alone," he said.

"I just thought since it was Valentine's Day . . ."

"So you'll be working it, huh?"

"I need the money for a car. Brady does a lot of these and I'm hoping he'll add me to his regular team."

"You used to like working at the inn." He couldn't help himself from brushing a speck of lint off her sweater.

"I still do, but I'm trying to cobble together as many hours as possible without interfering with school."

He'd give her part-time work at his motorcycle shop doing light bookkeeping or working at the convenience store at the Gas and Go, but it would be too much temptation. "I'll try to find a good car in your budget. In the meantime, don't rely too heavily on the Scout."

"Maddy and my brother insist I drive one of their cars at night. I'll be okay until I get something. I better get back to work, though."

It wasn't as if he was stopping her. The phone hadn't rung once. "Me too. See you around."

Griffin walked outside to a dark sky and a cool rush of air. A quarter of the way to his Range Rover the clouds opened up on him. He ran the rest of the way in a downpour. There had been no forecast of rain this morning. In fact, it had been clear and sunny when he'd left his house. As far as winters went in the Sierra, this was one of the driest on record.

By the time he got to the Gas and Go, the showers had stopped and the sun came peeking out over the mountain range. Griff couldn't help but wonder if his sudden soaking was Mother Nature's way of giving him a sign. A sign to stop dicking around and go after what he wanted. He just had to figure out what that was.

Chapter 13

Sloane got called out shortly after the squall. One dry winter and everyone forgets how to drive in the rain and snow. A Subaru Legacy crashed into a telephone pole off the highway, knocking out service to forty houses. At least there hadn't been any injuries, but there were wires all over the road and she needed to direct traffic until one of Griff's tow trucks and a Sierra Power crew arrived.

Nice way to spend a Saturday. Jake had offered to go, but Sloane figured he had better things to do just a week before his wedding. When she got to the scene, Clay McCreedy had parked his pickup at the side of the road and was guiding motorists around the mess.

"Happened to be passing by," he called to Sloane as she got out of her SUV.

"Glad you were." Clay was sure capable. Word had it he used to be a naval fighter pilot. That's probably where he got the swagger. It looked good on him. "You mind doing that for five more minutes while I get a statement from the driver?"

"Whatever you need." That's how it worked in this town. People pitched in. Sloane's dad said that's how it used to be in Chicago in the old days. Her brothers would laugh and say, "When was that, the Stone Age?"

Sloane talked to the driver, jotting down notes just in case she needed to make out a report. The Subaru looked pretty banged up. Griffin came with the tow truck and the driver said he would catch a ride back with him to town.

"Hey." She waved up at Griff.

"Good thing I came in today," he called out his window. "My weekend driver called in sick. I'll get the car out of here as fast as I can."

"Thanks."

Clay waved his cowboy hat in the air by way of a greeting to Griff and Griff tooted his horn. *Funny town*, Sloane thought as she walked over to Clay to relieve him.

"How's filling in for Rhys?" Clay asked.

"Good. But I'll be happy when he's back."

"He's sure singing your praises," Clay said. She suspected he was just being nice.

"Were you on your way to town?"

"Yep. I was headed to Owen's for a haircut. I stopped to make sure the guy was okay. He'd already called 9-1-1. I've been meaning to ask if there are any clues about that body my boy found?"

"I'm working on it. Hey, by any chance do you know if Justin is friendly with Rose Jones from school? She's a freshman."

"Can't say that I do. Why?"

She sighed. "Rose is going through a tough time at school, and that day at the Meet Up it seemed like Justin had a lot of friends. I just thought it would be nice for a popular upperclassman to show her a little support."

"Rose Jones?" When Sloane nodded, he said, "I'll pass the word on."

"Thanks. She'll be back to school in a couple of weeks." Sloane stopped southbound traffic so a few northbound cars could get around the power lines.

Clay raised his brows. "She okay?"

"It's a bully situation. But I think she'll be fine."

"Not Justin?"

"No no. Mean girls."

"I hear they can be brutal. I'll talk to him."

"I'd appreciate it. And thanks for being a Good Sam." She stopped cars coming both ways so that Clay could cross to his truck and get safely back on the road.

Not long after, Griffin left with the Subaru in tow and a couple of workers from the power company showed up and got the wires out of the road. Sloane's work here was done. Back in her SUV, she did a quick run up McCreedy Road, knowing that the chief lived up there somewhere. Clay too. From what she'd been told, the land, for as far as the eye could see, belonged to the McCreedy cattle ranch. Nice chunk of property. At the end of the road she saw a froufrou birdhouse mailbox engraved with the name Shepard.

"No way," she said aloud. And Brady thought she was girlie.

She took the driveway up to a big white Victorian farmhouse that looked like a smaller version of the Lumber Baron. "Holy shit."

An older lady, who Sloane assumed was Maddy's mom, came out onto the porch.

Sloane rolled down her window. "Hi. I was just on patrol and thought I'd cruise by and see how you were getting on."

"We're doing fine." Mrs. Breyer smiled. "Emma's taking her nap. Maddy and Rhys called a little while ago and are having a great time."

"I'm glad. If you need anything, just call."

Sloane turned around in the driveway and went back the way she came. Next, she tooled through Sierra Heights and found herself fantasizing what it would be like to live in one of the mini mansions. Despite all the bells and whistles, it sort of felt like a cozy place to live, nestled in the trees the way it was. A great environment to raise a family. Big community pool, tennis courts, rec room, golf course, the whole shebang.

She decided to head over to Rose's part of town. Skeeter's Camaro was parked on the street in front of the Jones's house. Sloane reminded herself to run him when she got back to the office, got out of her truck, and knocked on the door.

"What do you want?" Skeeter stood pressed to the screen, but didn't open it.

"Just checking on Rose."

"She's with my mother."

"Okay." Sloane couldn't force her way into their house. "I'll see her on Monday then." He slammed the door in her face before she could say more.

For the rest of the afternoon she patrolled neighborhoods and landed back at the station sometime around three to check messages. Connie stopped by a little later.

"Why aren't you enjoying your day off?" Sloane asked her.

"I wanted to make sure you weren't in over your head."

"So far, so good. But I'll be happy when Rhys is back. I cruised by his house today while on patrol. Nice digs."

"Clay McCreedy bought it and a bunch of land off the bank in a foreclosure sale, then sold the house and a couple of acres to Rhys. I heard Darla is moving in with Wyatt."

"Really? They seem like a good couple. I have a hair appointment with her before the wedding."

"She does good work."

They both jerked their heads up when Wyatt came in the door.

"How 'bout that little rainstorm we got today?" he called to them.

"A guy hydroplaned on the wet road and slammed into a telephone poll," Sloane said. Because around here that was big news.

"Whoa. You go out on that one?"

"Yep. Luckily, Clay McCreedy was driving by when it happened and directed traffic."

"Was the driver hurt?"

"No, thank goodness. His car is trashed, though."

"You got anything for me while I'm on rounds tonight?"

"Nope. Just the usual."

"I've got a date with a blackjack table in Reno," Connie said. "It looks like you've got everything handled without me." She put her coat back on. "See you guys Monday."

"I'm taking off pretty soon myself," Sloane said, and turned to Wyatt. "Text or call if you need backup."

"Will do. It's been nice having you as chief these last few days." Wyatt booted up his computer and logged on.

Sloane left with a smile on her face. Parked in the chief's spot— one of the few perks of the job—she started to get in the driver's seat when something across the square caught her attention: a lanky man in camouflage who'd just come out of the sporting goods store. She couldn't make out his face, but his body type and something about the way he moved was distinctly familiar. With a bad feeling in her gut, she ditched her vehicle and went after him.

The man crossed the green in the direction of the Lumber Baron but at the last minute doubled back toward the barbershop. Sloane did the same. There were people out—a mother toting two kids and a family of five heading to the Bun Boy. Donna Thurston got into her car, and Mariah came out of the Ponderosa and dumped a carton of empty liquor bottles into the recycling bin. The mayor, Dink Caruthers, stopped to ask her when Rhys would be back, and by the time she got to the barbershop the mystery man was gone.

Darla had Harlee in her chair when Sloane walked in. "Did either of you see a tall man in camouflage come by here?" She'd like to know what model car he drove.

Both shook their heads. "You don't look so good. You're pale," Darla said, and went into the back and brought Sloane a bottle of water. "You coming down with something?"

"No."

"Who's the guy?" Harlee wanted to know.

Sloane wanted to downplay it. "From a distance he looked like an old friend. But what's the likelihood?"

"It's a small world," Darla said. "You're still coming in this week for a trim, right?"

"Mm-hmm." She sat on one of the plastic chairs near the window. If he'd ducked into one of the shops, she'd see him as he came out. "How dressed up are you guys getting for the wedding?"

"I'm wearing my bridesmaid dress from Harlee's wedding. It's more conservative than what I usually go in for, but Wyatt really likes it."

Harlee, who was having her hair straightened, said, "I'm wearing a dress too, with a pair of stunning Badgley Mischka pumps I got for half price on my last trip to the Bay Area."

"Isn't the wedding in a barn?" Sloane asked, keeping one eye on the window.

"Yeah. But it's a pretty fancy barn and it's not like we get a lot of opportunities to dress up around here," Harlee said.

"It's a little tricky for me because I have to work a partial shift during the wedding."

"I can give you the key to the barbershop so you can use the dressing room to get ready after your shift," Darla said. "Wyatt said he'll just change in the police station in the locker room. But you'd probably be more comfortable in here."

"Maybe." Sloane was too distracted to think about it. "I actually feel a little queasy—probably something I ate. I'm gonna head home."

"I could go over to the Ponderosa and get you some ginger ale."

"I'll be fine," Sloane said. "I'm working tomorrow. If you guys are around we should get a bite."

"I'm in," Darla said.

"As long as there are no big breaking stories, I'm in too. Just text us."

Sloane programmed both their numbers into her phone while watching the square. No sign of him. On the drive home, she nearly convinced herself that she'd imagined him.

Brady came out onto the porch, took one look at her and said, "What's wrong?"

"I thought I saw Sweeney's partner, Roger Buck, here today."

"Where?" Brady took the key from her hand and unlocked the door. "Let me go in first."

Before she could argue that she was the sworn peace officer and the one with a gun, Brady went inside and searched her apartment.

"Nothing looks out of place. Take a look." He nearly stepped on her, she was so close. "I told you to wait."

She took a closer inspection. "It looks exactly the way I left it this morning."

"Sit and tell me everything." He patted the couch and sat next to her.

"Not a lot to tell. I got off duty, walked to my car, and saw a man coming out of the sporting goods store wearing fatigues. From a distance he looked like Roger, so I tried to move in closer. It was almost as if he knew I'd spotted him and he wanted to lead me on a chase. He walked to the Lumber Baron, then doubled back to the barbershop. I got waylaid by the mayor and lost him."

"Did you go in the sporting goods store and ask about him?"

"No. I didn't want to sound crazy. There are dozens of guys walking around here in camouflage. Hunters, fishermen, archers, even birdwatchers."

Brady got up, grabbed her landline, and dialed. "Lina, we have anyone by the name of Roger Buck staying with us?"

He held the phone to his ear with his shoulder and waited. "Thanks, Lina. Hey, while I've got you on the phone, what's Carl's number over at the sporting goods store?" He grabbed a pen off Sloane's hall tree and jotted the number down on the back of an envelope. "Thanks."

He dialed again. "Hey, Carl, it's Brady. Did a guy in camo leave his credit card in there? His name is Roger Buck . . . said you were the last place he remembered using his card . . . No? Hmm. I'd appreciate it." Brady muffled the phone with his hand and turned to Sloane. "He doesn't think so, but he's checking the cash register, and with his daughter, just to make sure."

Brady paced while he waited. "Okay, Carl, thanks." He hung up the phone and climbed over Sloane to reclaim his spot on the couch. "He says he doesn't have any credit card receipts for a Roger Buck, and according to his daughter, the only guy wearing camouflage today bought a pair of binoculars and paid in cash."

"Wow," Sloane said. "You might want to consider a career in law enforcement."

"We still don't know any more than we did before." Brady scrubbed his hand through his hair. "How sure are you this guy could be Roger?"

"Hard to say. At the time I saw him my heart started pounding and my fight-or-flight response kicked in, like I was certain. Now, I think I may have overreacted. Seriously, what are the chances he came all this way?"

"My feeling is your initial instinct is the one you go with. I'm not saying it was him. But we need to proceed as if it was."

Sloane dropped her head onto her chest. "I just want peace from these people."

"I know." Brady massaged the back of her neck.

"That feels good. Don't stop." Sloane moved her hair out of his way.

He kneaded her neck, moved down to her shoulders, and seemed to hesitate, like he was warring with himself, but never took his hands away. Then he whispered, "Take off your uniform, sweetness."

She unbuttoned her top and let it slide off her shoulders. He played with the lace on her bra and pushed her shirt off until it fell to the floor. Little by little he undressed her, removing her boots and socks first. He wrestled with her gun belt. She removed it while he worked his way up to her snap and zipper. He tugged down her pants, leaving her in nothing but her skivvies.

Thank goodness she'd put on good ones. Black and lacy.

"Cold." She shivered.

He lifted her like a bride, carried her into the bedroom, and laid her down on the floral duvet. "Frilly in here too."

She knocked a row of pillows off the bed and crawled under the blanket. Brady kicked off his shoes, pulled his shirt over his head, undid his belt, and whipped off his jeans. He stood over the bed and she thought she could stare up at him forever. His body reminded her of a marble statue—cut and solid. His arms ropey with muscle and inked in color. He got under the covers and touched her everywhere, making her breasts and nipples tingle.

"You feel good," he said as he kissed the curve of her shoulder. "Smell good too."

She shuddered when he unfastened the clasp on her bra and took her breasts in his callused hands, his erection pressing against her. "Oh, Brady."

He reached underneath her, pulling her closer and tighter . . . to that very spot that throbbed for him. And they kissed and kissed, rolling around in her ruffled, lavender-scented bedding. His fingers crawled under the elastic waist of her panties, making her hotter and wetter. She sucked in a breath, closed her eyes, and moaned her pleasure while he took her to heaven. Then he dragged her underwear down her legs and plunged into her, taking her up, higher and higher, until her pulse raced and her heart soared. He held her arms over her head and went deeper and faster. She wrapped her legs around his hips, feeling filled and completely surrounded. Connected, body and soul.

"Jesus, sweetness, I can't hold back any longer." The muscles in his neck strained.

"Don't . . . want . . . you . . . to," she said in a stuttered voice that didn't sound like her own. "Brady."

"I'm right there with you, baby."

They rode the crest together, clinging to each other, until they came crashing down. Brady gathered her in his arms and they just lay there, spooning and listening to the trees whistling in the evening breeze.

"What are you thinking?" she asked him, wondering if he was already having regrets.

"That it was even better than the first time and that we didn't use a condom."

"Oops." She flipped over to face him. "I'm healthy. You?"

"Yes. To tell you the truth, you're the first woman I've been with since I left LA. Are you on any form of birth control?"

"No." She hadn't been that sexually active to warrant it. At least not in the last six months.

"All right, we'll just have to monitor the situation." He seemed freaked out about it, not that she could blame him.

"I'm sure it'll be fine." Sloane wanted to be reassuring but frankly didn't even know where she was in her cycle. She hadn't had any reason to track it.

He bent over her and brushed a kiss across her lips. She thought he meant to leave, but he plopped down next to her and wrapped her in his arms.

"You hungry?"

"I could eat." Come to think about it, after Brady's big breakfast, she'd never had lunch. "What did you have in mind?"

"Whatever you want."

"You've been cooking all day," she said. "How was your confab with the Baker's Dozen?" She thought it was hilarious that Mr. Alpha Brady belonged to an all-woman's cooking group, especially given that all the ladies were happily married. Sloane had never met a man more secure in his masculinity.

"It just so happens that we made chicken tortilla soup—Donna's recipe—and I have leftovers."

"I'd definitely be down with that. Should we go over to your place?"

"Nah. You stay put. I'll get it and bring it here." He sat at the edge of the bed and put on his clothes.

"Do you miss Pig and Tangelo?"

"It was a good gig . . . helped me make a name for myself. If I'd stayed, I'd probably have my own restaurant by now." He stood to pull up his pants and button his fly.

"Do you ever think about moving to another big city, somewhere out of California, and starting there?"

He sighed. "In a big city, at a big restaurant, there would be publicity. The reason I came here is because I could still do my best cooking and stay incognito . . . at least until Sandra's dealt with."

What a life, to always be looking over your shoulder, Sloane mused. But as a cop she'd seen it before. Women running from abusive husbands or boyfriends. Movie stars threatened by deranged admirers. People victimized by ex-lovers. Unfortunately, a lot of times there wasn't anything the law could do about it.

Sloane stretched out in the bed, waiting for Brady, all worries of Roger banished from her head. The more she thought about it, the more convinced she became that the man on the square couldn't have been him. Just the same body type, is all.

A few minutes later, she heard Brady come through the door and head to the kitchen. She got up, wrapped herself in a robe, and headed to the bathroom for a quick shower, passing Brady on the way.

"Got room for two?" Not only had he brought soup, bread, and beer, but clothes too. Looked like he was bunking here for the night.

"Of course."

"Get the water hot while I get this into a pot." He held up the container of soup.

"Grab an extra towel from my closet."

By the time he joined her in the shower, she'd gotten a good steam going. Brady grabbed the soap out of her hand, started on her back, worked his way lower until he slid the bar between her legs. She snatched it away from him and took her time washing him. They both shampooed each other's hair and Brady kissed her.

"You know this is a really bad idea, don't you?"

"You'll have to be more specific," she said. "Showering? Because personally I'm a stickler for good hygiene."

He looked at her with those sexy hazel eyes and said, "Me staying the night, which I fully intend to do as long as there's a chance that this Roger loser is hanging around."

"I don't need you to protect me," she said and rested her forehead against his. "But I want you to stay."

He nudged her under the water so they could both rinse the shampoo from their heads. She reached up on tiptoe to put her lips on his, letting the hot water sluice over them while they kissed.

"You in a rush to eat?" he asked.

"No."

"Good," he said. "Because I'm hungry for something other than food."

Chapter 14

"Hey, boss, Lina just called. Her truck broke down on State Highway 70, near Chilcoot. She needs a tow. You want me to go out?"

Griffin only hesitated for a second. "Nah, I'll get her."

"You've got her cell phone number, right?" Rico's lips curved up in a smart-ass smile.

Griffin flipped him the bird. "Hold down the fort while I'm gone, will you?"

They had two oil changes and three appointments for smog checks. Not bad for a Monday. At three, Griff had a meeting with a Sacramento lobbyist who wanted a custom bike. He had a cabin up here and had seen some of Griff's work at the car show in Clio last month. That left him plenty of time to get Lina and haul her Scout back home. He grabbed a set of keys from his office, hopped into the cab of one of his tow trucks, and got on the road, not liking the idea of Lina stranded alone.

Despite the winter's lack of snow, his tow business did a booming business. This time last year, most of his calls had been weather-related accidents and cars stuck in the mud or snow. This year, not a lot of snow but plenty of breakdowns. Good thing he'd purchased the tow trucks against Owen's advice. The old man thought selling fish bait would be the secret to Griff's success. The barber wasn't exactly Jeff Bezos.

It took Griffin thirty minutes to reach Lina's truck, marooned on a barren stretch of high desert just past Chilcoot. He pulled ahead of the Scout, managing to weave around two telephone poles. Lina got out of the truck and rested her arms on Griffin's open window.

"Thanks for coming."

"No problem. What happened?"

"It started to sputter a few miles back like it was running out of gas. I pulled over here and the engine went dead. It said I had half a tank. But maybe my gas gauge isn't working."

Griff doubted it. The ancient truck had seen too many miles and was ready to go to that great junkyard in the sky. "Let's haul her in and check 'er out. Hop in and get out of the cold."

Lina got in on the passenger side while Griff adjusted his boom to get his tow chain as close as he could. He got out, fastened the chain and hook to the Scout's axle, and got back in the cab. With the boom, he lifted the Scout's two front tires onto the back of his truck and hung a U-turn on the highway.

"Sorry you had to wait out here by yourself."

"No big deal. I would've called Rhys, but he and Maddy are on their way home from San Francisco."

"You coming from school?"

"Mm-hmm. I don't have any more classes this week and Brady wants me to help prep for the wedding. I'll be screwed without a car."

"Let's see what we can do." He absently brushed her leg with his hand. "Don't remember you ever wearing pantyhose before."

"I interviewed for a summer internship today with an engineering firm that builds suspension bridges. I wanted to look professional."

He slid her a sideways glance. "You look good." Too damn good. "You get it?"

"I won't know for a while. A lot of people are applying. So if not this summer, maybe next."

That sounded logical and mature to him—and very unlike Lina. Typically she was the impatient type. Wanted what she wanted now, never later.

"You've got a lot of things you're juggling, don't you? Even working on Valentine's Day, huh?"

She shrugged. "I'm not seeing anyone, so it's no big deal. How about you and Dana? You have plans before or after the wedding, since she's not coming?"

Griffin cleared his throat and focused on the road. "We're not a couple, Lina."

"Oh." Her voice sounded surprised. "I'm sorry. When did you break up?"

"Uh, we were never really like that . . . a couple, I mean. We just dated for a while and decided we were better as friends."

"Really? I'd gotten the impression that the two of you were . . . serious."

"I don't know where you would've gotten that idea. Certainly nothing I ever told you."

"Yes, you did. That first time I saw you at the gas station after I got back."

"No. You said you'd heard I was seeing someone. I neither confirmed nor denied it. I figured you were still seeing that guy from USF."

"I wasn't . . . I'm not," she said. "Honestly, I'm too busy to be anything other than single. I don't even have time to date."

"That's what I tried to tell you." *Way to sound like a sanctimonious tool*, he silently scolded himself.

"You were right. About us . . . about everything."

He should've asked her if he could get that on tape. Instead, her easy acquiescence made him angry. What they'd had was the real deal, and maybe he shouldn't have been so consumed with how young she'd been . . . how young she still was. Age was just a number, after all.

He pulled to the side of the road, slammed on his brakes, twisted toward her side of the cab, and kissed her. Not some preppy college-boy kiss either. Nothing wet and sloppy. He kissed her like a man who knew what he was doing.

"Griffin," she said against his mouth, her hands in his hair, and the rest of her practically in his lap. "What are we doing?"

"I don't know." He pulled away and closed his eyes. "That shouldn't have happened."

"It's no big deal. We're just familiar to each other. Come on, let's get back on the road and forget it ever happened."

Who the hell was this woman? Back in the day, he'd been the one who'd had to put on the brakes. She'd wanted him like no one else had. And that was saying a lot, since Griffin had never suffered from a lack of females putting the moves on him.

"Sorry." He nosed the tow truck onto the road, and tried to pretend that he hadn't just made a fool of himself.

"Nothing to apologize for. What are you doing on the twenty-eighth?"

"Of this month? I don't know. Why?"

"Maddy and Rhys are throwing me a birthday party. If you're free, stop by. It's at the Lumber Baron. Nothing fancy, just food, drinks, family, and friends from school."

Ah, Jesus, all he needed was to see her around a bunch of drooling frat dudes or whoever she hung out with now. He'd have to figure out a way to get out of it. "Thanks for the invite. I'll try to stop by."

"I'd like it if you could, but if you're busy or something comes up, no worries." She actually sounded like she meant it, like she was 100 percent totally over him.

As they pulled past Nugget's welcome sign, Griffin asked if Lina wanted him to drop her at home.

"I was sort of hoping you could look at the Scout first and tell me what I'm facing. Then I can walk to the square and get a ride to Rhys and Maddy's."

"Okay. I'll see what I can do, but I've got an appointment at three." Griff looked at his watch.

At the Gas and Go, he maneuvered the Scout into an empty bay while Rico unchained the tow truck and parked it. Lina stood over Griffin's shoulder as he examined the engine. Nothing jumped out at him, but he'd have to do a complete diagnostic before he knew the problem. First, he wanted to check on her theory about the gas gauge. Griff stuck a hose in the tank to measure the amount of fuel she had left. The Scout held nineteen gallons. From the gas line on the hose he estimated that it had nearly ten left. So not a gas problem.

"This'll take a while," he told her. "I probably won't have an answer until tomorrow. Let me drop you somewhere."

"I can walk. You've got that meeting pretty soon."

"Lina, it'll take me five minutes to run you to the Lumber Baron. You've got heels on."

"All right. How much do I owe you for the tow?"

"Let's figure it out after I know what's wrong, okay?"

She nodded. He stood there for a few seconds just looking at her, because she was that pretty.

"What's wrong?" she asked.

"Uh, nothing. My truck's on the street." He led the way, unlocking the doors with his key fob. And because Griff wanted to touch her, he helped her in.

When they got to the Lumber Baron he leaned across her to unlock the door.

"Thanks for rescuing me today, Griff. You'll call me as soon as you know, right?"

"Yep. But, Lina, I don't think we're looking at good news here.

It's reached the point where it's mostly a money pit now, especially if you're planning to buy something anyway. If it's something small, I'll do my best to patch it up and get it running until you find something better. But if it's big, you should cut your losses."

She flashed a sad smile. "There are just a lot of memories attached to that truck is all."

"I know." The first time they'd met was after she'd flooded the Scout's engine and he'd helped her get it started. Remembering that day made him want to kiss her all over again.

"But I realize that it's probably time to let go." She climbed out of the truck and waved goodbye. "Talk to you later."

He watched Lina walk into the Lumber Baron, feeling like her old truck—nothing more than a fond memory.

Three things happened on Monday. Rhys came back to work. Rose showed up on time. And Sloane finally got a break in her bones case.

The state's forensic anthropologist believed the remains to be that of a Caucasian male in his early twenties. His best guess, based on the length of one of the legs that had been found—they'd never recovered his arms or hands—was that he was somewhere between five ten and six feet tall, and according to wear on certain bones, weighed approximately 180 pounds.

What amazed Sloane was that the anthropologist could tell, by looking at his teeth and the bones around his mouth, that their John Doe had likely played a woodwind instrument. Wild, but also extremely helpful in whittling down their missing-persons pool.

Because his hyoid bone was not fractured—usually a sign of strangulation—and no bullet holes or other signs of trauma were found, John Doe's cause of death remained a mystery. But based on animal bites, the anthropologist approximated the time of death to be roughly four months ago.

It wasn't a tremendous amount to go on, but it was a significant start, Sloane thought as she walked into the chief's office for a briefing with him and Jake.

"Why's there a high school kid working in my police station, McBride?"

"Sorry, Chief, I meant to tell you about Rose when you came in, but you seemed stressed." She looked at Jake for moral support and he nodded. "She got suspended for fighting with another girl . . . and, uh, bringing pepper spray to school. The girl and her friends have been bullying Rose for some time. I thought working here might build her confidence."

"So we're social workers now?" Rhys raised his brows. "Did she use the pepper spray on anyone?"

"She didn't do anything with it. I think she just brought it for protection. These girls have been pretty rough on her."

"Will I be getting calls from pissed-off parents?"

"Yes, sir," Sloane said, dreading his reaction. "The father of the instigator . . . Taylor Grant . . . is apparently on the warpath. He thinks we should've arrested Rose."

"How do you know this?"

"The principal gave me a heads-up."

"Okay. Just as long as I'm not blindsided. What's Rose doing for us?"

"Administrative work. I'm having her cull through missing-persons reports."

His brows winged up and he tilted his head, as if to say it was a big job for a fifteen-year-old. "Hey, it's your call."

"She just needs a little support, Chief." But Sloane worried that maybe she'd gone too far. She could've had the kid pick up trash on the highway.

"Just don't turn my department into a teen shelter."

With a great deal of relief she nodded.

"Let's talk about what you got from the California DOJ."

She detailed the forensic anthropologist's information on their John Doe, and told Rhys the theory about him being a musician.

"That might help narrow it down," Rhys said. "We still don't know if it's foul play, huh?"

"Nope. But no strangulation, head trauma, stab marks, broken bones, or bullet holes."

"I had one of these once," Jake said. "Never could determine the method or cause of death."

"The anthropologist thinks he's been dead since November, huh?" Rhys looked at Jake. "Seems older to me, considering we didn't have a full skeleton or any skin."

"First off, it's been a pretty mild winter," Jake said. "And between the bears, raccoons, vultures, and fish, he was picked pretty clean."

"That's right about the time the cattle rustling started . . . and the drug dealing on Lucky's ranch."

Rhys got up from his chair and sat on the corner of his desk. "Sloane, you talk to Lucky yet?"

"No. I'll go out there before my shift's over. Now that I have more to go on I was thinking of putting something out in the *Nugget Tribune*, maybe make up fliers."

"Let's give Harlee a hotline number, put it on the fliers too, and have the kid pass them out around town. Clay McCreedy's ranch was hit hard by those rustlers. Talk to him as well. Maybe he had a ranch hand who played the flute."

Jake laughed. "Aren't all cowboys required to have a harmonica on them at all times?"

"There you go," Rhys said. "We're halfway to solving this thing. You ready for Saturday?"

"Yup." Jake eyed both of them. "You two coming to the rehearsal dinner Friday night?"

"Wyatt's coming to the first half while I cover his shift," Rhys said. "I'll be over after, so be sure to save the good booze for last."

"I'm coming for the whole thing." Sloane planned to space out her four comp days but was taking Thursday and Friday off.

"Good." Jake peered at his watch. "Cecilia and I have a meeting with Brady over at the Lumber Baron."

"Take off," Rhys said, and turned to Sloane. "Why don't you head out to Lucky's and hit Clay's on the way back?"

"Okay." She waited until Jake left and said, "Can I talk to you for a couple of minutes?"

"Yep."

"Right after you left I got a disturbing text." She showed him the threat with the picture of Sweeney hanging.

"Ah, Christ." He fiddled with her phone. "Who sent this?"

"I don't know for sure but suspect it was Sweeney's partner, Roger Buck." She told him about the other texts and phone messages. *Sloane McBride, you can't hide. We're coming to get you.* And described the man she'd seen Saturday.

"You didn't see his face, though?"

"No. And now I'm thinking it probably wasn't him, but I thought I should tell you the whole thing."

"Damn right. You should've told me from the get-go. I've got a friend in Houston who's a genius at tracking these things." He held up her phone. "Let me call him. As soon as I find out who's behind this, I'll call LAPD internal affairs."

Sloane cringed. "That didn't work out so well for me the last time. I haven't gotten anything since that text; maybe it was their last hurrah, and now they're done with me. I'd rather just leave it alone."

"I don't like it, Sloane. No one—"

"Please, can't we just monitor it for now? Otherwise they'll make my life a living hell . . . I don't have the fortitude to go through it again."

He let out a breath. "We've got your back here, Sloane. All right, we'll do it your way. But I need your promise that you'll come to me if it starts up again."

"I will," she said, and when he gave her a hard look amended, "I swear I will."

He got off the desk. "Make sure Rose has enough to do before you get going."

She showed Rose to an empty computer, told her to get started on the flier, and popped into the *Nugget Tribune* office to give Harlee the scoop before heading out to Lucky's. During her short time in Nugget she'd only driven by the cowboy camp, never gone in.

The ranch was busy. Everywhere Sloane looked, she saw construction. She wasn't sure where to find Lucky, so she parked in front of a single-wide trailer and started there. A man answered the door, Sloane flashed her creds, and he directed her up the hill to a huge stack-stone, timber-log building. The door was open and she went in. It looked like the hall was getting rewired and she wondered if this was where Jake and Cecilia's reception would be held. Magnificent place with open-beam ceilings and pine-plank floors. Seemed like they were cutting it close to the party, though.

She'd never actually met Lucky Rodriguez, yet she picked him out of the crowd of workers without a second's thought. He just stood out. Had a certain kind of indefinable something.

"Mr. Rodriguez?"

He stopped what he was doing and looked at her. "No one ever calls me that. I'm Lucky." He stuck his hand out for a shake. "You must be Sloane. My fiancée told me all about you."

She did? "You have a couple of minutes to talk?"

Someone turned on a power saw. "Let's take it somewhere quiet," he shouted, and led her out of the lodge, down a paved road to a small building that served as an office. "Sorry, it's crazy around here. We're trying to make a deadline."

"For the wedding?"

"Nah, we're all set there. That'll be in the barn on the south side of the property. But we have a four-day event in the spring, and this place needs to be done."

"I won't take much of your time. You hear about the remains we found a few weeks ago at the Meet Up?"

"Sure did. What's going on with that?"

"A forensic anthropologist was able to determine that the person, a male in his early twenties, died sometime around November, about the same time all the trouble with the drug dealing and cattle thefts happened. There's a chance that our person might've been involved with that or witnessed something. Perhaps a ranch hand or one of your construction workers. Can you remember anyone failing to show up for work or just sort of disappearing?"

Lucky scratched his head under his cowboy hat. "Most of the original crew on this job was caught up in that drug sting. My daughter was real sick at the time, and unfortunately I didn't pay too much attention to their comings and goings."

"Just give it some thought," Sloane said, hoping that if he had time to mull it over something might jog his memory. "Sometimes people remember things that at the time didn't seem significant. Apparently, our mystery man was a musician—played a horn, clarinet, harmonica, something like that. If you can think of anything at all, give me a call." She handed him her card.

"I'll do that. You coming to my ma's wedding?"

"I am, and to the rehearsal dinner."

"We'll try to cut Brady loose long enough so that he can dance with you."

Oh boy, Sloane thought, word traveled fast in this town. She didn't say anything, just smiled and thanked him for taking the time.

Next, she hit McCreedy Ranch. Justin greeted her at the door of the enormous farmhouse.

"Hey, Justin, are your parents home?"

"Yeah. Come on in." The inside, Sloane noted, was even more impressive than the outside. "Everything okay?"

"I came to talk to them about the bones you kids found. We have a little bit more information about it and wanted to tell you in case any of it rings a bell."

"Okay. I'll get 'em."

"Hey, Justin, before you go, did your dad talk to you about Rose Jones?"

"Yeah." He shook his head. "I don't know her."

"She's only a freshman. I was hoping you could say hi to her every once in a while. Maybe just wave to her across the hall. Nothing big."

"I could do that if you think it'll help her." He hitched his shoulders like he didn't know how it would.

"I think it would, and I'd really appreciate it."

"Hey." Clay came into the foyer. "What brings you our way?"

She gave him the same spiel she'd given Lucky. "If there is anything at all you remember, even something small, it could be helpful."

"Sounds like you've got a real puzzle to solve. But I'll think on it and talk to Emily. I'm sure whoever his family is would like to give him a proper burial."

She figured no one would understand that better than the McCreedys after what Emily had gone through with her daughter. "Thanks. You have a beautiful place here."

"Come over anytime. Justin and Cody will take you out on horseback. It's a nice way to see the area."

Sloane didn't ride, but she'd like to try it. "I might take you up on that."

"Anytime. In the meantime, I assume we'll see you at the wedding Saturday."

"Yes, you will."

She said goodbye and got on the road. Back in the office, Rose had made a good start on the flier. The kid had found a flier template on the Internet and had gone to town. She got an A for being a self-starter. It was a little splashier than Sloane liked, so she toned it down a bit, added the Nugget PD logo, printed a stack, and sent Rose around the square to ask merchants to hang the fliers in their windows. While she was gone, Sloane downloaded a list from NamUs of people who were reported missing since November. Any one of them could've come through Nugget. During Sloane's days off, she wanted Rose to sort through the list, eliminating those who didn't fit their John Doe's description. Then Sloane could examine the ones that did.

She didn't know whether Brady would be too busy with preparations for the rehearsal and wedding reception on Thursday. If not, she wanted to make good on her promise to make him dinner. He'd stayed with her again Sunday night, genuinely concerned that the man she'd seen in the square was Buck. Secretly, she'd felt safer having him there. Of course there were other benefits to having him in her bed as well.

A man in an expensive suit came in the station demanding to talk to the chief. When Connie told him the chief was on the phone, he brushed by her like he owned the place. Sloane stepped in his pathway and asked if she could help him.

"I'd like to speak with the chief."

"As Connie explained, the chief is tied up on a phone call right now. But if you'll take a seat I'll let him know that you're here. Your name, please."

"Kenneth Grant."

Ah, Taylor's father. Here we go.

Sloane wondered how much Rhys would have her back when politics came into play. Based on the Italian shoes and silk tie, Kenneth Grant wasn't your typical Nugget railroad worker or cattle rancher. More than likely Grant had clout. Rhys served at the whim of the mayor, and the mayor served at the whim of the townsfolk. Being a third-generation civil servant—her grandfather had been a Chicago firefighter too—Sloane knew only too well how this worked. And political pressure in a small town had to be worse than a big city.

She waited until Rhys was off the phone and told him about their company.

"Send him back," he said.

She escorted Grant into Rhys's office, then left and shut the door and went back to her desk.

"When Rose gets back, I'll take her for a Coke at the Bun Boy," Connie said. "I'm due for a break anyway."

"Do you know the Grants?" Having grown up here, Connie seemed to know everyone.

"No. I'm guessing he's a fairly new addition to Nugget. Natives don't act so self-entitled unless they're the Addisons."

Sloane laughed.

"Officer McBride, could you come in here for a second?" Rhys called.

"Here we go," Sloane muttered so that only Connie could hear.

Connie grinned. "Don't take Grant's crap."

Sloane marched into Rhys's office like she was on her way to the guillotine. "You wanted to see me?"

"Grab a seat," Rhys said. "I believe you already met Mr. Grant. Mr. Grant is chief counsel for the Silver Luck Resort."

"We moved to Nugget because I wanted my children to go to safe schools." He looked pointedly at Rhys and then at Sloane.

"Right," Rhys said. "Mr. Grant wants to know why we've been so lenient on Rose Jones."

"She tried to assault my daughter with pepper spray, for God's sake."

"That's not exactly what happened, Mr. Grant," Sloane said. "She never used the pepper spray and only brought it to school because she's petrified of your daughter and your daughter's friends. Are you aware that they regularly verbally and physically abuse Rose? They even tried to hold her head down the toilet?"

"Is that what the girl is telling you? Because it's a bunch of lies. Taylor doesn't have a mean bone in her body."

"According to Mrs. Saddler, there are other girls who have complained about Taylor, Mr. Grant." Sloane held her ground.

"Then why is this the first I'm hearing of it?"

Rhys stepped in. "We can't speak for the school district, Mr. Grant. But when a student feels so threatened that she's afraid for her own safety, it becomes a police issue."

"Yes, exactly. That's why I'm here. Because Rose Jones threatened to blind my daughter."

"There were witnesses, Mr. Grant," Sloane said. "Rose dropped the pepper spray."

"Just bringing it to school is a crime. Need I remind you that I'm a lawyer?"

Sloane started to say something, but Rhys interrupted. "We're dealing with Rose. She's been suspended from school and she's part of a pilot program that Officer McBride is running for at-risk teens. She's a good student from a disadvantaged home. Certainly you wouldn't want us to turn our backs on her?"

Pilot program? Sloane had to give Rhys credit. She had no idea where he'd pulled that one from.

"And, Mr. Grant, a little unsolicited advice," Rhys continued. "This is a small town. Most of the Nugget High kids have grandparents who went to that school. Families here work hard and rely on each other for help. If indeed your daughter is bullying other students, this town won't tolerate it."

"I think what you're trying to tell me, Chief Shepard, is that I'm an outsider and I better watch my step. That kind of insular attitude will eventually make people like you irrelevant. Because more people like me are moving here and we won't put up with it."

Rhys stood. "It was nice meeting you, and thanks for stopping in." Grant had been spoiling for a fight and Rhys wouldn't give him one.

Sloane was a little bit in awe. After Grant left, she said, "Wow. You out-lawyered the lawyer."

"Just make sure our pilot program is a success."

"We don't have a pilot . . . you're kidding, right?"

"Do I look like I'm kidding?" He didn't. In fact, there was not so much as a trace of humor in his expression. What ever happened to *Just don't turn my department into a teen shelter?*

"No, sir." She wanted to throw her arms around him but got the distinct impression he wouldn't appreciate any overt displays of affection. Funny, a few weeks ago that's exactly what she'd thought he wanted. "I'll just get back to work now."

She'd barely made it to her desk when Wyatt and Connie cornered her.

"What happened?" Connie asked.

"Rhys kicked some booty."

"You don't mean literally, do you?" Wyatt said.

Connie rolled her eyes. "Don't mind Wyatt, he has a learning disability."

Sloane glanced around the room. "Where's Rose?"

"Her brother picked her up," Connie said. "Uh, nice Camaro. Not. It was okay that I let her go, right?"

Sloane looked at the clock. Jeez, it was late. "Yeah, of course. Hey, Wyatt, did Jake brief you on the info we got today about the John Doe?"

"Yep. You taking off?"

"I was thinking about it. There's nothing I have that needs following up on for the night shift. Today was pretty quiet."

"Okay. I'll just ride patrol, maybe take some of those fliers"—he motioned to the stack on her desk—"to the Gas and Go and the Nugget Market."

"Sounds good." She grabbed her jacket off the back of her chair and was just about to leave when Maddy came in with a big bouquet of flowers.

"These are for you." She handed the flowers to Sloane. "Thank you for filling in for Rhys and giving me four blissful days alone with my husband."

Sloane was at a loss for words. It hadn't been that bad. Some of it had even been kind of fun. "Uh, no problem."

"I just want you to know how much I appreciate it . . . how much Rhys appreciates it. Did he tell you how much?" When Sloane stood there silent, Maddy said, "He didn't, did he?"

"Yeah, he did. He totally did."

"I did what?" Rhys came down the hall and nuzzled his wife's neck.

"Tell her how much you appreciate her filling in for you," Maddy said.

"She knows I do."

"Rhys!" Maddy put her hands on her hips.

"What? You know I appreciate it, right, Sloane?"

"Absolutely. He gave me six days off just to show his appreciation."

"Four. Don't push it, McBride. You have a pilot program to run."

"What pilot program?" Maddy wanted to know.

"I'll tell you later. Let's go home, sugar." Rhys pulled his wife out the door and Sloane watched them hold hands across the square.

Ah, she thought. *I want that.*

Chapter 15

Brady waited on the porch for Sloane to get home. He knew she'd want to go for a run and didn't want her going alone. Not if this Buck guy was really in town. He could be renting one of the day cabins favored by hunters and fishermen, or even staying in one of the plethora of campgrounds in the state park. Hell, he might even have a room at the Beary Quaint, for all they knew.

Sloane had managed to convince herself that she'd only imagined it was him. But Brady was more inclined to trust her initial reaction. It's not like she over dramatized things. If anything, Sloane was more likely to downplay it.

He heard her truck before he saw it come over the hill. A few minutes later she came down the driveway and parked next to his van.

"Hey," she said, and hopped down onto the running board.

"Nice flowers." He cocked his brows. *Who the hell got her those?*

"Maddy gave them to me as a thanks for filling in for Rhys."

Ah. "Good having him back?"

"Oh yeah. A lot happened today. I'll tell you about it, but first I want to go for a run."

He'd called that one right. "I'll go with you. You can tell me on the trail."

"I can't even keep up with you, let alone talk at the same time."

"I'll slow down for you." He winked. "Go put your running clothes on."

While she went inside her apartment he quickly checked his laptop to see if Sandra had hit again. Nothing. Perhaps she had found someone new to obsess over. Doubtful, according to the textbooks. Although Brady wouldn't wish her on anyone else, he desperately wanted to be free of her.

"You ready?" Sloane came out onto the porch, slung her bare leg up on the railing, and did a few stretches. She really did have great legs, but was going to freeze her butt off in shorts.

Brady stashed the laptop back in his apartment.

"Anything?" she asked, and it struck Brady that they had each other's habits down.

"Nope. She's been quiet for a few days."

"That's something. Maybe both our troubles are over?"

Brady wasn't counting on it. Best-case scenario was that Sloane really had imagined Roger Buck being here and that the bad boys at LAPD would eventually stop the texting and phone calls. But he didn't think Sandra was ever going away. Not entirely. He'd read about women like her. They are called simple-obsession stalkers and are the most likely to be violent, even deadly. Just like Sandra, they need extreme control, can't take rejection, and exhibit obsessive and vengeful behavior. The worst part: They are incapable of taking responsibility for their actions. The studies and reports he'd read said that these types of stalkers bolster their self-esteem by terrorizing their victims. Their self-worth is so wrapped up in the object of their obsession that they'll stop at nothing to get him or her back. Nothing. So Brady would forever have to have eyes in the back of his head.

That's why this thing with him and Sloane couldn't go too far. As soon as he felt confident that she was safe, he'd back off. It was for the best in more ways than one. Sloane hadn't said it, but it was obvious that she wanted what they had to go further. And he didn't do long-term. Not with a woman. Not with much of anything. Working at Pig and Tangelo had been his longest commitment on record.

"Let's hope," he replied, and jogged down the steps. "You up for the fire trail loop?"

"I am if you are." She took off in front of him.

"You gonna tell me about your day?"

"We heard from the state's forensic anthropologist," she called over her shoulder, and slowed down to tell him what they'd learned and about their theory that John Doe could be connected to Nugget's November crime spree.

"Makes sense," he said.

"Rhys totally stood up for me today. You should've seen how he took on this hotshot lawyer guy. It was awesome."

"About the John Doe?" Brady was confused.

"No. I'm jumbling my stories. Sorry. I told you about Rose, right?"

"The kid with the pepper spray."

"Yep. Well, the other girl's father came in today to complain that we hadn't sent Rose to San Quentin." Brady laughed. "Yeah, can you believe it? Anyway, he's chief counsel for the Silver Luck Resort in Reno but moved here for the safe schools. And he really came on strong with Rhys, who I thought for sure would cater to him. But I was wrong. First he told the guy that we were running a pilot program for at-risk teens—just pulled that one out of nowhere. Then, in the nicest way imaginable, he told the guy to go screw himself."

"I don't know why you're surprised." Brady ran backwards. "Everyone knows that Rhys doesn't take crap. He's got a reputation for being a fair chief, but if you try to push him around, he pushes back. I also get the impression that when he was a kid he and his old man were the town outcasts. So perhaps he identifies with Rose."

"She's really a sweet girl. She tries to act apathetic, but you can tell that she's eager to please. I get the impression that her mother is so busy trying to keep a roof over her family's head that she doesn't have a lot of time for Rose."

"What about the father?"

"No father, just a super creepy brother named Skeeter." She made a face.

"Hey, don't make fun. Where I come from there were lots of Skeeters."

"What's it a nickname for?"

She was short of breath so he slowed down. "Mosquito."

"Get out. Seriously?"

"Yup. You know, like a pest. Skeeter." He went heavy on his South Carolina accent to give her the full flavor.

Her lips curved up. "You ready to go back?"

"Sure. Sloane, did you talk to Rhys about the text and Roger Buck?"

"I did. He wanted his friend in Houston to try to trace the text and go to LAPD internal affairs. I asked him not to."

"Why?"

"Because it would only make it worse. I haven't received any more messages, and the more I think about it, the more I'm sure that it wasn't Buck who I saw. But if Rhys goes to IA the harassment will start all over again."

Brady was quiet for a few seconds. Honestly, he had no clue about what to do in a situation like this. But he didn't like the idea of these guys getting away with menacing Sloane the way they had. Hell, he didn't like the idea that they were allowed to wear badges—and carry guns.

"Okay," he finally said. "But let's continue to be vigilant."

She tacitly agreed and they ran the rest of the way home in silence. When they got back, Sloane bent over and put her head between her knees. Brady did a few quad stretches.

"You should go inside before you catch a chill in those shorts."

She nodded, still trying to catch her breath. "You're in really good shape."

He shrugged. "My legs are twice as long as yours."

"You're not competitive in the least, are you?"

"Not with you." He tugged her against him and kissed her. "Want to take a shower?"

She grabbed his arm and pulled him toward her apartment.

"Hang on a sec. Let me get some clothes."

"Okay, but hurry."

Damn, he liked her. Inside, he grabbed his shaving kit, boxers, socks, sweatshirt, a pair of jeans, and the cowboy boots Tawny had made him. He didn't feel like cooking tonight and decided to see if Sloane was game for the Indian restaurant in Glory Junction.

Once in her apartment, he could hear the water running and picked up the pace. She was washing herself when he got in, letting the spray from the showerhead sluice over her. He took the washcloth and slowly soaped up her breasts. Sloane leaned the back of her head against the tile and moaned.

"Good?" he murmured in her ear as he moved the cloth down her body.

"So good."

He kissed her neck and then her shoulders while he sponged her belly and moved the washrag between her legs. She gasped and he smiled.

"You okay?"

"Never been better." She spread wider to give him more access and he pushed the ridge of his erection against her stomach while he brought her to orgasm with his hands, rubbing the terrycloth against her sensitive nub.

"More?"

"God, yes," she pleaded.

He reached outside the shower and fumbled around in his shaving kit until he found what he wanted and had the condom on in less than five seconds. Then he turned her around, told her to grip the wall, and made love to her until the water turned cold and they could no longer stand. Brady carried her to the bed where they lay in each other's arms, recovering.

"I'm excited about this restaurant," Sloane said.

"Then I guess you better get up."

"Ugh," she groaned, and he playfully slapped her bottom so they could get a move on.

She padded across the floor and rifled through her closet for something to wear. Brady enjoyed the way she unabashedly moved around naked. Not too many women he'd known did that.

"You don't have to dress up, Sloane. It's still the Sierra." He forced himself to get up too, and started putting on the clothes he'd brought.

"I know, but I want to. I feel like all I ever wear anymore is my uniform or exercise outfits." She pulled a black dress out of her closet and moved to her chest of drawers to find the right underthings.

He watched her shimmy into a black thong. "Nice."

She did a little stripper dance for him while she put on the matching bra.

"You're supposed to take it off, not put it on." He grinned. It scared him how much he liked her. "Hey, that time we didn't use a condom . . . we okay on that?"

"We're fine," she said.

Sloane rubbed lotion on her legs and slid into the dress. Holy Mother of God, she looked good.

"Those are gorgeous." She pointed at his cowboy boots. "I assume Tawny made them."

"Yup." He pulled them on.

"She copied the design of your tattoo—the fork and knife. Tell me the truth, did you guys used to have a thing?"

"Nope. She's always had a thing for Lucky."

"But you would've if she hadn't?"

"Who can say? But it was never like that. I count her as one of my best friends here . . . anywhere. She's good people and so is Lucky."

"The other day when I met him at his cowboy camp, he said that Tawny had told him all about me. You know what that's about?"

He grabbed her around the waist and bent her backwards for a kiss. "Can we go? I'm starved and it'll take a half hour to get there."

"Let me just dry my hair and put on some makeup."

"You don't need makeup."

But she put some on anyway. Finally they got in Brady's van and made their way to the resort town. Fifteen minutes into the drive, Brady pulled onto a side road that wended around a lake, the mountainside dotted with matching cabins.

"Where are we going?" Sloane asked, peering out the window at the view.

"This is Nate and Maddy's new acquisition—Gold Mountain. When they're done with the rehab, it'll be awesome."

"I think it's awesome now. Is it a resort or something?"

"Yeah. The same families rent the cabins summer after summer. Nate's winterizing them to take advantage of ski season . . . if we ever have snow again. They're also planning to put in a casual restaurant. I'm working on that with them."

"Will you cook for it?"

"Nah," he said. "We're talking really simple dishes. Sandwiches, pizzas, hamburgers, and hot dogs. Stuff people can take out and bring to the lake or the pool or eat at picnic tables inside the restaurant—a glorified hamburger joint, except we'll serve beer and wine for the adults."

"So where do you come in?" Sloane asked.

He loved how she was genuinely interested. "I'll do the business plan, design the menu, and come up with the recipes."

"The business plan? What does that entail?"

"Coming up with a concept, which is pretty much what I just described. Determining profit margins, that sort of thing. A lot of people are under the impression that restaurants make bank, when in fact there is very little markup on food. The money is in volume and liquor sales. That's why I'm trying to design a menu where they can do lots of turnover."

"You know how to do all that?"

"Yep. That's what executive chefs and restaurateurs do."

"So you did that at Pig and Tangelo?"

"Me and the owner, who didn't know dick about running a restaurant. Just thought it would be cool to have a place where he and his friends could hang out."

She continued to stare out the window. "This is totally the kind of place my family would go in the summer. Sometimes we took vacations at Table Rock Lake near Branson, Missouri. They were the best."

"I think the Breyers are on to something here. The place needs a lot of work. But when it's finished it's gonna be a beaut—and a money-maker."

Brady got back on the highway. "I wanted to show you while there was still daylight."

"I'm glad you did. How soon until they open?"

"Nate hopes that it'll be done by summer, since the place is al-ready booked out. He doesn't like losing money."

"Is it true that he owns nine other hotels?"

"Yep. He's a helluva businessman, and between him, Sam, and Maddy, the best bosses I've ever had."

"But wouldn't you like to go back to being your own boss?" she asked.

"At some point."

As they pulled into Glory Junction, Sloane sighed.

"What's that about?"

"It's so freaking cute here."

Brady found a parking space on Main, a cobblestone street flanked on both sides by cutesy shops with old-time wooden signs that catered to tourists. The town was at the bottom of five ski resorts and had lifts and gondolas going up and down the mountainside, with skiers and snowboarders in the winter and mountain bikers in the summer.

The Glory River and a boardwalk with concession stands bordered the western side. Picturesque as hell, but Brady preferred Nugget. When the skiing was good here, the place was awash with people and cars. Same thing in the summer, when the weekenders and sightseers came to take advantage of the rivers and lakes. Sometimes the traffic was so bad you couldn't move.

"What time do you think the stores close?" Sloane asked.

Brady pretended to look at his watch. "Now."

She smacked his shoulder playfully. "Let's just take a quick peek. Look, there's a cooking store over there."

Brady had seen it during his many ski visits. Filled with overpriced pots and pans and ridiculous gadgets, like chocolate fountains and snow-cone makers. He let Sloane drag him inside, and for her sake feigned interest in the shelves covered with salad bowls, pewter servers, and ceramic dishes. She painstakingly looked at everything, which he found cute. Sloane might be a kickass cop, but she was also a girlie girl.

Their next stop was a fudge shop—more Brady's speed. He bought them each a piece for after dinner. Sloane found a place that sold furniture, which had a couple of Colin's pieces. They talked to the owner for a while and Sloane bought cushions for her rocker. He put them in the van while she hit a couple more stores. Eventually, Brady found her in a combination gift and clothing boutique, trying on furry boots.

"They're on sale," she said. "And I don't have any."

He didn't bother to tell her that winter was almost over. In his experience women weren't that practical. To them "sale" was the magic word. The store had a nice plump chair, so Brady made himself comfortable. He figured they'd be there for a while.

"What do you think?" She stood in front of the mirror examining the boots.

"They're nice."

"But do you think they'll go with enough of my clothes?"

The saleswoman saw him struggling to answer and took pity, ticking off about twenty things that would work well with the boots.

"All right, I'll take them." Sloane went to the cash register, paid, and pulled him out of the chair. "Let's eat."

The Indian place was up a side street and owned by a nice couple. The wife immediately recognized Brady, greeted him with a big hug, and escorted them to a private table.

"You must come a lot." Sloane perused the menu.

"Occasionally while I'm here skiing."

"I always wondered why you never invited me."

"To go skiing or to eat here?"

"Since there hasn't been any snow, at least to eat," Sloane said. "You were a bit standoffish in the beginning."

"What? Are you used to men falling at your feet?" He grinned at her. Truthfully she probably was. Smart, beautiful, charming, athletic, self-sufficient. A man's dream woman.

"No. But I thought we could be friends."

"And so we are. What are you getting?"

"I don't know. What do you recommend?"

He looked down at the menu. "You want to share a few entrées and get a couple of side dishes?"

"That sounds like a lot of food," she said.

"So? We can take home what we don't eat."

She leaned across the table. "I like the way you think. Growing up in an Irish household, you either cleaned your plate or were tortured with stories about the potato famine."

He laughed and proceeded to order half the menu. When her eyes grew big, Brady said, "This is the way food people do it."

She held up her arms in surrender. "Works for me."

As it turned out, they took the bulk of it home, which was fine with him. He'd be so busy preparing for Jake and Cecilia's wedding that living off leftovers for a few days would save him from more cooking.

"I want to make you dinner Thursday night," Sloane said as he slowed down to take a curve. "I have the day off. But will the timing be bad?"

"Hard to say." He watched for deer crossing the road. With the dry weather there were even more of them coming down from the mountains, looking for water. It was not unusual for a mother and her babies to dart out onto the highway. "I've got a couple of people helping me with prep, but they aren't trained cooks. Let's see how it goes between now and then."

"If you can't, I won't take the day off. I'll save it for another time when I can make you dinner."

He put his hand on her leg. "You gonna dance with me at the wedding?"

"Are you as good a dancer as you are everything else?" In the faint light he could see her smiling.

"I'm not much of one, no. But for you I'll kick it up a notch."

Sloane wound up working Thursday since Brady was swamped. But Friday she took off. Darla had promised to do her hair for the rehearsal dinner. Apparently Maddy, Emily, and Donna had had the same idea.

"Hey, Sloane," the women chimed in unison as she entered the barbershop.

"Hi, everyone." She grabbed one of the plastic chairs and joined the party.

"Make sure this'll last through tomorrow night," Donna told Darla, who was setting her hair in fat curlers. "I'm not coming in twice."

"It'll be fine as long as you don't get it wet." Darla finished and pushed Donna under a drier and stuck a magazine in her face.

She signaled for Maddy to jump in her chair. Snapping a cape around her, Darla went to the back of the shop to mix her highlight color.

"You doing Cecilia's hair?" Donna called to her.

"Not for the rehearsal. She's wearing it loose. But I'm giving her an updo for the wedding. Now there's a woman with beautiful hair." Darla returned with a box of square foils and a bowl of color.

"You saying that we don't have beautiful hair?" With a quick glance around the room, Donna stuck her chin out at Darla, who was brushing on Maddy's highlights.

"Yours is better now that it's gotten my tender loving care. But no one has hair as healthy as Cecilia's. Hers is thick and luxurious and she doesn't even use product—just supermarket crap. She once told me that once a month she slathers it with mayonnaise. That's it. Even the streaks of gray look good on her."

"We don't have any gray," Emily said.

"You, Maddy, and Sloane don't," Darla corrected.

Donna gave her the finger. "What you need, besides respect for your elders, is a manicurist. I could be getting a mani-pedi while sitting here under the drier. Kill two birds with one stone. Then I wouldn't have to go to Graeagle."

Darla let out a sigh. "I've been thinking about it, but it'll take some convincing to get my dad on board. He already thinks I've turned this place into a"—she made finger quotes in the air—"hen parlor."

"When's Owen going to finally retire?" Donna asked.

"Who knows? It was supposed to happen more than a year ago." Darla put the last foil in Maddy's hair. "You're awfully quiet."

"Just making plans in my head," Maddy said. "We've got a full house with the wedding."

"How are you setting up for the rehearsal dinner tonight?" Donna asked.

"Just opening up all the common rooms where folks can mingle and eat. Brady is doing a lot of passed hors d'oeuvres and a buffet in the dining room. We're putting the bar where the reception desk is."

"Are Jake's kids staying at the inn?" Sloane asked.

"Yep. He's putting a few guests up at his cabin. But most everyone else traveling here is staying at the inn. A couple of Lucky's friends are bunking at his place. We even had to send a few to the Beary Quaint." Maddy made a face.

"Those Addisons weren't invited, were they?" Donna asked. "It would be worth it just to see what they'd wear. Formal attire with goddamn bears."

Sloane started to laugh and quickly shut her mouth. Not good for the law to participate in lady snark.

Sam came in the door and everyone greeted her. Darla had Donna and Maddy switch places under the drier and began taking out Donna's rollers in front of the mirror.

"You can still fit me in, right?" Sam asked.

"Of course." Darla did appear incredibly organized, moving from one client to the next. "Emily, do me a favor and take that sweater off. I don't want to get color on it."

Emily disappeared behind a screen made of picture frames that displayed various hair styles. Clever, Sloane thought.

"That the color you're sticking with for the wedding?" Donna asked Darla while she combed her hair out.

Today, Darla's hair was bright fuchsia. The hairstylist was known for her bold accessories and loud colors. In LA it would've been nothing. Here it was the talk of the town.

"Just plain old blond," she said.

Emily came back in a smock. "Sloane, anything new on the deceased man?"

"Not yet. But we're still sifting through missing persons reports. Harlee's story got picked up by the wire services, so hopefully that'll drum up some leads."

"I'd like to help," Emily said, and the room went quiet. "I could put a few hours in on the hotline or drive those fliers to neighboring towns. Whatever you need."

"Thank you, Emily." Sloane had heard that on account of her missing daughter, Emily volunteered for the National Center for Missing and Exploited Children. "At some point we'll definitely put you to work."

"I hear you've got Margaret Jones's girl working over at the police station," Donna said. Darla styled her hair into a poufy bob. Very flattering.

"Rose. You know her mother?"

"Oh sure. Poor woman. Four years ago her husband walked out on her and never came back. She's so busy trying to earn a living that those two kids of hers have to fend for themselves. I understand Skeeter's working at Union Pacific now. The extra income should help. So what did Rose do? Word is she got suspended from school and is paying penance at the police station."

"Fighting," Sloane said. "Some girls have been picking on her. Actually, Darla, I was thinking about bringing her in for a haircut and some of those skin products you sell. She could use a self-esteem boost."

"That's so nice of you." Darla scooted Donna out of her chair and crooked her finger at Emily. "After the wedding I've got lots of time."

"Hey, Darla, I want to run back to the inn and make sure Brady isn't slammed." Sam grabbed her purse. "Just text me when I'm up."

"I'll be right over," Maddy told her sister-in-law.

Darla sent Maddy back to the shampoo station while she put on Emily's color.

Donna left cash at the register. "I'll see you ladies tonight. And, Sloane, that is very sweet of you to take Rose under your wing. Poor girl could use a little help in the beauty department."

"Donna!" Emily shook her head.

"The girl is going through an awkward phase. Someone pretty like Sloane can help her with that."

After Donna left, Darla shampooed Maddy, then trimmed and blew out her hair. She finished with Emily and by the time she got to Sloane, most of the morning was gone. But it had been worth the wait. Sloane's hair looked fantastic. She didn't get this good a haircut even in Los Angeles.

Because she couldn't stop herself, she stuck her head inside the police station. "Anything going on?" she asked Connie.

Connie nudged her head to the back of the room, where Rose and some goth-looking boy wrote names on a dry-erase board.

Sloane made her way over to them. "Hi."

"Hi, Officer McBride." Rose went back to writing.

Sloane meaningfully looked at the boy and asked, "Who is this?"

"Sorry. This is Simpson. He's helping me with the John Doe. Chief Shepard said it was okay."

"I'll be right back," Sloane said, and went directly to Rhys's office. "You got a second?"

"I thought this was your day off." Rhys had his feet up on the desk and was eating a Bun Boy burger.

"It is. I came in just to say hello and met Simpson."

"Yeah. That kid is the bane of my existence. Has a thing about smashing people's mailboxes."

"Then why is he here?"

Rhys sat up. "Rose told him what she did and he wanted to help. I figure it's better than having him out, running around, vandalizing private property. Consider him part of the pilot program."

"Okay. I don't know if I have enough for them both to do."

"We'll come up with stuff. Hell, they can wash the police rigs."

"All right." She hitched her shoulders. The more the merrier, she supposed. "I better see what they're up to."

"Sloane, have your day off, for God's sake. It's bad enough you worked yesterday. And by the way, nice hair."

She went and checked on the kids anyway. They spent their time methodically sifting through each missing person's summary. The ones that fit their John Doe's description, Rose wrote on the board.

"You guys are doing great," she said.

"You think someone murdered him and then chopped off his arms?" Simpson asked.

"Probably not." But she couldn't say for sure. "We'll be able to figure out more once we know who he is."

"What if we never find out?" he asked.

"There's a chance we won't. That's where you two come in. This is an important job you're doing, so don't screw it up. I'm going now."

"Bye, Officer McBride," Rose said. "See you Monday."

"Pilot program," she muttered to herself as she crossed the square. But she had to admit that she kind of liked the idea of working with at-risk kids, especially in a town like this, where there weren't a lot of options for them.

She found Brady in the inn's kitchen, peeling and deveining more shrimp than Sloane had ever seen. Lina and a couple of people she didn't know stood over the sink and counter, trying to keep up with Brady. Still, he did six shrimp to everyone else's one.

"Pick up the pace, people. We've got other stuff to do." Surprisingly, he came around the counter and laid his lips on her. "Don't want to touch you . . . shrimp hands."

"You need help?"

"Nah. That's what I pay these lug-heads for. Your hair looks nice."

"Thanks. Darla's crazy busy."

"Yeah, Sam just went over and Maddy just came back. It pays to be a guy."

At the moment he had a folded bandana tied around his forehead, keeping his hair out of his face. The sleeves of his chef's jacket were scrunched up to his elbows. Sloane thought it was a good look. Between the headband and the tattoos he looked a wee bit disreputable.

"I guess I'll see you tonight then," she said.

"I'm not even planning to go home first." He glanced around the kitchen, which looked like a bomb had gone off. A pile of vegetables, which Sloane assumed was for a crudité platter, sat in a tray of ice. Serving dishes lined one of the counters and sheets of mini toasts had been stacked on vertical cooling racks.

"Good luck," she said, flashing him a commiserating smile.

"See you later." He went back to peeling shrimp.

On her way out she bumped into Andy.

"You coming tonight?" he asked her.

"I am."

"I'm working it," he said, and bobbed his chin at her. "But maybe you and I can have a drink."

The kid was barely legal, but she didn't want to hurt his feelings. "We'll see, Andy."

"I tried to get Jake to hire my band, but he's doing a playlist from an iPod. Cheesy."

"You ever hear Tater's band? What were they like?"

"Gold Country was before my time. But Tater's a legend. He used to sit in with freakin' Willie Nelson."

"Wow."

"Yeah. I'll probably have him jam with my band one of these days."

From everything she'd heard about Andy's band, Sloane doubted Tater would be interested. "I'll see you tonight, Andy."

She had her hand on the door when he said, "Some guy called here the other day, wanting to know how to get in touch with you. He said he'd heard you were staying here, which I thought was weird 'cause you'd only stayed that one time."

Sloane slowly turned around. "Did you get a name?"

"I can't remember whether I even asked."

"What did you tell him about me?" Sloane had a bad feeling.

"That he should call the police station. You didn't want me to tell him where you lived or anything, right? I mean it's not like he couldn't figure it out in this town but—"

"You did good, Andy. Don't ever tell anyone where I live."

Chapter 16

"That was one hell of a wedding." Griffin rested his elbows inside Tawny's truck window while he filled her tank.

"I'm still recovering," she said. "The last guests left Sunday after the big breakfast, and we drove Jake and Cecilia to Reno to catch their plane."

"Hawaii, huh?" Since coming into his money Griff had gone to the Big Island and spent some time on Maui. Beautiful place.

"Cecilia had never been and was dying to go."

"They'll have a great time. Ordinarily, it would've gotten them out of the snow." Griffin gazed out over the horizon at the mountains. Usually, the peaks looked like vanilla ice-cream cones. Now, not so much.

"It'll still be warmer." Tawny tugged her coat tighter and Griffin felt guilty for talking her ear off with the window open.

The gas nozzle clicked. He hung up the hose and screwed on her gas cap. "You're all set." He tapped on her roof and waved goodbye.

It really had been one hell of a wedding. The booze flowed like the Feather River, the food was about as gourmet as it got without being too fussy, and watching Lina work in a tight black skirt and fitted white blouse . . . well, that had been a nice extra.

All the servers had worn black and white, but none had worn it as well as Lina. For her part she'd pretty much ignored him. To be fair, she'd had a job to do and didn't have time to hang around, flirting with him all night. It was mystifying how much she'd changed. How responsible she'd gotten and how immune to him she'd become. It was like he was nothing but an old flame.

He got out of the cold and holed up in his office for a while doing paperwork. When he came back down about an hour later to grab a hot dog from the convenience store, a guy with a Lexus SUV asked him about getting an oil change.

"You want it done now or can you pick it up tomorrow?" Griffin asked.

"I put it on craigslist a few hours ago and have a couple of people coming to look at it first thing in the morning. Any way you can do it now?"

"Let me check." Griff gave the Lexus a once-over. It was a 2013. Sweet ride. He talked to Rico and motioned for the guy to pull it into the last bay on the right.

"I'll handle it, boss."

"Nah, I've got this one," Griffin told Rico. He wanted to get his head under the hood.

The owner climbed out of the driver's seat. Griffin got in and pulled it onto the ramps while Rico took over a brake job in the bay next to him. "You the original owner?"

"Yeah. I just bought the NX hybrid, figured I'd save on gas. My wife has an Outback. So what do I need with this?"

"Out of curiosity, how much you asking for it?" Griff checked the odometer. The guy must just drive it to church and back.

He rattled off a number that seemed more than fair to Griffin.

"It drives well?" Griffin flipped on the hydraulic lift, put on a pair of gloves, and slipped a drip pan underneath the vehicle.

"Drives great, especially in the snow. Be nice to get some, huh?"

"This drought is killing California." With a socket wrench Griff loosened the drain plug, then unscrewed it with his hand, letting the oil spill out.

"Man, don't I know it. This drought is killing my business. A couple of guys and I own a ski resort in Glory Junction. The place is deader than the off-season."

"Why'd you come all the way to Nugget for an oil change?" Hell, it was a thirty-minute drive.

"The truth. I don't trust my cars with the mechanic over there. I usually go to Tahoe, but someone told me you guys were fantastic—and cheaper."

"Nice to hear. I'm the owner, so I really appreciate that. We also build custom motorcycles." It sounded like the dude and his friends had money if they owned a ski resort. Good to get the word out.

"Yeah? What kind of stuff?"

"Something along the lines of a Ducati. But we can build any- thing." He mopped the underside of the Lexus with a rag and replaced the drain plug.

"Hmm. I don't ride, but I know a couple of guys who have BMWs and may be looking to trade up. I'll let 'em know."

"I appreciate that." Griffin moved the pan and started replacing the oil filter.

"Hey, it's not easy making a living up here. I used to work in ven- ture capital in Silicon Valley. Jeez, the money that poured through there. Kind of made you sick."

Griffin hadn't exactly earned his from hard labor either. Being half Wigluk Indian he was entitled to a huge draw of the tribe's profits, in- cluding money from one of the largest gaming casinos in the country.

He sealed everything up and lowered the vehicle, wiping his hands on a towel. While he added the oil, he checked the engine, transmission, and the brake lines. Everything looked clean as a whistle. Even the tires looked brand-new.

"You take care of this baby, don't you?"

"I take care of all my vehicles. They'll run forever that way. But what the hell am I telling you that for?"

Griff cracked a grin. "It should drive cleaner now."

"I doubt the average Joe will feel the difference, but it's like leav- ing the new owner a clean house. Pride of ownership and all that."

"You mind if I take it for a quick spin?"

"Not at all. If you hear or feel something that's off, let me know. I'm sure whoever is interested in buying it will get it checked out by a mechanic first."

"More than likely." Griffin got inside and backed the SUV out of the bay.

For the next fifteen minutes he drove it around Nugget, even took it out on the highway, testing the heater, AC, stereo, GPS, windows, and wipers. The first thing to go in these babies was usually the elec- trical system. But everything worked like a dream. And the ride was smooth—good suspension. Griffin suspected that by the time he re- turned to the Gas and Go, the Lexus's owner feared that he'd run off with the truck.

Parking it beside the convenience store, Griffin jumped out. "You want cash or a check?"

The man jerked in surprise. "You want to buy it?"

"Minus the price of the oil change, I do. If you want cash, we'll have to go to the bank."

"Cash would be good."

"You drive." Griffin tossed him the fob.

Two hours later, Griff returned in his new Lexus to the Gas and Go. After making the money exchange, signing the pink slip, and registering the paperwork with the DMV, Griffin had taken the former owner home and stopped off to grab a sandwich. He'd never gotten that hot dog.

Now he desperately needed coffee. Inside the convenience store he filled a cup and leaned against the counter while Rico rung up a woman for a smog check.

After she left, he cocked his head at the window and said, "What do you think of my new Lexus?"

"What do you need this car for, boss? You already have a Range Rover, a Ducati, and too many other motorcycles to count."

"It was a good deal."

Rico rolled his eyes. "It was exactly what the Kelley Blue Book said it was worth."

"You don't find vehicles in mint condition every day."

"You're full of crap, man. I know exactly what you're planning to do with it. Let Lina get her own car."

Griff followed his mechanic into the garage. "What's your problem with Lina?"

"I have no problem with her. Love her like a sister. But you're hot and cold when it comes to the girl. *She's too young*," Rico mimicked. "*I love her so much.* Make up your mind. But if you think she's too young, don't go leading her on by giving her a luxury car. It's douchey."

"She's got a birthday coming up." Griffin shrugged. "Besides, you weren't there when I had to tell her the Scout was dead. She cried."

"Dude, you're pathetic, and Lina's not a charity case."

Griffin pinched the bridge of his nose and walked away. "Do me a favor, Rico? Mind your own business."

Darla gave Rose the works. An adorable layered cut that flattered her face and made her look lighter. She even added highlights.

"Not too many," Sloane said.

The girl was only fifteen and should stay as natural as possible. At least that was Sloane's philosophy. Working in LA, she'd seen girls as young as sixteen getting boob jobs, nose jobs, even liposuction. Television, magazines, and advertisements had given girls such an unrealistic view of beauty that it made Sloane sick.

Working out, eating right—not that she wasn't prone to stuffing her face with junk food now and again—and making the best of what you were born with was the ticket to true beauty.

And for all of Darla's tacky plastic jewelry and outlandish hair colors, she knew how to play up a person's natural features. To accentuate Rose's beautiful brown eyes, Darla shaped her brows, giving them a wonderful arch. Afterward, Rose got a facial and a bag of cleansing products and instructions on how to use them.

"The key," Darla said, "is keeping your pores open and clean. Nothing is more attractive than healthy skin."

Harlee watched the whole process, regaling Rose with stories about her youth. How she'd had frizzy hair, a unibrow, and a mustache. No one looking at Harlee now would believe it, which had gone a long way toward perking up Rose's confidence.

Sloane could tell that the new hairstyle and Darla and Harlee's easy way with Rose had helped her come out of her shell. In just the short time she'd worked at the police department, Sloane had seen a difference in the teen. She was more self-assured. In less than a week, she'd be going back to school, and Sloane hoped that Taylor and her posse would leave Rose alone. It would also help if Rose's mother took a little more interest in her daughter.

Early that morning, Sloane had picked Rose up at her house with the express purpose of meeting Mrs. Jones and getting her permission for the makeover. In a raspy smoker's voice, Mrs. Jones had said, "As long as it doesn't cost me anything," and promptly got in her car and drove away. Well, the makeover hadn't cost anyone a cent because Darla did it pro bono. Sloane had insisted on at least paying for the products.

Harlee, who couldn't seem to resist a project, threw a couple of extras in the bag. "You look awesome, Rose."

Rose stared at her reflection in the mirror and Sloane could tell that she liked what she saw. They went back to the police station, where Connie, Jake, and Rhys made a big fuss.

"You at least look like a girl now," Simpson said, and Sloane wanted to beat him over the head with a billy club.

She'd give the kid credit, though. He'd thrown himself into the John Doe project like a mathematician with a problem to solve. Today he'd ridden over on his bike right after school and begun where he'd left off on Sunday. She'd come back from a call to find him hunkered over a list of missing persons reports, adding new names to the dry-erase board.

Rose didn't seem to mind the rude jibe. The two kids appeared to have a nice camaraderie. Sloane didn't think they were boyfriend and girlfriend, just two people who had the sad commonality of being teenage outcasts.

A horn honked outside and Rose gathered up her things, including Darla's goodie bag. "That's Skeeter. I've gotta go." She ran out the door, calling, "See you tomorrow."

"Don't you have homework to do, Simpson?" Sloane asked.

Simpson hitched his shoulders. "When do we start calling these people's families?" He nudged his head at the board, where there were at least fifteen missing persons listed.

"I'll start first thing tomorrow morning." All she wanted to do now was go home and take a nap.

The weekend, between the wedding and working, had worn her out. Not to mention that she'd spent much of it on high alert. Ever since Andy had told her that someone had called the Lumber Baron looking for her, she'd been a nervous wreck. She'd wanted to tell Brady, but he'd been so busy with catering Jake and Cecilia's three-day event, including a breakfast on Sunday, that she hadn't felt right about it. She should've told Rhys. But he would've demanded that they go to LAPD, and that was the last thing she needed.

For all she knew it was a friend from LA or even someone from Chicago. Still, her cop sense told her the call was suspect and that she needed to watch her back.

"I'll be at school in the morning," Simpson said, sounding disappointed.

"We'll have a briefing as soon as you come in. In the meantime, you should really go home, Simpson, and start your homework."

"Okay." He grabbed his jacket and bike helmet. "Rudy Mendoza, this kid who goes to school with Rose and me, wants to help too. Can he?"

"Um, sure." But they were getting down to the last of their missing persons.

She thought about Rhys's idea that they wash police rigs. Kids were pretty smart. They'd know that was just grunt work. The John Doe case made them feel like they were doing something important. She'd have to come up with some other tasks they could work on that would seem significant, like a real contribution.

After Simpson left, Sloane decided to cut out too. At home she found Brady on the porch, leaning back in his rocker, reading a book. It was a Jack Reacher novel. She loved those.

"You recovering?" She climbed the stairs.

"Yeah. Long weekend, huh?"

"I didn't get to thank you for the roses. They're beautiful. I have a present for you too."

"Not much of a Valentine's Day."

"I wouldn't say that. The food was amazing. Those shrimp skewers . . . I ate at least ten. And those pastry cup things and the plum tomatoes filled with ceviche . . . oh my God. It makes me want to have a party just so I can hire you as the caterer."

He laughed. "I think it went pretty well. The inn emptied out right after breakfast this morning and we don't have any bookings until tomorrow. So I'm off until tomorrow afternoon—get to sleep in."

"Lucky you."

"Want to go for a run?"

Sloane considered it. "Nah, I just want to relax, have a glass of wine, and do some laundry. But don't let me stop you."

"I'll probably go in a few minutes. We could have dinner after. I could cobble together a meal from the wedding and breakfast leftovers."

"I'm all in favor of that. I'll change, put in a wash, and set the table while you take your run. You don't mind if we do it in my place, do you?"

"Nope. I love ruffles and lace."

She poked him in the arm, went inside and quickly put on jeans. Throwing together a load of laundry, Sloane hauled it to the washer and turned it on. She was just about to set the table when her cell rang. It was her oldest brother, Aidan.

"Hey, everything okay?" Usually she and Aidan just emailed.

"Everything's fine. I'm just checking on you, little sister."

"Nothing to report," she lied.

"How's Nugget?" For some reason every time Aidan said the name of Sloane's new home he laughed.

"What are you laughing at, goofball? It's good here." Then even she started laughing. "Of all the McBrides, you would like it here the most." Aidan was the outdoorsman of the family. He liked nothing more than to hike up a mountain and sleep under the stars.

"If the pictures you sent are legit, I probably would. You still on bear patrol?"

"I'm still trying to hunt down the identity of the remains we found. And in my free time, I'm running a pilot program for at-risk teens." She rolled her eyes. Rhys came up with some doozies.

"That sounds right up your alley."

"Being a social worker instead of a cop? Thanks."

"Ah, Sloane, we're all social workers to some extent; otherwise we wouldn't have gone into public service. I just meant that you like helping people. Isn't that why you became a cop in the first place?"

Yeah. To solve crimes. Major crimes. "What's going on there?"

"Not much. Just finished Kids' Weekend." It was a huge event for the firehouses in Chicago. CFD opened its doors to the community, giving kids tours, letting them climb on the firetrucks, and helping parents put together ID kits for their children, to aid law enforcement if, God forbid, the kid ever went missing. Sloane's dad had always been the chief organizer.

"How did that go?"

"Exhausting, but nice, though it gets our folks riled up about not having any grandchildren."

"You and Sue better start cranking them out then."

"Yeah . . . about that." Long pause. "She got sick of waiting for a marriage proposal and is seeing someone else."

"She moved out?" Sloane was taken aback. When had this happened?

"It's been a few weeks . . . I should've told you."

"Ah, Aid, I'm so sorry." Now Sloane knew the real reason for the call. "You guys have been together forever . . . maybe she'll come back."

"Nah. I screwed up. She's done with me, Sloane."

Sue had wanted to get married and Aidan had kept putting it off. First he'd decided that they should wait until he got elevated to the arson detail. Then he'd decided they should wait until after Sue got her teaching credential. There had always been an excuse.

"Hey, Aid, you think maybe she wasn't the right one for you?"

"She was the one for me." His voice got quiet. "But I guess I wasn't the one for her."

"Why don't you take a few days off and come here? You could fly into Reno. I have a couple of days coming to me and we could go fishing, camping, or just hang out. Whatever you want to do."

"I'll think about it," he said. "I've got a call coming in. But it was good talking to you, little sister."

She hung up, feeling sad. Sue had been such a big part of their family. She and Aidan had been going together for three years. A year ago, she'd decided to change careers from technical writer to middle school teacher and moved in with Aidan so they could save money while she got her credential. Sloane suspected what Sue had really wanted was to start making a home and family with Aidan. But her brother had put it off and put it off until Sue probably felt like she was running out of time.

Apparently, her smart, ambitious big brother could sniff out a firebug a mile away but was clueless when it came to women and their biological clocks. Sloane considered calling her parents or Arron or Shane to get the full scoop, but someone was knocking on her door. Lately, she'd been real careful about keeping it dead-bolted. It seemed too soon for Brady if he'd gone on that run.

She looked out the peephole, grinned, and unlocked the door. "You didn't go?"

"I'm feeling lazy."

"You deserve a day off. You worked so hard this weekend."

Brady came in carrying two bags. "I need to heat some of this stuff up. You hungry?"

"Uh, yeah, I guess."

"What's wrong?"

"I just got off the phone with my brother Aidan. He and his long-term girlfriend broke up."

"I gather you liked her," Brady said.

"A lot. She was part of the family. Aid said she got tired of waiting for him to marry her and is dating someone else. He sounded depressed."

"Why didn't he marry her then?"

"Good question." She helped unload the sacks of food. "You brought the prime rib. God, that was delicious."

"Homemade horseradish, too." He held up a small jar. "Maybe he's just not into marriage. It's not for everyone, you know?"

"Well, then he probably should've told her that right off the bat, instead of making her think that a proposal was just around the corner."

"I agree. Everyone needs to be on the same page. It saves a lot of heartache in the end."

She wanted to know what page they were on, but felt self-conscious asking. As it turned out, she didn't have to.

"That's what I like about us," he said, and preheated the oven. "You understand that given my situation I'm in no way able to commit to anything. Hell, at any minute I may have to pull up stakes and go somewhere else."

"You're giving Sandra too much power."

"No, I'm keeping the people I care about safe."

But Sloane was starting to wonder if Sandra was just an excuse and whether Brady suffered from the same malady as her brother. Commitmentitis.

Chapter 17

"Let's talk about the menu you want for your birthday party, kiddo."

"'Beware, the chef is hot.'" Lina read the inscription on Brady's apron and cocked a brow. "Well, don't we think highly of ourselves?"

Brady laughed. "Sloane gave it to me yesterday." His Valentine's Day gift.

"Did she now?"

His and Sloane's relationship was starting to get complicated. He'd never given a woman flowers for Valentine's Day. It had always screamed obligation and a bunch of other pledges Brady had never been comfortable making. The fact was, he liked flying solo. Still did. The only reason he'd given the dozen roses to Sloane . . . Ah jeez, he didn't know why he'd done it. Just seemed like the right thing to do.

"Are you guys a couple now?"

"Menu, Lina. Focus."

She smirked at him knowingly and got back to the party. "I want it to be fun. Nothing over-the-top."

"You'll have to be more specific." Brady poured them both cups of coffee. He'd slept in and it was his first cup of the day.

"I loved what you did for Jake and Cecilia, but that's way too fancy for what I have in mind. If it wasn't February I'd want it to be a cookout—hamburgers, hot dogs, that sort of thing. Plus, I don't want this party costing my brother and sister-in-law an arm and a leg."

"Okay." That gave him something to work with. "What do you think of pigs in a blanket, mini fried-chicken sandwiches, sliders, and a variety of salads? We'd be playing on that cookout theme, only keeping everything indoors. For dessert we could go old-school—ice cream cake."

"You're a genius!" she said, and threw her arms around him. Lina backed up and read his apron again, and in a breathy voice said, "And a hot chef to boot."

"Yes, I am. So you better not touch or you'll get burned."

"Griffin might come to the party." She hopped up on a stool, sipped the coffee Brady had poured, and tried to act casual. Brady knew better.

"Oh yeah? How did that come about?"

"My truck broke down near Chilcoot. I called for a tow and he came to the rescue. He told me that the real estate agent isn't in the picture, kissed me, and afterward did what he always does. *Sorry. That shouldn't have happened.* I told him no big deal, mentioned the party, and told him to drop by if he was in the area."

She poured more cream into her coffee. "That's the shorthand version anyway. But more or less I did what you told me. I played hard-to-get."

"Wait a minute," he said. "I did not tell you to play hard-to-get. I told you to finish school and then worry about men."

"You also told me that men don't like needy women. So I'm being cool as a cucumber."

Brady looked at her and shook his head. "No, you're playing games. Men don't like that either."

"Frankly, Brady, I'm tired of the push me, pull me. Griff is full of mixed messages. He tells me I'm too young for him, then the next thing I know he's kissing me. I'm so over it."

"Then why did you invite him to your birthday party?" He bobbed his chin at her in challenge.

"Because he's a friend. No matter what, he'll always be a friend."

"Fair enough. Who else is coming to this shindig?"

"A bunch of my friends from school. Obviously Rhys, Maddy, Emma, and my little brother, Nate and Sam, the McCreedys, Donna and her husband, the entire police department, probably the mayor. You know how it works in this town."

Brady cracked a smile. "Yep. We're gonna have a full house." He'd have to make room in the deep freeze for the cake and the pigs in a blanket, which he could prepare in advance.

"I better get back to the desk," she said. "Nate's here and you know what a taskmaster he is."

"I am not." Nate breezed into the kitchen, opened the refrigerator, and popped his head in.

"What are you looking for?" Brady asked.

"Nothing. I just do it out of habit. That's why I've gotta lose five pounds."

"Brady just came up with the most excellent menu for my birthday party."

"Yeah?" Nate sat next to Lina at the island and she told him what they'd planned. "Andy is under the impression that his band is playing. I hope you disabuse him of that notion as quickly as possible."

Lina snorted and got to her feet. "I don't know where he got that idea. Not from me, that's for sure. But I'll go break the news to him right now." She rushed out of the kitchen.

"You want something to eat?" Brady asked Nate.

"I'm good. How's the menu for the restaurant at Gold Mountain coming along?"

"Fine. I cruised by the other day on the way to Glory Junction. Looks like you're making headway."

"I'd like to have it open in time for Memorial Day weekend."

Brady jerked his head in surprise. "That soon, huh?"

"Things have been going so well with the rehab that we're thinking we could actually make it happen in time for the holiday. If you think it's too ambitious for the restaurant, we could always roll that out later."

"No, we should do it all at the same time. Makes a statement that way. After Lina's party, I'll cut back on the catering and go at it full throttle."

Nate stared at him for a second. "If you think I don't know how overqualified for the Lumber Baron you are, you're kidding yourself. What happened at your last job, Brady? What are you running from?"

Brady really didn't want to have this conversation. But from the time he'd taken the job he'd known it was inevitable. "Nothing happened as far as Pig and Tangelo. I was a rock star there and that's the truth, Nate. I had some personal problems with a woman and felt it was best to leave."

Nate watched him closely, clearly not buying it. "And come to a Podunk town like Nugget, where you could flip pancakes at a bed and breakfast?" He shook his head. "I'd like you to play a bigger role in Breyer Hotels, Brady. I really would. But not until you're straight with me."

With that, Nate moseyed out of the kitchen, leaving Brady to wonder what a bigger role meant. And how welcome would he be after Nate learned that a deranged woman wanted to hunt Brady down and do God-knew-what with him.

Sloane thought she was being watched. Maybe she was just creeping herself out, but twice she'd heard footsteps on the porch and twice she'd looked outside her living room window to find no one there. Still, she had the bizarre sense, a gut instinct so to speak, that there were eyes on her. Like she was the focus of one of those Hollywood point-of-view shots that lets the viewer know something scary is about to happen.

She'd first felt it as she carried groceries in from her truck. The hairs on the back of her neck stood at attention, signaling that she wasn't alone. In the police academy, recruits were taught to be hyperaware of their surroundings, and suddenly her body had gone taut, on alert. Shielding her eyes from the sun, she'd searched the trees, only to spy a pair of squirrels chasing each other from branch to branch. She'd sniffed the air and for a second thought she detected cigarette smoke. And then, just like that, it was gone. Lord, how the mind played tricks.

Just the same, she checked the lock again, absently touched the handle of the Glock at her waist, and went back to the kitchen. Tonight she planned to finally deliver on that dinner she owed Brady. She'd gotten a recipe from her mother's beloved *Silver Palate Cookbook* for a French chicken dish made with olives, prunes, capers, and herbs. Just exotic enough to surprise the pants off Brady.

Getting Brady's pants off hadn't been all that difficult. But this evening she'd like to do it with a home-cooked meal. One she'd made, instead of him. While the chicken baked in the oven she prepared the vegetables for roasting, drizzling them with olive oil and sprinkling them with salt. She read the directions for the couscous a second time and filled a pot with water. That's when she heard the noise, a kind of *thump thump*, coming from the back of the duplex. Sloane peered out the window.

"This is ridiculous," she muttered to herself, and unlocked the back door with the key she kept in the drawer. Stepping out onto the deck, she called, "Anyone out there?"

Her answer came in a loud shriek from a crow. Three deer dashed down the ravine and leapt across the railroad tracks. For crying out loud, she chided herself. What was wrong with her? Sloane went back in the house and relocked the door.

With her prep work done, she began setting the table, thinking how she'd spend tomorrow. Two days off in a row. For an officer in a small, country police department, Sloane worked a lot of hours. Especially with the John Doe case hanging over her head. Now she had three kids to look after in her so-called pilot program. Rudy Mendoza had turned out to be a shy boy with a pronounced limp. He'd been born with one leg significantly shorter than the other. His parents had tried to compensate by putting a lift in one of his shoes, but he really needed custom-made orthotics, which were pricey.

Sloane planned to talk to Tawny, who'd designed plenty of boots for customers with special needs. They'd of course have to get guidance from a doctor, and Sloane didn't know whether the Mendozas had insurance—Rudy's father supported the family by getting seasonal work on local cattle ranches and farms.

Unlike her other kids, Rudy spoke fluent Spanish, which would come in handy for the new project she had in mind. Sloane wanted to organize a children's-ID-kit fair in which they'd help parents assemble fingerprints, updated photos, and medical information about their kids in case of an emergency. She'd gotten the idea when Aidan had mentioned CFD's Kids' Weekend. A big part of Nugget's population was Hispanic, and Rudy could act as an interpreter. She also wanted to bring Emily on board. Sloane thought it would fit in nicely with the volunteer work Emily did for the National Center for Missing and Exploited Children.

At the sink, she washed dishes, trying to get the kitchen presentable. That's when she heard a noise again. This time it was closer and sharper, like someone banging. Sloane immediately shut off the faucet to listen and realized someone was at her back door. No one ever used that door. Not even Brady, whose apartment shared the same deck. Whoever visited always came to the front.

She moved away from the windows, flattened her back against the wall, and withdrew her Glock. "Who's there?" Sloane called.

No answer. Just the sound of footsteps coming around the side of the house. Whoever it was continued to the front. Sloane confirmed that theory when she heard boots on the porch steps, then a tapping on her door. Possibly a ruse. Home-invasion robbers worked in teams. One person knocked on the front door while the others pushed their way in through the back. No home-invasion robberies in Nugget, but she hadn't ruled out Roger Buck and his merry band of assholes. Or maybe she was just being paranoid.

Pressing against the wall, she carefully peeked out the window over the sink. No one out there, unless they were hiding behind the trees. The knock came again and Sloane crept her way to the living room, avoiding windows. She plastered herself against the door, stuck her head out just enough to peer through the peephole, sighed, and un-latched the lock.

Opening the door a crack, she said, "How'd you find my house?"

"I asked around."

"You shouldn't have come here."

"Why? You come to my house . . . walk right in like you own the place."

"What do you have behind your back, Skeeter?"

He pulled out a bouquet of grocery-store flowers. She tucked the gun in the back of her waistband and walked out onto the porch.

"What's that for?" she asked, nudging her head at the flowers.

"A thank-you . . . for what you did for my sister. The haircut and letting her help you with the dead guy. She seems . . . I don't know, less depressed."

She let out a breath and looked for Skeeter's car. "How did you get here?"

"I walked over from the railroad yard."

"Did you come to my back door first?"

"Yeah." He looked at her like she was a kook. "I wasn't sure if anyone was home, so I planned on leaving the flowers on the front porch where I thought you'd see 'em better. What's the big deal?"

"Did you ask Andy where I live?"

"Andy who?"

"The reservationist at the Lumber Baron."

"I might've. Rosie didn't know, so I put some feelers out. What the hell you so spooked about?"

"Cops don't like house calls," she said, and immediately felt bad. He was just trying to show his appreciation. "Before coming here I worked in Los Angeles. It was different there . . . lots of scary people. The flowers are very thoughtful. I'm glad that working at the police department has been a positive experience for Rose. She's a smart girl."

"Yeah, she is." He shoved the bouquet at her. "If she could get a scholarship, she could go to college, do something better with her life than working on the railroad."

"I think that's a possibility," Sloane agreed. "But she'll have to behave at school."

"Nothing wrong with her protecting herself from those little bitches."

"She can't take matters into her own hands, Skeeter. Her best course of action is going to an adult."

He snorted. "Yeah, right. That did her a lot of good. Will she be able to work at the police department when her suspension is up?"

"Yep. As long as she keeps on top of her homework. We can sure use her assistance."

"That'll help her with a scholarship, right?"

Sloane hadn't thought of it. "I suppose it might. It certainly can't hurt." Maybe when the time came, Rhys would write her a letter of recommendation. "In the meantime, she has to keep her grades and attendance up. I know you and your mom have a lot on your plates, but she needs encouragement at home."

"I try to do that."

Sloane's mouth slid up. Perhaps she'd misjudged the guy. He really did seem to have Rose's best interests at heart. "Good."

"I've gotta get back to the yard." He turned to go, but stopped. "You're not like other cops, are you?"

"What do you mean?"

"You actually give a shit." He jogged down the steps and Sloane watched him go down the ravine behind the duplex and follow the train tracks back to town.

She started to go inside but Brady pulled up in his van. Uh-oh, her chicken. Sloane ran to the kitchen and opened the oven. Some of the juices had dripped to the bottom and had begun smoking. She pulled the pan out, wiped out the mess as best she could, and cranked up the heat to roast the vegetables.

"Smells good in here." Brady came in still wearing his chef's pants and jacket.

"You have to go," she said.

"Why?"

"Because timing all the food is crucial and I can't concentrate with you here. Go change, get comfortable, and come back at"—she looked at the clock—"six-oh-five."

He chuckled. "You sure you don't want my help?"

"No. But I want it to be perfect and got distracted. So go." She shooed him out, slid the baking sheet with the vegetables into the oven, put her pot for the couscous on to boil, and opened a bottle of wine to breathe.

With a slotted spoon, she arranged the chicken on a platter, found another serving dish for the vegetables and a bowl for the couscous. By the time Brady came back, everything was on the table, including a baguette she'd gotten at the Nugget Market. So it wasn't home-made. Baking bread was above her pay grade.

"Sit." She swooshed her arm over the table.

"It looks amazing, Sloane." He spied Skeeter's bouquet on the counter. "You want me to put those in water?"

"The food will get cold. I'll do it while you start eating."

"Relax, sweetness." He kissed her neck. "It's gonna be perfect."

She found a vase, filled it, and stuck in the flowers. "Don't judge. This is my first real meal."

He sat, placed the cloth napkin in his lap, and poured them each a glass of wine. Shoot, she should've done that.

"Chicken Marbella, huh?" he said with appreciation.

"You know it?"

"*Silver Palate Cookbook*. It's a classic." He looked up from serving himself and must've seen her face drop. "Come on, it's one of my favorites. You want a breast?"

"Sure." He put chicken, a scoop of couscous, and a helping of vegetables on her plate and lifted his fork to take a bite of his own.

She watched him swallow and take a few more bites. "Well?"

"You nailed it. Seriously, Sloane, it's fantastic."

She leaned back in her chair and let out a breath. "Thank God."

He looked highly amused. "It stressed you out that much?"

"Easy for you to be nonchalant, Chef Boyardee." She leaned over the table. "How's the couscous?"

"Nice," he said with his mouth full. "Not mushy, bright flavor, and the pine nuts were a smart touch—gives a little crunch."

"My mom told me to add them."

"You did good, baby." He was dishing out a lot of endearments that he usually only used during sex. God, she liked him. Maybe more than liked him. "You do anything else on your day off besides cooking up a feast?"

"Skeeter Jones came over." She nudged her head at the vase. "Brought me the flowers."

"This is Rose's delinquent brother you told me about?" Brady continued to eat with gusto, which did Sloane's heart good.

"Yeah. Except now I'm starting to think he might be a good guy. Just rough around the edges. He wanted to thank me for helping his sister."

The corner of his lips tugged up, his mouth full. "I bet he did."

"It's not like that," she said, nibbling on chicken, which she had to admit turned out good. "But it did freak me out that he'd called the Lumber Baron looking for me. When Andy told me about it, I assumed it was Roger Buck."

Brady stopped eating. "When did this happen?"

"A few days ago."

"Why didn't you tell me?" He sounded angry.

"You were busy with the rehearsal dinner . . . the wedding."

"Walk me through it."

"Not much to walk you through. Someone called the inn, said they'd heard I'd been staying there and wanted to get in touch with me. They didn't give Andy a name and he told the person he could reach me at the police department."

"And Skeeter said it was him?"

She shrugged. "Skeeter said it may have been. That he'd been asking around to find out where I live. But he didn't remember specifically asking Andy."

"I don't like this." Brady pulled his cell out of his pocket.

"What are you doing?"

"Calling Andy."

She pushed her plate out of the way, reached across the table, and put her hand on his arm. "You think you have better interrogation skills than I do? I was a homicide detective, for goodness' sake. That's all Andy knows. It had to have been Skeeter."

"Andy said it was a man's voice?"

"Absolutely." She knew exactly where his mind had headed. "Look, there isn't a boogeyman hiding around every corner. Sandra has been quiet for a while, and I haven't gotten any more threatening texts. Maybe it's over."

He shook his head. "I'm not letting my guard down on either front. You tell Rhys?"

"There's nothing to tell him."

"Bullshit. He could trace the call." He filled his mouth with couscous.

She rolled her eyes. "If it's Buck or anyone else from LAPD, the call's untraceable. More than likely they used a burner or a random pay phone."

He got to his feet, picked her up, carried her to the living room, and put her down on the couch. "You matter to me, Sloane." He pinched the bridge of his nose like he wanted to say more but couldn't get the words out.

"You matter to me too, Brady." Sloane knew if she said any more she'd scare him off. He was an easy read, flighty when it came to relationships, especially given his situation.

With a little time, though, she hoped to change all that.

Chapter 18

"Hey, Lina, I think I may have found a car for you . . . it's actually an SUV. When you get a chance, give me a call or just stop by the Gas and Go." Griffin finished leaving his message and took the stairs down from his office to the convenience store.

Owen and a couple of other mafia guys sat in the garage around the space heater. He'd bought a few truck bench seats off eBay and turned it into a seating area for customers. But most days the old dudes camped out there to play pinochle and drink Griff's coffee.

"Where've you been?" Owen asked him, as if it was Griff's sole responsibility to provide entertainment.

"Work. That's why they call it a job."

"Bah!" Owen called. "Dink says that little jail-bait girlfriend of yours is having a birthday party."

"She's not my girlfriend and I already know about her party. What of it?"

"You going?"

"I've got a conflict," he lied, and tried to walk away.

"We took a vote and we think you should go."

"I didn't realize my social calendar was under democratic rule."

"We're all going," Owen said.

"So? What does that have to do with me?"

"Brady is doing the food," Dink, Nugget's illustrious mayor, said. "You don't want to miss that."

"I can't . . . get out of the other thing. Why don't one of you guys bring home a doggie bag for me?" He went into the store, where Rico had been listening to the conversation through the pay window.

"Why do you lie to them, boss?"

"It's easier." Griffin grabbed a hot dog off the steamer machine and loaded it up with onions, relish, and mustard.

"Better question: What's the big deal about going? It's not like you and Lina are fighting."

"All her school friends will be there. I'll feel . . . I don't know."

"Old?" Rico let out a loud belly laugh, and Griff gave him the finger. "Come on, boss. Half of Nugget will be there. I'm going. Harlee, Colin, Darla, and Wyatt are going. That little bitch Andy will probably be there."

It had not gone beyond Griffin's notice that Andy was always checking out Lina's rack. Every time he'd been at the inn, the jerk's eyes had been all over her.

"We'll see," he said, which was the universal code for "not happening."

Griff took a bite of his dog and grabbed a soda from the cooler to wash it down. "What's going on with the Chevy?"

"It needs a new fan belt. I'm just waiting for Calhoun to give me the go-ahead."

"Well, get it out of the bay until you hear from him." Griffin motioned at three cars parked near the air pumps. "They all need oil changes."

"Will do," Rico said, and fiddled with his phone. "Hey, when is your open house at Sierra Heights? I want to put it on my calendar."

"First Saturday in March." Hopefully he'd sell a few goddamned houses.

"We've got the bowling party that night. You know that, right?"

"Yep." Griffin gazed out the plate-glass window at an Outback that had just pulled in, threw the rest of his hot dog in the trash, grabbed a box of mints near the cash register, and poured a dozen in his mouth.

Lina got out of the car and Griffin headed for the door.

"Hey." He waved at her, noting that it felt more like spring than winter. He'd left the house only needing a fleece pullover.

"You found a car for me?"

"Maybe." He led her behind the store, where he parked whatever vehicle he was driving for the day. "What do you think?"

She squinted at the Lexus and walked closer to get a better look. "It's brand-new."

"Nah, it's a few years old. The owner just took good care of it. You want to take it for a test drive?"

"Uh, yeah." Her eyes sparkled. "But how much is it?"

"Four thousand. You may be able to whittle it down, though."

"You know the owner?" she asked, reverently running her hand over the Lexus's silver finish.

"Yup. Good guy. Knows his cars."

"Can I look inside?"

Griffin popped the locks with the fob. "Of course. Take it out on the highway, see if you like the ride." He handed her the key.

"Leather seats," she said with awe as he watched her climb in.

"It's got the full package: all-wheel drive, seat warmers, navigation system, upgraded sound system, the works."

She looked at the odometer. "Not much mileage on it. Do you think they may have done the thing where they roll back the numbers to make it look better than what it really is?"

The corners of his mouth curved up. "I don't think so."

"I'm scared to drive it, it's so nice."

"Want me to come?" Now why had he offered that?

"Could you? I don't know where everything is."

"No problem." He got into the passenger seat and buckled up. "It's an automatic. You won't have a problem."

She backed out and pulled onto Main Street. "I'll take it around the square and then to the highway."

She drove like a granny, but Griff didn't say anything. Clearly she needed to get used to the vehicle.

"It's different than Maddy's Outback," Lina said. "It's so smooth."

Griff turned on the radio. A country station. "This making you nervous?"

"I'm okay." She checked all the mirrors and adjusted the one on her side. Griffin thought she looked good in the SUV. Then again, she'd look good in a Vega hatchback.

She wiggled her butt in the seat, oblivious to what it was doing to him. "It's comfortable."

They went around the square, took the road out of Nugget to the entrance of the highway.

"How about driving over fifty?" Griffin said.

"I will when I'm ready." She shot him a look and he grinned. *Fiery thing*. "Four thousand, huh? It seems that a truck like this would be worth more."

"That's what he's asking." Griffin looked down at his boots.

"I've only got three thousand. I could probably borrow five hundred from my brother. But he and Maddy are paying to throw me a big party. I wouldn't feel right about asking for any more."

Griff nodded in understanding. "See if the owner will take thirty-five hundred. Can't hurt to ask."

"I'll have to talk to Rhys first. He'll probably want you to check the engine and all the other stuff a mechanic is supposed to look at before buying a car."

"No problem." Griff glanced over at the speedometer. And what do you know? She was doing sixty.

"I really love it, Griff. How did you find the car?"

"The guy came in for an oil change, said he'd just bought a hybrid and wanted to unload this one."

She'd pulled over to the side of the road, hung a U-turn, and headed back to Nugget. "It seems like it would be super reliable."

Anything would be more reliable than the Scout. Rhys had given him the go-ahead to junk it. "It'll definitely get you to Reno and back for a lot of years."

"It's so luxurious." She gazed at the dashboard with its gauges and screens.

"Lexus makes a nice vehicle."

Feeling more comfortable in the driver's seat, Lina played with the windshield wipers, the heater, and the radio.

"How are plans for your party coming?" He didn't know why he asked. But idle conversation seemed like a better alternative than what he'd like to do.

"Brady has a great menu planned, and a lot of people are coming. My mom couldn't afford a *quinceañera*, so this is my first big birthday party."

Griffin knew that a *quinceañera* was the equivalent of a sweet sixteen for fifteen-year-old Mexican girls, only fancier. They wore big poufy dresses that looked like wedding gowns, had attendants, and there was some kind of religious ceremony involved. Parties like that took a chunk of change to throw, and like Griff, Lina had grown up dirt-floor poor. Griff hadn't come into his wealth until he was twenty-five. Lina had lost her mother when she was seventeen. She and her brother, Samuel, had come to Nugget to live with their half-brother, Rhys, and their father, who'd died a short time later.

So this damned party was a big freaking deal.

"You're coming, right?" Lina turned into the Gas and Go, pulled the Lexus around back, turned off the engine, and pressed the emergency brake.

"I have another commitment," he said, and couldn't look her in the eye. "But I'm gonna try."

"Okay," she said, like she couldn't care less. "I'll talk to Rhys and get back to you on the SUV as soon as possible. Are there a lot of people who want it?"

"You've got first dibs," he said and hopped out of the cab.

She handed him the key. "I can't thank you enough, Griffin. I hope I get it." Lina crossed her fingers and Griffin wanted to tell her that the Lexus was hers. Instead he kind of stared at her, slack-jawed. She was just that beautiful.

The next day, Rhys showed up at the Gas and Go wanting to see the Lexus. Griffin took him to where he'd parked it. He walked around the truck a few times, peeked in the windows and kicked the tires.

"What the hell are you trying to pull, Parks?" Griffin feigned innocence, but Rhys wasn't buying it. "This vehicle is worth five times four thousand bucks."

More than that, but Griff didn't say anything.

Rhys waggled his hand for the keys, got inside the truck, slid the seat back, and took off.

Rico sidled up to Griffin. "What do you plan to tell him when he gets back?"

"Don't know yet." Griff went inside the store and poured himself a cup of coffee.

A few customers filtered in and out. Griffin rang up their purchases. The kid he'd hired didn't come in until after school, leaving him and Rico to handle the cash register in the morning. He could really use another mechanic who could also help out in the store.

Rhys returned about a half hour later. Apparently he'd wanted to put the Lexus through its paces. He walked into the shop, dangling the key from his finger.

"You trying to give the car to my sister?"

"No, I'm trying to sell it to her for somewhere close to four thousand dollars."

Rhys huffed out a breath. "You're giving it away, Griffin. Why?"

"You know why." Griffin pretended to organize the maps on the counter.

"No. You need to explain it to me."

"Because I love her. There, are you satisfied?"

"If you love her, do something about it. I'm sick of watching the two of you moon over each other. It gives me heartburn."

Griff jerked his head up. Lina wasn't mooning over him anymore. "What about the age difference?"

Rhys shrugged. "She's a grown woman. I can't stop her from wanting an old man."

He laid four thousand dollars cash on the counter. "I take it you've already gone over the Lexus with a fine-tooth comb?" Clearly, Rhys was being facetious.

Griff nodded.

"Good." Rhys made his way to the door. "Tell her, Griffin."

Brady was getting in deeper and deeper with Sloane. Every night he stayed at her place, telling himself it was for her safety. The woman was a cop, armed to the hilt, for God's sake. She could take care of herself.

But he liked being with her, talking with her, eating with her, and feeling her nestled next to him in bed. The sex was great, but the waking up together was even better.

And that's not the way it was supposed to be. Not for him, anyway. He didn't like roots, he didn't like commitments, and he especially didn't like embroiling a person he cared about in his personal hell.

Although Sandra had been oddly quiet these last few weeks, she was like a rattlesnake in the grass, coiled and ready to strike. Brady just never knew when. A few times, he'd considered flying to Los Angeles on a reconnaissance mission. But why tempt fate? He liked things quiet, even if it was only temporary.

As much as he knew it would be best to cool it with Sloane, he just couldn't do it. Running with her after work, having dinner in her kitchen, listening to her talk about her day . . . well, it had become an addiction. She'd become an addiction.

Here he was, preparing food for Lina's party tonight, doing what he loved, and he couldn't stop watching the clock. Waiting for the minute she'd walk in the room and rock his world. He'd never been in this position before, and frankly it scared the hell out of him. What happened when it all blew up?

"How's it going?" Sam danced into the kitchen. Maddy and Rhys were hosting the party, but there could be no mistaking who was orchestrating it. Sam, event planner extraordinaire.

"Piece of cake," he said. "The pigs and cake have been done for days. I fried the chicken this morning and made the sliders. Just have to pop them under the broiler when the time comes. I'm working on the salads now. Slaw, potato, green, and macaroni. We're going retro, baby."

"What's the big hunk of cheese for?" she asked, a big smile lighting her face.

"I decided, in addition to the potato chips and onion dip, to throw in a nacho bar, which reminds me, I've gotta make the *queso fundido*—Cecilia's recipe."

"They'll be back in time from their honeymoon, right?"

"Yep. No one is missing this party."

"It's gonna be pretty great. You should see what Nate and I got her." She could barely contain her excitement.

"What?"

She ran out of the room only to return a few minutes later, holding a small rectangular velvet box. "I still have to wrap it." She flipped up the lid and a gold necklace with a diamond pendant twinkled under the lights.

Brady whistled. "Big-ticket item."

"Every young woman should have a special piece of jewelry from her family," Sam said, and Brady wanted to say, *Spoken like a true socialite.* "Anyway, it doesn't compare to what Griffin gave her . . . well, may as well have given her."

"What's that?"

"A Lexus SUV."

"Get out," Brady said. "He gave her a freaking car?"

"It's used, but barely. Rhys says it's worth nearly thirty-five-thousand dollars and Griff sold it to her for four thousand."

"That certainly trumps my fifty-dollar iTunes card."

"Griffin is a good guy." Sam assessed the kitchen. "You need help in here? I could do the dishes."

"I've got it covered, unless you're done with everything else."

"I am," she said, sounding surprised. "This is the easiest party I've ever organized. The birthday girl is incredibly low maintenance. Told Maddy and me to do whatever we wanted."

"Same with the food," Brady said. "She had a vision for a cook-out. Since it's February, we did the next best thing."

"I can't tell you how much I'm looking forward to the food. I'm so sick of Richard's pretentious dishes. Every Breyer hotel event has to have beef Wellington. Do you know how tired that dish is?"

"Tell that to Gordon Ramsay." But secretly Brady agreed that it was pretty tired. "Richard is okay. Nothing wrong with sticking to the classics."

"Nothing wrong with it as long as you're not an insufferable ass too."

"What's going on now?" Sam had never gotten along with Nate's corporate chef. Brady would never come out and say it, but Richard was a prick.

"He just fights everything," Sam said. "Any suggestion to switch up the menu with lighter dishes or something more festive, and he balks. People, especially in California, don't eat all those rich foods anymore."

"Has Nate talked to him?"

"Nate shouldn't have to intercede. I'm Breyer Hotels' corporate event planner. Richard needs to take direction from me. But he doesn't like women."

It wasn't that Richard didn't like women; he didn't like having them as his boss. Brady could understand Sam's frustration, but he didn't like bad-mouthing other chefs.

"Sorry," Sam said. "I was just venting and you don't need to hear this while you're in the middle of preparing for a big party. Did you see the beautiful pastries Emily brought?"

"I did. It's gonna be one hell of a dessert table."

Brady looked at the time and got to work on the cheese sauce for the nachos. While that was cooking, he began slicing cabbage for a spicy slaw he planned to use as a topping for his mini fried-chicken sandwiches. By the time all his prep work was done, salads made, and oven preheated, some of his helpers had arrived. He'd assembled an experienced catering team that he used regularly. A number of the servers and line cooks moonlighted from their permanent jobs at hotels and restaurants in Reno and Glory Junction. Brady put them to work building sandwiches and sliders and plating.

When the first gaggle of guests streamed in, Brady sent servers out with passed hors d' oeuvres. Sam had seen to the setup of the bar and had hired Floyd from the Ponderosa to serve drinks, wine, and beer.

"Hey." Sloane wandered in wearing a simple black cocktail dress that clung to her curves and showed enough cleavage to make him hyperventilate. She'd dressed up for Jake and Cecilia's wedding, but tonight she took his breath away.

"You look beautiful." He couldn't restrain himself and kissed her in the middle of the kitchen for anyone to see. If she stood there much longer in that dress, he'd hoist her up on the counter and have it over her head in no time. And wouldn't that be a show?

The things this woman did to him.

"Will you be able to come out and mingle for a little while?" she asked.

"I'm planning on it once everything is under control in the kitchen. Even brought a change of clothes."

She beamed up at him and again he felt that magic pull. Shit, he was so unprepared for these feelings, so ill equipped to parse and compartmentalize them and put them in the proper place. Under different circumstances he might've let himself go and just enjoy the euphoria of being this deeply infatuated with a woman. But how could he?

And it seemed as if the powers wanted to reinforce that point because right at that moment his phone vibrated with a call from Santa Monica Police Department's Detective Rinek.

Griffin planned to stay for thirty minutes, no more. Just enough time to circle the room, show his face, and wish Lina happy birthday. Then he'd be on his way, social obligation taken care of. Someone passed with a tray of sliders and he grabbed one. May as well eat, he figured, and hit the buffet table, where he loaded up a plate.

"Hey, Griff." Nate rushed by him.

It looked like the family was about to make a toast. Maddy, holding Emma, along with Rhys, Samuel, and Sam, stood by the bar waiting for Nate. Once they were all assembled, Rhys cleared his throat. In an effort to hush the room, a few guests clinked their glasses with pieces of flatware.

Rhys stepped up as the room finally grew quiet. "We just wanted to thank everyone for coming and celebrating my sister's birthday. Ordinarily, we would've waited to do something like this for her twenty-first. But given that she was accepted into the prestigious engineering department at the University of Nevada and she's home again with the people who love her, we figured we had a lot to celebrate. So why wait? Lina"—he searched the room—"where are you?" She waved her arm in the middle of the crowd and a shout went up. "Just wanted to say how very proud we are of you. Happy birthday, little sister."

The guests hooted and hollered as they broke up to mingle, leaving Griffin with his first glimpse of Lina. She was so stunning that his mouth went dry. Her hair had been swept back in an intricate twist that involved a braid with loose tendrils framing her face. Griff took in her strapless dress, shapely shoulders, tiny waist, and mile-long legs. He'd never seen her look so sophisticated.

"Gorgeous, right?" Darla came up alongside him. "I did her hair."

"Incredible," was all he could manage to say.

"Check it out." Harlee, who'd squeezed in next to them, showed Griffin a photo of a beaming Lina on her camera. "I just posted it on the *Trib*'s website. She's a star. What's wrong with you?"

"Nothing," Griff said.

"You looked really far away there for a second." Harlee felt his head and smirked. "A little hot, perhaps? Go say hi." She pushed him directly at Lina. Damn, she was strong. Griff stumbled and almost lost his plate. He put it on an empty tray and walked toward Lina. She was surrounded by people he didn't know, probably her friends from school. A few of the guys stood way too close for Griff's taste.

"You came." Lina separated herself from the group and smiled up at him. Griffin thought for sure his heart would pound out of his chest.

"Happy birthday." He'd forgotten to bring a gift and felt a little stupid.

"Thank you. Come meet my friends." She took his arm and introduced him to the circle of folks she'd been hanging with.

As they all stood, talking, Griffin absently put his arm around Lina. She didn't seem to be bothered by it, so he left it there. He couldn't help but notice that a few of the clingier dudes had backed off. One had even started scoping out other women, which suited Griff just fine.

"Hey, you two, I want to get a picture." Maddy motioned for Griffin and Lina to move closer and snapped a photo. "Now with the whole group." Lina's school friends gathered around and Maddy got the shot.

The two McCreedy boys and Lina's little brother came running up. Maddy wanted a picture of Lina with them, too. Griff started to move away, but Maddy told him to stay put.

"All five of you." She shot a few more, then did a couple with just Lina and Samuel.

"Let me take one of you, Lina, Samuel, Emma, and Rhys," Griff suggested.

"That would be great." Maddy sent Samuel after Rhys, who had baby Emma.

They returned a few minutes later and Griff got a family shot of them standing on the inn's killer staircase.

"Now that's a good picture," Clay said, and put his drink down on a nearby table. "Griff, get on the staircase with them and I'll take it."

Griffin waited for someone to point out the fact that he wasn't part of the family. But when no one did, he caved and got in the shot. Rhys wanted a picture of the McCreedy clan. So they spent another fifteen minutes switching people in and out of various shots—some taken on the veranda. There was a family portrait of the Shepards and Nate and Samantha Breyer, which Griff took. The whole thing was getting kind of out of hand.

All Griff wanted to do was steal some private time with Lina. But as she was the guest of honor, no one would leave her alone. Donna and her husband, Trevor, Ethel and Stu, the Millers, who owned Nugget Farm Supply, the Gaitlins, whose son played basketball with Samuel, and Pam from the yoga studio and her husband. Griffin couldn't even remember his name. They all wanted a piece of Lina.

So he just waited with his hands shoved in his pockets. Colin stood with him for a few minutes, but after a while the crush of people became too much for Colin. He had a social anxiety disorder that he'd nearly whupped. Still, this many people sent him over the edge.

Finally, sensing that Griffin wanted a few minutes alone, Lina took him by the hand to one of the upstairs rooms. Maddy and Nate had closed the place to overnight guests for the party. Given Lina's dress and the way she looked tonight, Griffin didn't think a vacant room with a bed was the best choice for a private place to talk.

As he looked around the suite, he realized something. "This was my room when I first came to Nugget. This was the first place you and I made out." It had been more than making out. They'd done everything but the deed itself.

Lina's face turned red. "I snuck in and made a fool of myself."

"That's not the way I remember it."

He wrapped his arms around her, backed her up to the foot of the bed, and kissed her like a starving man. Carried away, he found the zipper on the back of her dress, pulled it down, and tugged the hemline until the little number floated around her feet like froth in a milkshake. Her bra, like the dress, was strapless, held up only by two perfect breasts, and her panties consisted of nothing more than a strip of lace.

"You make me crazy," he whispered in her ear. "You're so beautiful."

"I have a room full of guests downstairs." But she continued to kiss him back, pulling Griffin against her until he thought he'd explode.

He slipped away just fast enough to lock the door, came back, peeled Lina's panties down her silky legs, and found her wet center with his hand. She moaned, going down on the bed, and pushing herself up with her elbows.

"Ah, Jesus, I want to take a picture of you like that." With her breasts thrust forward and naked from the waist down. He came down on top of her, spreading her legs apart with his knee so he could feel her heat.

"Don't you dare." She kept kissing him. "Griff? We have to stop."

"What? You don't like this?" She'd always been the one to initiate sex in the past. He'd always been the one to stop her before they went too far.

"I like it so much that pretty soon I won't be able to stop. But it's completely inappropriate."

As much as it gave him blue balls to admit it, she was right. When had impulsive little Lina Shepard shown good judgment? When they'd first started seeing each other, she used to pull all kinds of stunts to get him to take her virginity, including stripping naked in places where they could easily have gotten caught.

He rolled off her and tried to catch his breath. And she started putting her clothes back on.

"One of us should go down first," Lina said, and tried to zip the back of her dress.

He finished the job and spun her around. "Where are we at, Lina?"

She held his gaze. "You tell me, since you're always the one with the rules."

He wanted to say that someone had had to be the adult. "I miss you. Do you miss me?"

There was a long pause before she said, "Yes. But you hurt me, Griffin."

"I was trying to do what was right. I was trying to give you a chance to be a college student. You know that, because we've been over it a hundred times before."

"If you'd really loved me you wouldn't have let me go."

"I loved . . . love . . . you so much it hurts. You were eighteen when I met you. Eighteen, Lina."

"And what, twenty is the magic number?"

"It's still too damn young. But not being with you . . . it's killing me. Did Rhys tell you that we talked?"

"No. What did he say?"

"He said he was sick of seeing us moon over each other."

She smiled. "I didn't realize we were that obvious."

"You're not."

Her face grew somber. "I've got a lot going on right now. School, work, my family. Maybe we could just go slow. Date. See where things go."

"That didn't work for you before."

"I'm a different person now." Definitely more mature, Griffin thought. "Do you think we could try that?"

He nodded. "Does that rule out us seeing each other tonight, after the party?"

"Tonight is for my family. Now, I have to get down there before

Rhys and Maddy send a search party looking for me." She started for the door, but he stopped her.

"Happy birthday, Lina. I've loved you since I first saw you in the parking lot of the Sierra Heights clubhouse, and I love the woman you've become."

She didn't say anything back. She didn't have to. Her love for him was written in her eyes. But the new, grown-up Lina had become more circumspect. He could live with that. At least for now.

Chapter 19

Sandra was gone.

She hadn't been to work in five days. No one had been able to reach her. And someone from her job had gone to her home and found her mailbox overflowing. According to neighbors, she hadn't been seen around her apartment in at least a week. Sandra's family had reported her missing and Santa Monica police were investigating.

"I've put in calls to your police chief and Officer McBride," Detective Rinek said. "I'm waiting to hear back from them."

That wouldn't be tonight.

Brady tried to find a quiet spot to finish the call. He had a lot of questions and it was difficult to hear over the crescendo of partygoers.

"Give me a second, Detective. I'm right in the middle of a catering gig." He stepped out onto the veranda, pulled one of Colin's rockers to the far corner, and sat down. "Why, you think she's coming for me?"

"There is no evidence to suggest that, but I think it's prudent to be prepared regardless."

"Did you go inside her apartment?"

"We did. Her things . . . furniture, clothes, jewelry . . . are still there. Only thing missing is her car. Investigators found nothing to indicate she was up to something nefarious. However, her computer showed recent searches for you. It doesn't look like she got any hits, but it's impossible to tell for sure."

"You don't think the mere fact that she's searching for me is *nefarious*?"

"It's not enough for us to jump to the conclusion that she's coming after you . . . or even knows where to find you." Brady got the distinct impression that Rinek knew more and was holding out on him. "For all we know she's been in an accident and is in a hospital somewhere."

"Are you checking that out?" Brady knew that he sounded confrontational, but he couldn't help it. Sandra had turned his life upside down and he just wanted the cops to be straight with him. Enough of the double-talk.

"Of course we are. We're checking everything, Mr. Benson. In the meantime, exercise an abundance of caution and we'll be in touch."

The detective clicked off. Despite the work waiting for him in the kitchen, Brady continued to sit there, watching what was left of the sun disappear behind the Sierra. A cricket chirped in the not-too-far distance, and wood smoke from the chimney wafted over the porch, eliciting memories of camping, roasting marshmallows, and firelight. It all seemed so idyllic that it was hard to believe that a lunatic was out there, lying in wait, ready to ambush him at any moment.

"I've been looking all over for you." Sloane stepped out of the shadows, and he jumped. "My God, what's wrong? You look like you've seen a ghost."

Guests started drifting out onto the porch, and suddenly it wasn't so quiet. Brady took Sloane by the wrist and pulled her close.

"Detective Rinek called. Sandra is missing."

She tilted her head back so she could look up at him. "What do you mean, missing?"

"She didn't show up to her job all week, which according to her coworkers is completely uncharacteristic for her. The police searched her house, and her stuff is still there. But they found recent searches for me on her computer."

Sloane blew out a breath. "We need to talk to Rhys and Jake."

"Detective Rinek left messages for you and Rhys."

"Let's go find him." She grabbed his arm, but Brady pulled her back.

"Not tonight. I need to finish with the food."

"We can't put this off."

"I don't want you involved with this, Sloane."

"Too bad."

He didn't want to fight with her. Not now, not in the middle of an event. "All right. As soon as the party's over we'll talk and make a plan."

Sloane reluctantly agreed and they both went back inside, where

Brady spent the rest of the evening sending out food from the kitchen and mingling with the guests. He would've liked to have finished off the night with a stiff drink but needed to have his wits about him.

"I told Rhys that we want to meet with him first thing in the morning." Sloane came up behind him and wrapped her arms around his waist.

"It's Saturday, Sloane." Just this afternoon, he'd been looking forward to the prospect of sleeping in the next morning, since there would be no guests to feed.

"We work weekends. You ready to go home?"

"Sloane, I don't think it's a good idea for you and me to go together."

"I'm the one with the gun. So I think it's an excellent idea for us to go together."

His mouth quirked. "A lesser man would take issue with that, you know?"

"Good thing you're not a lesser man." Her gaze took him in. "We'll leave your van here and go in the batmobile."

"Sloane, listen to me. This is reckless. If she's coming for me and gets even an inkling that you and I are together, she's gonna go batshit. I've done a lot of research on obsession stalkers, and they're extremely possessive—violently jealous."

"That's why we're taking my vehicle. If she's out there, she'll see the Nugget PD logo and figure that you're under guard."

He highly doubted it, especially if Sandra got a load of Sloane in that dress. But it was no use arguing with her. She was one of the most bullheaded women he'd ever met. And definitely the one he trusted most in a bad situation. So he got in the passenger seat and let her drive.

She let out a yawn. "It was a beautiful party tonight. The food, Brady, was off the charts. Those little chicken sandwiches, to die for."

"You might not want to use that phraseology." They both laughed. A moment of levity was good. Ah hell, they were probably overreacting to Sandra's disappearance. Maybe she'd finally checked herself into a funny farm.

All such fantasies died when Brady saw the unfamiliar car parked in their driveway.

"Wait in here," Sloane said, and grabbed her Glock from the glove box before getting out of the rig.

The hell he would. He grabbed the Mossberg 500 pump-action

shotgun off the rack in the back of the SUV, made sure it was loaded, and went after her.

"I told you to stay in the truck," she whispered.

The motion lights went on, illuminating the front porch. Whoever the car belonged to was nowhere in sight. He put his finger to his lips and led the way around the side of the duplex. Brady planned to circle the perimeter of the building and check for signs of a break-in. Sloane caught up and stared daggers at him.

She pointed at the shotgun and whispered, "It's against department policy for you to have that."

He rolled his eyes, shushed her again, and motioned for her to crouch down under the windows in case their visitor was inside one of the apartments.

"Don't tell me how to do my job," she said.

He pulled her down until they were both squatting, and pointed to Sloane's living room window. "Look for broken glass."

"Duh." She duck walked ahead of him.

He couldn't help but grin at how funny she looked doing that in a dress and high heels. At least his shoes were practical. Whoever their guest was knew they were here. Only a deaf person would've missed the sound of Sloane's police truck crunching gravel. Then again, Sandra hadn't exactly gone for the element of surprise by parking her car in plain view. She was just delusional enough to greet him at the door in an apron. *Honey, you're home.*

He held the shotgun firmly at his side and motioned for Sloane to stop just as they reached the end of the duplex. Before they turned the corner to the back of the building, he wanted to come up with a plan. The only escape route behind them involved the ravine and railroad tracks. He didn't like those options.

Sloane of course didn't listen and continued around the rear, gun drawn, yelling, "Put your hands up or I'll shoot."

"For God's sake, calm down," came a man's voice.

"Aidan? Is that you?" She lowered the gun.

"Look at you, all dressed up."

The man—Aidan—came down the deck stairs, circled her in his arms, and lifted her off the ground in a bear hug. A few seconds later he took notice of Brady with the butt of the shotgun planted against his shoulder, his finger on the safety button.

"What, are you people nuts here?" Aidan asked, in a thick Chicago accent.

Sloane let out a breath. "It's a long story. I can't believe you're here."

"I know it seems spur of the moment. But after you invited me . . . maybe I should've called first." He eyed Brady, who'd relaxed his hold on the Mossberg.

"Of course you didn't need to call first." Sloane went in for another hug. "I'm just so glad you came, Aid. When did you get here?"

"I flew into Reno, rented a car, and crossed Nugget city limits about five p.m. Sloane, you weren't kidding, this place is awesome."

"Why are you sitting back here? I don't even know where that ratty chair came from," Sloane said. Brady was pretty sure it had been left by the last tenant.

Aidan shrugged. "I waited for you on the front porch at first. But when the train went by I wanted to watch it." He nudged his head at Brady. "You work with my sister at the police department?"

"No. I live in the apartment next door. I'm a chef."

Aidan eyed the shotgun speculatively. "Okay."

"Let's go inside," Sloane said. "You've been sitting out here for hours. You have to be starved."

"I could eat," he said. "But I could really use a bathroom."

Sloane grabbed the shotgun from Brady's hand, led Aidan around front, and unlocked the door. "I'll be back in a second."

Brady watched her return the Mossberg to the rack in her SUV and waited for her on the porch. Aidan had rushed inside.

"Hey," he said, and slipped his arm around her. "Go spend time with your brother and I'll see you in the morning."

She chewed on her bottom lip as if she was contemplating what to do.

"Sloane, we'll only be separated by a thin wall. It's no different than if we were in the same house together."

"At least let me check your apartment first." She didn't wait for his permission, just grabbed his keys out of his hand and let herself in. Going room to room, she opened closets and searched any space where a person could hide. "It's clear. Does anything look out of place?"

The apartment looked exactly the way he'd left it. "Nope."

"Bang on your wall if you need me," she said.

"I will. Go tend to your brother. You got anything to feed him? Had I known, I would've brought home party leftovers."

"I've got stuff. You get a good night's sleep. Remember, we're meeting with Rhys in the morning."

Brady watched her walk next door. Standing on the porch, he felt the night chill cut through his dress shirt like a knife. He'd forgotten his jacket at the inn. For a moment, he considered going back to get it and his car, then driving away to a new town with new people where he could once again hide in plain sight. Staying here was only borrowing trouble.

He heard laughter from Sloane's apartment. It was a little contagious, that laugh. So genuine that it spread through his chest like warm liquid. He thought about the prospect of leaving and never seeing her again. Never hearing that laugh or about her pilot kids or the orgasmic sounds she made while eating his food, and his heart constricted like it was being smashed in a garlic press. That's when he walked inside and went to bed.

When they arrived in the morning to meet with Rhys, he was already on the phone with Detective Rinek. Brady made coffee on Connie's fancy grind-and-brew while Sloane checked her messages. Technically she was off today. Now that Jake was back from his honeymoon, they were fully staffed again and she could go back to a forty-hour work week. Still, she was curious to see if she'd gotten any hits on her John Doe. So far, none of the missing persons on their possibility list had checked out. Several had already been found, some had never been missing, and on closer examination it was unlikely that the others had ever stepped foot in Nugget. Some of their trails had ended in other states entirely.

Sloane was beginning to believe that her person had never been reported missing, because he was either a transient with no family or friends, or a migrant worker whose people lived in another country and didn't know how to contact authorities here. Those possibilities would make the case nearly impossible to solve.

But the poor man at least deserved a headstone with his name. And she wanted her three junior investigators (i.e., the pilot program) to have the satisfaction of solving the case. They'd worked so hard. Sloane glanced over at Rhys's glass office and could tell his conversation was wrapping up.

Brady brought her a cup of coffee—her first one, since there hadn't been time this morning. When they'd left the duplex, Aidan had still been sound asleep on her sofa bed. She and her brother had stayed up talking much of the night about Sue and Brady. He'd told her that Sue seemed to be getting serious with another school teacher, and she'd filled Aidan in on Brady's stalker situation—the reason why they'd come home locked and loaded.

Rhys waved his hand for them to sit in his office, and Brady grabbed him a cup of coffee.

"Thanks." Rhys warmed his hands on the mug. "Jesus Christ, Brady, what the hell have you gotten yourself into?"

Sloane didn't like the implication of that sentence. It sounded a lot like blaming the victim. If the victim had been a woman, Rhys would have selected his words more wisely. At least she hoped he would've.

"Brady didn't do anything wrong. This woman is a terror."

"I didn't mean to imply that he did, Sloane."

Brady cut in. "What did Rinek say?"

"That they don't know where this Sandra Lockhart is and that there is some indication that she may have disappeared on purpose. According to her computer searches, they think she may have been planning a road trip, though she hadn't put in for vacation. According to her coworkers, she's very conscientious about her job. There were also recent searches for you and for another male, who Santa Monica PD is trying to reach."

"Rinek didn't tell me there was anyone else."

"This guy may be completely immaterial to the investigation."

"What kind of road trip?" Sloane asked.

Rhys shrugged. "She'd made a list of gas stations. From the list, her trajectory is unclear. The stations are all over the map."

It sounded bizarre to Sloane, like she had a bad case of OCD. Any smartphone could find the nearest gas station and navigate her there. "In California?"

Rhys deliberated and eventually said, "And Nevada."

"Where in Nevada?" Brady asked.

"Beatty, Tonopah, Carson City."

"That's the route you would take here from Los Angeles if you wanted to go via Nevada." And if you wanted to tack on another four hours to your drive, instead of taking I-5 across California, Sloane noted.

"Except, she also researched gas stations along the Arizona border, in El Centro, Blythe, and Lake Havasu City." Rhys looked at their puzzled faces. "See what I mean? There's no way to tell what she had planned. For all we know she's a gas station buff."

"Bottom-line it for me, Rhys." Brady leaned forward in his chair. "Does Rinek think she's coming here?"

"There's no way to tell that, Brady. There hasn't been any activity on her credit or ATM cards and no large cash withdrawals in recent weeks. It's as if she disappeared into thin air. Our best course of action is to stay on our toes. I've printed her DMV picture and a photo I got off Facebook. I want to pass them around, let people in town know that we're looking for her. That way if she shows up we'll be notified. I also plan to have one of us regularly patrol Donner Road, and we've got Sloane living right next door to you. We've also got the inn to think about. Sometime today I'd like to gather Maddy, Nate, Sam, Lina, and Andy and have a frank conversation about this. Who knows? She may try to check in there. Everyone needs to be on alert."

He got up from his desk. "I asked Connie to come in for a few hours today. Let me see if she's out there and can set up something. I know Maddy is at the inn right now with Emma. She's making sure everything is in order after last night's party."

After Rhys stepped out, Sloane put her hand on Brady's leg. "This may finally be our chance to get her."

Yeah, right he conveyed with his eyes, and it killed her to see him so deflated. She'd fallen for the man and his hurt was her hurt. And right now he was feeling a lot of pain.

Rhys came back in and sat on the corner of his desk. "We can do it at one—before the guests start checking in. Does that work?"

"Yeah," Brady said, and Sloane nodded.

When they left the police station and got into the van, Brady said, "You don't have to come to this, Sloane. Hang out with your brother, show him the sights."

"I will, but I'm coming to the meeting. You're not embarrassed, are you?"

"No, it was bound to come out anyway. All along Nate's been suspicious of my past, thinking that someone with my experience must be hiding something to be satisfied to cook for a tiny inn. I think he'll be relieved that I'm not wanted by the mob—or the FBI."

"When this is over, you'll be able to cook anywhere you want." And she wondered where that would leave her. Because if he went away she'd miss him like crazy. Ah, who was she kidding? If he went away, he'd leave a great big hole in her heart. In just the short time she'd known Brady, he'd become everything to her. Her best friend, her sounding board, and her lover.

"Look, when we get home, you go spend some time with Aidan," Brady said. "I want to call my sister and tell her what's up and make a month's worth of menus for the Lumber Baron. I don't want to stay there if I'm putting the staff and guests at risk. At the meeting I'm gonna recommend that I take a leave of absence."

"No one will want you to do that. We don't even know what the deal is with this woman. It would be ridiculous to jump to conclusions, Brady."

He reached across the console of his van, cupped her face with his hands, and kissed her. Sweet and gentle at first. Then he cradled her head and went all the way in until she was practically lying across his lap.

"What's this for?" Sloane murmured against his lips.

"For being a good friend."

"Is that what I am?" She lifted her face to look into his eyes.

"You are." He didn't say any more, just turned his key in the ignition and started the engine.

She didn't dare press it on the way to Donner Road. A man under his kind of stress shouldn't have to answer relationship questions. Anyway, Aidan was waiting when they got there, which didn't leave them time to talk.

He'd commandeered Brady's rocker and had his feet up on the railing while sipping a cup of coffee. "How'd it go?"

"Frustrating." Sloane climbed the stairs. "They don't know where she is or what she's doing, other than making a list of gas stations across California and Nevada."

"Gas stations?"

"They think she might've been planning a road trip," Brady said. "But the locations of her gas stations are all over the map."

"But the woman's crazy, right? So you can't apply logic to anything she does." Sloane thought Aidan had a point. "In my line of business

I'd be thinking accelerant. Amateur arsonists will often use gasoline to start fires and they'll go to extremes to get it from places that aren't likely to be traced back to them."

"Eventually, she will need money and have to use one of her cards," Sloane said. "When that happens, they'll nab her. You ready to do some sightseeing, Aid?"

He got to his feet. "Absolutely. Let me just put the mug inside."

Sloane hooked her arms around Brady's neck. "Call your sister."

He pulled her against him and she felt his warmth and solidness and the stubble on his chin when he rubbed his face against her cheek. The smell of him—soap, shampoo, and man—made her want to burrow against his broad chest.

"Be safe," she said in his ear.

Chapter 20

On Sunday, Griffin decided he'd waited long enough for Lina to recuperate from her party and call him. He picked up the phone and dialed her cell.

"What are you doing today?" he said by way of greeting.

"Laundry. I've got homework and classes in the morning. Why? What did you have in mind?"

"Breakfast at the Ponderosa." It was the first thing that popped into his head since he hadn't planned anything in particular. He just wanted to be with her.

"It's noon, Griff."

"Okay, lunch."

He could hear her hesitate at first. "I can't take too long, though. I want to get to my apartment in Reno before dark, and I still have a bunch of things to do in Nugget."

He'd hoped they could spend the whole day together. "You've got to eat."

"Give me twenty minutes and I'll meet you there."

Griffin got to the restaurant early and snagged them a quiet booth at the back of the dining room.

"How's it going?" Mariah called from behind the bar.

"Can't complain. Business is good. I'd just like to sell some damn houses."

She tossed him a commiserating smile and came over to his table. "I heard you're having an open house next weekend. That should help."

Griff didn't know that he'd sell anything, but at least they'd continue to get the word out. "We'll see how it goes. How are you, Soph, and the baby doing?"

"We're doing fine and Lilly is getting big." She looked around the restaurant, crowded with families and tourists taking advantage of the unseasonably mild weather. "And business has never been better. We're even thinking of hiring on a few more servers."

"That's great. If you hear of a good mechanic looking for work, let me know."

"I will certainly do that. You want to order?" Mariah searched the dining room for a free waitress.

"I'm waiting for Lina, so no rush."

"Lina, huh?" She grinned. "That was a great party Friday night."

"Between Jake and Cecilia getting married and Lina's birthday, we've been having a lot of them lately. Pretty soon it'll be Lucky and Tawny's wedding."

"Always a party in Nugget." Mariah laughed.

Lina came in the door, saw Griffin, and made her way to the back. Mariah gave her a hug and told them she'd send a waitress over shortly.

"Those Tawny's boots?" Griffin asked Lina, who had her skintight jeans tucked into a pair of red shit-kickers. The woman looked so good, he wanted to carry her off to his bedroom.

"Are you kidding? I can't afford her boots. I got these at Boot Barn in Reno."

"They're nice."

She sat across from him and bent across the table. "Rhys told me how much my Lexus is worth. Griff, why'd you do that?"

"Because I can." She started to argue, but he stopped her. "Just accept it graciously because I don't want to spend my one day off talking about cars." That shut her up. "Did you enjoy your party?"

"It was the best birthday I've ever had. But something bad happened later."

Griffin stiffened, worried that someone might've had too much to drink and gotten into an accident.

Lina told him about Brady, his troubles in Los Angeles and how his stalker had mysteriously fallen off the radar.

"They think she's coming here?" Griffin asked with disbelief.

"No one knows for sure. But we had a meeting at the Lumber Baron to talk safety measures. Brady wanted to take a leave of absence, Maddy and Sam started to cry, and Nate threatened to kill him if he left us in the lurch. Even Andy got all up in his grill about how we have to stick together in times like this. I think in the end Brady was pretty touched."

"Crazy," Griffin said. "It reminds me of that movie, *Fatal Attraction*."

"I never heard of it."

"It's a classic. With Glenn Close and Michael Douglas."

She shook her head. A server came to take their order. Neither one of them had to look at the menu. Lina got the Cobb salad and Griff got a tri-tip sandwich.

"So you're going back to Reno today?"

"As soon as I finish my laundry at Maddy and Rhys's. It's so much nicer than having to do the quarter thing in the laundry room at the apartment. I always run out."

He realized she had a whole life that he knew very little about. "Do you live near the friends who were at the party?"

"Mm-hmm. Mostly everyone lives near campus. Mine is a nice apartment complex with a pool and an exercise room. But I'm starting to wonder if I made a mistake living there, since I'm here most of the time. My classes are Monday, Wednesday, and only a half day Friday. I could save my family a lot of money by commuting, especially now that I have an amazing SUV." She beamed at him like he'd hung the moon for getting it for her.

"You like living at home?"

"I have a beautiful room, my own bathroom, even a sitting room. And I get to see Emma and Samuel more. What's not to like?"

Your overprotective big brother, Griff thought to himself. "Hey, I'm in favor of it."

"I heard through the grapevine you're having that open house next weekend."

Their food came and Lina stole a fry off his plate like she used to do at the Bun Boy that first summer they'd met. He turned the plate so she could have as many fries as she wanted.

"You coming?" he asked.

"I'll help if you want."

"Dana's got it pretty well covered. But having a smoking-hot woman hanging around might help business."

She didn't respond, just picked at her salad. "It might be awkward for both Dana and me to be there."

"I told you there is nothing between us. You're the only woman I'm interested in."

She lifted her eyes from her plate. "I'm not going to lie to you, it'll bother me. I've never met her and I'm sure she's a nice woman . . . I just think it'll be better for me not to come."

He tilted his head. "For a jealous woman, you've been awfully standoffish toward me."

She lifted her brows. "Is that what you would call Saturday night? Standoffish?" A laugh bubbled out of her and it took all his willpower not to pack her into his truck, drive home, and perform a reenactment of that night. And this time they would go all the way.

"Could we do that again sometime soon?" He dipped one of his fries in catsup and fed it to her.

"You never know." She chewed and her lips tipped up in a flirtatious smile.

"How about after lunch? You could do your laundry at my house."

"I want to take this slow, Griff."

Now she wants to take it slow. "I was just kidding," he lied. "I could come to Reno one night this week and take you out to dinner— just dinner."

"There's a great burger place near campus that you would love."

"I'd rather take you somewhere nice." She deserved to be wined and dined, unlike the last time. "We can do the burger place another time."

"All right." She whipped out her phone and checked the calendar. Griff snuck a peek. She had a lot of things going on. "I could do Thursday night."

He didn't need to check his calendar. "That'll work. Text me your address and I'll pick you up around six."

They finished eating and Griffin paid the bill. Outside, it was sunny and so crisp that the air crackled. He could smell the Ponderosa sap and it reminded him of home-baked cookies. Impulsively, he took Lina's hand and locked his fingers with hers while they walked to her truck. She pressed the key fob and the Lexus chirped twice.

"It's running okay?" Griffin looked at the rear right tire. It appeared a little low. But on closer inspection he saw that it was fine.

"I've never driven a car that ran this well. Griff, this is a crazy expensive gift you gave me and I don't feel right about it. I want to make payments."

"Don't offend me, okay?"

"Remember when you used to fix the Scout for me and how I paid you in enchiladas?"

A corner of his mouth slid up. "They were the best enchiladas I ever had."

"I could make them for you one night at Maddy and Rhys's, like I used to."

He cupped her chin in his hand. "I'd like that," he said, and covered her mouth with his. She wrapped her arms around his waist and they continued to kiss right there on the square, in front of the police station.

"Rhys is in there," she said against his lips.

"You think he'll shoot me?"

She giggled. "I've got to go, Griff."

"You never used to have to go." He maneuvered her against the side of the SUV and boxed her in.

"That was before I was an adult with things to do." She ducked under his arm and got into the driver's seat. "I'll see you Thursday night."

She started the Lexus and Griff watched her drive away as her words sank in. She was definitely an adult now.

After breakfast service at the Lumber Baron, Brady took Aidan fishing. Sloane was tied up with her pilot-program kids, putting on the children-ID-kit fair she'd been planning. Ethel and Stu offered to let them set up shop in the parking lot of the Nugget Market and had even donated cookies, coffee, and cider to the cause. Clay brought a canopy tent to set up near the entrance and Rhys supplied a couple of folding tables from the Lumber Baron.

Before they'd completely set up, a long queue of parents began to form. Rose, Simpson, and Rudy walked up and down the line getting people started on filling out forms, and handed out stickers and balloons to the little ones.

The turnout was even better than Sloane had expected, which she chalked up to her pilot kids. They'd made posters and fliers, advertising the heck out of the event. She saw Maddy in the crowd with little Emma. And Tawny had brought Katie.

"You done good, Sloane." Rhys gazed out over the crowd and lit up when he saw his wife and daughter. "This is the kind of community service a department like ours should be doing. But it took you to organize it. All these people have you to thank."

"Don't forget Rose, Simpson, and Rudy," she said, but her chest expanded with pride.

"Your doing, too." Before she could thank him for the praise, he wandered off to say hi to Maddy.

They set up an assembly line, with Wyatt taking Polaroid pictures of the kids and Sloane getting their fingerprints. Emily explained the process to the parents, including how to fill out a description card of their child and make a body map that detailed scars, moles, birthmarks, and any other unique identifiers.

Harlee showed up with a laptop and camera, shooting pictures for the *Tribune*. She got a few quotes from Sloane about why the kits were so important and what other steps parents could take to keep their children safe.

"Hey, Harlee, do me a favor and get a few quotes from the chief."

"I tried. He said to talk to you. That it was your program."

"I may have organized it, but he finagled the funding." Rhys seemed to have the magic touch when it came to squeezing money out of city hall. "It may not look like much, but we don't have money in our budget to fund projects like this. Rhys fought for it. And those kids"—she pointed at Rose, Simpson, and Rudy—"put their heart and soul into it. If you could get a picture of them in the paper they'd sure be thrilled."

"I'll see what I can do." Harlee interviewed a few parents, talked to Emily, and made her way to Rhys. The two of them had a combative relationship, but Sloane could tell he liked Harlee. He seemed to admire strong women in general.

Eventually, Harlee circled around back to Sloane. "Nothing new on the John Doe, huh?"

"Nope. But I may have something for you later this week."

"Tell me now, off the record." Harlee, always the consummate reporter.

"Since I haven't had luck with matching him to a missing person, I'm talking to a forensic sculptor, who can reconstruct his face. If she can do it, I'd like to release pictures to the press."

"But to me first?"

Sloane nodded. "I'll give them to you first, but I want this to go national in case our John Doe is from somewhere else."

"My stuff goes on the wire," Harlee said defensively.

"Good." Sloane observed Rudy explaining how the kits worked to a few Spanish-speaking parents and she smiled. "Just get my kids in your article today."

Rhys's crazy pilot program had become incredibly important to her. Even though Rose had gone back to school, she still showed up at the station most weekday afternoons. Same with Simpson and Rudy. It gave them purpose and confidence. Sloane already had plans to do outreach at the high school and bring in a few more kids. Maybe expand the program to include other after-school activities besides quasi police work, like cooking classes with Brady or horseback riding lessons from Clay or Lucky Rodriguez. Perhaps a tutoring clinic. She had lots of ideas up her sleeve.

As the fair wound down, Sloane checked her phone to see if Brady had messaged. Ever since Sandra's disappearance, she'd been on edge. He'd sent a picture of Aidan in a kayak. They must've gone out on the lake. Luckily it wasn't too cold.

The parking lot started to clear out, Ethel collected her coffee urn, and Rhys folded up the tables while Clay took down the canopy tent.

"It went really well, Sloane," Emily said. "We had fifty-two parents make kits."

"Thank you so much for your help. We couldn't have done it without you." Sloane wondered if the day had been hard on Emily, bringing back too many memories of her own missing daughter, Hope.

"It was good for me, Sloane. Thank you for organizing it. I know Rhys was really pleased."

"You ready to go?" Clay wrapped his arm around his wife and said goodbye.

Rudy's parents came to pick him up and agreed to take Simpson home since it was on their way. Rose waited for Skeeter, who roared into the parking lot driving his Camaro. Only this car looked like he'd just driven it off the showroom floor. The dents were gone and the primer gray had been painted glossy banana yellow with black trim. Her mouth must've hung open because Skeeter got out of the car, smiling from ear to ear.

"You like it?"

Sloane wasn't into muscle cars, but she had to admit that the Camaro had a certain sex appeal. "That is your old car, right?"

"Yep. I did the body work myself."

"You're insanely talented, Skeeter." The car was virtually unrecognizable.

"Thanks." He turned a little red. "When I bought the car it barely ran. Now it purrs like a kitten."

"Did you do the mechanical work too?"

"Every last bit of it. It took me six months and I had to scour for parts. But now she's a dream."

"You ever think of getting a job in an auto repair shop?"

"The only one here is that snooty Gas and Go, owned by the rich dude."

"Griffin Parks," she corrected. "You ever talk to him? Because he's a really nice guy. Maybe he could use someone like you."

Skeeter shrugged. "I doubt it."

"I know him; you want me to introduce you?" She had to tell herself to stop pushing. But working as a mechanic seemed to hold a better future than working in the railroad yard, not that she knew much about either. She'd just never seen Skeeter so enthusiastic.

"Why would you do that?"

"Why not? If you can help him with his business, I'd be doing him a favor. And I like Griffin."

"I might be willing to talk to him."

"You should, Skeeter," Rose chimed in. "You love fixing cars."

He put Rose in a headlock. The move reminded Sloane of her big brothers and how they used to roughhouse with her. "It's up to you."

"When?" Skeeter surprised Sloane by asking.

The Gas and Go was just across Main Street. "We could go right now. I don't know if Griff's working on a Sunday, though. Why don't we meet there?"

They caravanned over, Rose riding in Skeeter's car, and parked in front of the convenience store. Rico waved to Sloane and came out from the garage.

"What up?" he asked, but didn't wait for her answer when he caught a glimpse of the Camaro. "Whoa, nice wheels." He circled the car.

"Griffin wouldn't happen to be around? I want you guys to meet a friend of mine."

"You're in luck. He just stopped by. I'll get him." Rico climbed the stairs to Griff's office and the two of them came down.

Griff got one look at Skeeter's car and ignored his visitors. "Holy cow, you weren't kidding." Like Rico, he walked around the Camaro a few times. "What is it, a Z28?"

"Yup," Skeeter said, stepping forward. "A 1993."

"A freaking classic." He looked up at Skeeter. "It's in mint condition."

Skeeter pulled out his phone and showed Griff some pictures. "That's what it looked like before."

"Who did the body work?"

"I did."

"Get out. You've got mad skills, dude."

Sloane cleared her throat. "This is Skeeter Jones. I told him I'd introduce him to you and Rico."

"Yeah? Nice to meet you, man." Griff motioned at the car. "Can I drive it? I'll just take it around the block."

"Okay," Skeeter said, though he seemed reluctant.

"Looks like you guys don't need me anymore," Sloane said. "I'm taking off." Before she left, she sent Skeeter a silent message: *If you're interested in a job, let him know.* "I'll see you on Monday, Rose."

On her way home, Sloane thought about dinner. Lately, she'd left that decision up to Brady. They'd been eating nearly every meal together, especially on the days she could break away from work and have lunch at the inn. But with Aidan here she needed a plan. Her brother could eat an entire side of beef. Cruising down the driveway, she noted that her Rav4 could use a washing, since it only sat and gathered dust these days.

The minute she got out of the SUV, the smell of barbecue assaulted her nose. She saw smoke coming from the side of the duplex, where she found Brady and Aidan standing over a Weber. Brady had dragged his small kitchen table outside to use for prep. A couple of large rainbow trout were on the grill and Brady brushed them with some sort of marinade.

"You caught fish?"

"Yeah, we did." Aidan's smile split his big, happy face. "Man, I envy you, Sloane. This place . . . it's flippin' paradise. We spent the whole day on Lake Davis. I just can't get over this town. And this dude"—he pointed at Brady—"best tour guide ever."

And that made her own face split into a grin. High praise from Aidan for her guy was like winning the lottery. The McBride men had never met a boyfriend of hers they liked. In their minds, no one was good enough for their little sister.

Brady gazed up from what he was doing and winked at her. "Dinner is in ten minutes." He added a few aluminum foil pouches to the grill.

"What are those?"

"Rosemary potatoes and flatbread. I've got a big salad tossed. You planning to eat in that?" He nodded at her uniform.

"I'll change real quick. We eating in my place?"

"Yeah. Unless you want to eat out here," Brady said.

"Too cold."

Aidan laughed. "You've been away from Chicago too long."

Sloane threw on a pair of jeans and sweater and set the table. Brady and Aidan came in carrying platters and bowls of food. She pulled a bottle of chardonnay out of the fridge and Brady put it back.

"What?" she asked.

He didn't answer, just went next door and returned with a bottle of sauvignon blanc. "Better with lake trout."

To her, trout was trout and white wine was white wine. Whatever. "You hear anything today about Sandra?"

"Nope." He passed her the bowl of salad. "Not a word. How did the kid kits go?"

"We had more than fifty parents come by. Rhys was thrilled."

"That's your boss?" Aidan asked, his mouth full.

"Police chief. His wife, Maddy, came with their little girl. And my pilot kids were really into it." She'd told Aidan all about Rose, Simpson, and Rudy.

Brady's cell phone rang. Checking the caller ID, he stepped away from the table and spoke in a low tone. When he sat back down, she and Aidan looked at him expectantly.

"That was Nate." Brady took a big bite of trout. "He wanted to know the oven temperature for heating my artichoke turnovers."

"Nate's doing the wine and cheese service today?" Sloane tried not to laugh. Nate owned a fleet of luxury hotels.

"Someone had to do it." Brady had taken the day off for her, to entertain Aidan while she had to work, even if it meant that the owner of the company had to fill in for him.

She leaned across the table and kissed him. That's when she felt it. A tugging in her insides, like someone had pulled a chain and the light came on. Sloane loved him. It probably shouldn't have come as a big shock. They'd been headed in that direction all along. But with everything going on, she'd missed the big picture. Now here it was, staring her in the face in twenty-four-bit color. The million-dollar question: Did he feel the same way?

Chapter 21

"You really want to go to this?" Brady curved his body around Sloane's, rubbing against her sweet behind.

"I'd like to support Griffin, and I have the day off."

He laughed. "Support Griffin. You just want to get a look at those big-ass houses." He glanced at his alarm clock. "I've got to get going. Breakfast is in two hours."

"Just five more minutes. You're warm."

"If I stay any longer it'll be more than five minutes and then I'll be late." They'd already made love twice that morning. With Aidan gone they were making up for lost time. Sloane had driven him to the airport in Reno yesterday. "Come over to the inn and I'll feed you. Afterward we'll go over to Sierra Heights and check out the mansionettes."

She rolled over to face him. "I'll give you ten minutes in the bathroom, then I'm coming in."

He gave her a long kiss and scooted out of bed before he changed his mind. Good to her word, Sloane met him in the shower and despite his better judgment, they did it again.

"It's gotta be a quickie, sweetness." He turned her around, pressed the palms of her hands against the tile, and took her from behind. But it wasn't enough.

Brady lifted her out of the shower and carried her to the bed, where he made love to her again, this time slower so he could feel every intake of her breath. Feel every plane of her body, which he'd already committed to memory. He held her face in his hands and the passion he saw there both excited and scared him. When had he ever let himself feel this much?

He rocked into her, back and forth, trying to make it about sex, just the pure carnal pleasure of it. But when they climaxed together, he knew it was so much more. And suddenly he couldn't get out of her bed . . . her room . . . fast enough.

"I've got to get a move on." He rolled off her, and she reached for him, laughing.

"I'm not kidding, Sloane. You want me to be late?" He tossed on his clothes, tied his tennis shoes, and gave her a quick kiss goodbye. "Lock up behind me."

At the inn, Sam greeted him with a big smile. "Lina's helping Griff, so I'll be your server today." She made a little curtsy.

"The girl can't make up her mind. She told me she wasn't going to the open house—didn't want to see Dana."

"Apparently she decided to go after all. Those two have been inseparable lately, and from what I can tell, Griffin is heavily pursuing her."

"As long as she's happy." Brady started mixing the ingredients for basil and goat cheese frittatas.

The French-toast bread pudding had sat overnight, soaking. He popped it in the oven to start baking. They had a full house, so Brady wanted plenty of variety. Sam started putting the cereals, yogurts, pastries, and fruit out on the buffet table. On the stovetop, bacon and sausages sizzled.

"Can you bring me the pans for the chafing dishes?"

Nate, holding a pastry in one hand—he must've swiped it from the dining room—and his laptop in the other, wandered into the kitchen and plopped down at the center island. "Coff—"

Brady slid him a mug and handed him the half-and-half. "Sloane's dragging me to Griff's open house today."

"You in the market for a house?"

"Hell no. But women like that kind of stuff."

"Speaking of, what's going on with your whackjob?"

"Police still don't know where she is. I hate to say this"—Brady knocked on one of the wooden cabinets—"but I think she would've struck by now if she'd been coming for me."

"What does Rhys think?" Nate took a sip of his coffee.

"I don't know what Rhys thinks, but the detective from Santa Monica agrees. He said she most likely would've shown up here before anyone noticed her missing."

"So what does he think happened to her?"

"No way to know at this point. But it's peculiar that she hasn't been using her credit or bank cards."

"Could she be dead?"

"Anything is possible." Brady poured his frittata batter into three cast-iron pans and slipped them into one of the wall ovens. "But police have checked area hospitals and morgues and there has been no one who fits her description."

"Maybe she has credit cards in someone else's name."

"Nothing would surprise me. That's why I'm not letting my guard down." Although that was a lie, because he'd stayed at Sloane's last night. He just hadn't been able to stay away from her.

"I'd like to talk to you soon about something. You're busy now with breakfast. Perhaps we could do it on Monday after the breakfast service. What do you say?"

"Sure." Brady wondered what Nate had on his mind. He didn't like surprises and didn't want to wait two days to hear what Nate had to say. "You don't want to give me a heads-up?"

"Nah. It's something we need to sit across from each other on."

A small part of him worried that Nate was thinking about firing him. As long as this thing with Sandra dragged on, it made him a liability to the inn. Brady couldn't blame Nate for wanting to protect his business and family. And it wasn't like he couldn't find another job. He could make more working at a white-tablecloth restaurant than cooking for the Lumber Baron.

"All right," Brady said. "I'll wait till Monday then."

Sloane got to the inn just as the last guests finished eating. Brady loaded a plate with frittata, French-toast bread pudding, bacon, and fresh fruit, and put it in front of her with a mug of coffee.

"Jeez, Brady, do you think I'm a lumberjack?" In tight jeans and a chambray shirt that cinched in at her small waist, she was the shapeliest lumberjack he'd ever seen.

A corner of Brady's mouth lifted. "Not even close." He grabbed a fork and sat next to her at the island. "I'll share with you."

"My forensic sculptor emailed." She took a bite of the French toast and closed her eyes in appreciation. "She has a bust of my John Doe already. Someone from the sheriff's department is delivering it on Monday. We're holding a press conference on Tuesday. But I'm giving Harlee the story as soon as the bust arrives."

"You think it'll be enough to find out who he is?"

"I hope so." She sighed. "This poor guy needs a proper burial."

He kissed her. "Nugget is lucky to have such a dedicated officer."

"Yeah, it is." She smiled and kissed him back. "I know you don't want to go, but I'm excited about seeing the big houses at Sierra Heights."

"I can think of better things to do with our time off, but I'm game. What time does it start?"

"Noon. What time do you have to be back here for wine and cheese?"

"I'm in good shape prep-wise, so as late as four. Maybe we'll have time for a nooner." He waggled his brows.

She stifled a giggle. "Didn't you get your fill this morning?"

"Hey, I'm making up for a week's worth of Aidan."

Her smile faded. "You think he'll get back with Sue?"

"He's your brother. You'd know better than me. But in my experience, when a guy puts off marriage with a woman he's been with for three years, he either doesn't want to get married—period—or she's not the one."

"It's sad. Poor Sue is in her late thirties; she wasted some of her best child-bearing years on my idiot big brother."

This kind of conversation made Brady itch. So he got busy cleaning the kitchen. They had about an hour to kill before heading to Sierra Heights.

Sam hauled in the last of the dirty dishes. "Everyone has eaten. What time are you guys going over?"

"When I'm done here," Brady said.

"Are you going?" Sloane asked, then shook her head. "Duh, you live there."

"I'm still planning to look at the homes. Griffin wants it to look busy, and frankly I'd like to see him sell some places. The neighborhood feels like a ghost town."

"Other than the empty houses, do you like living there?" Sloane brought her dishes to the sink.

"Love it. The golf course, the tennis courts, the pool, it's like having your own country club. I'm also thinking that it'll be a great place to raise kids when Nate and I . . ." She blushed. "Anyway, it's pretty terrific. Are you interested, Sloane?"

"I can't afford one of those places. But a girl can dream."

Brady wondered, if Sloane had the money would she actually buy one of Griff's mini mansions? Because that kind of investment suggested permanence to Brady, and he'd always gotten the impression that Nugget was a placeholder for Sloane until her part in taking down the corrupt cops at LAPD was a distant memory and she could go elsewhere.

By the time he finished with KP, they still had thirty minutes to spare. They burned it by browsing in the sporting goods store. For a small country shop it had a surprisingly good selection. Everything from skis and sleds to kayaks and fishing equipment. Brady hadn't been in for a while and it looked like Carl had begun stocking up for spring. Lots of biking gear and boating paraphernalia.

At a rack of bathing suits, Brady grabbed the skimpiest one he could find and held it up to Sloane. "You want me to get this for you?"

She gave him a little shove. "Shush. People can hear you." Nevertheless, she was laughing.

Brady gazed at his watch. "We can go now."

They took her Rav4 because it needed the exercise. Brady drove the short distance to Sierra Heights. Today there was a guard in the kiosk and he stopped them on their way in.

"Hey, guys." It was actually Wyatt.

Sloane bent over Brady and stuck her head out of the driver's window. "You moonlighting as Sierra Heights security now?"

"It was Darla's idea. She thought it would make a good impression on prospective buyers."

Brady checked out Wyatt's khaki pants, khaki shirt, and ridiculous hat. "Dude, you look like you're going on safari."

"Again, Darla's idea." Wyatt motioned at the line of cars behind them. "Move it along. Nothing to see here."

They zoomed past him, Sloane snorting with laughter. Brady parked in the spaces designated for the pro shop. He'd played golf here a time or two with Nate. It was a great course. He, though, was not such a great player. Then again, neither was Nate. For the most part they'd cruised around in a cart, drinking beer. Not a bad way to spend an afternoon.

Halfway to the sales office they met up with Connie and Tater. Tater was a surprise. He usually didn't participate in overly social events. Although Brady had noticed that Tater showed up at Lina's party. And come to think of it, he'd been hanging out with Connie. Sloane hadn't mentioned anything about the two of them and she was pretty tight with Connie.

"You see Wyatt at the guard station?" Connie rolled her eyes.

"Hilarious," Sloane replied.

The four of them walked into the sales office together and Dana's face dropped, knowing full well that they weren't buying any houses.

"Hey, Dana. How's it hanging?" Connie said, and Brady coughed to cover up a laugh. The dispatcher was loyal to Rhys, and by extension to Lina, he assumed.

"Welcome." Dana plastered on a fake smile and Brady had to give her credit. She looked as professional as any other big-city real estate agent with her wool suit, silk scarf, and expensive shoes. Carol Spartan used to be the only game in town, but she'd hired Dana to split duties so she could have more time to spend with her family. "A map with all the models, price sheets, and refreshments are in the clubhouse. If you have any questions you just let me or my partner, Carol, know."

"Thanks, Dana," Brady said, and led their group to the clubhouse.

"Yo, Griff," Connie called, her voice echoing through the large building that reminded Brady of a ski lodge, complete with an enormous fireplace, picture windows, and leather sofas. The flat-screen TV alone was the size of his living room.

Startled, a few people who'd been looking at a wall map of the property marked with pins to denote available homes, jerked up to stare at them. Griffin and Lina came over holding hands.

"Thanks for coming. I was worried no one would show up," Griffin said.

"Who are they?" Connie pointed at the map people.

"They saw the ads Dana placed and have been interested in the area for some time," Griffin said in a soft voice. He sounded hopeful.

Connie gave him a thumbs-up. "Hey, Tater, food." She dragged him to a table with platters of Costco cookies and coffee.

"We want to look at the models." Sloane bounced on her heels.

"They're amazing," Lina said, and waved to someone just arriving.

Brady turned around and spotted Harlee and Darla dressed to the nines. Apparently they were pretending to be real house hunters, walking around, reading the literature, and pretending not to know anyone.

"Are you guys coming to bowling tonight?" Lina reached over and grabbed two packets off a table and handed them to him and Sloane.

"We are." Sloane pretended to roll a ball down the middle of the clubhouse. "I'm ready to take Wyatt on." Everyone was aware that Wyatt belonged to a league, and Brady knew Sloane couldn't bowl.

"It'll be fun. I think my brother and Maddy may even come if they can find a sitter." Lina pointed to their packets. "That shows you where the models are. Go enjoy."

Before they went on the tour, Sloane walked up to Harlee and whispered something in her ear.

"What was that about?" Brady asked.

"I told her I had a scoop for her on Monday."

"What are you, WikiLeaks?"

"We women have to stick together." She looked down at the diagram in her packet. "Let's go to the Pine Cone first. It's the smallest at twenty-eight hundred square feet."

"Lead the way."

The place had skyscraper ceilings, twenty-foot windows, and a master bathroom the size of a two-car garage. Brady liked the log walls and oak floors. He supposed he could live here if he was forced to.

"Ehh." Sloane rocked her hand back and forth, clearly unimpressed. "Onward and upward."

Their next stop was the Sierra.

As soon as they walked into the massive foyer, Sloane said, "Now this is what I'm talking about."

Yeah, Brady had to admit, the space was pretty spectacular. The great room had so much glass that he wondered how much it would cost to heat the place. There was a loft with a wet bar and a built-in for a humongous flat-screen. He could definitely spend some quality time in this room.

"Brady, come check out the kitchen," Sloane called from downstairs.

He went down, walked through an imposing dining room with built-ins, and into the sickest kitchen he'd ever seen in a private home. First off, the architect got the layout exactly right. The sink, refrigerator, and stove formed a perfect triangle. There was so much counter top that he'd never run out of space. Miles of cupboards and pantry space and a wine refrigerator. All the stainless steel appliances were top of the line, the center island had a vegetable sink and enough room to seat six, and there was a wood-burning fireplace that could easily double as a pizza and bread oven.

"Just out of curiosity, how much is this place?"

Sloane rifled through the packet and started to laugh. "It ranges from eight hundred thousand to more than a million, depending where on the property it is. For example, golf course view, you're looking at top price. And everything in this kitchen"—she made a swirling gesture with her finger—"is an upgrade. If I had to guess, an easy hundred thou extra."

"What about this one?" He looked out the window. It didn't have a golf course view, but it looked out onto forest, mountains, and a slice of river. It worked for him. "How much?"

She laughed again. "It's the model. I don't think it's for sale."

"Griff would sell it to me," Brady said, and joined in her laughter. "You like it?"

"Uh, yeah. It's like my freaking dream home. But if we sold everything we owned we still couldn't scrounge up enough for a down payment." She grabbed his arm. "Let's go see the next one. This is fun."

It was. Brady never expected looking at model homes to be fun—in fact, he held it right up there with being waterboarded—but he was enjoying himself. He credited Sloane with that because she was fun. She had a difficult job, solving tough crimes and seeing the worst of humanity. Yet, when her work day was done, she knew how to let loose and have a good time. Life was too tenuous not to. She saw the fragility of it every day in the line of duty.

They walked through a couple more models. But he liked the Sierra the best.

"Do you think all my shabby chic stuff would go with one of these places?" Sloane joked.

"Sure. Why not? I'm doing leather couches and club chairs in mine."

Sloane's smile slipped. "Yeah . . . uh . . . that sounds perfect. Very masculine." She walked a little ways ahead of him.

When they got back into the clubhouse, Griff winked. "What did you think?"

"They're beautiful, Griffin." Sloane lowered her voice. "Any action?"

"Two parties seem really interested. Dana and Carol are working them over."

"Which ones—" Brady's phone rang. He pulled it out of his jacket pocket and checked the display. "I've got to get this." Sloane followed him to a corner of the room.

"Do you have something?" Brady didn't even bother to say hello. He figured the detective wouldn't be calling on a Saturday to make small talk.

"Yuma PD found her car," Rinek said.

"But not her?"

The detective let out an audible sigh. "Not yet. Her car was ticketed more than a week ago, before she was reported missing. An annoyed neighbor got sick of looking at it, called the Department of Public Safety, and had it towed. They ran the plate numbers and it came back to us. We're working with Yuma PD. But I'm not gonna lie to you; they won't give it high priority. She's a missing adult from California."

"Why would she leave her car parked for more than a week?" The whole thing sounded strange to Brady.

"Don't know. It was a residential neighborhood, so maybe she was visiting someone. It's a newer Toyota Camry, so I can't see her ditching the car. I just don't know, Brady. But stay vigilant and hopefully I'll have more for you next week."

Frustrated, Brady hung up. Sloane had given him space but was close enough to have heard his side of the conversation.

"They found her car?"

"In Yuma," he said. "But they don't have the first clue where she is."

Sloane scraped her upper lip with her teeth. "Rhys said her recent computer searches showed that she was looking for someone else besides you. I bet he lives in Arizona. She ever say anything about having a friend in Yuma?"

"Sloane, we didn't do much talking. And when she did talk, it was crazy stuff about how I was her destiny and that she would make me love her even though I'd only known her one night." He scrubbed his hand through his hair. "Is this ever gonna end?"

She put her arms around his waist, her cheek against his chest, and simply said, "Yes." And as much as he wanted to believe her, he couldn't.

Chapter 22

On Monday, Sloane got the bust of John Doe. It was so lifelike that it gave her the willies. Deep-set eyes, a nose with a slight bump—it had probably been broken—and a strong jaw.

The forensic sculptor had done a masterful job of reconstructing his face. She'd made a plaster cast of the skull and used modeling clay to reproduce his facial features. Of course, without knowing his hair or eye color, the thickness of his lips or how much fat tissue covered the bone, the likeness was only an approximation of what he looked like. Still, Sloane had heard that facial reconstruction—while fairly rare—had worked for other police departments to identify people who had been otherwise unidentifiable.

So, she'd thought, why not give it a crack?

She wheeled the bust, which sat on a cart, into the conference room and covered it with a blanket. Harlee had already been over to have a look and was given professional photographs of the reconstruction to feature in her article. The hope was that her story and pictures would get picked up by the wire services, including the Associated Press, since the big news outlets had zero interest in coming to Nugget for a press conference. Reporters from Sacramento and San Francisco didn't want to travel so far. So Sloane had written a press release and sent the photos by email, hoping that some of them would pick up the story that way.

The goal was to spread the photographs of the bust far and wide, in hopes that someone would recognize him. In the meantime, John Doe's reconstructed face had attracted the interest of Nugget residents to the point that they were cycling in and out of the police station like it was the Louvre.

"He looks like an ornery cuss," Owen had said, inspecting the bust like an art critic. "Shifty eyes."

"Those are glass, Owen. We don't have his real eyes."

Donna was convinced John Doe had an eating disorder. "Look how sharp his cheekbones are. He looks hungry."

Just about everyone who came in had an opinion. Her pilot kids would arrive after school. They'd been following the entire process, and Sloane couldn't wait to see their reaction. Simpson was doing a report on facial reconstruction and forensic anthropology for his science class. The mean girls had stopped picking on Rose. Sloane wasn't sure if it was because of Rhys's warning to Mr. Grant or that Rose's new-found self-esteem had repelled the bullies.

"What are you smiling about?" Rhys asked on his way back from the coffeemaker.

"I was just thinking about the pilot program."

"Griffin was over for dinner Sunday night and told me he hired Rose's big brother. From what I gathered, you set that up?"

"I just introduced them." She shrugged her shoulders.

"Right. I could've used someone like you when I was a kid." He pulled up a chair and straddled it. "You hear anything more from Rinek?"

"Not a word. Why would she just leave her car on a residential street in Yuma?"

Rhys huffed out a breath. "She have family there? Friends?"

"Not that Santa Monica PD is aware of. None of it makes sense. That other guy she was searching for on the Internet, did Rinek tell you whether her computer showed that she'd found him? Where he lives?"

"I was wondering the same thing," Rhys said. "Unfortunately, Rinek didn't tell me much. I got the feeling that I'm only on a need-to-know basis; otherwise I would've told you. You thinking he might be in Yuma?"

"It's as good a guess as any."

"You want me to give Rinek a call, see what I can get out of him?"

"Let's wait a few days."

Rhys got to his feet. "How about you? Any more texts or phone calls?"

"Nothing."

"I figured they'd eventually stop. They just wanted to mess with you. Guys like them give the rest of us a bad name." He went in his office and shut the door.

It was still a little early for lunch, but Sloane decided to take a walk across the square and say hi to Brady. But Brady was cloistered in an office with Nate.

"What's going on?" she asked Andy, and nudged her head at Nate's closed door.

"You think anyone tells me anything around here?"

She popped her head into Maddy's office, but it was empty. Deciding to come back later, she left the inn and had started back to the police station when her phone rang. Harlee.

"What's up?"

"If you've got a sec, come over. I want to show you something."

"Okay." Sloane crossed the square to the *Trib*'s office and found Harlee sitting at her desk in front of a computer.

"Look." Harlee pointed to her monitor.

It was an AP story about how Nugget PD was using facial reconstruction as last resort in finding the identity of skeletal remains that had washed up on the shore of the Feather River. There were quotes from Sloane attributed to the *Trib*. "That's great. Is there any way to find out how many papers and TV stations picked up the story?"

"No, but we can see if some of the big ones did by going to their websites." Harlee quickly searched the *New York Times*. "Nothing here yet, but the story just went out. Let me search for it on Google News." She typed *forensic facial reconstruction* into the bar. "Aha, Fox has it and so does CNN. *USA Today* and the *Sacramento Bee*. It's getting picked up."

"Wow." Sloane was surprised it was getting this much traction. And so soon. "Thanks, Harlee."

"Just remember who your buddy is when you crack this case wide open."

"I won't forget," Sloane said as she left to go back to the station to tell Rhys.

When she got back she had at least a dozen messages from the media, including *Dateline*.

* * *

"Look, if you want me to leave, I'll leave. I won't hold it against you, Nate. In fact, if the shoe was on the other foot . . . You've gotta take care of your business . . . your family."

Nate scrubbed his hand over his jaw. "What the hell are you talking about?"

Brady gave him a long look. "You're not terminating me?"

"What, over the wingnut? I thought they were hot on her heels in Arizona."

"They found her car but have no idea where she is."

"I thought we went over this already. As I recall, you offered to leave and we all said no. So why are we revisiting it?"

"I just assumed that when you wanted to have a sit-down, you'd reevaluated."

"Well, you were wrong. I'm firing Richard. Sam hates his guts and I'm quickly getting there. I'd like to replace him with his chef de cuisine. He's not a control freak and can actually take direction. He'll be fine as far as handling the food for the Theodore. But he doesn't have the chops to oversee food service for all my hotels. That, my friend, would be you, if you want it."

Brady blinked, stunned. This had not been what he'd expected.

Nate held up his hand. "Don't say no yet. I get that hotels are not your bag, and if it weren't for your current circumstances you'd likely be working toward starting your own trendy restaurant group. But it's time to come out of hiding, and this is a great opportunity, Brady. You'd have free rein over the kitchens and menus in my nine San Francisco hotels, the Lumber Baron, and Gold Mountain. Not to mention a huge budget and staff at your disposal. If somewhere down the line you want to do your own restaurant, that's a possibility too. Think of the investors you would have access to."

"What about the Lumber Baron?"

"Obviously, you would no longer have time to be making breakfast and snacks for a twenty-room inn. You'd hire someone here."

"Would I have to work out of Breyer Hotels' corporate office in San Francisco?"

"Some of the time, yeah. But you can do like Sam does and make your base here. We'll give you an office in the Lumber Baron. When you work in the city, we'll give you a suite to stay in at the Theodore."

That was Nate's flagship and one of the most decadent hotels Brady had ever seen.

Nate grabbed a Post-it pad and scribbled a figure on it. "This work for a salary?"

Brady's jaw about fell open. It was more than he'd ever made in his life—even at Pig and Tangelo, which paid just shy of six figures.

"That's not counting bonuses and benefits," Nate said, and scribbled another figure on the pad before pushing it at Brady. "You're looking at a package worth at least that."

Being an executive chef for a hotel corporation might not be as high profile as running a Michelin three-star restaurant, but it sure the hell paid better. And as long as Sandra was still on the loose, being low profile was a good thing. But would it be as creative? For the most part he'd be fine-tuning banquet and room service food. At least at the Lumber Baron he could modernize and tart up the kind of comfort dishes he'd grown up with. But hotels typically served continental cuisine in order to appeal to a large clientele. That really wasn't his thing.

"I've got to sleep on it," he told Nate.

"Absolutely. Talk to Samantha about it too. As Breyer Hotels' event planner, she'd be working with you a great deal."

They'd been buddies since his first day at the Lumber Baron, so that wouldn't be a problem. The truth was, he liked the whole Breyer clan. "I'll do that."

First person he wanted to bounce it off, though, was Sloane. Not that she factored into his decision making. The only reason was that she'd tell him whether or not taking the job would be the same as selling out. He crossed the green to the police station.

"Did you come to see the bust?" Connie asked him.

"What bust?"

Connie grabbed his sleeve, dragged him into the conference room, and whipped a blanket off . . . someone's head.

"Whoa." He jerked his head back, at first thinking it was real. "Is that the John Doe?"

"Yep. Freaky, right?"

He touched it. "It's realistic, that's for sure."

"Who knows if it really looks like him, but it looks like someone. Matt Lauer called. He wants Sloane to go on the *Today* show."

"So it's drumming up publicity, huh?"

"Harlee's story has been picked up all over the place, and the AP did something too. Apparently forensic facial reconstruction isn't all that common and it's kind of controversial as far as using it in court. Although you'd never know it from watching *CSI*."

"Why's it controversial?"

"Because there are too many unknown variables and often the sculptor is relying on artistic interpretation. A lot of people think it's too subjective. But what the hell, right? It's worth a try."

"Where's Sloane?" He hadn't seen her when he came in.

"She got called out on a DWHUA." Connie must've known he had no idea what she was talking about and supplied, "Driving with head up ass."

Brady laughed, then realized it might not be funny. Connie wasn't exactly sensitive. "Anyone hurt?"

"Nah."

"That's good. Tell Sloane I dropped by, okay?"

"Sure thing."

He decided to kill time at home and do some laundry before the afternoon service. His place could use a good cleaning too. Since he'd been spending most of his nights at Sloane's, he couldn't remember when he'd vacuumed last or thrown away the expired food in his refrigerator.

Today, he had Sloane's Rav4. She'd wanted him to drive it so it wouldn't get rusty. He parked it next to his van, did the usual security check on the windows and doors, and let himself in. The place was stuffy as hell. He opened a few windows despite it being about fifty degrees outside, and put a load of laundry in the washer. For the next half hour he tidied up, went through his mail, and cleaned the kitchen and bathroom. Sloane, he'd noticed, was a neat freak. In spite of her crazy hours, she managed to keep her place spic and span. He thought about all her ruffles, curlicues, and flowers, and smiled to himself. Yeah, he liked a girlie girl who could kick ass. Once again, he wondered what she'd think of his job offer.

If he decided to take it, the first thing he'd do was change the room-service menus. They were a good twenty years behind the times. Baked Alaska. Who did that anymore? He'd be willing to bet that not one had been sold in the last year or so. The menus needed to be seasonal. Dungeness crab in fall and winter. Squash in summer. Fresher, lighter food. For events, he'd do the same. The wedding fare at Breyer Hotels reminded him of something out of the eighties. Blackened seafood, salads drenched in raspberry vinaigrette, and pesto. Tons and tons of pesto.

No question, he could improve things at Breyer Hotels. And working for Nate and Sam would be easy peasy. They were great bosses. He got the electric broom out of the hall closet, plugged it in, and ran it through the living room. Over the whir, he heard a faint noise, like something scraping against the hardwood floor, coming from next door. Turning off the vacuum, he thought Sloane must be home. But her police rig wasn't in the driveway. He put his ear against the wall and listened. Nothing. It had probably been the broom cord slapping against the floor.

About to turn on the vacuum again, he heard something else. This time it sounded like a thumping coming from the back of the duplex. He went to the kitchen, looked out the rear window, and saw a shadow. It appeared that a person was coming around the side. Brady grabbed a cast-iron skillet on his way out and crept along the living room wall. He'd gotten as far as the front door when someone knocked.

"Ah, Jesus," he said aloud as he peeked outside. The psyching himself out had to stop. Brady put down the pan and opened the door. "Hey, Skeeter."

He'd never actually met the kid, but had seen him and his Camaro around town a few times. "Where's your car?"

"I hiked up from the train yard. I knocked on Officer McBride's back door, but I don't think she's home."

That must've been what Brady heard. "What do you got there?"

Skeeter turned red and handed Brady a box of drugstore chocolates. "It's a finder's fee for helping me get the job at the Gas and Go."

Between bringing her flowers and candy, Brady thought the kid might be harboring a crush on Sloane. "You want me to give them to her for you? I'll see her tonight." Brady made sure to say it in a way that Skeeter understood that he and Sloane were together. Petty, since the boy couldn't be more than twenty. Twenty-one at the most.

"Yeah, I don't want the critters to get it."

"No problem."

Skeeter started to walk away but stopped. "What happened to her back window?"

"What are you talking about?"

"The pane is gone." Not when Brady had done his routine check less than an hour ago. "If she's getting a new one, she shouldn't leave it open like that. Raccoons will get in and tear the place apart."

"Come in the house!" he told Skeeter, and grabbed his cell off the entry table where he'd left it when he first came in. "Call 9-1-1."

Brady picked up the skillet, went outside, and silently made his way to the rear of the duplex. Sonofabitch! Sure enough, the pane above Sloane's kitchen door was missing. Someone had used a glass cutter to pop it out. Brady didn't have time to check the door because he saw movement behind a copse of trees a few feet from the house. Crouching down, he used the propane tank enclosure for cover, and like a ghost made his way toward the grove. Slowly and as quietly as possible, Brady inched closer, desperately trying to stay out of sight. He used to hike with a former Green Beret who could sneak up on a person without so much as a faint rustle. What he wouldn't do for those skills right now.

He heard voices. They were too low to make out, but for a second Brady thought he'd been discovered. That's when he saw a gun trained on Skeeter.

I told you to stay in the house. Dammit, dammit, dammit! Brady continued toward the trees, skulking through the bushes. The armed person faced Skeeter with his back hidden from Brady's view by a giant redwood. At least Skeeter acted as a diversion as Brady tried to get closer without being detected.

He continued to hear hushed voices, but still couldn't tell what was being said. If only he could create another distraction, just enough of one that he could get to Skeeter without being detected. He considered throwing a rock down the ravine, but worried that the sudden move-ment could trip someone with a hair trigger. Almost there, he took a couple of deep breaths, wondering if Skeeter had at least called 9-1-1 before stupidly wandering into the line of fire. Idiot kid. But if any-thing happened to the boy, it would be Brady's fault. He'd always known that this would end badly.

At the grove now, he maneuvered himself behind the thick trunk of a tree, waiting for his moment. Because he knew he'd only have one. He saw the muzzle of the gun but couldn't see who held it. Brady didn't need to. In his gut he knew.

He could see Skeeter. The fear in the boy's eyes reminded Brady of a feral cat calculating a way to escape danger. He wished he could signal to him some way; get him to draw the shooter out where Brady had a clear shot. But it was too risky. So he stood stock-still, ready to pounce.

Sirens rent the silence and the gun holder spooked, lunging for Skeeter. Brady didn't think or breathe or even flinch. Lifting the skillet high, he ran closer and slammed it over the assailant's head. It wasn't until the shooter crumpled to the ground that Brady realized he hadn't hit Sandra.

"You okay?" he asked Skeeter.

"What the hell is going on?" The kid was shaken.

"I'm not entirely sure." Brady looked up from the body to see Sloane running at him with Rhys and Jake taking up the rear.

"What happened?" she yelled, skidding to a halt when she saw the man on the ground, his gun a few feet away. Brady still clutched the skillet. "My God, it's Roger Buck."

She knelt down and checked his pulse. "He's still alive," she told Rhys, and pulled her radio from her belt to call for an ambulance.

Rhys put on gloves, pried the cast-iron pan from Brady's hand, and said, "You're out of this, McBride. Jake, bag the weapon."

Sloane threw her arms around Brady. "Are you all right?"

"Yup." Brady stared down at Buck. "I thought he was Sandra."

Sloane put her finger on Brady's lips. "Don't talk without a lawyer."

Rhys rolled his eyes and read Brady his rights.

"What the hell do I need a lawyer for? He tried to break into Sloane's apartment and held a gun on Skeeter." Brady watched Jake seal the gun in a plastic bag.

An ambulance stopped at the top of the driveway and two paramedics came down carrying a gurney. Jake went with Buck and the medics and Brady and Skeeter went with Rhys to the police station, where they each gave statements. Sloane was not allowed to be present, since her being romantically involved with Brady and a former colleague of Buck's amounted to a double conflict of interest.

Brady told Rhys everything, including about the missing pane from Sloane's kitchen door, how Skeeter had likely interrupted Buck before he'd had a chance to go into the apartment. After Skeeter gave his statement, both were told they could go home. Sloane was waiting for him outside the conference room.

Rhys took one look at her and said, "That must have been Buck you saw last month. He came to case your place, I'm sure of it now. And I'm kicking myself for not having done more. If Brady hadn't been home, if Skeeter hadn't come when he had . . . God knows what you would've walked into. Dammit, Sloane, I screwed up."

"No you didn't. I wasn't sure it was even him. And then the harassing messages stopped. How could anyone have known?"

"I'll tell you this: He's not walking away. I'm gonna have his badge and anyone else's involved in harassing you. Come here." Sloane obeyed the command and Rhys wrapped her in a hug. "I'm sorry I let you down."

"No, LAPD let me down. I know you have my back, and Brady . . . he saved the day."

"He sure the hell did." Rhys shook his head. "And with a fry pan, no less."

Chapter 23

"What are you doing?" Lina lounged in Griffin's bed, watching him empty the dresser in his room.

"Making space for you to put your stuff. There's also plenty of room in the closet." Together, they couldn't fill the giant walk-in unless Lina owned a department store.

"Griff, it's bad enough that my family thinks I was in my Reno apartment last night. It's a small town. I don't want to be caught in a lie."

"I don't want you to lie, I want you to move in. Officially. You already said that keeping the Reno place was a waste of money."

"Griffin, slow down. All of a sudden you seem like you're in such a rush. Is there something you're not telling me?"

"Of course not. It's just that we can finally be a real couple now."

"We can be a real couple without me moving in." She got out of bed and Griff watched her walk to the bathroom. Lina took his breath away. A few minutes later she came out, wearing his robe. The thing swallowed her. "I'll stay when I can. But it seems a little soon to be moving in."

"Lina, do you love me?"

She blinked at him in surprise. "I've loved you since the first day I met you. What kind of question is that?"

"I don't know. You just don't seem as committed to this as I do."

"When I was committed to it, you weren't. In fact, I overwhelmed you with my commitment." She laughed. "I don't want to do that again."

He pulled her into his arms, tugged open her belt, and let his hands roam over her body. "You won't. I'm all the way in this time."

She tilted her head back as he fondled her breasts. "Mmm."

"I love you." He slid the robe off her shoulders and let it fall to the floor and walked her backwards to the bed. "I've always loved you. But now the time is right."

"Because you say it is?" she teased.

Griffin stopped touching her. "Because you're truly a grown-up now. You have to admit, Lina, you weren't back then."

She went down on the bed and took him with her. "I've done some maturing."

He let his gaze sweep over her. "Yes, you have."

She started to say something and he covered her mouth with his lips. "No more talking."

He caressed every inch of her with his hands and lips. She pushed his shorts down. They bunched around his feet and he kicked them off.

"You smell good," he whispered in her ear. "And taste good."

"Am I allowed to talk now?" She let out a giggle when he swirled his tongue around her ear and nibbled on her lobe.

"Only sex talk." He licked and laved his way down her body.

"Mmm. Lower," she pleaded in a breathy voice that drove Griff wild.

He lifted up, cocked his brows, and went directly to the spot she begged for. She clutched his head, wound her fingers through his hair, arched her back, and screamed out his name when he brought her to orgasm. It hadn't taken long. She went off like an air-raid siren.

He moved over her, molding her breasts in his hands. God, how he'd missed these breasts. They were round and firm and larger than expected for such a petite woman. Her brown nipples puckered prettily and he whorled his tongue over each one while she moaned with pleasure.

He still couldn't believe she'd waited for him. Nearly two years of college and she hadn't been with a man. Not until last night, with him. In the beginning, when they'd first started seeing each other, it had been a constant fight. She'd wanted to make love with him and he'd wanted her to wait. After they'd broken up and she started seeing students her own age, Griffin had been convinced that she'd lose her virginity to one of them.

"You sore?" He wanted her again but was afraid it was too much so soon.

"No. Please."

He touched her between her legs. "You sure?"

She ground into his hand just to let him know she meant business. Damn, he loved this woman. Griffin reached for a condom on the nightstand, rolled it on, and slid into her. Gazing down on her, he slowly took her up, loving her until they were both so close that he quickened the tempo. When she gave a little shudder and closed her eyes, he knew he'd hit the sweet spot.

She wrapped her legs around his waist and he plunged into her, deeper and faster. As she called out, he ravaged her mouth with hunger. He could feel her heat and her heart thudding. His own heart felt ready to burst. He pumped once, twice, three more times and let himself go. For a few seconds his mind and body went numb. He just lay like a human blanket over Lina. If he stayed pressed against her much longer, he'd be hard again in no time.

He rolled to his side and tugged her so that her head rested on his chest like a pillow. "You okay?"

"I don't believe I've ever been better." She kissed his shoulder as the morning light filtered in between the blinds, making shadow lines on the wall.

He sifted his hand through her dark hair, rubbing a long lock between his fingers. "If you moved in we could do this every night."

"And then I'd never get my studying done." She turned, resting her forearms on his chest so she could look at him. "What if I kept the apartment in Reno and stayed with you when I'm in Nugget? That way when I need to knuckle down on my studies I'll stay there."

If that's all he could get, he'd take it. "That would work."

"Rhys won't like it."

That was an understatement.

"I'll talk to him," Griffin said. "Make sure he understands that we're serious. Because we are serious, right?"

"I've always been serious about you, Griffin. Always. But I'm only twenty. I need to finish school, and when I'm done I want to build bridges, make something of myself before I settle down."

"That doesn't mean we can't be a couple. I'll go with you while you build bridges."

Her lips curved up and she kissed him. "I'd like that."

"I'll get another dresser then." He cocked his head at the one he'd already emptied.

* * *

For three days straight, people had been calling the hotline with tips about John Doe. Ever since Sloane had done the *Today* show, the phone had been ringing off the hook. Yet nothing had panned out.

Sloane hadn't even gotten to meet Matt Lauer. Although the show had offered to fly her to New York, Sloane had opted to go to the NBC studio in Reno to do the live interview remotely. Easier, and after what had happened with Buck, she'd wanted to stay close to home for a while. For that reason the closest she'd gotten to Lauer was having his voice transmitted to her through a tiny bug in her ear. *Today* had sent a camera person to Nugget to film the bust and get B-roll footage of the station. Sloane's entire family had seen the show in Chicago and hadn't stopped razzing her about it.

Brady had been less enthusiastic, worrying that the publicity would bring more trouble to her door. At Brady's hand—or skillet— Buck had suffered a bad concussion. In the meantime, he'd been put on unpaid administrative leave from the department, pending an investigation. That was pretty much cop code for he was getting fired. Rhys had come through, raising holy hell with LAPD, threatening to go to the FBI and the press if the chief didn't take action against the men harassing Sloane.

Internal affairs had launched a full-blown inquiry. So far, it looked as if Roger Buck, distraught over his partner's suicide, had been the main instigator. The original posse of trouble makers had let their anger go after Sloane left the department. But Roger had held on to his grudge like it was life support. He'd told Jake, who'd known the detective since his days at LAPD, that he'd only meant to vandalize her apartment. "Put a little fear into the bitch," is what he'd said.

Sloane hoped Buck got the help he needed. As for Brady, these last few days he'd seemed to be somewhere else entirely. Quiet, distant, and broody. She suspected that he was waiting for the other shoe to drop with Sandra or preparing to bolt—from her, from Nugget, from anything that held roots. The thought of him leaving ripped her heart out. She'd tried to talk to him about it, but he wasn't receptive to conversation.

"Sloane, you've got a call on line two," Connie called across the room.

"Who is it?"

"Someone who saw *Today* and claims to have information." Connie rolled her eyes.

They'd gotten a lot of nuts, as was common in high-profile cases. People claiming to be psychic, people wanting a substantial reward for information, people saying they have known John Doe in a past life. You name it, they got it. Every once in a while a legit tip came in. But nothing that had led to anything substantive. Sloane was starting to come to terms with the possibility that they might never solve the case.

"This is Officer McBride." She waited for the person on the other end to respond. "Hello."

"I think the man you found may be my son." There was something in the woman's voice, a tremor of such utter despair, that Sloane sat up straighter.

"Why is that, ma'am?"

"I have a photo. Is there a number or an email address I can send it to?"

Sloane gave the department's email address and waited while the caller sent the photo. A short time later an email appeared, and Sloane clicked on the attachment. The picture, a young man maybe nineteen or twenty, bore a close resemblance to the bust.

"This is your son?"

"Yes. He disappeared four years ago."

They hadn't gone back that far in NamUs because the forensic folks speculated that he'd died in November. Those were some well-preserved bones if he'd actually been lying in the outdoors for that long.

"From where, ma'am?"

"We're from Pennsylvania, but Kevin was attending the San Francisco Conservatory of Music. He was there less than a year when we stopped hearing from him. The school told us he'd stopped attending classes after six months."

"Did you file a missing persons report?"

"With the San Francisco Police Department. When they discovered that he'd terminated the rental agreement on his apartment and friends told investigators that he'd left to travel, they stopped looking for him. He was an adult, Officer McBride."

"And during those four years you never heard from him?"

"My son suffered from debilitating depression. He was better when he took his medication. Without it, he was erratic. We just prayed that he was okay and would eventually contact us again."

Wanting to check Kevin's missing person report, Sloane got his full name, date of birth, and social security number. She had his mother's contact information from the email, but double-checked it with her. "Mrs. Fagan, did Kevin have a dentist we can contact?"

"Both his dental records and DNA are with your state's Department of Justice." She'd started to cry, clearly understanding the implications of what Sloane was asking. They would use Kevin's dental records and DNA to match the teeth and DNA they'd extracted from John Doe's skull. "For a long time I worried that this day would come. Having a child with a mental illness . . . it's difficult, to say the least. Although the San Francisco police stopped looking for him, they submitted his information to the Missing and Unidentified Persons Unit at our request. It's all right there, Officer McBride."

"Mrs. Fagan, do you know why your son would've come to Nugget?"

"I didn't even know of the town's existence until I saw you on television. My husband and I have only been to California three times—the first time to bring Kevin to school, the other two to search for him."

"I understand," Sloane said. This had to be sheer hell for her. "You said your son went to a music school. What instrument did he play?" She hadn't mentioned to Matt Lauer the forensic findings that John Doe had likely played a woodwind instrument.

"He could play everything. By the time he was ten, his instructors told us we had a virtuoso on our hands. But Kevin's main instrument was the clarinet."

From everything Mrs. Fagan had told Sloane, it sounded like Kevin could very well be their John Doe. It still, however, didn't answer how he'd died. But as soon as Sloane could confirm his identity, she'd get to work on the next piece of the puzzle.

"Officer McBride, if it is our son, we'd like to come there and see to the transfer of the remains ourselves. We want Kevin home."

The coroner would handle that, and Sloane didn't know if for health reasons it was even allowed for a private party to transport bones across country. She would check to see if they could make arrangements with a mortuary, but at this point they were jumping the gun.

"Let's take this one step at a time. I'm going to try to rush these tests to make a positive ID and then I'll be in touch. In the meantime, if you have any questions at all, you call me." She gave Mrs. Fagan her cell phone number. Her heart went out to the woman. Even if this wasn't Kevin, it had to be unbearable to not hear from your son in four years.

When Sloane got off the phone, she found Rhys, Jake, and Connie hovering around her desk. No doubt Wyatt would've been there too, if he wasn't riding patrol.

"You get something?" Rhys asked.

Sloane let out a long sigh. "I think so." She told them what she'd learned, starting with Kevin's disappearance four years ago.

Rhys let out a whistle when he saw the photograph. "Pretty damn close. The cheeks are a little sharper and the nose slightly wider on our dummy, but good enough for government work."

"You think he died four years ago and we just found him now?" she asked.

"Not likely," Jake said. "The forensic anthropologist could tell from the lack of soft tissue left on the skeleton and cracks on the bones from weather. There is certainly room for error. But four years? I don't think so."

"He could've become a drifter, falling off the grid for the last four years . . . especially if he was mentally ill and off his meds . . . and died recently," Rhys said. "The question is, did he die of natural causes or was it a homicide? Since there's no physical evidence of a homicide, I'm leaning toward natural causes. But if you're able to confirm his ID, you'll have a little more to go on. Maybe someone will remember a Kevin Fagan, if he continued to use that name."

Rhys slung his jacket over his shoulder and headed for the door. "Good work, McBride. Go home."

It was too late to contact the Missing and Unidentified Persons Unit at the state DOJ. She'd get on it first thing in the morning.

"You going home too?" she asked Jake.

"Pretty soon. Just have to finish a report." He'd gone back to his desk and was on the computer. "You hear anything new about Buck?"

"No. I was gonna ask you the same."

"He'll be out on his ass. The question is, will they let him keep his pension? I hope not."

Sloane didn't care. She just wanted to be left alone. "I seem to attract trouble, don't I?"

He looked up from what he was doing. "You're one of the good guys, Sloane. Trouble's over and we've got your back."

They did indeed. Rhys, Jake, Connie, and Wyatt were colleagues she could depend on. Especially Rhys, who'd taken a chance on her and had remained her stalwart supporter, even going up against a department a thousand times the size of Nugget PD on her behalf.

She went home, hoping to drag Brady to the Ponderosa. At least go for a run. It didn't get dark until seven now, and the evenings had gotten warmer. It took a few minutes for him to answer the door. Usually he waited on the porch for her. Sloane caught a glimpse of his laptop on the coffee table and asked what he was up to.

"Research," he said.

"Research about what?"

"Restaurants."

One word answers weren't really her thing, so she didn't press. Clearly he was looking for jobs. With Sandra in the wind for so long, maybe he felt safer about resuming his old life. Without her. She couldn't think about it right now. The prospect of him leaving made her chest squeeze to the point that she couldn't breathe. So she changed the subject entirely.

"I may have found the identity of John Doe."

"Seriously?" He ushered her in and she grabbed the spot on the sofa where he'd been sitting so she could snoop at what he'd been looking at on the computer. But the screen was on Google. "What happened?"

She told him the story like she had Rhys, Jake, and Connie. "Sad, huh?"

"Really sad. You think it's for sure him?"

"I do. Everything fits. It's just weird that he goes missing four years ago and dies in November. Doesn't it seem odd to you?"

"Not necessarily." Brady's theory was similar to Rhys's. "Strange that he would come to Nugget, though. And how did he get here? No one ever found an abandoned car, right?"

"Nope. That was one of the first things I checked. A bus perhaps. As soon as the DNA test is done and I know for sure it's him, I'll look at bus records." Although it was a railroad town, the trains only carried cargo. Presumably, he could've been a freight hopper. But there would be no way to tell unless railroad personnel busted him and kept records. Doubtful.

"You hungry?" he asked.

"I thought we'd go to the Ponderosa. Give you a little break from cooking."

"Okay. Let me just put on a different shirt." He had on a sweat-shirt that had seen better days but looked comfy.

She followed him into his bedroom, sat on the edge of the bed, and watched as he tugged the ratty hoody over his head. He stretched, grabbing the top of the door frame, and his arms and chest rippled with muscle. She could never get enough of looking at him. His broad shoulders. The smattering of hair that sprinkled his chest and disappeared under the waistband of his jeans. Washboard abs to die for.

And the thing about Brady was that he was as nice and kind as he was good-looking. Finding both in a man was a rarity in Sloane's opinion. Most of the handsome men she'd known had been conceited and self-entitled.

"Brady?"

"Hmm?"

"What's going on? You seem different lately . . . quiet."

He pulled a long-sleeved thermal over his head, followed by a T-shirt, and sat next to her on the bed. "If it hadn't been for Skeeter, I would've missed Roger Buck breaking into your apartment. More than likely he would've been there waiting for you when you got home."

"But you didn't miss it. You clocked him, knocked him out cold."

"Yeah, what if I hadn't?"

"Then I would've clocked him and knocked him out cold."

"With all due respect, Sloane, you're what? Five seven? A hundred and forty pounds? I don't care if you're trained in self-defense or carry a gun. So is Buck, and he could've crushed you."

"Brady, why are you doing this? Everything turned out all right. You saved the day and it's over."

"That's the thing, Sloane. Who knows if it's over?" She knew he was talking about Sandra. "Next time it might not turn out so lucky."

"Brady, it's honesty time. What are you really trying to tell me? I feel like the past few days . . . the Buck drama . . . should have brought us closer together. Instead, it's driven a wedge between us. You've hardly talked to me and you seem a million miles away—like you're done with this, with us. So, I'll just lay it on the line for you because I don't want to wind up like Aidan and Sue. And after everything that's happened, it's become crystal clear to me that I'm in love with you. I want the house and the kids. Maybe not right now, but some-day." She looked at him, hard. "I'm not asking for an instant proposal. But we go to Sierra Heights to look at those houses, and even playing around you made sure to let me know that the idea of us living together was out of the question. You once said that couples should be on the same page. Brady, are we on different pages?"

He just sat there, stiffly. Minutes went by and he said nothing. Sloane could hear him breathing—or perhaps that was her taking in nervous gulps of air—and the low hum of the heater. More time ticked by and still nothing. It seemed like an eternity. Finally, Sloane realized that the silence spoke louder than words.

She got to her feet and left.

Chapter 24

Sloane drove off. Brady could hear her studded tires churning the gravel on the driveway. He should've said something. But when she'd thrown out the confession that she loved him, he froze like the proverbial animal caught in the headlights. The words had paralyzed him. Not because he'd never heard them before, but because he wasn't ready to return them.

Love was too complicated, came with strings attached, and in his experience usually involved loss. Case in point his parents. Rationally, he knew he was emotionally stunted. People died, they got divorced, they went away. That was life. So when someone perfect came along, like Sloane, you embraced and cherished every moment together.

Except he wasn't made that way. For him, feelings were messy, constricting, and petrifying. As soon as they got too intense, he packed a duffle and said sayonara.

After Buck, he'd put off telling Sloane about his job offer. He was starting to think that working for Breyer Hotels was all wrong for him. Initially, he'd been seduced by the money and the opportunity to make his mark. But Brady liked the restaurant scene, liked partying, liked being his own man. And it was getting time for him to move on anyway. Nugget was starting to feel too permanent—like roots. And leaving now might put psycho Sandra off his scent.

He'd tell Nate tomorrow. Breyer had waited long enough, probably figuring that Brady was still recovering from the Roger Buck ordeal. The only thing he regretted was not hitting that bastard harder. Every time Brady thought about Sloane walking into her apartment with Buck lying in wait, it made his stomach knot.

He got off the bed, went into the kitchen, and got a few ingredients out of the refrigerator. Breaking a couple of eggs into a bowl, he started an omelet. He wasn't the least bit hungry but he needed something to do. Something to keep busy.

The night dragged on, with him jumping up every hour or so to look for Sloane's SUV. Around nine he saw her headlights come down the driveway and felt a combination of relief and anxiety. He needed to tell her he was leaving. Not tonight, but soon. He at least owed her a face-to-face goodbye. The hardest part was that he loved her—he wasn't so emotionally stunted that he didn't know what that felt like—and if he were a settling-down kind of guy she'd be the one. But he wasn't.

He slept badly and was happy to finally see daylight filter through his blinds so he could stop tossing and turning and get up. This morning he planned to make bacon-and-egg soufflés for the inn's guests. It took a little longer than most of his breakfast dishes, but he had the time.

After a quick shower he got dressed and arrived at the inn before the day shift. Andy sat slumped over with his head cradled on the front desk, sleeping.

"Hey, wake up." Brady gave him a little shove. "Not too professional there, buddy." Why the hell hadn't Nate fired the guy?

He continued to the kitchen and gathered up his ingredients, starting on the soufflés. While he was at it, he might as well make the coffee cake Nate liked so much, and got started on that too. Lina popped her head in.

"What are you doing here so early?"

He looked up from the flour canister. "It's not that early. Want coffee?"

"Yes!"

Brady poured in the beans, filled the water reservoir in the grind-and-brew, and flipped the switch. "You send Andy home?"

"Not yet." She looked at her watch and smiled evilly. "He's got fifteen more minutes on the clock."

Brady chuckled, then took a few seconds to look at her. She glowed like a woman who was in love. "You and Griffin working out?"

She lit up like the Las Vegas strip. "We're good."

He tilted his head sideways and grinned. "What, did you run off and elope?"

"No. We're being very mature. I've got school and he's got his businesses, so we're staying super chill. When I'm in Nugget I'll stay with him at the Heights, and he'll stay with me some of the time in Reno."

"The Heights?" Brady lifted his brows.

"That's what Nate calls it."

Yeah, that would be Nate. "Sounds... mature." The coffee was finished brewing and he poured them each a cup.

Sam came in a few minutes later and Brady poured her one too.

"You're early," she said to Brady, and turned to Lina. "Look how cute you look."

"Thanks, you too." Lina looked at her watch again. "I guess it's time to let Andy go home." She hopped off the stool and took her coffee with her.

As soon as Lina was out of earshot, Sam said, "She and Griffin are officially an item."

"So I heard."

"Rhys doesn't like her sleeping over at his house."

"Nope, I suspect he doesn't. But my guess is he partook in plenty of sleepovers when he was her age."

"I bet you're right." Sam let out a laugh. "So how are you doing, Brady? I understand that the cop you clobbered is losing his job. Thank God. Rhys is trying to get a bunch of them fired."

"Yep," was all he said.

She watched him for a little while as he spread out a number of ramekins for his soufflés. "Please tell me you're taking the job."

Brady exhaled. "I'm sorry, Sam, but it's not for me."

Her face fell. "If it's the money, Nate will give you more. He'd kill me if he knew I told you that. But I want you to take the position so badly. You're so great to work with—and fun. Richard is as far from fun as a nuclear holocaust. Come on, why don't you want to do it?"

"I'm leaving, Sam."

"What?" Her expression turned shocked. "The Lumber Baron? Nugget? What about Sloane? You two are so great together. Everyone thinks so."

Brady's phone rang and for once he was happy for the interruption. "I've got to take this," he said and looked at the caller ID. He really did have to take it. "Hello, Detective."

"You sitting down? Sandra Lockhart is dead. Yuma PD just called.

She's been in the morgue this whole time. They just got around to linking her to our missing person."

Brady staggered to the stool Lina had left empty and sat down. "Are you absolutely sure?"

"Without a doubt, unless the DNA tests lied."

"This is gonna sound horrible, but can I see a picture?" Brady was having trouble grasping that she was really dead.

"Won't do you any good. She was burnt beyond recognition."

"Burnt?"

"Investigators believe she was trying to set a house on fire and got caught in the flames. An arson team is still looking at it, though."

Brady remembered Aidan's off-the-cuff remark on the gas stations. "Whose house?"

"A former boyfriend. Apparently she thought he was home when she climbed up on his roof, poured a five-gallon mixture of gasoline and diesel down the chimney, and tossed in a propane lighter rigged with a zip tie to keep it lit. She was scrambling down the ladder when pressure from the fire blew the roof off. Luckily, her intended target was working late. But the guy had a friend staying in the house . . . she probably mistook him for the ex. The friend smelled smoke and got out before the explosion. The owner came home to find what was left of his house teeming with firefighters. Turns out her car was parked only a few blocks away. They found something like nine gas cans in her trunk."

Brady got a sick feeling. "Was she coming for me next?"

"That's the working theory. But who knows? The broad was crazy. The good news: You have your life back, amigo. Go ahead and live it."

Brady hung up and put his phone away, stunned.

"That was about your stalker, wasn't it?"

He'd forgotten that Sam was still there. "Yeah. She's dead, burned to death in a fire."

The soufflés. He got up and went back to his batter.

"Brady, I think you should sit down." She hovered over him. "I can do that."

"I've got it." He poured the mixture into the individual ramekins and finished buttering the pans for the coffee cake.

"Wouldn't you like to go over to the police station and tell Sloane?"

"After breakfast." He was having enough trouble digesting the information. Sandra was dead. He hadn't wanted her to die, but knowing that his nightmare was over, that he was free . . .

When the last guest finished breakfast, Brady went home. He needed some time alone to think his life through and get used to the idea that he no longer had to hide. Or compulsively watch his back. Flipping open his laptop, he went on Facebook. Never again would he have to see himself with Sandra in Photoshopped pictures or read posts about their fabricated vacations—or worry about her coming to Nugget to burn his house down.

He still couldn't wrap his head around the fact that she died while trying to kill an ex-lover. On a whim, he picked up his phone and called Frank Klein. The last time he'd talked to him was to give notice at Pig and Tangelo.

"Frank, it's Brady Benson."

"Jesus Christ, I've been looking for you for months. What, you go to Nepal to find yourself or something?"

"Nope. I've been living in this small town in the Sierra Nevada, cooking for a beautiful bed and breakfast." Brady could actually divulge that information now. Damn, it felt good.

"You changed your number. I didn't recognize the area code. Any chance you can come back? My chef, a prima donna who couldn't cook his way out of a hospital commissary, left. I have Paulie running the place."

"Seriously?" Brady laughed. Paulie used to be his sous chef. Nice kid, but nowhere ready for prime time. "I'll have to think about it." He was actually considering heading for Portland. Good restaurant scene there.

"Brady, I'll make you a partner in Pig and Tangelo. Fifty-fifty split." The restaurant must be in real trouble.

"I'll think about it, Frank. Hey, it was good talking to you."

He'd just pocketed the phone when Sloane's police rig came down the driveway. Through the window he saw her get out of the driver's seat. He walked out on the porch.

"I heard the news," she said, and climbed the stairs.

"Yeah. Wild, huh?"

"Could we sit for a second?"

He sat on the swing and patted the space next to him. She took the rocker instead.

"Sam said you were pretty shaken up after getting the call. She got the impression from your side of the conversation that Sandra may have been coming for you too."

"It seems clear that it was like what Aidan said. She was looking for gas stations to buy her accelerant. Beatty, Tonopah, Carson City. Next stop Nugget. I keep thinking, what if you'd been sleeping with me when she set the place on fire?"

"But she didn't, Brady. She never even made it to the Nevada border."

He put his face in his hands. From the minute Rinek had called and he'd realized Sandra's grand scheme, the horrific thought of Sloane being in the duplex while Sandra set it ablaze looped through his head.

"I'm leaving in two weeks," he blurted, planning to give notice as soon as he got back to the inn for the afternoon service.

Sloane tensed. "For good?"

"Who's to say? But I thought I'd check out Portland. The van's been packed since I got here, so I guess I never meant to stay."

"I thought you liked it here, that it reminded you of home?"

"I do and it does. But it's time to go. Look at my history, Sloane. I never stay in one place too long."

She got up and crouched down in front of him. Her eyes were wet and she quickly tried to wipe them with the back of her hand. "You've been through a lot these past few days. Buck. Sandra. Take a few days off and go away. Give yourself time to think."

He stood, holding his hand out to help her up. When they were facing each other he said, "I'm sorry, Sloane. I never said it, but I do love you. I just can't give you what you want. The house, the kids . . . just not in my DNA."

"I understand," she said, but it came out like a croak. "No hard feelings."

He wiped her tears with his hand. "Ah, Sloane, I can't stand to see you cry."

"I'm gonna go now." She backed up. "Take care of yourself, Brady."

She practically ran to her truck, started the engine and took off. He continued to stand on the porch while a couple of blackbirds, perched on a sugar pine branch, chuckled at each other. Or maybe they were chuckling at him for being a fool.

* * *

Sloane went back to the station, parked, and sat long enough to compose herself. One look in her rearview mirror and she knew there was no way to get rid of the puffy eyes. The bell over the door in the station rang as she walked in, and Connie looked up from her computer.

"The Fagans are en route. They booked a room at the Lumber Baron."

Sloane threw up her arms. "We don't even know for sure that it's their son. The DNA tests could take weeks, even months."

Connie hitched her shoulders. "They're probably on a plane by now. What happened to your face? You look like you got hit by the ugly stick."

"Allergies. I get 'em in March."

"You want a Zyrtec?"

"Nah, they make me sleepy." Sloane started for her desk to check the progress of the case. She at least wanted to have something to tell the Fagans when they got here.

"McBride, you got a second?" Rhys stood over her.

"Sure." She followed him into his office, where he shut the door and signaled for her to take a seat. "Everything okay?"

"Buck got his walking papers today and two other detectives were moved out of robbery-homicide. They won't be fired, not enough evidence that they were in on the harassment. But the department knows it has a problem on its hands and is trying to break up the group and make enough people's lives miserable so that they'll quit. They're worried about a lawsuit."

"I never said anything about suing."

"I may have mentioned it." Rhys wore a grin the size of Texas. "Between that and pressures of a federal investigation, I don't think you have anything to worry about. Buck's getting his pension. But if he so much as sends you a birthday card, LAPD will pull it. I don't like that he's getting it after what he put you through. Still, the threat of cutting him off is a nice insurance policy that he'll leave you alone."

"Thank you, Rhys, for doing everything you did. I'm happy to have this behind me."

Rhys leaned back in his chair. "You could probably go anywhere you want now. With all your good press—the *Today* show, *48 Hours*, the newspaper clippings—Officer Sloane McBride is a hot property.

During our first interview you told me that you went into law enforcement because you wanted to make a difference. You've made a difference here. The pilot program and the child-ID-kit fair made a big impact on this town. Probably bigger than you'll ever know. And the John Doe case you're about to solve . . . well, I don't have to tell you what that kind of closure means to a grieving family. Just ask Emily Mathews McCreedy what it's like to never know."

He pulled forward. "The thing is, Sloane, it's difficult to make a dent in the big city. In a town the size of Nugget a little bit goes a long way. We need you here."

"Thank you, Chief." Tears sprung to her eyes. If she didn't get out of his office soon, Sloane would start bawling all over him. "I appreciate it."

"No pressure." And there it was again. That damn Texas-sized grin.

Sloane went back to her desk. What she really wanted to do was go to the bathroom, lock herself in, and cry her eyes out. Through the window she could see Brady parking his van in front of the Lumber Baron. If she continued to watch him, she'd start blubbering in the middle of the police station. Instead, she buried herself in her email. Someone from the DNA lab at the DOJ's Bureau of Forensic Services wrote to say that they were working on the analysis. But Sloane wasn't given a time frame for when the results would be in. Likely there was a long line ahead of her. She hoped the Fagans hadn't gotten on a plane for nothing.

Her kids came after school, anxious to hear if there'd been a conclusive match between John Doe and Kevin Fagan. She explained that it might take a while, depending on how backed up the lab was. She put them to work passing out Neighborhood Watch fliers. At some point she'd like to get them badges or vests, something similar to what the Scouts wore, to make them feel official.

By six o'clock she realized that she was just going through the motions and went home. Brady's van was gone. She figured he was out, celebrating his newfound freedom. On second thought, Brady wasn't the type to rejoice in Sandra's death, even if she had made his life a living hell. More than likely he'd gone out after work for a bite. The next two weeks would be excruciating living next door to him, knowing that he was leaving.

She went inside her apartment and rummaged through the refrigerator for something to make for dinner. Aidan had left a message, but Sloane didn't have the energy to call him back. She was angry with him anyway. He and Brady were cut from the same cloth—men who couldn't commit. Channel surfing, she tried to immerse herself in a TV show but couldn't find a program to hold her attention for long. As far as she could tell, Brady still wasn't home. Not that she listened or watched for him.

Since Jake was on call tonight, Sloane decided to pop a couple of Advil PMs and call it an early night. She woke up groggy the next morning, padded into the kitchen to make a pot of coffee, and noticed that Brady's van was still gone. Either he'd come and left or he'd stayed out all night. She made a mental note to make sure that he showed up for work today. Perhaps he'd taken her advice and put in for a vacation.

Sloane showered, dressed, and slurped down a cup of coffee. On her way out, she slyly peeked through Brady's window to see if she could tell whether he'd been home. Everything looked the same. But then again, it always did in that sparsely furnished apartment of his. She supposed not accumulating a lot of stuff made it easy for him to leave.

She made the short drive to work, trying to put him out of her head, and parked in her usual space in front of the police station. Across the square, Brady's van was also in its usual spot. There went her theory about him taking time off.

"Hey, some guy keeps calling you," Connie said, shoving a handful of Post-its at Sloane as she walked into the station house. "Says it's urgent."

Sloane glanced down at the messages and didn't recognize the name or the number. The area code was San Francisco, though. "Have the Fagans come in yet?"

"Not yet."

She supposed she could stroll over to the inn and greet them. The problem with that was she'd likely bump into Brady. Instead, she plopped down at her desk and called back Urgent Guy.

"Zattrell Liquor," a man answered, and Sloane checked to make sure she'd dialed correctly.

"I'm looking for Steve Bucci."

"Speaking. You that lady cop?"

"I'm Officer McBride. What can I do for you?"

"I know the guy you made that sculpture of, the one on the morning show. The kid used to do odd jobs for me, not quite right in the head."

"Do you remember his name, Mr. Bucci?"

"Of course I do. Kevin Fagan."

Sloane jerked her head in surprise. For once, all the stars seemed to be aligning. "When was the last time you saw Kevin, Mr. Bucci?"

"It was right around Halloween. I remember that because he and I laughed at some of the people walking around in the Tenderloin in their costumes. I told Kevin, 'Don't those idiots know that they'll get knifed down here?' I don't remember seeing him too much after that."

"Do you know where he was living or who his friends were?"

"He lived on the streets. Sometimes under the Bay Bridge on Fifth Street. His friends were a bunch of junkies who I wouldn't let in the store. But he sometimes talked to one of my regulars, a musician."

"You know how to get ahold of him?" Sloane asked.

"No. But he usually comes in the store a couple times a week. I could ask him to give you a call."

"He can call me collect, Mr Bucci. And here's the number for my cell." She asked him to read it back to her just to make sure he'd taken it down accurately. "Thank you for passing this information along. You've been extremely helpful."

"So it wasn't a prank?" Connie said as soon as Sloane got off the phone.

"Nope. He also recognized our bust as Kevin Fagan. Apparently, he'd been living on the streets of San Francisco—at least until the end of October."

"So how did he wind up here?" Rhys had come out of his office.

"I was waiting for the DNA results before I talked to Greyhound, Amtrak, and Plumas County Transit. But I'll start today."

She got on the phone and started calling every transportation company she could find between Nugget and San Francisco, working on the premise that Kevin probably hadn't had a lot of money for traveling expenses. At least she had the picture of Kevin that Mrs. Fagan had sent her. Even though it was four years old, she could send it to the companies and ask that they show it to drivers on the route. It might spark a memory. As a last resort she'd check flight manifests, but she'd need a court order for that. For the next couple of hours,

Sloane made call after call. Just before noon, Connie waved to her from across the room.

"A David Salzmann is on line four. He says a Steve Bucci told him to call."

"Thanks, Connie." Sloane grabbed line four. "Hi, Mr. Salzmann, this is Officer McBride. I appreciate you calling."

"Steve from Zattrell Liquor informed me of your investigation. I had no idea that Kevin had passed."

"We're not sure that he has, Mr. Salzmann. But he apparently looks a lot like a man who died here in the fall."

"It must be him. Did you find the body near my cabin?"

"Your cabin?" Sloane took a deep breath.

"Yes. I inherited a small cabin in your quaint little town six years ago. I lent use of it to Kevin."

"You must've been very good friends."

"Not precisely. But we both shared a love of music." Salzmann took a long pause and Sloane waited him out. "I was a violinist for the San Francisco Chamber Orchestra. Unfortunately, like Kevin, I had a substance abuse problem. I'm now three years sober. Kevin was still grappling with his addiction. And living on the streets is filled with temptation. We both thought my little cabin in the woods would be a good place for him to get clean. Sadly, it doesn't look like it turned out that way."

"When was the last time you were at the cabin, Mr. Salzmann?"

"Not since six years ago. It's a dusty, rustic shack, really. At the time I inherited, it wasn't even worth selling. I've held on to it all this time, thinking that at some point the market for a plot of country land might improve."

"Where is the cabin? And do we have your permission to search it?"

"Of course. It's a little difficult to find." He gave Sloane directions. She had a vague idea of where it was, but hoped that Rhys, who knew every inch of the area, could find the cabin.

"Do you know how Kevin got here?"

"Right before leaving San Francisco he traded one of his Buffet Crampon clarinets for a used Volkswagen Beetle. I helped him with the transaction."

"Mr. Salzmann, do you know when he left San Francisco?"

"I believe he left early November. That's when I had the utilities turned on at the cabin. But Kevin wasn't the most reliable person. And I wasn't sure that he'd actually follow through. In fact, I planned to visit in spring to determine whether to keep the power on."

"Kevin didn't have a phone?"

"Not that I'm aware of."

"You've been extremely helpful, Mr. Salzmann." Sloane took down his contact information.

"Officer McBride, will you please let me know the outcome of your investigation?"

"I'll do what I can." She hung up and headed straight for Rhys's office. "I've got a good lead on our John Doe case. Wanna take a drive?"

It took them some time to find the cabin, which sat in a remote spot, perched in the pines above the Feather River. Sloane had never been up there before. The area was beautiful, with heart-stopping views of the Sierra, and so peaceful. No cars, no people, only nature.

"There's the car." Rhys pulled up behind the Volkswagen in the driveway.

They got out and Rhys knocked on the cabin's front door. When no one answered, he tried the knob. It was unlocked.

"Hello," Rhys called. "We're here from the Nugget Police Department to do a welfare check. Anyone home?"

Still no answer. Rhys directed Sloane to go around the cabin in case there was a back door. With his gun drawn, he went in the front. No door in the rear. The place was tiny, no more than a couple of rooms. Sloane returned to the front.

"The place is clear," Rhys called from the doorway. "Check it out."

The musty cabin smelled like rotting food and rodent urine, but it was neat as a pin. There was a sleeping bag laid out on a daybed against the wall and a corduroy couch that had seen better days in the middle of the room. Behind it, next to a miniscule kitchenette, sat a wooden table and two chairs. On top were a bag of needles, a shoelace, cotton balls, a vial of pills, a deflated red balloon tied in a knot at the top, and an opened soda can. Rhys photographed everything with his phone, put on a pair of gloves, shook the can, and turned it so that a used syringe slid out. After taking more pictures, he untied the balloon and poured out a small stream of white powder. The former Houston narcotics detective knew his stuff.

Sloane searched two brown shopping bags that lined the wall next to the daybed. They were filled with clothes. One had a wallet with Kevin's Pennsylvania driver's license. She held it up for Rhys to see.

"Looks like we're getting closer to our confirmation," he said, and continued to take photos.

At the foot of the bed were two leather instrument cases. The one on top was empty. In the second, Sloane found five pieces of a clarinet stored in individual plush compartments.

"I thought he traded his clarinet for the Bug?" Rhys snapped pictures of the cases and the instrument.

"I got the impression he had more than one. We'll have to ask the Fagans."

"No sign of a struggle in here." Rhys went inside the bathroom and came out. "Nothing in there except a few toiletries. My guess is he shot up, went outside, and died."

"But how?"

"Since the forensic anthropologist didn't find signs of trauma, I'm gonna guess an overdose." Rhys looked at the table with the paraphernalia. Apparently, Kevin hadn't done too well getting clean.

They went outside and searched the grounds. After four months, though, the likelihood of finding anything constructive was next to nil. Even footprints would've been washed away by what little rain they'd had. Rhys traced what seemed like the most probable path from the cabin to the river, with Sloane following. An easy walk, even for someone stoned. Level and less than a quarter of a mile.

"I heard Brady put in his notice," Rhys said.

"I suppose you heard about Sandra too."

"Yup." Of everyone she knew in Nugget, Rhys was the most tapped in and the least gossipy. "You thinking of going with him?"

"Nope." She didn't know yet whether she was staying, but Brady had made it clear that he had no intention of asking her to come with him.

He turned back to look at her. "I'm happy to hear that. But are you?"

"What do you mean?"

He let out a sigh. "I almost made the mistake of letting the best thing that ever happened to me go because I was afraid of commitment. I wouldn't want to see that happen to you."

How had she ever misjudged this man? "I'm not the one afraid to commit."

"Ah." He leaned up against a big shade tree. "I'm sorry, Sloane."

"I'll get over it." If she cried now she'd shoot herself. "What's that?"

Something near the tree was glinting in the sun. From where she was standing it looked like a coin. A quarter, maybe. She walked closer and bent down to get a better look. It was half covered in leaves and dirt. Rhys came over and helped her clear away the debris.

"Is that what I think it is?" she asked, staring down at what they'd uncovered.

"The clarinet from the empty case." They both just stood there staring at it. "I'm speculating that he got high, came out here to sit by the river and play a little music, fell asleep, and stopped breathing." Rhys looked up at the blue, cloudless sky. It was about sixty degrees. "In November we had some nice days like this."

"So this is where you think he died?"

"Right under this tree . . . with his clarinet."

"How awful."

"Nah. It was probably painless," Rhys said. Sloane knew he'd seen the horrors of the drug trade up close. "And at least he died doing what he loved in a scenic spot. I think we should offer the Fagans the opportunity to come see it for themselves."

"Just leave everything the way it is?"

"We'll take the drugs and the clarinet into evidence, but it's not a crime scene. The coroner's office will classify this as an undetermined death, you can bet on it. We wouldn't be violating any police protocol by letting the Fagans see it."

Rhys leaned against the tree once more and took in the area. Sloane had to admit that the spot was so tranquil and picturesque—it smelled like fresh pine needles, bark, and sage—that seeing it might help the Fagans with their grief. The pain of losing a child had to be the worst, but knowing that this idyllic spot was his final resting place could be succor. It sure beat the hell out of a garbage Dumpster or a rat-infested alleyway.

"I'll bring them here today if they want to come," she said, and he nodded.

Chapter 25

"They're out there," Maddy whispered to Brady.

"Who?" Brady whispered back. "And why are we whispering?" He was tired from tossing and turning in a tent all night, pissy from taking an ice-cold shower in the state park this morning, and generally in a foul mood.

"The parents of the missing man."

"I thought they didn't know for sure . . . not until they matched the dental records or the DNA."

"The parents seem positive it's him. It's so sad."

Yeah, it was. Brady wondered how Sloane was holding up.

It was after eleven and most of the guests had already eaten. "They sleep in?"

"They got in very late last night—from Philadelphia."

"I'll take them some breakfast." He'd done omelets because they were easy and he wasn't up for hard. "You know if they have any food restrictions?"

"I'll ask." She headed to the dining room and returned a short time later. "None. They seem very nice and a little shell-shocked."

Brady broke five eggs into a bowl. "Get me out that serrano ham. I'm thinking they need hearty."

Maddy stuck her head in the refrigerator. "Brady?"

"Hmm?"

"Don't go. Even if you don't want Nate's job, stay at the Lumber Baron. Or open your own restaurant. But you're family to us. Losing you . . . it's a big hit, Brady."

It moved him knowing that people here cared. At the same time it made him itchy to leave. Not healthy, he supposed. But he was what he was. A screwed-up individual with fears of attachment. At least he knew his weaknesses. "I'll probably come back," he lied.

The omelets were finished and he'd reheated the potatoes from earlier. Muffins and Danish were still out, along with coffee. He carried the plates to the dining room, where he found Sloane sitting with the couple. They were in deep conversation, but stopped when he came to the table.

He nodded at the man and woman and said hi to Sloane. She returned a faint smile. After leaving, he stood in an inconspicuous place behind the doorway and watched her. Clearly she was in the midst of imparting some heavy stuff. The couple's heads were bowed as Sloane said something. The man eventually nodded and the woman wiped her eyes with a napkin.

He didn't envy Sloane her job. But she did it with grace and empathy. The way her hand gently rested on the woman's arm, how she spoke softly and calmly, giving the couple time to process. No judgment in her eyes, just warmth and caring. He loved her so much his body ached with it.

"Hey." Nate slapped him on the back. "What're you doing?"

"Finishing the breakfast service." He nudged his head at the couple. "They got in late last night."

"They the ones with the missing son?" Brady nodded in response. "Come into my office for a sec."

Brady followed Nate, who shut the door. "Look, you've gotta do what you've gotta do, but I'm prepared to up the salary to this." He handed Brady a piece of paper with a figure that made him reel. It was a very nice chunk of change.

"It's not the money, Nate. Although if I stayed that's more in line with what I'd be looking for." He smirked at Nate, who appreciated a good game of dickering. "There are other places I want to go . . . see, especially now that my situation has changed."

"Your stalker?"

"Yep. I can finally breathe again."

"I always figured you'd leave us for the big city," Nate said. "What about Sloane? You two seem good together."

Even though Nate was as much a friend as he was a boss, Brady wasn't going to answer that. "It's time for me to move on, Nate."

"I'm sorry to see you go. Not just because I wanted you to be

Breyer's executive chef, although I think you're a moron for turning it down. But hey, buddy, we'll always have Nugget." Nate wrapped him in a hug. "I love you, man."

Brady chuckled. "You find anyone to replace me at the Lumber Baron yet?"

"Working on it. There's some ski bum Emily knows who just finished culinary school. I might give him a try."

Brady should've felt relief that Nate, Sam, and Maddy wouldn't be left in the lurch. Instead, a swift punch of melancholia hit him in the gut.

"We might rent him your side of the duplex too."

Brady didn't want a man living next door to Sloane, not even a ski bum just out of culinary school. "I'm not out of it yet."

Nate held up his hands. "Take your time. You're the one who wants to leave us." He eyed Brady closely. "What's up with your hair?"

"I camped last night. Didn't have a comb." Nate cocked his brows and Brady shook his head. "I've gotta finish up in the kitchen."

On the way to a sink full of dirty dishes, he bumped into Sloane leaving. "Can I talk to you?"

"Not now," she said.

Back in the kitchen, Maddy had already made a big dent in the cleanup. He started wiping down the counters and together they finished putting everything away. In a little while, after the couple had had time to finish their breakfast, he'd clear away the foodstuff and dishes in the dining room.

"Rhys just called," Maddy said. "He and Sloane found a cabin where the young man was living. They found a pile of drug things and think he may have overdosed. But Rhys says they'll probably never know for sure. His poor parents. Sloane is coming over to talk to them and take them to the cabin if they want to go."

"She was already here." He let out a breath. So that's what that was all about. Tough thing to have to tell someone.

"Hey." Lina came in carrying dirty dishes. "The folks from 207 are done. They're apparently going with Sloane somewhere. What's going on?"

Maddy explained the situation and for the second time that morning Brady worried how Sloane was handling all this. He put up a pot of water to boil and pulled a bag of pasta from the pantry. He'd leave her macaroni and cheese for dinner. After a day like this she'd need comfort food. Later, Brady delivered the dish to her apartment, stowed it in the refrigerator, and had just enough time for a hot shower before getting back to the inn for the afternoon service.

The whole place was abuzz. Apparently the Fagans' visit to the cabin had been trying, to say the least. Maddy told Brady that they'd seen their son's possessions and were convinced now more than ever that Sloane's John Doe was Kevin. Of course the DNA tests would be the official determiner, which Rhys had requested a rush job on. In the meantime, the Fagans wanted to hold a small memorial for their son at the very spot where they believed he died.

"They're not religious, so they just want to say a short eulogy. Their other son is flying in tonight. Sloane's pilot-program kids want to go." Maddy made a face. "Rhys thinks it'll be good for them, and the Fagans said they didn't mind. I'll go with Rhys. I think it'll be nice to show support."

"You think we should do some kind of food thing back here?"

"I hadn't even thought of that. Would it be too presumptuous?"

"I don't know. Should we ask them?"

Maddy pondered it a minute. "Would you mind calling Emily and asking her what she thinks? I don't want to bother the Fagans. Emily will know what's appropriate in a situation like this."

"Will do."

A little while later Brady had his answer and a kitchen full of the Baker's Dozen.

"They don't want to eat, they don't have to," Donna said, muscling him out of the way while she put together her famous bean dip. "But this is the right thing to do. Those poor people shouldn't have to face this alone."

She got busy chopping tomatoes for the salsa. "And you, Brady Benson, I'm pissed at you. Just because you no longer have a stalker, doesn't mean you can just up and leave. I'll stalk you all the way to Oregon, and you don't want to mess with me."

Emily winked at Brady and whispered, "Do you really have to go?"

Brady didn't answer. "Hey, crazy women," he called. "Huddle together." With his phone he snapped a few pictures. He'd never forget these ladies.

That night he went home to a dark duplex. Sloane must've been fast asleep because both her SUV and Rav4 were parked in the driveway. He and the Baker's Dozen had made enough food for a proper memorial. The ladies wanted to make sure that not all of the Fagans' memories of Nugget were bad. It was tragic what happened to their son. Not knowing where he was for four years and then him dying alone like that. What he'd learned through the town grapevine was that the kid had suffered from depression. Brady assumed he was using the drugs to self-medicate. *Terrible.*

He stared at Sloane's door before dragging himself through his own. It hadn't been that long and he already missed sleeping with her. Tomorrow he planned to go to the service at the cabin. Not for the Fagans, who he didn't know, but for Sloane.

Practically the whole town had turned out by the big tree near the river's edge to pay their respects to the Fagans. The crowd stood back, giving the couple plenty of room to say their goodbyes and prayers in private. Sloane couldn't be more proud of her kids. Skeeter had dropped them off. Rose in a dark dress and the boys in suits. They behaved so respectfully that Sloane's heart filled with pride. Rhys and Maddy had gotten there early and set up chairs for the Fagans and their son Lucas, letting them know they should take as much time as they needed.

Even the Nugget Mafia, the Baker's Dozen, Griffin, and Lina had shown up. Harlee was there too, but in an official capacity as a reporter. Darla and Wyatt stood off to the side. The only ones from the department who hadn't come were Jake and Connie. Someone had to hold down the fort. But it was Brady who Sloane noticed the most. He kept looking over at her like he wanted to make sure she was okay. Between that and the mac and cheese he'd left in her fridge, she wrestled against her pride, wanting so badly to wrap her arms around him and beg him to stay.

The Fagans took turns eulogizing Kevin. Mrs. Fagan read a Native American prayer and each laid a rose on the spot where she and Rhys had found Kevin's clarinet. The family then shook everyone's hands and thanked them for coming. Mr. Fagan nodded at Sloane, who escorted them to her SUV so she could drive them back to the inn.

Before getting into the backseat, Mrs. Fagan took Sloane's hands in her own. "Thank you for finding our son. Chief Shepard told us how hard you worked on this case and I just want you to know that you've given us our lives back. All those years of not knowing whether Kevin was dead or alive was slowly killing us. You're a very dedicated officer."

Sloane's throat clogged. All she could say was thanks.

Brady and the Baker's Dozen must've raced back to the inn, because when Sloane and the Fagans got there a full spread had been laid out. Rhys, Maddy, and Sloane's pilot-program kids were just seconds behind.

"This is absolutely lovely," Mrs. Fagan said, taking in the table loaded with food.

"We understand that you're grieving and are under no obligation to mingle," Sloane told her. "In fact, if you want to take plates up to your room everyone would understand."

Sloane gazed around the dining room. All these people had come first to the cabin and now here to help total strangers through their sorrow. What a special town Nugget was. And what a fool Brady was for leaving.

Right then and there Sloane decided she wasn't going anywhere. Like Rhys had said, this was where she could make the most difference. All she had to do was look at the faces of the Fagans, who wandered through the crowd as Dink, Owen, Mariah, Sophie, Lucky, and so many others offered their condolences. All she had to do was look at Mrs. Fagan hugging Rose, Simpson, and Rudy to know that she'd made a contribution. That she'd left a mark, even a small one.

"You okay?" Brady sidled up to Sloane.

"Yeah." She sighed. "Thanks for doing this. It was incredibly thoughtful. And thanks for the mac and cheese. Only you would've known how much I needed that."

She walked away. Out of the dining room and out of his life. Lina and Griffin sat in the living room sharing a plate of food.

"You want to hang out with us?" Lina asked her.

The two of them looked so happy together Sloane didn't want to intrude. "Nah, I'm heading home."

On her way out she bumped into Rhys. "I don't know if I've ever told you this, but you're the best boss I've ever had."

He scrutinized her. "You're quitting, aren't you?"

"Nope. You're stuck with me, Chief."

* * *

Brady woke early the next morning. Lying in bed, he listened for any sign of movement next door. Last night, like the night before, Sloane's lights had been out by the time he'd gotten home. He could tell that the last couple of days had been exhausting for her.

Before jumping in the shower he went into the kitchen and made himself a cup of coffee. He'd tank up on more at the inn. The Lumber Baron, unlike the rest of Nate's hotels, had good brew. Brady had made sure of it. Coffee was one of the first things he'd have changed at Breyer Hotels. No one in a great city like San Francisco should be forced to drink swill.

After showering, he dressed and sat out on the porch to enjoy the morning. He didn't have to leave for a while and wanted to take advantage of the sunrise and the quiet. Other than the river rushing and the birds chirping, it was as peaceful as you could get in civilization. Perfect for contemplation. Boy, would he miss it.

Sloane's door creaked open and she stepped out. Early day at the office, he supposed.

"Hey," he said, the sound of his voice clearly startling her.

"I didn't see you."

"Just taking a moment before I head to the inn."

She'd swapped out her uniform for a pair of jeans tucked into boots, and a suede jacket. Her blond hair was down and she looked heart-stoppingly beautiful. His first impulse was to forget work, forget that he was leaving, and drag her to bed.

"You off today?" he asked.

"No. But the kids and I are going to Lucky's cowboy camp today for our first riding lesson."

Rays of sunlight backlit her, and from where Brady was sitting she looked like an apparition. An angel. She embodied everything he'd ever wanted in a woman—beauty, kindness, and kickassness—and here he was walking away.

He scrubbed his hand over the stubble on his jaw and got to his feet. "I better get going."

At the inn he went through the breakfast routine in a haze, reaching for ingredients by rote and popping dishes in and out of the oven without a lot of conscious regard. Luckily, Lina had school, Maddy was out, and Nate and Sam were meeting with a vendor in the conference room. He had the kitchen to himself with only a few guests to serve. The Fagans had left early in the morning to catch a flight home.

He took a couple of French-toast soufflés to the dining room and quickly escaped back to the kitchen. The phone rang and Brady figured Andy would get it. When he didn't, Brady forced himself to pick it up.

"Lumber Baron Inn."

"Why haven't you returned any of my calls?" Tawny asked.

"Didn't want to." Brady smiled. "I heard Sloane's coming over to the ranch with her pilot kids to go horseback riding."

"I heard you're an imbecile. Furthermore, if you don't cater our wedding, I will never speak to you again." There was a long silence. "Some people search a whole lifetime to find what you've got here. Cowboy up and stop running."

Click.

Brady couldn't believe she'd hung up on him.

For the rest of the morning he cleared and cleaned in the same blur he'd cooked in. There wasn't much to do for the afternoon wine and cheese, so he took off his apron, grabbed his jacket, and got in his van. He drove the backcountry, taking any road that looked interesting. Despite the drought, the Sierra was awash with color. Greens, purples, oranges, and browns.

In a blink of an eye, the landscape changed from forest to high desert and everything in between. A person, he realized, could never get bored here because nothing ever stayed the same. The land was a constantly evolving canvas. He thought of all the places he'd been, the people he'd known . . . the women. And his mind kept coming back to Sloane.

Somehow he'd wound up on the highway, just before the turnoff to Sierra Heights. He pulled in through the gate. No security guard this time, and he cruised the streets aimlessly. Last he'd heard, Griffin had sold three more houses. He parked at the clubhouse, took the flagstone path past the swimming pool and tennis courts, and found himself peeking in the window of the model with the pimped-out kitchen. Sloane's words came back to haunt him.

We go to Sierra Heights to look at those houses and even playing around you made sure to let me know that the idea of us living together was out of the question.

"What's up?" Griffin came up behind Brady and he jumped.

"Jesus, you scared the hell out of me. Will you sell me this one?"

Griffin looked at him like he was joking. "It's the model. I thought you were leaving town."

"Change of plans. I want this one, Griff. Will you sell it to me?"

Griffin just kept staring at him. "I guess I can turn one of the others into a model. Are you just yanking my chain?"

"Nope. Who do I have to talk to? Dana? Carol?"

"Sure. But we're friends. If you really want the place, we'll work something out."

"I've got a few things to do, but I'll get back to you."

"Okay." Griffin shoved his hands in his pockets, dumbfounded.

Brady ran to the van, floored it out of the parking lot as fast as he could, and tried not to break any traffic laws on the way back to the inn. Andy was checking a couple out of the Lumber Baron as Brady came through the door.

"Where's Nate?"

"His office."

He nearly collided with Sam as he jogged down the hall.

"Where's the fire?" she called to him.

"I need to talk to Nate." He knocked, then burst through Nate's door. "I need to talk to you."

"So I heard. They also heard you in China."

"The job for Breyer Hotels . . . is it still open?"

Nate swiveled his chair away from his desk. "Hell yeah, it's still open."

"I'll take it then."

Behind him someone shouted, "Yes." Brady turned around to find Sam loitering near Nate's doorway. She wrapped her arms around him and jumped up and down.

"I've gotta go," Brady said, and pulled loose from Sam's grasp and kissed her on the forehead.

"We have to talk salary," Nate called after him.

"I want your last dollar offer, four weeks paid vacation, and complete creative control over anything food- and beverage-related."

"Within reason." Nate followed him to the front door.

"Nope. It's my way or the highway."

"Sounds fair. Come back later and sign the paperwork."

"Sam, you heard what he just said. Complete creative control.

You're my witness." Brady took off across the square to the police station and pushed through the office. "Where's Sloane?"

"She's on her way to Lucky's cowboy camp," Connie said.

"It's not even three. I thought she was taking the kids." He rushed for the door.

"They have half—"

Brady didn't let her finish her sentence, just ran for his van and started the engine. Halfway to Lucky's ranch, he hung a U-turn. That's when he realized he was making a huge mistake.

Chapter 26

Sloane's radio went off just as Lucky taught them how to put the bit in the horse's mouth.

"What's your 10-20, Officer McBride?" Connie knew what her location was. Sloane had been talking about the cowboy camp all day.

"I'm at Lucky's," she said, not bothering to hold back her annoyance.

"We need you to go to 1240 Pine Cone Lane for a house call."

A house call? What the hell was Connie talking about?

"I don't copy you."

"The chief says when you get there to stand by. That's a direct order."

"Ten-four." What the . . . Couldn't they send Jake, who was already on patrol? Unless something big was going down. Then, of course, Sloane didn't want to miss it.

"Hey, guys, I just got called out," she said to her group now huddled around Lucky's daughter, Katie, who was demonstrating how to put a saddle on the horse.

"I'll make sure they get home safely," Lucky said. "Do what you got to do."

Sloane headed to her SUV. She didn't even know where Pine Cone Lane was, and turned on her GPS. It seemed to be taking her on a circuitous route away from town, past McCreedy Road, to Sierra Heights. Sierra Heights? Nothing ever happened there. She drove through the gate, following the GPS's instructions, wondering if she was lost. Now wouldn't that be embarrassing?

"You have arrived at your location," the disembodied GPS voice said. The location happened to be the clubhouse and pro shop parking lot in the planned community.

Ah hell, this couldn't be right. Just to make sure, she hopped out of her truck and followed the flagstone path past the clubhouse, the pool, and tennis courts to catch an address. Sure enough, she stood on Pine Cone Lane. Tracing the addresses she found 1240—the model she and Brady had liked so much. The one he didn't want to live in with her.

Stand by, Connie had told her. Impatient, she radioed back. "I'm here. What am I supposed to do?"

"The chief says to go inside but stand down. This is not an emergency. I repeat: This is not an emergency."

Sloane signed off and cursed. What was it then, a freaking scavenger hunt? She went inside. It was still a breathtaking house with its soaring ceilings, huge picture windows, and polished hardwood floors, but quiet as a library. And a bit unnerving. Despite the chief's command to stand down, Sloane's hand automatically reached inside her purse for the butt of her gun.

"Anyone here?" she called, and the words echoed through the big space. "Hello?"

She walked through the front room, down the long dining room, and into the kitchen. A giant bouquet of red roses had been arranged in a crystal vase on the counter. Next to it was a champagne bucket, filled with ice and a bottle of bubbly. Two glasses stood at the ready.

Someone in the corner cleared his throat. Sloane jerked up and did a double take.

"What is this?"

"Crappy champagne because it was all I could find at the Nugget Market on short notice."

She wouldn't know the difference between André and Dom Pérignon. "Brady?"

"Sloane?" He came for her, grabbed her around the waist, and pulled her close. "Change of plans."

"What's that?"

"I'm staying, I'm buying this house, and I'd appreciate it if you'd at least allow me to make the loft my man cave before you fill the rest of the place with your frilly, floral stuff." His lips were so close to her ear it tickled.

"You can't afford this house."

"Says who?"

She pushed away to read his face. "What's going on, Brady?"

"Today . . . maybe yesterday . . . hell, I don't know when. Maybe I knew all along that I couldn't live without you . . . that if I ran away, I'd regret it for the rest of my life. You're the best thing that's ever happened to me. Be with me, Sloane. Make a life with me and I promise to love you forever."

Sloane choked on a sob. "I love you, Brady Benson. So if you're messing with me, I swear I'll shoot you. Don't test me."

He kissed her, bent her over the miles of granite countertop, and continued to kiss her into sheer oblivion. "This is the only kind of messing with you I want to do." His hand went for the zipper on her jeans.

"Wait a minute. Are we really buying this house?"

"If you want it, I'll buy it. I've been saving forever for a restaurant, which I'll use for the down payment. With my new job as executive chef of Breyer Hotels, we should have no problem making the mortgage. What do you think?"

"Executive chef of Breyer Hotels." Her eyes grew big. "You've been busy. When did this happen?"

His hand reached for her zipper again. "I'll tell you all about it as soon as we're done initiating these countertops. One question first: Will you have me?"

Sloane stifled a sob. "That was never in doubt."

Epilogue

"You promised that the loft and the kitchen were my domain," Brady said as he blocked Sloane from bringing one of her frou-frou chairs up the stairs.

"There's no room for it downstairs and I really like it." She pouted.

"It doesn't go with the leather stuff." They had something like five thousand square feet of space. She couldn't find a spot for the chair?

"But it could be my chair when I come up here to watch TV with you."

"All right," he said, giving in without much of a fight. He was finding that he had a hard time saying no to her. "I draw the line at the kitchen, though, Sloane."

Ah hell, who was he kidding? If she wanted to put up lacy curtains and block their fantastic views, he'd let her. That's how much he was in love with her.

Sloane climbed to the loft landing, handed Brady the chair, and let her gaze drift around their new house. "Are you sure we can afford this?"

Brady chuckled. "With what Nate's paying me . . . hell yeah."

It had been two months since he'd taken the job with Breyer Hotels and he was loving it. Gold Mountain had opened early—and with a bang. Longtime guests, who Nate had feared would balk at rate hikes due to all the renovations, were so smitten with the changes—especially the restaurant—that they'd renewed their weeklong leases. Some had left, vowing to never come back, but that was to be expected.

Slowly but surely, Brady was changing the menus at Nate's other hotels. So far, Nate had kept his word on giving Brady full control over food and beverages. Occasionally he missed slinging hash at the Lumber Baron, but the two extra hours he got to stay in bed with Sloane made up for it. Man, did he love her. He'd never been this happy in his entire life.

"You think we'll have this place in shape by the time your family comes next week?" Brady asked. The week after, his family was coming.

Everyone wanted to meet each other. Brady supposed they were all waiting for a marriage announcement, which would come in good time. Right now, he and Sloane wanted to enjoy their new house and take their time planning the big day. Oddly enough, Brady would've marched down to Nugget City Hall and had Dink, the mayor, perform the ceremony this very minute. It was Sloane who wanted to wait. He suspected that she had her heart set on July, the same month as Tawny and Lucky's wedding, and didn't think they could pull it together fast enough.

"Yep," Sloane said. "All five of them are coming, and the way I talked up this place, it better be ready."

He grinned at her like a lovesick fool. "Then we'll have it ready."

"The kids are coming over this afternoon to help us unpack." Rose, Rudy, and Simpson would walk through fire for Sloane. Next fall, she had five more kids wanting to sign up for Rhys's crazy pilot program.

"Hey, Brady, I think Aidan might go for that job at Cal Fire. Would you have a problem if he stayed with us for a while? The thing with Sue . . . he's having a rough time."

"Would it mean we'd have to stop having sex?"

"Uh, definitely not. My hospitality only extends so far."

"Okay, then he can stay. But let's start now." He wrapped his arm around her waist and tugged her backwards to the couch. "We need to break this place in."

And that's when his badass cop girlfriend giggled. Giggled. "We've been breaking it in for two months. If Griff knew what we were doing in this house before escrow closed, he'd have a heart attack."

"Nah, he's got his own good stuff going on. You have a problem with us breaking it in some more?" He went down on the sofa and pulled her on top of him.

"Nope. Not a bit."

"Good." He got to work undressing the both of them.

"I love you, Brady."

And for the next hour he took his time loving her back.

Printed in the United States
by Baker & Taylor Publisher Services